The Lords of Leftovers

The Lords of Leftovers

Dan Williams

Copyright © 2013 by Dan Williams
All Rights Reserved

This book is a work of fiction. Names, characters, places, and incidents are products of the author's imagination. Any resemblance to actual events or locales, or to persons living or dead, is purely coincidental.

ISBN: 978-0-9883839-7-5
Library of Congress Control Number: 2013945379

Manufactured in the United States of America

Ink Brush Press
Temple and Dallas

For all those left behind

Fiction from Ink Brush Press

Laurie Champion, ed., *Texas Told'em*
Terry Dalrymple, *Fishing for Trouble*
Terry Dalrymple, ed., *Texas Soundtrack*
Andrew Geyer, *Dixie Fish*
Andrew Geyer, *Siren Songs from the Heart of Austin*
H. Palmer Hall, *Into the Thicket*
Dave Kuhne, *The Road to Roma*
Myra McLarey, *The Last Will and Testament of Rosetta Sugars Tramble*
Eric Muirhead, *Cab Tales*
Brett Riley, *The Subtle Dance of Impulse and light*
Jim Sanderson, *Faded Love*
Jim Sanderson, *Dolph's Team*
Melvin Sterne, *Zara*

For information on these and other IBP books, go to
www.inkbrushpress.com

Chapter 1

The little barman flipped a page in his ledger book and ran a fat finger down a column of numbers. "Ill tell you what I can do for you. Ill let you have the whole bottle cheap."

I nodded and sipped a tiny sip, just enough to taste what he had poured, and smiled back at him, trying not to cough. Whenever someone starts a transaction using the word cheap, I take him to mean the opposite.

"Lets see, Ill let you have the whole bottle, or better yet, one just like it unopened, firstrate leftover stuff, for your horse and rig."

He had seen me ride up and tie up in the alley. I was just trying to get out of the rain, and a sign like "Leftover Whiskey" is as likely as anything to get my attention.

"Lots of places around Aurora are selling gallon jugs for one of the Princes little silver coins," I said and smiled. Outside it was drizzlycold and windy, so it was a good day to sip whiskey and swap stories. No reason to be unfriendly.

"Those gallon jugsll leave you blind and twitchy. I am offering you the best whiskey anywhere on the front range, and premiums always going to cost more. You get what you pay for. Im sure you can understand that. Its one of the foundations of good business."

He looked back at his ledger book and added a mark with a stubby pencil, his round belly spilling over his belt. I had never seen him around before, and I wondered how in lean times he had got fat and stayed fat. He had opened up an overnight whiskeyshop not too far from the Princes Square in one of the old bigbuildings, hammering enough splintery lumber together to create four walls and a rough loppy bar. As soon as I walked in I thought there was a good chance he had more in mind than trading whiskey shots.

"You want that bottle? I am an honest man offering you a fair deal." He looked up from his ledger book, waiting for me to agree.

I should have nodded and kept my mouth shut, but I couldnt. "Pouring rustbucket swill into fancy bottles aint none too honest or fair."

The little barman stared hard for a moment. He moved to the end of the bar and pulled out a rag and shook it a couple of times before making a show of wiping his hands. "Theres lot of folk around who like my whiskey. Just the other day the Prince and some of his troopers came in for a drink, and they liked it just fine. Say, whats your name?"

I ignored the name question, as I usually do, and I didnt fault him for lying. In trade, lying is expected. But the truth was I could find better whiskey. With the times improving, and with the Princes rangers close by, there were a number of places around selling tolerable whiskey, and some even with a couple leftover bottles hidden away.

I held the shotglass, spilling a few drops, and wondered some more on how he fatted up when most people still handtomouthed to get by. I expected lies and deceit from someone selling rotgut for leftover, and seeing how he didnt have much else to sell, I more or less expected the other two slugs when they drifted in and set down in a corner in behind me. The barman made no move to pour for them, so I sideways around and give them a look. Both were taller than the little barman, but one just as fat with a big round baldhead, while the other was just as tall but thinner and squinteyed with long graygreasy hair. Both looked like they were half asleep. I didnt doubt but that they were an essential part of the little barmans transactions. They were armed with handguns stuffed into their belts.

I opened up my coat to shake off some of the rain, but also to show both the gun belts I had strapped on. I pulled an old revolver and shook it, wiped it, and blew on the cartridge chambers.

"Wet out there, aint it?" I smiled at them all and held the revolver a moment, just a polite show, and then stuffed it back under my coat again.

"I think Ill pass on the bottle. Im just an old nameless fool of a scavenger and have no taste for your fancy stuff. Up ahead at the Princes my partners waiting for me. Maybe youve heard of him, Joe Cruz? Lots of folks have. Hes well known along the front range. If Im lucky, maybe the Prince will pour me a drink of his whiskey before we set out for the mountains. If Im real lucky, maybe Ill find my own bottle up in high country. You never whats left up there between those peaks."

I set the drink back on the bar unfinished and edged around towards the door, one hand under my coat. "Hope the rain leaves off. Hate to start a long trek in the rain. Good weather to stay bottledup safe under a roof somewhere."

"Hold on, we got accounts to settle," the little barman called out. "You just insulted me, and you owe me three silver coins for the drink. And youre a liar if you say you know the Prince and Joe Cruz. Around here every grubber and rateater claims the same. Too bad neither one is here to back you up. You just tried to rob me. Aint that right, boys?"

The little fat mans associates nodded without blinking and got to their feet, the bigger one moving around left, while the skinnier one drifted to the right. Behind me the little barman pulled something up from under the bar and hid it behind his ledger book. I thought I would have a lively time dropping all three of them.

"Ill be taking your horse and rig." The barman dropped his ledger and was holding a small black automatic.

I felt a flash of anger and thought about clunking him on the head and stuffing the shot glass down his throat, but then eased back. "And what are you giving me in exchange?"

"Nothing."

"Aint but nothing to be had for nothing."

"Ill still be taking your horse and rig."

"Robbery one of the foundations of good business too?"

I motioned the two slugs to back off but they ignored me and pulled their pistols. I considered taking a run at them, but before I could the door crashed open and Joe stepped in. He looked around and smiled.

"Is this a private affair, or can anyone join in the fun? I can come back later."

The two slugs melted back towards their corner, while the little barman emptied his hand underneath the bar.

"You can go back out in the rain, if you want. The barman and his two associates were just negotiating for my horse."

Joe moved to the middle of the room. He was cradling a little machine pistol that sprayed a ton of bullets. He shook off some of the wet. "Whats he offering for it?"

"Nothing."

"Nothing? That dont sound like much of a deal."

"Hes good at managing his accounts. Hes also trying to gouge me three silvers for a shot of turpentine, which hes claiming is leftover."

Joe waved his machine pistol towards the barman. "I thought you were better at negotiating than that. Why dont you decline the offer and lets get going. The rains letting up, and the boy is up the street with the mules, all agitated to start the trek. The Princell be tapping his foot and snarling by the time we get to him."

I went over to the bar and picked up the little fat mans ledger book, flipping through a few pages. "I aint too good at keeping numbers, but I can read well enough. You should mark down that there aint much profit in bad whiskey. You can pour that rotgut back into your bottle. Thats a fairer deal than the one you and your associates were offering me."

The little fat man pointed towards Joe. "I thought you said he was waiting for you."

I dropped the ledger book and went towards the door, Joe backing out with me, but paused before ducking out. "I lied. I was waiting for him and the wildboy to catch up with me. But you best believe that the Prince is waiting for us and that Ill be sure to give him your regards. You might consider closing up shop and moving on. You aint got a much of a future in Aurora."

I am a trader of lost things and leftovers, sometimes a thief, and mostly a scavenger. I live in Aurora by the dead city with Joe and his clan, and we trade in the mountains, loading up with the wreckage of the lost years, taking up just about anything that didnt get scorched in the Fires.

If the little fat barman had been interested in dealing, we could have done some business. Me and Joe could have filled his rickety spidertrap with a load of leftovers. But he and his two backshooters were set on riskier work.

Truth is a tradable commodity, and generally I am an active wholesaler. But I had not lied about hooking up with the Prince. Me and Joe were fixin to head back up to Nineveh and the magic mountain with him and a sizable portion of his rangers. There was serious dealing to be done up there. No telling what we would bring back down. We had stumbled down from Nineveh and the magic mountain a couple weeks earlier, and now we were hot to get back up there before the snows set in, and before all the saints and sinners slaughtered each another.

But this aint exactly the beginning of my story. Sometimes beginnings and endings get all mushed up and confused. The little barman and his wackers are more like an ending getting ready to jump over into the beginning of a story that aint been spun yet. This story is about how me and Joe first went up to Nineveh and the magic mountain, and most likely it takes off with the wildboy stealing one of our packs. Only before that it began with a couple of old liars down in the foothills north of Aurora. They were the ones who got us set on going into the high country.

Me and Joe had been scouting trades along an old twisty road that ran through the hill country, and we had stopped at what was left of a town at a crossroads. There wasnt much left beyond splinters and char and a couple tradeshops and whiskeyshops, but the locals kept an open market where, sometimes, a good deal was possible. When the afternoon dusted up with high winds, we gave up on the market and hauled ourselves into one of the whiskeyshops. We bought a round for the barman and three spongers, and before long we were trading halfcups of passable whiskey for stories with all four of them, and it was then we got a jiggers worth of Nineveh given back to us. One of the spongers was an old jittery fellow, thin and wiry and creasy with age, and at first he sat off by himself, but after guzzling two cups of the barmans shine, he got more sociable.

"I know a place thats got electricity."

I poured him another halfcup. "We like electricity."

So the jittery old man poured us a story about Nineveh. It was an old mining town set alongside a lake where the water was icecold all year round, and where there were supposed to be a thousand or so people who lived mucking around in an old silver mine. The town was run by some sort of fiery church of truebelievers.

We didnt hear a lot more about it, and what we did hear wasnt all that good. Half the town or more were all saintedup with deacons and elders and such, and they were all hostile to outsiders, especially to hunters and skinners who wandered into their valley.

"And they got witches and demons up there and that Church burns em regularly. And they got packs of wolves and wild dogs ranging the hills up there and the people stay huddled around the lake listening to sermons."

"Hellfire and the apocalypse?"

The old man gulped our whiskey, shrugged, and sputtered on about the church. Joe yawned, closed his eyes, and leaned back, but I knew he was listening.

"They got people living in big buildings filled with leftovers, hundreds of rooms all full of old stuff still boxedup and new. They got electric coffee makers, flashlights, electric blankets, and paper towels, and all kinds of stuff to eat. And they got generators and gasoline and they turn on all the lights and give stuff out as earthly rewards to the faithful. Them church people is coldblooded though."

I thought he was only spinning stories for drink. All the spinners and liars will tell you just about every little splinter of a charredup town is packed with witches, wolves, demons, zombies, and all manner of misshapen creatures at loose in the night. With straight faces and solemn vows these old liars will tell you theres bloodsucking monsters roaming the ranges, devouring cattle and children. But in all our years trading me and Joe aint ever seen anything so monstrous as a pack of wackers gunnedup and bloodyminded. Even a freakedup church packed with saints and a messiah aint actually all that freaky. Since the Fires, theres all manner of saviors roaming around, some more pernicious than others. The old man wasnt even sure where this place was, but his stories were worth the whiskey. He had us listening.

"Yall go up there and see. They got batteries and little headlamps, and every single day they drink coffee and eat peanutbutter and jelly sandwiches on white bread and scoop silver out of that old mine." The old man looked back at us earnestly, hoping his words were good enough for another round. I poured and smiled.

"Me and Joe like peanutbutter."

We werent too sure if there was a Nineveh, but we wanted to see what was up there west beyond the high peaks. Theres lots of isolated valleys in between the ranges, and long ago before the Fires there had been hundreds of towns scattered around up there. The hard times and troubles killed off or chased off most of the people, but there were still pockets here and there, little settlements of hard, stubborn highlanders hidden away between the rocky spines and peaks, living in the wrecks of what used to be fancy little resort towns where preFired people played in the snow. Even if there wasnt a Nineveh with a silver mine, we thought maybe we would find something to trade or scavenge. Theres always the hope that across the next ridge we will stumble across something that aint been touched since the burnings began. If there were people way back beyond, then maybe we would do business.

Theres always some something someone will want, some little thing that someone thinks will make him feel better or live better. And somebody else will always come along to barter it. Me and Joe have found that most anything can be bartered, and most times with anyone. Sometimes even the bloodiest, murderminded militias will put up their guns to trade for a little can of leftover fruit cocktail. Tradings a part of being human. And since the Fires have finally begun to cool down people are generally more inclined to feel human again.

I could have explained this to the little barman, though I doubt he would have listened. He had his mind set on the quick and the bloody.

Values aint constant. The price you put on a horse or a leftover bag of peppermint candy is always negotiable, and what you offer one day is liable to double the next. A pack of sewing needles that was worth next to nothing before the Fires is likely to fetch a handful of silver today, and maybe a couple handfuls if someone was in dire need of a patch.

But gold and silver hold their worth, as do guns and bullets. We can always find a buyer all feverish for leftovers like canned foods, toilet paper, tupperware, and juicedup batteries. Tools and livestock go well, and leftover tobacco and coffee run like gold. And a sealedup bottle of leftover whiskey will fetch just about anything, maybe even a horse or two. There are plenty of craving fools around who would trade the farm for a fortyeight hour soaking.

For those bloodied and desperate, the cutthroats and wackers, killings easier than trading. But these days there are fewer of them brutes roaming the edges of Aurora and the dead city. The Prince and his rangers gather them up for hanging in the Square when they catch them, which is often enough. If the Prince wasnt in such a hurry for us to take him up to Nineveh and the magic mountain, he would probably go after the little fat barman. Selling bad whiskey aint a crime, of course, but if youre going to kill a man for his horse, you might as well give him a sip of real leftover.

Those in the mountains, those that are left up there, keep to themselves and dont care much for flatlanders and strangers. But me and Joe get along okay, trading most anything for anything. Any sort of leftovers will go, and sometimes it dont matter what it actually is. Its just something from before, something that connects. Some of the old stuff is being made again in Aurora, when the lights are turned on and things are working, but its not always good stuff, and most people crave the leftovers. Mostly they want the old labels, preFired stuff, the stuff that brings back the memories of before.

Once me and Joe once came across a whole carton of little disposable lighters, those old thin plastic ones with adjustable flames, and people up in the ranges went crazy to give us stuff. For a handful of lighters, one grizzly old man wanted to give us three goats and one of his daughters. We took the goats but left the daughter, since we aint slavers, thoughs theres plenty of them about. Mostly we want gold and silver, old jewelry and pretty stuff thats been kept buried away in a family since before the Fires got lit up. People will usually have something tucked away, old coins or a couple of rings, or maybe an old necklace that once belonged to somebodys grandmother or great aunt. Most times all it takes is to flash some sort of leftover, like those little lighters, or a nice pocketknife without a lot of crust or crud. I once got a handful of pretty stuff for one of those fancy old redhandled pocketknives with all the little foldable gadgets. A man up by the north pass traded away all his familys pretty stuff for a pocketknife with a can opener and a corkscrew, though he didnt have any cans or bottles to open.

You cant own what you cant keep. These days the Prince can give you a piece of paper that says you own a whole town, or whats left of it, but that doesnt mean much if a bunch of gunnedup wackers come through and think different. But a little gold ring, though, will likely get you a weeks lodging and the best leftovers in Aurora.

But trading aint easy. Somebodys always trying to cheat you on a deal or jump you on a trail. Weve been shot at and robbed, and nearly dropped more than a few times. We got enemies that want to put us down, and we even got friends that would do the same if they got the chance. For a long while there wasnt much warmheartedness going around. Most people stayed hunkered down and didnt have much feeling for those they werent connected to. But people in the front ranges dont seem so flinty these days since the Prince took over. Its mostly out on the old roads where a human life remains a cheap commodity.

Me and Joe have always been lucky. Weve always run loose, going where we wanted and doing what we wanted, though theres been times weve been locked away. Once the Prince got mad at us enough to keep us bolted in a little room for a few dreary days over a small dispute about a couple brokedown barely rideable horses. But that wasnt our fault. And once we got chained up by some surly scavs who mistakenly claimed they had a right to a couple boxes of shoes and old clothing that me and Joe had found shutup in an old splittery house. Those fools had intended our ruination, but they were dumb enough to hammer our chains into the floor and a ceiling beam, which Joe pulled out after a couple hours of tugging, and then our halfwit guard was too thick to realize he should not step within a swingable chainlength of Joe, which reduced him to a nowit. One way or another, weve always been lucky enough to slip out of tight places.

But once, way back when I was real young, and before the old couple took me up and kept me for a while, I got locked up in a dark place. I was herded into an underground garage of an old bigbuilding with a hundred or so other throwaways. The Fires were burning redhot then, and we all got plucked off the streets by one of the peacock militias that had been strutting around the dead city. We were stood in a long line and inspected by the peacock in charge, and he hauled the bigger kids out of line to join his glorious cause. And had I been chosen I wouldve gone. I would have strapped on a cutter, one of those old assault rifles everyone was carrying back then, and I would have shot at whoever I was supposed to shoot at. I wouldnt have cared if the rifle was as big as I was. I wanted to go. I wanted somebody to take me up. But I was too small or too dirty or too something, and the peacock commander strutted by me.

The rest of us, the runts and the damaged, were led into the dark underground and lockedup. And left there to die. Maybe one of the peacock fighters was supposed to come back and let us out, or feed and water us, but no one returned for us. We spent a couple days in the dark, fighting with each other for the water that was left in the restrooms and to stand near the crack of light that squeezed in under the big doors, all of us screaming and crying. I can still remember how thick the darkness was and how all of us throwaways stumbled around in the dark touching and punching. That was pretty much my worst time. Finally a couple of scavs heard our screaming and let us out. They wanted silver or something from us, but those of us who made it to the entrance scattered like rats. I remember tripping over several who never made it to the doors. That blackness was a hell I want no part of ever again. Me and Joe wont stand for getting locked up in the dark.

Knowing is the first step in connecting, and these days the Prince knows us well enough to let us come and go. There aint been any more misunderstandings since those worthless horses, though he knows we scavenge in the dead city, which for some contrary reason he claims as his. But I knew his mother a long time before she knew his father, so he lets us slip. And many of the people along the front ranges know us well enough to trade, even though most are still liable to pull out guns when a stranger appears.

We even trade with the skinners, those that are half insane, half naked, and mostly wild, the ravers and the roamers who have gone primitive, banding up into loose clans to follow the elk herds in the high ranges. Refusing to get settled, they live in patchwork tents of hides, plastic wrap, old canvas, window drapes, or whatever, which they pick up and move whenever they have a mind to. They raid scattered settlements for cattle, horses, and children, and as they are hunted, they will kill most anyone they catch. But we get along okay. Me and Joe have traded at their camps when others could not. Weve been at it so long that we now truck with the children of them that we traded with back when the Fires were still scorching.

Dealings the easy part. Its fetching and hauling that gets touchy. All of the old roads are chancy, especially the old highways. Theres always the chance that a group of strutting peacocks have set up a roadblock somewheres to collect tolls, though its only their guns that gives them the right. And stretched along those old roads, waiting for travelers, are the crazy ones, those that have gone bloody and savage, the wackers and killers and the like. Theyre the ones who trail after us, hoping to shoot us down.

The wild country is worth the risk. Theres always the chance that we might stumble on a big old house somewhere up there that aint been scavenged or singed, or some secluded clan tucked away in a valley with a herd of horses and a sackful of gold. And theres always stories being passed around about clumps of hideaways still walledup on top of some ridge somewhere who aint been hunted out and stripped. To get the best deals, we keep going higher and farther into the unfamiliar, following the stories of the old spinners and liars.

And that was how we first got up to Nineveh and the magic mountain, and that was why me and Joe were headed back up there with the Prince and his rangers.

Chapter 2

The wildboy came crashing through the underbrush , and I nearly shot him. And I wouldve too if I hadnt stumbled over a pack, the damned little fool.

We were holed up in a rocky bowl above a series of small beaver ponds, resting up after having finally made our way up from the front range, and waiting to see if some wackers were going to come after us. Theyd been trailing after us ever since we had started up the low hills, and Joe had dropped back to trail them trailing us while I had taken the mules ahead. There were five of them four adults and the boy, all nasty and mean and cruddy, scavenger trash from the new settlements. Hardhearted and murderous, they lived by killing and stealing, and they would kill us if they got the chance. It was their way. As soon as we straggled up the foothills, we spotted them coming after us, and we knew we would have to deal with them. They didnt try to hide from sight, didnt care if we saw them. And so when the boy came crashing through the underbrush, I nearly shot him. It was a close moment.

There was a scream that startled the mules, then the sound of someone running through the pine. I thought it was one of the wackers gone screamer. Joe was off, having circled back behind them, leaving me with the mules and packs when I heard the screamer. By the time I had stumbled and had a gun out the boy had crashed over the barricade of branches and brush and was in our camp, crouching, growling like some sort of wild beast about to spring. I brought the gun up to fire, but in an instant the boy grabbed a small pack and was gone.

I couldve shot him as he crashed back through the brush, I couldve put a large hole into his small back, but I hesitated, and he then jumped a big sappy pine trunk and was gone. I stood for a moment, wondering if I had seen what I had seen. The boy was small, maybe ten or so, and he was all raggy and scabby and muddy, looking just like a throwaway. In the second our eyes made contact he had seemed more beast than boy, a little wolfboy if there ever was one. I saw him, but I cant be sure he saw me. He had looked right through me.

I got several other guns out, as we keep more than a few around. Two were old cutters, and I cradled one with several clips, then blew out the lantern and waited. I didnt know what to expect, whether Joe, the boy, or the wackers. In all the years I had been trading, I hadnt ever been attacked by a wild boy.

Joe had been a scrawny, dirty throwaway kid when we first met years ago. Like me, he didnt know his birthday or his age, but I guessed he was about ten. I had been drinking in a brokedown whiskey shack on the edge of the dead city when I first saw him. Only I didnt see much at first, just a swirling mass of stick arms and legs. Two men had caught him stealing from their packs, and they were beating him. Hard men, scarred and mostly wild themselves, they were wackers or hunters or both. Either way, they were killers, as they carried enough guns and knives to indicate their inclination and capacity. One of the men had Joe in a headlock and was gouging out an eye, while the other was kicking him from behind. They were both laughing, and Joe, just a wild bit of stick and rag, was screaming and thrashing, scratching and kicking, but it looked like he was about to lose an eye.

Later on I told Joe I did what I did because I took a liking to a pair of boots one of the men was wearing. Maybe that aint exactly true. Maybe I did not even think about it except, maybe, that I did not want to see a boys eyeball roll across that dirty floor. Or maybe for a second I remembered way back about another throwaway who mightve been me getting smashed up and gutted like a fish. And I had made a promise when I scarredup to help when I could help. I dont know for sure. It all happened too fast to tell. Explaining always comes afterwards.

I shouted at them, then I waved a gun, and the kicker waved a gun back at me, then we started to do more than just wave at each other. Everything got real slow and deadly, although I was spinning around the room as fast as I could. The first few shots went wide, and then suddenly the whole world went calm, and my hand went steady like its never been before or since. Though he was running around some tables and chairs and firing at me, and though I was running around to keep ahead of his fire, I plugged him square in the chest. At the sound of the shots the other one quit eyegouging long enough to pick up a gun and fire, his shots zipping past my head. I shot him too, my hand as calm and steady as the other, another killshot. And in the midst of the smoke and bloodsplatter Joe sprung up and looked back at me kind of surprised, one eye blinking and bleeding, the rest of his face swelled up and bruised. He wobbled for a moment, wiped away blood from his mouth, and halfstared out of one good eye. He had a small blunty knife in his hand that he had pulled from somewhere, like he was ready for a fight. Then he began tugging at the dead mens pockets.

"If I had known you had a knife I might have let you fight it out with them two. I think you were tiring them out."

He looked at me for a moment, blinking and bloody, before turning back to the meat.

"I get the guns," he said. Those were his first words to me.

Chapter 3

I got the boots, he got the guns, and we split the packs between us and the brokedown whiskeyseller, who had sidedup with us once the meat was on the floor.

That was more than a quarter century ago, maybe longer, and me and Joe still split up even between us. And no one has ever tried to gouge out his eyes since. The scrawny little thievin stickboy grew to be as big as a mountain. Hes strong, fast, smart, and lethal, and only a few crazies are ever crazy enough to take him on. These days the stragglers and scavs in the whiskeyshacks along the front rangers pass around stories about Joe Cruz.

Funny thing about what happened back then. I aint a great shot, not like Joe at least. He grew to be as good a shooter as he grew big. Sometimes when I pick up one of those big old handguns, I can fire over, under, and around a target without hitting it. Those old automatics jump around in my hands as if they were alive, squirming to get away from my grip. Not Joe, though. Hes rocksteady, and even the biggest of those old blasters seem small in his hands. He doesnt miss often. Between the two of us, hes the shooter, which leaves me to do the talking and dealing. Its a fair arrangement. Those two wackers were the only men Ive ever killed in a fight like that, and if someone bet me to shoot across a room on the run and kill two men who were bobbing about and shooting back at me, Id bet against myself. I remember tugging at the dead mans boots and packs wondering how I done it and thinking I was lucky. Somehow the world went still and my hand went steady. It aint happened all that often since.

I hoped I could shoot steady now, and I hoped Joe was close by. I had no idea where he was, or the snarling wild boy with our pack, or the wackers. They all had to be close up somewhere. The night was cold and clear, and there was only a little slice of moon and the distant stars to break up the night. I wrapped up again in my blanket, still gripping the cutters and clips, waiting for whatever, and hoping for not much of whatever.

But within moments the stillness was broken by bursts of cutterfire, more guns than I could count. Joe had a couple cutters with him and enough clips to clear a forest, and by the sound I could tell he was chewing up the landscape down to the south of our camp. The mules were jumping and snorting, pulling against their ropes, and since there wasnt much else for me to do I went over to calm them, hoping Joe got the last shots in. The firing lasted only a minute or so, several bursts of what I hoped were Joes mixed with scattered cutterfire from a couple other guns. Then silence. Then some final bursts. I left the mules and went back to the rocks, figuring in a few minutes either Joe or the wackers would show up. The night air had gotten colder, and the cold metal of the guns seemed to burn against my fingers.

Joe showed up, only it took him awhile, and only he didnt come alone. After a half hour or so of silence I had started to get downright agitated when he materialized out of the darkness. He carried a couple packs on his back, had his guns slung over his shoulders, had our stolen pack under one arm, and under the other he carried the wild boy. He dropped everything but the boy and motioned for me to light a lantern.

"We can light a fire now if you want," he said, still holding the boy. "I persuaded our friends to head back down to the low hills. There was four of them plus this boy here."

"Was?"

"Still is, I guess. A couple are kind of leaky, and another is downright damaged, but they aint altogether spoiled. This boy here is in fine shape."

For a wild thing dangling from an unfriendly arm, the boy didnt do much. He didnt snarl or squirm. He didnt bite, scratch, or kick. As I lit the lantern, I inspected the boy, and in the light he looked worse than before, filthy, scratchedup and welted, wearing nothing but layers of rags. He wore old scarredup leather shoes tucked up in more rags.

"Its cold enough for a fire, I guess." I moved out of the small circle of light to gather up some wood. When I came back with my arms full, Joe was wrapped up in a couple of blankets. He had gotten his pipe out and was stoking. The boy was seated on the ground by the lantern, gnawing on biscuit and jerky. He had a couple cans of leftovers between his raggedy legs and was keeping an eye on the food sack Joe had fetched out. He wasnt tied up, and he didnt seem to be ready to run, so I figured him and Joe had reached an agreement.

I got the fire started and settled back to warm myself. The whole time I was fixing the fire the boy went on gnawing and chewing. Joe came out from under his blankets and began to sort through the food sack, and he soon extracted a little glass jar of leftover coffee and set to boil some water. I picked up the jar to inspect it. Part of the red and gold label had been rubbed off.

"It says, 'Mountain Grown.'"

"Where?" Joe asked, leaning over to peer at the lettering.

I pointed to the words, and he shrugged.

"Never seen jars of coffee powder grown in these mountains." He went back to his blankets and began refilling his pipe. After a few moments he spoke. "What mountains grow coffee?"

I looked away and watched the boy grab another handful of hard crackers out of the food sack. I figured we woud have to turn him loose before he starved us out. The boy looked up at me, giving me that empty animal stare of his, looking at me like hed look at a rock.

"Hell if I know," I said, wondering how many biscuits could a wild boy eat. "He got a name?" I asked.

Joe shrugged and puffed. "Ask him."

"You got a name?" I asked. The boy responded with another animal stare, then began tearing at a piece of jerky. I didnt care. Names dont matter much to me.

"Can he talk?" I turned back to Joe.

He shrugged again. "Dont know. Never asked him."

For a few moments I watched the fire and waited for the water to boil. I could tell Joe was smiling, waiting on me to ask.

"You got him pretty well calmed down. During his first visit he seemed a bit anxious."

Joe shrugged again. He dipped his pipe and relit it. The smoke was pungent, almost sweet.

The boy stopped eating long enough to look up at me again. I still saw nothing familiar and sociable in his gaze. Keeping his distance from me, he moved closer to the fire and resumed his chewing, dragging the food sack with him. After a while he got up and looked around. I thought he might grab another pack and run. Instead he moved over to the barricade and wrapped his skinny self up in my blanket until only his scabby legs showed. Like some kind of monstrous insect, he shuffled back to the fire. The silence was broken by only the crackling of the pine as it burned.

"Cold tonight, huh? Maybe you should give the boy another blanket."

I ignored them both, waiting for the water to boil.

Chapter 4

For several days we travelled along an old crackedup fourlaner that traced a river swollen with early spring thaw through a series of steep valleys. The pavement was brokedup and weedy in places, and there had been mud and rock slides that covered it up in other places, and there was still plenty of ice left in the dark corners, but all in all it was still a pretty passable road. Usually we avoided old roads in unfamiliar areas, preferring to travel along the high ridges rather than risk running into packs of wackers or skinners who kill and plunder out of habit and delight. Up in the ranges there are still a few too many crazies waiting for prey, trolls and trappers, bombers and screamers, and the like. Mostly all of them are nightcrawlers who come out at sunset to hunt. And they aint particular about what they hunt. I still hear stories of packs of raiders large enough to plunder entire settlements. The worlds cooling down, but in some places its still festeredup with killers and slavers, and old roads are a special kind of risk.

We figured we were alone, though. Since Joe had turned the wackers around we seemed to have the middle ranges to ourselves. Joe scouted ahead and behind, and since the night of the boyattack he had discovered no other human traces except for a few scattered homesteaders grubbing in the muck. So we figured it was better to follow an old road that led somewhere than take a chance climbing the ridges that might lead nowhere. As bad they were, roads eventually take you some place, even if there was no one left at the end. Theres always rock slides and wackers to worry about, and up high it was still a bad time of year for avalanches with the snow so wet and heavy. But mainly we followed the road because of the river flowed west.

From the start, the wildboy trailed along with us. I awoke on that first morning to find his head again in the food sack and my blanket dropped among the rocks like a discarded wrapper. He never spoke, or even grunted or groaned, since he first came screaming through the underbrush. But I took to conversing with him. Right from the beginning I set to informing him about people we had encountered, some good and some rather not good, and about all the places we had been and all the trails we had followed. And all the trading. I figured he needed to know who we were, and if he was going to stick around then he should learn the business. But also the older I get the more I want to go back and do everything again, doing a few things better but mostly just following the same paths. Every road comes to an end somewhere, and theres no going back to the beginning. Storying gives me a chance to recover some of that ground, and here and there I might have improved upon the original in my relations.

For someone who couldnt talk, the wildboy wasnt a bad conversationalist, and I figured he owed me for stealing my blanket and for my not shooting him. Sometimes I would get his vacant animal stare, or sometimes in response to my tellings he would scratch himself, pick at a scab, or slap at the mules. Some mightve thought he paid more attention to the wolves howling at night than to me, but I believed he was taking in my stories, especially when I described Joes many accomplishments. He paid Joe considerable attention. We would be picking our way along the road when he would dart ahead or to the side, looking into the forest. Then off a ways Joe would emerge from the shadows, a distant shape appearing before us. The boy had a decent talent for keeping track of Joe and the food sacks.

He had a talent for the mules too. Most of the time he stayed with them, walking with them, grazing them in the patches of wild grass that grew along the road. I was careful to teach him their names, for even old stubborn mules deserve a name, even if some people dont. I would point to a mule and say its name, like Eveready, Duracell, or Toshiba, but hed just stare at me like I was talking nonesense. Sometimes he would wander off a ways, but he never got too far from the packs. He showed no inclination to run off screaming through the pines. At the stops he would always show up, eat his fill, and then a couple more fills, and at night he would wrap himself up in my blanket. I tried to give him Joes one night, but the foolboy would not take it.

A curious wildboy. We dressed him a bit better than when he first arrived. The morning after his arrival Joe opened up the packs and got him out an old leftover redwool shirt, an old blueblack jacket, and bluejeans so big he could have fit his two sticklegs into one pantleg. He made a curious appearance with everything rolledup and foldedup to fit his scratchedup, scrawny self.

"Looks good, dont he?"

Joe was stuffing his pipe, amusing himself. I give the wildboy a glance.

"Kinda looks like a scarecrow set out in corn."

But the boots were the most curious part. While Joe was being so downright motherly and generous, the boy went to pulling out whatever his eyes fixed upon from the packs, pulling handfuls of leftovers he probably had never seen before and had not the slightest use of, things like adhesive tape, a bottle opener, and a toothbrush. Then he pulled out the boots. An old scruffy pair of fancy western boots with pointy toes and big heels. They were stitched with curly goldsilver designs, and once his gaze was upon them, once he had them gripped in his muggy hands and hugged to his chest, there was no tearing boots and boy apart. I tried, but it wasnt no use.

"I think you better let him have them boots. Unless you want to shoot him."

I stood back and considered. "Well, maybe I wont shoot him this time. Youre not going to give him anything else, are you?"

So the boy got his boots. They were about a hundred sizes too big for him, but they well matched his oversized balloonpants. All was well and good though, because there was more than enough boot to fit the excess pant legs inside of. Only it was a goshwonderful curious appearance. The boots added a few inches to the boy, but they came up nearly to his knees. The boy was all boots, and he would go clumping and stomping around like he was a drunken fool at a whiskey parade. He must have stuffed the boots with all the rags we took off of him in order to keep them on his feet. I could tell he had gone from being altogether wild and beastlike to being downright vain and humanlike. The wackers had used him as a packanimal and woodgatherer, and probably worse, but he was quick to learn the fine arts of mulekeeping and selfadmiring.

I remarked upon this with Joe later that night. "I aint sure we improved the boys appearance. Maybe we better give him those old rags back. Hes wearing enough clothing for a tent and enough leather for a saddle."

"Youre just jealous hes cutting such a fine figure. Hes ok. Just needs a little time to get settled. He aint so educated as you."

I wondered where the boy was going to get settled and get educated. Or get civilized. He was about as fond of bathing as the mules, and he certainly smelled like them. I had taken him down to the river, but I could not make him wash, which tended not to improve his appearance much either. He preferred to stay muddiedup.

"He looks like a skinner and smells like a mule."

Joe seemed not to care about this, shrugging and sipping his mountaingrown instant coffee, not at all disturbed by the oddity of either the boys appearance or smell.

They got along well with each other, Joe and the boy. About the third or fourth night I again took up the theme on how we had changed, but not improved, the wildboy.

"You try getting down to the river. If you want to civilize that wildboy, you teach him the etiquette of bathing."

Joe coughed up a laugh. "The what of what? Where do you come up with that stuff. You been wasting time in one of them old books you got stuffed away? Here, Ill fix him up."

Joe got up and reached back into one of his bags and then, giving me a quick smile like he knew he was sticking a muddy hand into a food sack, pulled out an old rusty hunting knife. He held it up and examined the blade. The wildboy was all eyes. Joe waited another few seconds, resheathed it, and then tossed it to him, who clutched it with both scabby hands like it was slippery fish. In an instant the boy strung it on the piece of rope he used for a belt, and it drooped between his knees, so when he was clomping and stomping around the knife would be skimming around the rims of his boots. I believed it was downright dangerous.

"When he gets caught up in knife and boots and trips over a rock face, youll have to bury him. I aint going to help."

Joe added the knife to tease me. I did not exactly feel threatened, as though the wildboy might cut my throat some night, but I did not hesitate to tell Joe that I thought it did nothing to improve either the his appearance or our security.

"This dont make good business sense. What are we getting out of this deal? Dressing a wildboy up in our tradable goods, and then giving him a still quite serviceable knife, this aint good business."

"Hell pay us back double for what were giving him. You wait and see. Its good business. Its what you call an investment."

The Lords of Leftovers

We got along as we went along that old crackedup road. I disregarded his attire, and the boy never once protested when I set to educating him, never seeming to care if I amplified what memory gave me. And he was handy with the mules. So I did not care too much about him clomping around in boots and knife. All in all, we travelled well that first week. The weather was good despite the chill at night. The mules were in good shape, there was enough of for all of us to eat, and the road was heading somewhere we hadnt been before. I was content to let the wildboy accompany us.

But I was not content when we encountered the old man. He was trolly and squirrely, looking like hed been living underground, and of course he was crazy as a screamer. No one who wasnt crazy would live in some old abandoned mine or hole in the ground, hiding from the light of day. This one had been living in the grease pit of an brokedup gas station, or at least seemed to be on familiar terms with it since he was slathered over with black greasy grunge. If it had not been for the wildboy, I would have detoured around the old man without stopping, as encounters with those deranged and unhinged generally dont result in anything profitable. But as soon as he came scuttling out of his hole the boy was overcome with an irresistible urge to be sociable, and before I could change the course of events the two of them were grinning at each other like they were kin, or leastways kindred spirits. The old man stood there blinking in the light and wiping grease from one part of himself to another, while the boy stood there in front of him, scuffing the cracked pavement with one of his ginormous boots, as bashful as if he were with a woman. For a moment I considered the possibility of calling up a rockslide to cover them both up. I tried to warn the wildboy but he had run off to the old man as soon as his greasy head popped up.

"Hold up there, that old man might not intend you kindness."

But the boy paid me no mind, and he and that squirrelbrained old fool kept on grinning at each other.

But grinning and smiling dont mean much. You cant ever tell. Often times somebody being all friendlylike aint all that friendly. Like that little fatman in the whiskeyshack, all a smiling and cheery. As soon as you turn your back someone like that will shoot you down in a second, as if you werent worth a moments thought. I was agitated the foolboy did not know this.

Dan Williams

We had followed the road down a wide, curving ridge into another steep valley when we came upon the crossroads. At the base of the ridge there was what was left of an old village—fifty or so old houses and buildings, most of which had cavedin and splinteredup years ago under the heavy winter snows. Most had been burned, and all of them had been picked over. There three old gas stations with big lots spaced between our road and another old road, and a row of old brokedup stores that faced the crossroads. Our road continued to follow the river snaking west, while the new road came from the southwest and angled back towards the northeast. Seemed like this spot had been charredup long ago.

Joe had come through shortly after daybreak and had discovered nothing worth salvaging. The houses werent much more than twisty mounds of chips and shards, pieces of old roofs and the jagged ends of broken boards. He had circled back to us earlier to let us know, and according to him the only inhabitants were multilegged and ratty. We didnt figure on stopping until the old man and the boy decided to have themselves a grinning contest. Wasnt much for me to do except either join in the fun, since I didnt have much luck breaking it up.

I was touchy, though, on account of Joe missing a creature as big as a greasy old twolegged man. If he had missed something as large as an old greasy troll, maybe he might have missed something else as large or larger too. After all the wackers, I did not want to conclude my days being surprised by a troll and a wildboy. I eased a cutter off of my shoulder and opened my coat to expose pistols and gunbelts. Just to avoid misunderstandings and be sociable. I stepped towards the old man until I was close enough to press the mule rope into the wildboys hand. I listened hard but heard nothing except the wind and the river below us, not even a hawk or jay screaming in the distance.

"Old man, you seem well lubricated today. You been in tight places?"

The old man shifted his gaze to me, still blinking and smiling. His eyes were red and watery, but his gaze was steady enough.

"Got any food?" he asked. His voice was whispery.

"Sure, plenty of food." I motioned the boy to drag off the mules to a patch of tall grass by the edge of the pavement. He seemed disinclined but clumped off, turning his head back to us.

"Got all kinds of tasty leftovers. Got cans of apple sauce. You ever had any apple sauce? Got cans of sweet corn and peas. Might even have coffee and whiskey. But were just poor traders trying to get by as best we can.

What can you give me, old man? We take most anything in trade except slaves." I smiled, relaxing a bit. I figured he was safe enough and that he wasnt packing an arsenal under his grease and clothes. I also figured he didnt have much worth trading except maybe some information or directions. Still, theres no way of telling what someones got hid away. Maybe he was carrying around his grandmothers gold locket like it was some holy relic. But the old man just kept blinking and smiling back at me.

But before I could conclude this interview and move on the boy had dragged out a food sack and was preparing to have himself another picnic, probably his third or fourth of the morning, only this time inviting a greasy old guest.

I might have sighed, sputtered, or maybe cursed. The boy was clutching a food sack and moving towards us, looking quite focused. I wondered if Joe was back in the trees watching us, waiting to see if some other nightcrawler would appear. I kept my hand on the cutter.

After each meal I had been trying to tie up and hide the food sacks so the wildboy could not be helping himself whenever we stopped, or whenever he thought I wasnt looking. I had come up with some fancy knots, and I had been moving the food sacks around in various packs from mule to mule. I finally had settled on Sony, which is the crankiest mule and known to bite. But the wildboy had made friends with that old creature and had found my hiding place. He had a respectable gift for locating food sacks and untying knots. He had equal facility with fingers and teeth, and one time I caught him carving up a knot with that old knife, which I complained was unfair and against the rules. Only the wildboy didnt bother much with fairness and rules.

Before I could spit he was plunging his head and shoulders into the food sack like he was trying to sack himself up. The old troll turned towards him, nodding and smiling, and letting out a little laugh like he had just won a lottery. I wished a rockslide would come, or maybe a black thunderhead would appear.

The boy had no business sense, and sure as hell that old greasey, raggy man didnt care a hoot for profits and loss. With the times what they are, I am about as charitable as anyone can be, and I like most people I encounter, at least those not inclined to kill or steal. But I dont give tradable goods away, not unless Im getting something back, and so far I wasnt getting much of a return from the wildboy, and I had little expectation of anything from the old man. Joe seemed right fond of both the boy, and teasing me with the boy, and I wasnt sure why.

In all our years we had far too often met up with far too many people starving and suffering to remember. When the Fires got heatedup, near everyone got to hurting. Some of those suffering we helped a little, maybe a biscuit or something like an old tornup shirt, and maybe even an old blanket, and sometimes I tried to bind up those bleeding and broken, but it was just patchwork. Many, maybe most, we just had to pass by, giving them only a nod and wish for better times, knowing how it could just as well be us. Us or them. You cant stop a flood.

Joe knew this. We had limits, and we werent in the giveaway business. Back in the foothills he had set himself up in a couple big old stone houses down at the end of twisty road in what used to be a fancy development where rich people lived. He had a handful of wives and a fair quantity of children and a couple old uncles, and he had more than enough of both to worry about with all of them. I wasnt sure why he carted that wildboy back into camp.

But the boy was none too worried about his place in camp or creation. He squatted on the crackedup pavement stabbing at a can of sardines with that big knife of his. The old man squatted down with him, nodding, blinking, and smiling, like he was offering thanks to all the gods he could think of. I believe I sighed again, or sputtered, or maybe it was something louder I muttered.

"Damn, boy, youre going to slice off your fingers before you figure out how to open that can. You even know what it is?"

I went over and grabbed the knife out of his hands. The boy had a gift for food and theft, but he was downright dumb when it came to simple things like opening up cans and building camp fires. But then maybe he wasnt so dumb after all. Cans got opened and fires got made while he just stood around looking loopy. When I gave him back his knife, which he licked off and resheathed real careful like, he handed me the sardine can and sat down to wait for his snack. The old man squatted there along with him. And I was thinking on rockslides and thunderheads and business profits, but for some unknown reason I got hit with feeling easy and generous. I pulled out a pocket knife and opened that little tin of oily fish. The old man leaned in like he was assisting the process. He smelled worse than the boy, the mules, or even the sardines.

There wasnt much I could do but shoot them or join them. I had no idea where Joe was but figured he was off at the edge of the forest watching us, enjoying the scene. The mules were still chewing at the grass and weeds, and the day was more or less pleasant. And anyway they were my sardines. I tied up the mule rope, which the boy left dragging on the ground in his feeding frenzy, got myself a biscuit and a little oily fish, and settled in. But I kept the cutter swung over my side.

  The old man was chewing and swallowing, and making grunty noises like he hadnt had sardines or much else in a good while. The boy seemed to be enjoying himself too, maybe too much. Soon as the sardines were devoured he dove back into the food sack, and before I could grab either him or the sack he had hauled out a couple more littlefish tins and another little sack of biscuits. Instead of stabbing at the flat tops, though, he held them up to me with that blank animal look of his, as if giving away food to a greasy troll was just a natural and perfectly acceptable part of my day. As soon as the old man finished licking all the sardine grease from the first tin, he leaned in on me, wheezing and sniffling, waiting on a second helping. I give up hoping for rockslides and thunderheads and opened up another tin just to get the old troll away from me.

Chapter 5

But the gunshots busted up our picnic, which is exactly what gunshots will do. And maybe that was just as well. If the stillness of that splintered crossroads had not been shattered, we just might have spent the rest of our lives setting there chewing on oily sardines and being foolish. But gunshots make quick work of picnics and people.

There were dozens of rounds fired in short bursts, serious gutbusting, lifebreaking activity. Somewhere nearby someone was trying to cut down someone else, or maybe more than a couple were getting cut. Even the craziest bloodletters wont waste bullets unless theyre killing or getting killed. I couldnt tell for sure where the shots were coming from, down a ways around a bend, and I had no idea who was shooting and who was getting shot. Maybe Joe at either end. I couldnt tell.

I dropped the fish and swung around pointing my cutter in the general direction of the fire, while calling for the wild boy to grab the mule rope and pull them back behind a broken cinderblock wall towards the trees. The shots werent too close, but close enough to get ready for hell and havoc, not knowing who or what might come around that bend or out of the treeline. Joe dont ever open up his guns unless hes hunting or getting shot at, and he dont hunt much.

The moment I dropped the sardines, though, that wildboy went after them, snagging the tin in the air and stuffing it grease and all into his baggy pockets before gathering up the mules and tugging them out of the crossroads, his boots thumping across the empty lot and his big knife thumping against his knees. The old man just stood there wheezing and sniffling, looking like he didnt know which way to go or how to get there.

"You got any friends around here, old man?"

He shook his head and started to move off after the boy. I figured he might scuttle back down his hole.

"Its been a real treat, but I think well be going now." I moved off a few steps trying to get between the boy and the mules and the road. I figured the best thing to do was get into the trees and gain some elevation and then disappear for awhile. Joe could track us wherever we went. I wasnt particularly attached to the idea of waiting out in the open to find out who was shooting and who was getting shot. And even the dumbest rateater will tell you that moving targets are the hardest to hit. The mules were somewhat skittish to cross a ditch and climb the first bank, but we pulled and tugged and I finally kicked Kawasaki and Hitachi until we got them into the trees above the broken crossroads. I didnt notice that the old man was still with us until I saw him trailing along behind Kawasaki. I wished it was Sony he was trailing.

"Old man, you best not stand behind that mule. Its a vengeful creature. You best go back underground or wherever it was you came from," I said, turning to face him. "Aint no more sardines."

But the old man just blinked, wheezed, and ignored me, although he did move off a ways from behind that surly mule. I didnt want to boot him or shoot him, but I couldnt see trying to deal with a bunch of cuttercrazies while attached to a greasy old troll. A wildboy around was bad enough, but a wildboy and wheezy old man was too much. The old man squatted down next to me behind the trunk of a tall pine, peering out at the crossroads below. The knees of his greasy pants were already covered with a coating of dirt and pine needles. I decided to ignore him for the moment and focused on the crossroads, cradling the cutter, waiting for Joe or whatever.

"Youve got guns," the old man whispered in my ear, "Maybe you need some hellfire rockets too."

I considered shooting him. He was more rattleheaded than I had thought. I wasnt sure if he was asking or telling, but either way he could see what I was holding, which was ample fire. Worrying about rockets and ordnance was way too much worrying. I leveled the cutter at his bony chest, figuring it was answer enough. But the old man reached out and grabbed the gun barrel.

"Old man, let go of my gun," I jerked the barrel out of his hands. "Dont ever grab a mans gun."

I was not happy. I had not been happy about the sardinefeast, and now I was a lot unhappier.

"I wont go back. I wont do it. I wont let them do it," he whispered, reaching for a pistol I had holstered. I batted his hand away.

"Go back where. Wont do what? Wont let who do what? Whats going on? I got a partner out there somewhere."

"Youre going to have to kill them, or theyre going to kill you."

"Aint that a surprise. But who, old man, whos shooting?"

The old man gave me a watery-eyed look and shrugged. "Its just smoke."

I tried to ignore the old man, figuring that somewhere out there in front of us was a bigger problem. There still wasnt anything to see that I hadnt already been seeing. Just the wreck of an old crossroads and the river beyond. All was quiet, the only sounds from the wind through the trees, the river currents, and a couple of jays squawking in the distance. But those squawky birds dont have enough sense to shut up. Out in the distance there was a buzzard circling high up, but not much else moving. It wouldve been a pleasant day in a pretty place if not for guns and a greasy old man. I began to consider relocating to higher ground, hopefully behind some rocks. Joe would find us as long as he wasnt too bloodiedup, and I couldnt imagine him getting bloodiedup. Most times he reacts before theres a need to react, and I hoped it was so this time. The mules and the wildboy were fidgety, pulling at each other. I motioned for him to take the mules further up the slope, but he ignored me.

"Theres too many of them."

I turned back to the old man.

"Whos them, and how many of them? I dont want to ask again."

The old man shook his head. "Dont know."

I was not getting any happier.

There was movement behind us, and I swung around to fire. But I let up and sat down. The old man jumped up but just as quickly dropped back down behind the log.

"We having fun or what?" Joe called to us. He was about forty yards above us, picking his way down the slope, moving casually enough like no one had been intent on killing nobody. He didnt seem concerned about anything, nor had he tried to soften his voice, but still I could tell he was in a hurry to get somewhere. I eased back and leaned against the tree, resting the cutter in my lap. There were sardine prints on the barrel, and I considered grabbing a handful of old man tatters to wipe the print off. The boy stood up from where hed been crouching and barked a greeting, and before Joe could ease off his pack the boy was poking him with his sardines. The old man seemed a little uncertain.

"Nice party. Good food and fresh air. Whos your friend?" Joe nodded towards the old man.

"He aint exactly revealed his name, though he has demonstrated a fondness for grease pits and sardines. Not too smart around mules and guns, though. And I assumed he was your friend, seeing how you left him here to surprise us."

"Havent had the pleasure, myself," Joe said, and then turned to the old man. "He is a might mucky, though. Been living in the ground, old man?"

"How come you missed him this morning?"

Joe shrugged. "I guess I didnt look underneath everything around here. I saw plenty of rats, but hes a too big for them. Saw some wolves too, but hes a bit scawny and feebled to be running with them. "

The boy again poked Joe with his sardine can, and he took it, opening it with his pocket knife and handing it back to the boy. The old man went over and sat down one the log next to the boy, reaching over for a share.

"Likes them smelly little fish, dont he?" Joe said, smiling. "The boys being right generous, too, making friends and all. Sure is a nice party. And I sure hate to break up a party, but we best be getting out of here, or else we will be having some real fun. Theres a dozen or so slavers a ways up the road who would love to have us join them, and they got plenty enough guns too." Joe got up and began to gather up his pack.

"Slavers?"

"Wackers, or screamers, I aint sure what they are cept bloodyminded and irritated. They had some captives tied up in a line."

"Had?"

Joe shrugged.

"What kind of fun were you having awhile back?" I glanced back at the crossroads and gathering myself up.

"The shooting? The ones with the guns were expressing their displeasure at the sudden departure of a couple that had no guns."

"What did you do up there? You couldve let them alone."

"I borrowed a couple of things." Joe grinned.

"We couldve traded."

"We dont truck with slavers. We aint never traded people. Now we better get going or we might end up yokedup and carted off." Joe began to move back up the slope.

The boy finished licking the sardine mush off his fingers and pulled at the mules to follow.

"Hold on a minute. The old man knows something about your friends." I gathered myself up.

"That right?" Joe asked, but didnt slow down to get an answer. "Well, bring him along too. Lets have some more fun. But lets do it up a ways. You take the boy and the mules and the old man up this way, going off towards your right just a bit, until you come to a wide rocky ledge. Around on the other side of the rocks is a couple of the things I borrowed. Pick them up for me, will you? Aint too far up a ways. Maybe a half mile at most."

Joe gave me one of his big grins. I just nodded. He was having fun.

"Ill follow later after I see if them wackers are smart enough to figure out which way we went. Ill watch for a while."

"What if the old man gets us into more trouble?"

"I dunno know. Shoot him, I guess."

One of the things Joe wanted me to pick up was a brokenfooted woman. We sweated up a steep hill for thirty minutes or so, dragging the mules up after us, zigzagging as fast as we could, until we came to a large crust of rocks overlooking the crossroads. And there we found her. She was waiting for us, watching us as we came over the rocks.

The boy and the old man pulled ahead of me, and by the time I got the mules to follow the three of them were staring at each other, she sitting and them standing sweatsoaked and heaving, catching their breath. She had a little silver pistol in her hands, a little pocket gun that Joe kept squirreled away in a boot or pocket in case of an emergency.

I was startled, and for a few moments I just stared, heaving along with the wild boy and the old man. Then she spoke.

"You are Trader."

She was more telling than asking.

"I am Bern. Your friend Joe told me to wait for you." She smiled, barely.

She had been beaten, savagely by the look. One side of her face was swelledup all purple and bruised, and she held herself real steady like people in pain always do. But she still was pretty, a kind of deep pretty that the pain and the bruises couldnt destroy. She had honeycolored hair that brightened in the sun, dark turquoise eyes, and a face without any of the scowl, rage, or misery that most people generally carry. Except for the swelling and bruises, she didnt appear too nickedup or scarred—even her hands, which are most times the first thing I look at on a woman. I couldnt tell her age, not young or old. She wore leftovers, a baggy blue shirt and old canvas pants that were tied around her waist and rolled up. Then I noticed the walking stick by her side.

"You hurt bad?" I asked.

She pulled out her right foot from beneath the folds of her pants. It was wrapped tightly with strips of an old red blanket. Joes blanket. I nodded and went over to her, moving the boy gently to the side. Between the two of us, me and Joe, I do most of the mending, having learned long ago how to set a bone or stop a bleed. I can sewup and patchup, and maybe even root around for a bullet—but only if the damage is not too bad. These days most deep wounds are killers one way or another. Infections kill as many as bullets. I looked at her foot.

"Your friend said you were a healer," she said.

"I am a thief, mostly," I answered, concentrating on unwrapping the remains of Joes blanket. I was afraid at what Id find. I could tell she was swelled up badly. "Least thats what most peoplell say. Sometimes they say worse."

"You have a healers touch."

I stopped myself from asking what that meant and focused on her ankle. It was probably broken. Joe hadnt had time to clean the cuts and bruises, so I cleaned them, trying to pour enough water over the scratches to get the grit out, but there wasnt much else I could do except try to keep it clean and then wrap it with a couple of splints. This would take time, though, and I wasnt sure how much time we had. I told the boy to go up to the top of the rocks and keep a watch for what was coming up behind us. I began to rewrap it as best as I could. I knew she would not be going anyplace soon without literally picking her up.

"You got any more of this?" I held up one end of a blanket strip.

She pulled out what was left of Joes blanket from her bundle, and I tore off a couple of more strips. The wild boy came over to offer his big knife, and I let him cut a couple more strips. Which he seemed to like.

"Theres nothing I can do now except try to wrap it better. Maybe later you can—" I stopped myself. What later, I wondered. We werent in a good situation, not hardly. Joe had told me to pick her up, and pick her up I aimed to, since she couldnt walk too far or too fast. I had no idea how soon someone would catch up to us. I figured shed been yoked up with the slavers, and for some reason Joe cut her loose. I imagined the slavers werent none too happy about the situation. I was hoping on Joe, but theres always a chance some wacker might have get around him, or through him. And she knew. She watched me wrap her broken foot, and she knew.

"You can leave me and get on your way. Take these packs. Theres food in one and things in the other."

"Things?" I asked.

She nodded. "Some guns. And some silver. Take it all and leave me here."

I finished wrapping. The old man leaned over to watch, and I rearranged him out of the way. I was starting to have a lot of questions.

"What happened to you?"

She studied me. "What do you want to know?" she asked after a moment. "What happened years ago or yesterday?"

"I was asking about your ankle," I said.

"The big one called Smoke did it. I ran away, and they caught me. Then I ran away again, and when they caught me again Smoke had three men hold my leg down over a rock. Then he did this to my ankle. With his boot. Twice he kicked my ankle against the rock. I cannot walk."

I looked at her directly. Again she smiled faintly, looking back at me. Her mouth was a bit cut up and swollen. I realized that her pain was intense and that she was still feeling it. But pains a cheap commodity. Other than your own, theres too much generally to worry much about. Just too much misery to waste time over. I thought about this. I had survived longer than most by keeping this in mind. But she looked back at me calmly, half smiling again. Other than the tight lines of her pain I couldnt see much else. None of the pleading thats usually in the eyes of the wounded and the damaged.

"Thats why you should leave me."

I went over to the rocks by the boy and looked over. The view was pretty and peaceful like the way faraway views usually are. The only sound was the wind moving through the trees in the forest. Over the valley a couple more buzzards turned slow circles as they climbed. I like these kind of spots. I like the mountains on sunbright bluesky days like this. All the colors seem too deep and too rich to fade. Against the dark blue the few slow clouds drifted along, they were an unearthly white, like snow that never touched the ground. The pines were sweet and green. And even the granite seemed alive with streaks of silver, gray, black, and gold that sparkled in the bright light. Down below the river glistened with the glint of the sun.

A pretty place, I thought, a nice spot for a cabin with a sturdy porch. Sometimes I thought about living in a spot like this, just setting out and watching hawks and buzzards circle in the wind over the valley below, watching the river endlessly marking time as the days passed. A peaceful, quiet place. Sometimes in a pretty spot like this Id start thinking that maybe I was done enough dodging about. But I knew Id start to itch. If I ever settled down to keep watch over a pretty view Id go screamer in a week and start chasing after a whiskey bottle. I tend to get anxious without at least a few people around to talk to. I usually cant keep my mouth shut. No matter the situation, I never have been able to keep shut up for too long, even when I was a scavvy kid hiding in a dark corner, and even when there was someone bigger and meaner telling me to shut up.

People dont talk much anymore, not about things other than the things in front of their noses. Grunts and coughs and hand gestures are about as thoughtful as most people get these days, and telling about things and unraveling complicated thoughts are things most people dont have an interest in, or a talent for. But I tend to talk, and ask questions, and tell stories about all the dealing and all the tight places me and Joe have been in and out of. I tell stories about the Fires too, since I can remember some of the early days after things got lit up. And I can even read a bit, and Ive read books about times before the Fires, which gives me no end of talking material. Set me around a table with a bottle of acceptable gutburn, and Ill start to tell people about what it was like before most things got charredup or fought over till nothing was left but splinters and leftovers, when there were hundreds of thousands of people living in big cities doing city kinds of jobs, and mostly getting along. Some dont want to listen, like the Prince when we first met, and some have done unusual things like walk away from decent whiskey so they didnt have to listen. But some are curious. Some are even eager to hear about the times before the lights went out and the toilets stopped flushing, and some eager just to hear something other than a grunt or a curse. Theres usually somebody wholl listen. Joes brood of children love to listen, and I am fond of narrating their fathers achievements.

I didnt waste anymore time. I hauled the wildboy over to the mules and made him point out the ones that carried food, and he knew which ones. Then I began unloading two that he didnt point to, Rayovac and Duracell. We use a simple xframe for the mules, a couple of boards with canvas straps, and in a moment I had both side packs off the mules. I started to open them up, thinking I would transfer some of the really good stuff to my own backpack, batteries and toilet paper maybe, or knives, nails, and matches and other little stuff like that, the stuff people go crazy for, but then I stopped and give it up. My own backpack was heavy enough, and if I started looking inside these packs I wouldnt be able to decide what to leave or take. I wasnt real happy, and looking at what to leave behind wouldnt make me any happier.

"Here boy, you drag these packs over to that ledge and stuff them under real tight. Then use some rocks and brush to hide them. Old man, you help him. Lets get over the top of this ridge."

The old man seemed a bit goofy and shy, but he pitched in. They began dragging the packs over to the rocks, and I began folding up what remained of Joes blanket for a saddle. The woman watched me.

"You should go now," she called over.

I nodded, not thinking about what I was doing. I live by picking things up and exchanging them for other things. I dont hide things under rocks. I dont give away boots, knives, or sardines. I dont like giving anything away. And I dont pick up wildboys, wheezy trolls, or brokenfooted women either. But I guess I didnt want the woman to know about all of the many things I dont do.

I picked her up and set her on Rayovac, which of the two unburdened mules seemed the more docile. She weighed a lot less than the packs, so I figured the mule wouldnt care much, although we dont set people on top of them. I checked the packs we were leaving behind and figured that a legless blind man could find them. The boy had done what he could, but the packs were just too big to hide, even though he was chopping away at pine branches with his big knife. So I gave up worrying about them. Sometimes its best just to give up worrying about something you cant do anything about. The whole trip had turned out strange anyway.

"Thats enough, boy. Joell have a fit if you chop a finger or two off. Come on, lets get on over to the other side."

That night we camped by a small lake surrounded by a series of steep, rocky ridgepeaks. We had followed the ridge up to a pass between two higher ridges, and over on the other side we had found the lake. Most of the time we had followed what mustve been an old trail, though no one seemed to have used it lately, and certainly no mules. We climbed slowly with the mules and the woman and the old man, switchbacking across the steep slopes, me leading and tugging and uttering the usual mulethreats, the boy stomping ahead or sometimes dropping off behind to check for Joe. The climb had been steep, and often the woman got jerked and jostled about. But she held on as best she could with one good leg, and though she was in pain the whole time she never did more than set her teeth and shudder a bit.

We camped in a small stand of twisty pine a hundred paces or so above where we tied the mules and the packs, and we didnt light a fire. I was afraid that them slavers would keep coming on, and it doesnt take much of a tracker to follow mules, even in the dark. I had half a dozen cutters loaded and close by. The woman and the old man were anxious too, and the wildboy kept staring back up the way we had come, waiting on Joe. There was only a sliver of a moon, and we werent much more than dark shapes that moved around and made sounds. But for a long while no one moved around much or made too many sounds. We werent in a bad situation, but we werent in a good one either. All we could do was wait for Joe or sunlight. I hoped the weather would hold.

I thought about when Joe would arrive and what wed do in the morning if he didnt, figuring I might even doubleback down to the crossroads. I figured that while I was gone the wildboy and the old man would eat everythying they could get out of the packs, then theyd eat the mules and end up eating each other. They wouldnt be the first maneaters to come out of these mountains.

I thought about the woman too, wondering why Joe had bothered with her, who she was, where she belonged, and what we were supposed to do with her. We hadnt talked much after we settled in. I had set the boy and the old man with her and then had moved down a ways to interrupt any night visitors, but I got to thinking about her. More than anything I wanted to know what she was running from so Id know what would be chasing us. The slavers probably figured she was valuable property. Unless Joe had bloodiedup the whole lot of them, theyd keep coming.

I get kind of itchy to find out what I dont know. After a while, after a couple hours of nothing but wind and night noise, I give up sitting off alone and went back up to the woman, so I could scratch a little.

I poked her with a few questions.

"I dont know what happened," she said, offering up her words real careful like.

I stared at her dark shape, waiting to throw another question at her. The wildboy dragged his blanket, which once had been my blanket, over and rolled himself up between us. He was chewing on something. Sardines and crackers probably. I didnt understand how he could sleep with his boots and knife, but he never seemed a mind to part with them. I listened to the mules breathing deeply and asked again.

"I dont know why. They came to take me, the Bishops men. I live in a cabin above the big lake, and I left before they arrived. I left the valley and I found an old road. I followed it down to the river. But then those men found me."

I waited some more to see if anything else would spill out and asked the obvious question. For a time she said nothing. Off to the side near the packs the old man snuffled and coughed. The boy had fallen asleep.

"The Bishop had left me alone for a long time. Then last week I was accused of heresy and witchcraft. I was accused of casting spells, and some of the Bishops elders complained that my spirit shape visited them at night. The Bishop called on me to confess my crimes, only I had not committed any crimes and had nothing to confess. They said I was guilty.

I waited some more, ready with the next obvious question, but she answered before I could ask. Maybe she was getting the hang of it.

"I am a midwife and gatherer. I attend the women during birth and sickness. I am also a healer like you. But now the people of Nineveh will forget my name. They are accustomed to forgetting names. They are forbidden to speak the names of people who are sent away or killed. No one has spoken my mothers name since she was taken away, nor did I ever hear my fathers name. I barely knew her before she lost her name. I was raised by an old woman. She was a midwife and gatherer, and she raised me to follow after her. She never spoke the names of my parents. As a little girl I learned not speak of many things. Every once in a while someone would be accused of heresy and taken away. No one could ever again speak that persons name."

I asked what else she learned not to speak about, but she said nothing. I asked about the Bishop

"When I was little he looked at me but never smiled. Everyone said he was our Savior, our Redeemer, that he and only he would bring us salvation. Everyone loves the Bishop as a Father. They still love him. They still say he is our Savior. But I was always scared of him. And I think secretly many others were scared of him, even those who worshipped him as our Lord. No one said anything else. Sometimes someone would whisper about those who did say other things and what happened to those people. Sometimes I would hear about the Inquisitors and the mines. Everyone said he was our Father, and we all wanted to be saved. No one in the Church ever starved.

"The Bishop arranges all marriages, and when I was still a little girl he arranged a marriage for me with an Elder, a soursmelling old man who could barely walk without bending his back. But I wouldnt talk to him and ran away into the hills until the old woman came to get me. She told me that the Bishop had changed his mind and that I could remain with her.

"She taught me her ways, and I gathered with her and attended her when she was called to birth. When she died I took her place. I was still young. I have lived in the old womans cabin above Nineveh ever since. Until now I have been left alone. I am sent for when I am needed, attending those who are at birth or those who are sick. Now I must confess myself or suffer punishment. People will stop speaking my name."

She stopped, and silence settled around us. I started wondering why me and Joe ever got the notion to visit up around here. Back in Aurora we dont have too many bishops and witches running around. Not too many inquisitors either though the Prince is generally inquisitive.

"Why did Joe steal you away from them slavers," I asked.

"Why, I dont know. He suddenly appeared. Smoke and most of the others had left to hunt for another runaway, someone they were anxious to find, someone the Bishop wanted. Two of the hunters had been left to guard me. Your friend was a shadow that suddenly appeared behind the guards. They cried out, but then both fell to the ground, one right after the other. Then he cut the ropes with a bloody knife. I didnt know whether I was being saved or killed, and I didnt really care. There was another guard who started shooting, and then your friend shot back. I waited for a bullet or the knife."

After a while a crash off in the forest startled us, and grabbing a cutter I rolled towards the sound. Then I knew and eased up. Somehow the boy knew too. He rolled himself out of my blanket and ran off into the darkness.

"What is it?" the woman asked.

"Just an old scavvy nightcrawler is all."

Before she could ask again two shapes emerged from the darkness, one huge and misshapen and a smaller shape hopping around in front.

"Brought you a couple of presents." Joe said. He dropped the mule packs we had left down below, then eased off his own pack. I was impressed. I have come to expect him to accomplish what most would think impossible, but I was surprised by his feat. He had climbed the long ridge and had come over the pass loaded down with heavy mule packs, each one probably weighing more than twice what he carried on his own back. But I did my best to appear unsurprised.

"Took you long enough," I said.

Joe chuckled and sat down between us with the boy attached to him. He opened up a food sack and began unwrapping something. The boy began to poke his bony arms in to help.

"I would have loved to have been there, seeing it for myself," he said.

I could barely make out the boy sticking his head in the food sack. The old man shifted himself over to them too. The woman sat a couple of yards off.

I waited for a few moments before swallowing the bait.

"Been where and seen what?"

"Been back down below on that rocky point and seen you choose between which packs to drop off," he chuckled again. Off to the side the woman coughed. In the darkness I smiled.

"It was too much for me. I let the boy choose."

"It mustve just about broke your heart to leave those packs behind, so I figured Id drag them up with me. You didnt have them hid too well, either. The squirrels and camprobbers were already picking at them. And you mightve just as well put up a sign for that pack of raiders."

"I didnt think we had a lot of time. Will anyone else be coming over the ridge tonight? We can open up some more of the boys sardines and get out the whiskey and be real hospitable." I asked, but I knew the answer. Joe would never settle down and get comfortable with wackers trailing us.

"No. We just have to make do with each other tonight. Maybe later tomorrow we might have company, though." He stretched out against one of the packs, then lit up his pipe. For a moment the match lit up our circle, and I could see the sweat and strain still left on his face. The boy was busy unwrapping and swallowing while the old man helped to forage. The woman had wrapped herself up in canvas.

"Where are her friends going to spend the night?" I nodded towards the woman.

"Bout halfway down the ridge, or a bit further. It took them a while to get started at the crossroads. Then they missed their way a couple of times. I wouldnt hire them as guides or trackers, especially that big ugly one. He aint exactly an impressive intellect like me and you. But theyll probably be able to follow our trail eventually. By the way," he turned towards the women, the fire of his pipe pointing towards her, "I didnt kill them two standing over you. I knocked one on the head and opened up the other a bit. They would have survived if they didnt pus up with infection. I aint no hardhearted killer like this one here. The man is a avalanche of death and destruction." Joe pointed towards me with considerable effect.

I let his joke go and asked, "Would have."

He sucked from his pipe and sighed. The boy grabbed at it, and in an instant he was gagging, and Joe was giggling.

"Thats right, would have. See how quick he is to pick up on words that just spill out?" he asked the woman. Then he turned back to me.

"I doublebacked behind them to see what was going on and found what was left of them. Their heads had been pretty near blown off. I believe the bigugly did it. Hes got a temper, and I dont believe he tolerates a sudden change of plans, specially when someones changed his plans. He was screaming and raging most of the time I watched him. I was a good quarter mile up in the trees, but I could still hear on. He has this long wild grayblack hair and beard that makes him look right brutelike."

"Smoke," I said.

Joe lit the pipe again and passed it to me.

"No," I shook my head, "the woman said his name was Smoke. She tells a pretty story about your Nineveh. You oughta hear her tell it. She stands accused of heresy and withcraft." I got up and checked the mules.

"My name is Bern," she called after me.

I could hear them talking without making out what they were saying. Just a rustle of words in the darkness, his and hers. I felt a little odd standing among the mules, which is always to be expected when standing among mules. But I was thinking that me and Joe had never been taken up with anyone before, and the only times we ever spent time around women was in whiskeyshacks or back in Aurora with his wives. Sometimes when there aint no men around, we trade with women, and they generally make sharp deals. I figured I just wasnt used to being around women who werent connected to either whiskey or Joe. I figured he was fixin to take another wife.

"Tell her your name."

I sat down again and spread myself out, preparing to sleep. I had slipped another blanket out of the packs, and I could tell the wildboy already had his eye on it.

"What is your name," the woman asked.

"He says he dont know his name. Or leastwise he never settled down to one name," Joe said. "People call him whatevers handy. Some have made right colorful choices, and a few have even been polite"

She turned to me. "What did people call you when you were a child?"

"Thief mostly, and then Kid or Heyyou, Getoutahere, Fuckoff, and Sumbitch were popular too," I said. "There were others."

She laughed. "What did your birth mother call you? What name were you given at birth?"

There was nothing to say, so I said nothing. In the darkness I shrugged. The nightsky was blasted with thousands of tiny jagged tips of light. I could have told her that I once had a book that gave names to a lot of the stars, but I said nothing. Just watched the nightsky. Names aint ever a favorite subject.

"I know the names of a few stars. I know theyve been there for millions and millions of years and theyll be there for millions more after were all dust and ashes. You cant count time with stars. A year, a lifetime, is nothing to a star.

"He dont know. He was a wild child like the boy here, brought up by wolves," Joe said. The woman was about to ask something else, but Joe changed the subject. "Old man, whats your story?"

The old man coughed and sputtered, shifting himself from one side to the other. The boy had given him a new blanket from the pack where I had gotten mine. I made a mental note that the old man owed for us for everything he had eaten and a practically brand new leftover blanket.

"No story," he said.

"No? Well, who the hell are you? Whats your name? Where are you from? You aint no real troll. You been living somewhere. You aint been hiding in a mud hole your whole life. Whats your story? Everyones got something to tell. Aint that right, Trader? Aint everyone got some kind of story?"

The old man swung his head around, watching the darkness. "No story, nothing to tell. Just an old man. Been living in these mountains all my life. Never been down to the flatlands. Never had even been down to the river valley before. Thought I might go down and look around. Never been nowhere. Never done nothing."

"You got a name?" I asked.

"Maybe like you people have called me a lot of names. You been calling me greasy old man all day. So thats who I am now, greasy old man."

"Well, listen here, Greasy, you with us or against us? You joining up or just looking for a mouthful to swallow?" Joe asked.

The old man grunted. "Dont know yet."

"Well, Greasy, you better think on it. Tomorrow we go to trading with skinners and savages. You got anything to trade?" Joe waited for a reply, but the old man only wheezed. After a moment he shook his head, settled back, and wrapped himself up in his blanket, which I could not help but still consider our blanket until payment was received. The boy imitated him, pulling my old blanket out from behind a pack and wrapping himself up in it. I made a mental to note to remember where he stashed it, thinking I would steal it back. I wasnt about to let a wildboy or a greasy old man get the best of me. But the brokenfooted woman was another matter, and I was more inclined to steer around her.

Chapter 6

The old fool acted like he knew the way to somewheres. At least he and Joe kept us moving along without getting stuck in some nasty noplace. For much of the day we moved in a northwest direction, switchbacking the sides up several rocky ridges, climbing most of the time. Then in the afternoon we hit an old chunkedup road that curved and twisted along just below the spine of another ridge. A lonely kind of place, the narrow road had been cut into the ridge so that one side dropped off while the other rose up to a high embankment of sandy dirt and rock. The boy was dumbfoolish enough to step right up to the steep fallaways and peer over, and I kept imagining him and them boots slipping off into a big drop. Time and weather had worn the embankment down so that alot of the road was already taken back by the forest, and we had the scramble over the patches where the road was coveredup. Except for the wildboy, we were careful.

    The old man kept shuffling ahead and then pausing, looking around. Pointing a bony finger, he gestured for us to follow the road. I was skeptical of his directions, but maybe Joe was right. Looking at him, he didnt seem so trolly and ravy now, or like he had spent too much time hiding in some hole someplace, coming out at night to steal. He wasnt too cut up or scarred, and he didnt have that battereddown look some of the rough ones get from living a hard life. For all his wheezing and sputtering, he seemed healthy enough. Even after trekking for most of the day he seemed able to keep up with the mules, who keep their own pace. He was no rateater.

    We stopped for a short rest after midday, and I watched as the old man grabbed a stickypine branch for support while he pulled himself around some rocks and then try to wipe off the pitch against his pant leg. I could tell he hadnt been out in the woods for too long. I picked my way around a broken chunk of roadway and caught up with him.

    "Them little knobbly pines are sticky, aint they? Cant hardly get that pitchy stuff off."

The old man gave me a quick look and a slow nod. Then he turned back to stare across the steep valley. Fat gray clouds were starting to roll in from the west, catching the next ridge.

"Where we going, old man?"

He wheezed and pointed up the road again.

"Whats up ahead there? I dont like traveling on roads I aint familiar with. I like to know whats around the bend."

He bent his head sideways and looked at me kind of strangely.

"No one knows whats ahead of them."

"You better know, old man. You get us into a tight spot, and Im going to send you back to the grease pit." I looked back at him with what I hoped was an equally strange look.

He coughed and spit. "Certainty, is that what you want? You certainly got more guns than them killers behind us. Isnt that certain enough, more guns? Dont guns and killers make things certain?"

I was about to explain the metaphysics of destruction when he gestured me away.

"Aint no one up the road. I came through here a week back and didnt see a thing but squirrels and a few birds. Aint no one around these parts. Go on up this old road a ways, and youll get where you want to go a lot quicker than trying to drag those mules through the forest. Aint no one been on this road in years. Aint no one anywhere around here except until you get over the pass."

I smiled. "Old man, you surprise me. Thats the most words I had out of you since you come out of your grease pit yesterday to steal some sardines. Sounds like you can communicate just fine. Now tell me where you came from and where is it you want to get to?"

The old man heaved his shoulders once and then again looked up ahead and behind again.

I didnt get any more out of him, or for that matter out of anybody else. Joe was off behind us someplace. Early on, he had dropped back, but by noon he had caught up with us, staying with us long enough to tell us that Smoke and his friends had either lost their way again or had given up. Then he was off again. In one day he covered three times the distance me and the mules traveled. The old man and I stayed up front. I tried to pry some more words out of him, but the most he would do was to cough,

The Lords of Leftovers

shrug, and point a bony finger in the direction we were supposed to go. I kept a couple of handguns and cutters ready. All the certainty I had available.

The boy and the woman trailed behind us with the mules. I had made some splints out of greenwood that I had smoothed and set her ankle in the early morning, wrapping with a roll of stretchy tape I kept hidden away. It was sprained, probably fractured, and all purpled and swollen. She never cried out or said much while I wrapped and taped, and only cried out once when I tugged to make sure the bones were set. When I finished she thanked me, a tight bloodless smile. She was pale and in a lot of pain, and there was nothing to give her except for some leftover pills, but I knew they would not do much more than dull the pain. She just clenched her jaw and rode along, doing her best to stay on top of a mule that wasnt accustomed to carrying riders. She got bumped and jostled plenty, as even on flat land a mule is no easy ride. But she never said much. The old man was right about the road. Even though it was brokedup and covered in places with mudslides and rocks, it was easier on the woman.

"So where is this Nineveh of yours?"

After clambering over another rough patch, we had paused before heading up a stretch to another break. She steadied herself atop her mule and swallowed some water.

"I am not sure. I never really left it before. I know the valley and the lake, and I know the hills and forest above Nineveh. But I never left that area before. We were always told that the whole world beyond Nineveh was damned and evil."

I thought she was right in a lot of ways, but then not all ways. I didnt count me and Joe among the damned, nor his wives and children. And there were tranquil moments when I looked around and thought things werent so bad.

"So how did you get out of your valley?"

"I climbed as high as I could until I went over and started coming down. I followed a stream through a gorge between two high peaks."

There were a lot of streams and peaks around, and neither she nor I had any idea where we were in relation to where shed been. Up ahead of us the boy and the old man were rooting around for another food sack. Up the slope a few small chirpy birds were twittering to each other. A heavy set of grayblack clouds were now rolling in.

"So why do you want to go back brokenfooted to the place you just ran away from, and where some fool Bishop wants to burn you for witchery? You dont seem the vengeful type."

"Are you the vengeful type?"

"No, not usually. There aint much profit in the business of being vengeful."

"Are profits always so important?"

I wondered what kind of answer she wanted. Theres easy answers, and then theres notsoeasy answers. Most times most people just want the easy answers.

"Its just a way of getting by. Times are still hard, and you got to figure out a way to get by. Some grub in the ground, and some hammer at things, and others tinker with things. Some tear stuff apart, and others build stuff up. Like a lot of unfixed people, me and Joe just move around, scavenging and trading, picking up something that someone aint using so someone else can use it."

"I thought you were a thief, mostly." She offered another tightlipped smile.

"How come you didnt answer my question. You want to go back down to this little world of yours, with slavers and bishops and wolves running around loose? Or you want us to set you someplace else a might safer?"

"What place?"

I shrugged. I had no idea.

"I dont know. Maybe we can find a place. Back down in the hills the Prince keeps things generally safe."

She patted the mule, which didnt much matter to the mule but probably made her feel warm and friendly.

"Then maybe well find a safe place."

I let go of her and the mule, thinking a brokenfooted woman didnt have a lot possibilities. I didnt know why Joe stole her from the slavers. She couldnt do much for herself, and the kind of healing she needed would take time and rest. There aint a lot you can do for brokenup people except wish them a little luck.

The afternoon had darkenedup, threatening to rain but never raining. Thick grayblack clouds rolled over the sky, dimming the forest until dark shapes filled the distance. Maybe it was the weather, but I went along the road feeling heavy and overcast. I dont like cold rain. I dont like unfamiliar roads. I dont like traveling with people I dont know much about. And

The Lords of Leftovers

before I realized what was happening I was heading off somewhere unfamiliar with a brokenfooted woman, a greasy old man, and a wildboy. And none of them of any particular advantage. There wasnt a pocketful of profit in the lot of them.

I had a bad feeling all afternoon, and when we got jumped I surely didnt feel any better.

They came out of the shadows and surrounded us. A dozen or so with cutters and flinty expressions. They were all dressed in military leftovers, greenblack camouflage, and much of it looking new and stiff. We had been picking our way along the broken ridge road, giving the mules plenty of time to work their way through the broken spots, no one saying much of anything, as if waiting for the shadows to move in on us. I had been thinking that maybe a silver mine wasnt worth it, when three of them dropped down the bank and pointed their guns at my head. Sonsabitches had me dead if they wanted me dead. Which they seemed to be considering.

I had been staring at my feet instead of the shadows, thinking when I should have been watching, and felt stupid with three rifles in my face. At first all I could think of was how Joe was going to rag on me for being so careless.

"You move, you die," one of the three said. They looked about the same. One was taller, one stockier, and the third somewhere in the middle, but they looked as if they had been carved out of the same stump. Young men with a grim purpose. Their ammo belts looked new too. Highquality leftovers.

"Can I scratch? I got this terrible itch."

"Shut up," the one nearest snarled, poking his rifle into my face.

Then they were on me, ripping off the pack and relieving me of the cutters I had slung about me. From behind, one of them clubbed me in the back with a rifle butt, and I went down. Out of the corner of my eye I saw the old man on the ground a few feet away with a black shiny boot on the back of his neck.

"Ill trade you for those boots?" I said from the ground.

Someone yanked a handful of hair and shoved my face into the brokenup roadway. Behind us I could hear someone shout, "Get him," followed by two bursts of cutterfire. They were yelling and firing after the wildboy, who had bolted into the woods below the road. I couldnt tell if he had gotten away or gotten killed. Only a crazy wildboy would try to outrun assault rifles. The woman was screaming now, fierce howls of pain. I tried to turn and roll, and for a moment caught a glimpse of her being dragged off Kawasaki. Then someone began to kick me from the side, and I felt my own deep dose of pain. I curled into a ball, trying to protect myself, but the kicks rained down on me. Then someone in front of me stepped in and rifle butted me again, this time on the side of the head, and in one instant the world went bright white, and then hazy. As I settled into a gray mist all I could think about was Joe coming back and killing them all.

When the mist lifted and I began to focus again, I was still on the ground, only rolled over now and staring up towards the tops of the pines and the blackedup sky. My head was throbbing, and I felt the burning coldness of an open wound on the back of my head. The bloodflow had stopped, but I could feel it down the side of my head and neck. Two of the raiders were standing over me, their guns pointed at me. Off to the side both the old man and the woman sat silently, another two standing over them, one of them smiling like he had just done something good. I raised my head, and then carefully sat up. The two over me watched with disinterest. My left side and back ached, and I felt sick in my stomach. It had been a good beating, and I was sort of glad that I had not been around for all of it.

"You boys having a good time?" I asked.

"Keep silent, Infidel," one of them spat back at me.

I knew the word, but I dont believe anyone ever had called me it before. That mightve been the first time. I thought about being an infidel, trying it on as a name, while I tried to shake more of the grogginess out of my head, but the movement only made the throbbing worse. Black clouds continued to boil over the high ridge ahead of us, and I suddenly looked forward to the rain.

"A nonbeliever—is that what I am?" I asked. "What am I a nonbeliever of, the holy word of assault, the church of carnage, the temple of pillage? Whats your creed, wack and attack? I at least ought to know what I dont believe in."

Another one of the raiders walked up to me. He was dressed about the same, but he wore purple and blue ribbons on his sleeves, and another set on his chest. His boots were new and shiny. He looked at me, without expression, and without interest.

"You have trespassed," he said.

"Forgive us our trespasses," I responded.

He smiled, but without warmth. With his rifle barrel he turned my head, examining the wound. "You and these two," he said, pointing to the old man and the woman, "will return with us. If you cause us problems, we will cause you great pain."

"Do unto others as they do unto you." I tried to look fierce. I kept waiting for Joe to open up and kill them all.

He stuck his rifle into my forehead. "I do not need you. I need them," he said pointing to the old man and the woman. "Decide, this moment, if you wish to live."

"Let him be," the woman called, "he has traveled many places and has knowledge of lands beyond the mountains. The Bishop will want to talk with him."

He went to where she lay. "Sister Bern, the Bishop will be pleased to see you again."

I was about to join the conversation when there was a call off to the side in the woods. In a moment half a dozen more raiders showed up on top of the embankment with Joe trussedup between them. They shoved him down the bank, and he fell, rolling to within a few feet of where I sat. He sat himself up and smiled.

"Im having fun," he said, "how bout you?" He was bleeding and bruised in several places. One eye was riflebutted shut.

I give him a moment to adjust. The believers guarding us seemed happy with the addition.

"I dont believe I have ever seen you all tiedup before. Hows it feel?"

Joe spit and rubbed a smear of blood on his cheek against his shoulder. "Peculiar." "How you feeling?"

"About the same."

Joe nodded towards the old man and the woman. "Them?"

"About the same."

"The boy?"

I shook my head. "He departed suddenly, but I aint certain his departure was successful. They fired off a lot of rounds after him, trying to persuade him to stay."

Joe spit again. "I might have to fire off a lot of rounds too when I get loose."

* * *

Nineveh was carved into a series of three hills that seemed to rise in tiers from the immense lake before it. With the morningfog and cookfire smoke, it seemed to move in and out of sight as we moved towards it. I wished it wouldve disappeared.

We had traveled most of the night, staying on the broken ridgeroad until it ran into another old fourlaner, which we had followed, picking our way around the broken concrete and mudslides, until climbing the last pass sometime late morningtime. Over the crest a wide valley opened up before us, with the long bluegreen lake running from one end to the other, and with Nineveh stretched along the left side. A jagged, irregular line of buildings, houses, and streets, the town was a mile or so long and half a mile wide. Scattered above it old mines opened up like gaping wounds, the discolored tailings and debris around the entrances looking swollen and infected. Old mining towns aint never too pretty.

The lake twisted along the farside of the valley, taking up enough space to make Nineveh look stunted and meager. Streams swollen with winter runoff rushed down the far slopes, the white foam of the rapids spilling into the dark bluegreen water. Most of the clouds had disappeared during the night, and the morning was filled with bright light and blue sky.

"Pretty picture," Joe said.

We were still trussedup. They had used some of the nylon cord out of one of the mule packs and, after getting our own backpacks on, they had tied our arms behind our backs. Joe hadnt said much the whole time, and everytime I had tried to talk to him I had gotten gunpoked back into silence. But we were okay.

But the old man wasnt so ok. Our believers had tied him up so that he could only take little shufflesteps, and he had a hard time to keep from tripping or choking every time he moved. And he had fallen a lot, only to get dragged up and pushed on. After a couple hours of falling down and getting dragged back up I thought that maybe the next time he fell one of the guards would simply shoot him where he lay. They were using him up, and they didnt seem to care.

Up ahead of us were the mules and the woman. She was guarded by about four of the believers and the two of the fancyribbons. When the early dawn began to lighten up she had turned back to gaze at us, but I couldnt get much from her expression. I couldnt get much of anything from anyone. The believers ignored us, walking on either side of us, smoking leftover cigarettes as they went, talking in low voices. Maybe it was the head wound, but I felt fairly numb and indifferent. Seeing Joe ropedup sort of ruined my plans for wrecking vengeance and havoc on our guards and their holy minescarred town. I occupied myself trying to stay on my feet. I had spent a lot of the night considering how to slip by the guards who surrounded us, waiting for a moment when they were preoccupied with the woman and the mules. But there wasnt much more to do than stumble along. Even with the dark nightsky there was still too much light to slip away unnoticed, and there wasnt much chance of slipping away while tied up and loaded down. There wasnt anything much to do except to march into Nineveh and try to talk our way out. I thought maybe the wildboy had found the quickest route out.

We came down into the valley and stopped at a couple of old gas stations. On the roofs of each and across the road in the broken storefront nests of soldiers sat with cutters and machine guns. Evidently our believers were garrisoned here, as they dispersed into one of the storefronts as soon as another group took their place. They were all dressed pretty much the same way, leftover camos with shiny black boots, all of the officers were purpledup with plenty of ribbons. I wondered if they hadnt all bumped into an old military base somewhere that hadnt been charred or looted. I hadnt seen unpatched military leftovers in a long time. Even the Princes boys are a motely group.

We were untied long enough for our packs to be stripped from us, then retied again. My arms were pinched and sore where the cord had cut off circulation, and my head hadnt improved much. I tried to engage the new guards in conversation, but they werent conversant. Several of them led the woman and all the mules and packs up a narrow road the zigzaged up the hill. The guards didnt pay me much attention when I tried to explain to them about property rights. The damn mules didnt pay me much attention either. They were all headed towards a series of squat redbrick buildings that were perched on a flat ledge high above the town.

"Sister Bern and your gifts are being taken to the Sanctuary. The Bishop will be pleased." It was the same purpled Ribbons as before, offering the same vacant smile.

"What gifts?" I asked. "I dont recall giving anything. I dont recall making any kind of gift. And for sure yall didnt offer me anything except a sore head." I paused, then thought I might try a different route. "Look, theres been a misunderstanding. Why dont you untie us? Were just poor scavvy traders trying to keep from getting bustedup and split open. We aint infidels comes to pollute the saintly."

Ignoring me, he turned away and walked up the road towards the town. Pushing us from behind, the guards herded us after him. It was hard to be ignored like I wasnt even worth the grunt of a response.

The old man stumbled and fell, only to be jerked up by one of the two guards who pushed him along. He was moving slower now, and shuffling carefully along as if he had a bucket of something he was afraid to spill. I was surprised he was still alive.

"Hold on minute. Where you taking us? This old man aint even ours. He just showed up to swallow a few little oily fish out of a tin can. You might as well just let him go. He aint worth your time. And you might as well just let us go too. We aint worth none of this trouble."

I walked a little, shutting up for a second or two. Slowly moving away from us up the twisty road was just about everything we owned, a years worth of truck and trouble. "Hey Ribbons, you fancy sleeves. Hold on. I got something to trade. Lets talk about your shiny boots. I got something youll really like."

No one wanted to trade. No one wanted anything of us other than to march us up to a big, square brick building in the towncenter. The people we passed didnt seem curious about us. A few sideways glances, but they generally ignored both us and our shinybooted guards. At least half or more of the people were dressed out in camos and boots, and what was left were dressed in raggy layers of leftovers, but they too had boots and shoes of good leather, though not as spitpolished as the saints.

Nineveh wasnt so spitpolished either. An old mining town long before the Fires, it was built below the mines and stopped where the gravel and rock debris began. There were a few brick buildings clustered around the center, but most of the houses were wood, and a number of those were split and cracked, with porches and roofs fallen in from the heavy winter snows. Many of the livable houses had windows either boardedup or stuffedup with rags and whatever. Nineveh had a lot of leather but little glass.

We were untied and left locked into a bare basement room. And we were left in better shape than we should have been. Over the years me and Joe had learned that it was a tolerable idea to carry concealed weapons, and we both still had a few that the shinyboots had missed. I kept a thin, singlebladed pocket knife and a couple of small steel lockpickers hidden inside my belt, while Joe kept knives tucked away in each boot, a couple long nails and a few matches hidden inside his belt, small razor blades sewn into his cuffs, and another little blade into his collar. The shinyboots had emptied our pockets of a couple of knives and little pocket pistols, and then patted us over, but they werent accustomed enough to their business to catch everything. That gave us an edge.

The old man curled himself up in a corner, while Joe spread himself out on a long table in the rooms center. There were no windows, and the only light was what slipped under the crack of the door. I felt my way around the room but found nothing except two old plastic buckets. One of them was filled with water. After drinking my fill, I used a little more to wash away the blood from my head. Then I took the bucket over to the old man.
"Here old man. Clean yourself up. Wash off some of that dirt and blood."
Instead of washing, the old man leaned his scrawny head into the bucket and drank like a mule, slurping and gurgling and gasping. After a moment he leaned back and balledup again, peering at me sideways with one round eye, all drippy and strange.
"Well old man, I surely am glad you stuck your greasy head in the only water we got to drink."
The old man kept peering at me, goggleyed and wheezy.
"I got something to trade," he whispered.
I paused a moment. The old man got me wondering. Our pack of shiny boots had seemed quite pleased with themselves to have taken him. I settled down beside him. "What do you got, old man?"
He was quiet for a moment. "Tell me the things you trade for."
I thought that this was a right peculiar question coming from a greasy old man who had just been kicked and dragged along a couple of mountain ridges. Half his face was swollen up, and he kept one arm tucked carefully away at his side. When he moved, he moved slowly and stiffly.
"What are you asking, old man?"
"Making deals. Just wanna know how you make your deals."
"Tell him, Trader," Joe called over, "tell him the secrets of our success."
I studied the crack of light that seaped into the room under the door,

tracing its borders until it gave out in the darkness. "Aint no secrets to tell, old man. You find people who want something you got, and you give them whatever it is they want, and they give you something back that you can give to somebody else. And sometimes if youre lucky you can make people think you got something they want, whether they want it or not."

The old man sniffled and coughed.

"What do you want?" he asked me.

I didnt need much asking. "I want to get the hell out of here. I want our packs and mules back. I want to be back down in the hills along the front range. I want to be someplace with leftover whiskey and a womans laughter. And on our way out of here I want Joe to wreck havoc and destruction on this stupid foolish town. Of course, I wouldnt mind taking a few dozen of them shiny boots, a couple leftover cartons each of chocolate, batteries, and tissue paper, and maybe a couple of those heavy guns they got guarding the main road."

He coughed a whispery laugh. "Is that all? What if you got all these things? What would you want then?"

"Quit, old man. Tell me what you want. Im not in a real good mood here. Ive been beatup, tiedup, and now locked up, and Im not real happy. What do you want with me, old man?"

The old man sort of sniffled again, and from the center of the room I could hear Joe chuckling from atop his table.

"Want to make you a trade, is all. Youre a trader, right? Thats what you do, go round places trading stuff?"

"What do you got that I want, old man, and what do you want from me?"

For a moment he said nothing. "Ill trade you a story."

I laughed, and he snorted. "Old man, Ive got plenty enough stories. Thats about all I hang on to."

"Not one I can tell, not mine. Ill tell you about a place where people live like they lived before all the troubles and darkness. Where theres electricity and lights, and where theres tons, literally tons, of food and clothing and anything else you could ever want. Whole warehouses where tons of stuffs been left in crates on shelves for years, still boxed up and new. Theres only a few people left there, and they have everything and need nothing. They even have cars and trucks and a helicopter and enough fuel to go wherever they want, but they are afraid to go anywhere. And they have computers that will run forever, filled with more information than a hundred thousand men could read their entire lifetimes, all the wisdom of all the ages stored away in tiny indestructible microchips. While all the rest of world lives in the dark, starving and killing each other for scraps, they all live in warm cozy apartments, where they can turn on lights at night, listen to music from their own little radio station. And hot water whenever they turn on a faucet. Whens the last time you had a hot bath?"

I sniffed around but then thought about it. You cant ever smell your own stink like others do. But I knew for damn sure I wasnt be any worse than the old man.

"Old man, I have heard your story before. Fact is, Ive heard it hundreds of times. Theres always some tearful fool telling about the paradise beyond the next ridgeline. But truth is, whenever me and Joe have got up there and beyond, we aint ever found anything but another ridgeline. There aint no paradise of leftovers. Everythings been charredup and scavenged. Its just a drunken story that gets told in every whiskey shop and sleazepit every time someone gets all drunkedup and mournful. Ive even heard crazyeyed screamers and stonethrowers who could barely talk tell about such places. Me and Joe have been around, old man, and we aint never come across any sort of happy valley. There just aint no such place that aint been usedup, and picked over. And there aint no secret society of saviors or governments out there trying to help anyone of us who got left in the dark. There just aint no one whos suddenly going to show up and turn the lights back on. There just aint."

The old man gave me another one of his fisheye stares and smiled.

"Not a valley. Its a mountain, a whole giant mountain carved up into tunnels and levels and compartments. Its a army base, one that was built to last forever, miles and miles of tunnels and chambers dug deep into the mountains, a fortress of underground bunkers and compounds built to withstand every kind of bomb or missile. When all the rioting and burning began, when the old government began to lose control, everything was stored up and hidden away. The whole complex became one huge warehouse for stockpiling military supplies. The military spent years hiding things away.

"Youre crazy, old man. A place like that would have been gutted a long time ago. You cant hide a place like that without someone telling something to somebody."

"Not this place. Its not a place thats accessible or hospitable. A few hunters and wild tribes have crossed the land, but theres nothing to see if you dont know what youre looking for. There aint much to see. There aint but little outside construction, and thats high up on the steep side of the mountain, where a few privileged people can sit behind their little windows and look down at the rest of the world. And besides, them out there kill anybody they catch that comes into the area."

The old man pointed toward the door. He seemed crazy enough to believe what he was saying.

"All right, old man, you got secrets to a happy mountain. Youre going to tell me where I can go for a hot bath. What do you want for your secrets?"

"Want you to do me a favor."

From the center of the room Joe laughed. "You got the right old man. Traders always doing people favors, a fountain of human kindness, he is."

"What do you want, old man? Tell me quick."

"A promise, is all. Just want you to promise that youll do something."

"Old man. I dont trade promises. They aint got much value these days. Now you tell me what you really want."

The old man shifted himself around. "Heres your deal. Ill tell you where this place is and how to get in. Ill even take you there and show you how to get in. And in return you swear to me that youll go there and that youll bust it wide open. Promise me that youll go there and get the people out. Theres more than hundred people in there that havent been outside in years. Make them get out and live in the world. Make them stop hoarding and start living. Make them stop playing computer games like theyre saving the world when they arent even a part of the world. Make them go out and grow something in the mud. It isnt right for them to go on any longer."

Joe laughed again, but I didnt see what was so funny. I thought maybe I would sleep, so I slid down the wall until I was on the floor. Seemed like the old man had been kicked in the head once too often during the march. I had been around ravers and screamers enough to know the signs. Sometimes some of the craziest seemed the most sane. There wasnt anything I could do for the old man. But before I got real comfortable the old man leaned over to me, pegging me with his one good eye.

"We got a deal? You swear that youll get everyone out. Ill give you more than just stories. I got something a lot better."

"Go away. Go talk to Joe. I want to scrounge up my own dreams."

But he didnt go. He just sat there next to me sniffling and snuffling. After a moment I sat up.

"I dont understand what you want. If you know where theres a happy mountain, why dont you just go and do what you want done? If you want to go turn off the hot water, why dont you just go and do it?"

The old man coughed. "Dont think Ill get the chance. "

"Why, old man? Why? What do you want to do this for?"

The old man sighed. "Long story. I come from there. Spent most of my whole life there sucking on stale air and playing computer games. Battle games mostly. Strategies for world domination. You see, dont you? While the real world was fighting real battles we were locked away underground playing games. We kept them computers going and kept that whole place going for what seemed like forever. Not one of us knew anything different, not one of us. We all believed we were doing something important. We all thought we were saving the world. Then the years passed, decades even, and the longer we stayed hidden away in the ground the less I believed."

Long story or not, I didnt get any more of it. The lock suddenly clicked, and the door swung open. Before I could get up the room filled with bright lights and shiny boots. In the door stood another one of the fancy sleeves, all purpleribboned up from his arms to his shoulders. He looked us over intently, then spoke to the guards.

"Get them on their feet. The Bishop will see them."

Chapter 7

The Bishop was a tall man with an intense blueeyed stare, and he stared across his big waxy desk at us as if he wanted to scratch out our eyeballs. He was old, but I couldnt tell how old. Maybe forever old. With his long graywhite hair, lean face, and angry look, he seemed removed from time, like he might have stepped out of some leftover picturebook of tenthousand year old prophets and might disappear back into its pages if you blinked. Most people carry their years in obvious ways, worn down and scarredup from all the grind and sweat of getting through hard times. But the Bishop was a picturebook man. He was dressed in black, and both his shirt and pants were unwrinkled and unpatched. His desk was an old wooden thing, dark and massive, and carved on the sides and legs with curly designs. He had four guards standing behind him, all stiff and solemn. They were so stiffedup and severe that they made him seem like he was some kind of almighty lordgodandsavior, and they were downright gratified just to stand woodenly behind him like they were part of the furniture. I imagined that the Bishop must have really thought he was almighty lordgodandsavior with his black suit, fancy desk, and rigid men. Though it was still daylight, and a bit of afternoon sun had crept through the clouds into his big windows, he had electric lights turned on.

Me and Joe had been led up a long series of long central stairs to the sixth floor while the crazy old man had been dragged off in a different direction. He goggleyed me once and smiled as they carted him off. There were shinybooted men along the halls and around nearly every door, and not a one of them talked or coughed, or even looked at us. Some were old, but some no older than the wildboy. The whole building was graveyardsilent. We had been trooped into the Bishops office and left standing until he arrived, facing his empty desk and the windows beyond. After a while the Bishop entered, followed by his stiffbacked, shinybooted guards. He had offered us a thin smile and a sullen stare while somebody else all ribbonedup solemnly proclaimed him to be the Bishop of Nineveh and Redeemer of the Lost. From that point the conversation had deteriorated rapidly.

"Why have you come to Nineveh?"

"I didnt come, I was dragged."

"You have violated sacred boundaries. We cannot allow outside pollutions to contaminate the Church."

"I guarantee me and Joe aint ever polluted a church before and aint inclined to now. If yall give us our mules and goods back, and maybe the brokenfooted woman and the old man, we will remove ourselves from your sacred boundaries. We are just poor traders and dont want to cause any trouble."

I tried to get Joe involved, but he went into his idiot routine, nodding, halfsmiling with his mouth open, and every so often making wordless sounds like he wanted to be petted or fed. When he put his mind to it, he could look about as stupid as the stupidest rockhead.

The Bishop sat and stared, and I assumed the intensity of his stare was intended to reinforce his message that he was almighty and that I was some kind of disagreeable stain he wanted to wash away.

"Why do you want to take Sister Bern from us?"

"We were trying to help her. She had been ropedup by a gang of slavers, and one of them had stomped on her foot. We were following an old road and found her."

"Sister Bern is condemned as a witch and heretic. Helping her to escape atonement means that you are devils."

"I aint no devil. A scavenger, and maybe a time or two Ive tried my hand at other things, but I aint ever took on the devil business. Joe neither. You must have us confused with some other contaminations. We aint toxic."

"You are devils in need of atonement."

"We mostly need bathing, and then a good meal and a clean bed." And maybe a bottle of whiskey. Do devils drink whiskey? I aint ever read about that. I dont think we are in need of atoning. Bathing would do us fine.

"You are covered in a filth that only fire can cleanse."

The Bishop stared a lot, and asked a lot of repetitive questions. He liked to stare. He wanted information about the woman and the old man, where we found them, what we were doing with them, where we were taking them, and whether there had been others with them. He thought we had come to his happy valley to defile his church. Who we were, where we were from, and where we had been mattered only slightly. He had only a moments curiosity about Aurora and the dead city, and not the slightest in my pleas and protests. All he wanted were the details of what we had seen, who sent us, and who we had met while traveling.

I tried to impress him with the urgency of returning the mules and packs and letting us go on our way, but the Bishop was not the type to be impressed upon. There wasnt much we could trade. You cant deal with devils.

We sat for a while, silent, waiting, Joe rocking and nodding, me looking around and trying to look agreeable, ignoring the Bishops stare. The stiffbacked guards kept staring without seeing, and in fact there wasnt much to see. The Bishop kept his office uncluttered. Besides his fancy desk and a couple of chairs, there wasnt much else. No saints hanging on the walls. No old books or little statues set on his desk.

"You mind if I get up and flip your light switch a couple of times? Its a fine thing to have illumination. Me and Joe aint used to being illuminated."

The Bishop broke off his stare and picked at something on his shiny black shirt, though from where I sat there wasnt anything to pick at.

"You are impure, but I offer you a chance for salvation. Which will it be? Salvation or damnation? I offer you a chance to choose," he finally said. He had stopped picking at himself and returned to his usual stare.

"I aint altogether sure what you mean by those words. I mean in practical, every day dumb people terms. They aint the sort of words I hear too often. Damnation dont sound attractive, but what does salvation mean?"

I hoped to convince his almighty self that I was ignorant and harmless and unused to solemn stares, shiny boots, and theological concepts, but the Bishop only stared back. Wed run up this trail a couple times already.

"You must serve the Church. You must commit your lives to the Church. You must evidence your sanctification by yielding your lives to the Church in every way. If you fail to demonstrate sanctification, if you cannot demonstrate true repentance and conversion, you will be cast into the flames of eternal damnation."

I figured the deal was skewed, but I considered the alternatives.

"Joes got a handful of wives and a sizable number of children and kin. Do they get salvation along with us?"

The Bishop stared some more, and I looked back at his guards, trying to catch one in a blink.

"If we choose salvation, do we get to wear shiny boots and to stand behind you like these emptyheaded stiffbacks. I would be honored to take on that responsibility."

"Your insolence will damn you," he said in curt voice.

"This mean we wont get the shiny boots."

Again a thin smile and an abundant stare. His stiffbacks, all dressed out in green camos and fancy purpledribbons, stood around like statues. They didnt react to my words. And they didnt do anything but stare off at some point beyond the backs of our heads. I imagine the Bishop liked creating rituals and protocols to display his control. It was a bit like a little boy playing with little leftover plastic armymen. I wondered what he would do if he caught one of his stiffbacks yawning or scratching.

"This is your last chance to escape the fires of perdition. Tell me why you brought Sister Bern and her friend, the old man, back to us. Tell me why you have invaded Gods land."

I didnt know how to answer. We hadnt been bringing the woman and the old man back to anyone. I also didnt know God was in the real estate business, but I thought it best not to dispute this.

"Some slavers had the woman, and she was hurt, so we borrowed her, since she wasnt of much value being brokenfooted. The old man just popped up out of the ground like some muddy troll, looking for a mouthful of something to chew. We didnt know which way we was going, and we certainly didnt expect to get jumped by a bunch of shinybooted headsmashers. We didnt know we had crossed over into Gods land. Do you think he can forgive our trespasses? Were just a couple of poor mountain traders."

"What were you plotting?"

I was talking, but he wasnt listening. "The only thing me and Joe ever plotted was how to get an edge in a deal. We brought up a load of leftovers to trade for silver. Me and Joe was hoping do a little business."

"Silver? You think we mine silver here?" The Bishop actually smiled, then turned serious again. "We bring up silver, but its a byproduct. What we mine is lead."

I should have figured it out as soon as I saw the shinyboots. Theres them that trade, and theres them that take. The Bishop and his boys were takers. They probably used up a lot of lead. I smiled back at the Bishop.

"Then youll give us back our mules and packs and let us go. Seems like we just made a simple mistake thinking you might want to trade with us. Most people up in the mountains are glad to see us and give us all kinds of stuff for what we drag up into the mountains."

He bowed his head and mumbled some. Then he took out a piece of paper and scribbled some. After a moment he handed it to one of his purpledribbons. "You have illegally intruded on Church land. You have conspired against the Church. And you have consorted with a witch and a runaway. Sadly you have refused the Churchs gracious offer of sanctuary and salvation. Your possessions have been confiscated, and your lives are forfeited. I will pray for your souls." A final thin smile and stare, then the Bishop stood up and began to leave. The stiffbacks still hadnt moved.

"Excuse me, but could you explain what you mean by that last part about our lives are forfeited? I aint got such a big stock of words like you."

He paused halfway across the room. "Tomorrow morning after prayer service you will be taken into the square and hanged. The Church must have atonement." No smile or stare this time.

Me and Joe were hardly repentant, or resigned to our fate. In all of the years weve been stumbling around the mountains, weve never taken kindly to strangers trying to kill us, and we were not about to play along now while a bunch of stuffedup, stiffbacked, rockbrained, shinybooted fools dangled us at the end of a rope.

After our last supper, some stale bread, some cheese that tasted worse than it smelled, and something resembling porridge, we considered our possibilities. We were tucked away back in the same basement room, only this time there was even less light. Night had fallen, and the outside hallway was lit only by a few candles, so that only a palegray line of light seeped into the room underneath the door. In the darkness the world had lost most of its shape and contour, and all lines, angles, and curves had disappeared into blotches of dark without depth or distance. I hate getting locked up in the dark.

We mightve tried luring the guards in and banging them on the head, but the profit margin wasnt great, knives against cutters, so we groped around the walls in the darkness, hoping to find something, anything that would give us a better chance. We had the knives out, and if nothing else we were planning on opening up a couple of saints in the morning, and maybe a hangman too. But then Joe found a crumbly spot in a back corner.

    The walls were cinderblock, and for the most part they were in good shape, but Joe found a corner where the masonry was soft and rotedup. All these old bigbuildings are crumbly in places, and often falling apart, and this one wasnt even intended to keep people locked away. It might have been a great and grand cityhall once way back, but I doubt the Bishop worried much about keeping it up. He had grander plans. Like rats gnawing at holes, we went to work busting through the crumbly corner. It aint right to keep someone lockedup in the dark.

    We went at it, Joe doing most of the scraping and gouging, scratching away with his nails and big knife, trying to loosen up a couple of blocks. The room was big enough, and we were quiet enough, so that we didnt worry about the guards posted at the ends of the hallway. I didnt make much progress other than blunting my blade and then breaking off its tip, but Joe worked miracles. He kept at it until he had chunked out bits of masonry, and after a while he could move a block enough to begin doing some serious damage. I hunched around him, clearing away the crumbles and dust and offering him advice.

    "You think we ought to let the Bishop know his walls aint too sanctified? When you get done, maybe we should go back up stairs and apprise his holiness."

    Joe moved away from the wall, resting, stretching his arms and back. In the dimness of the room he was a dark shadow.

    "I would enjoy letting him know. And you want to know how Im going let him know when we get out of here?"

    I noped in the dark, though knowing Joe I had a fair idea. Me and Joe have always attempted to balance our accounts, one way or another. But there are times I take a more practical approach. Sometimes you have to take a loss so that later you dont take bigger loss. "Lets just get the hell out of here."

    "Hell or salvation? Im thinking we need to give the Bishop and his Nineveh some damn damnation. Were gonna get payback for the boy, then get our mules and packs back, get the woman back, find that crazy old man and get him back too, and then we can all go see about his mountain. I wouldnt mind hurrying the Bishop and his stickmen along to another world."

"How about me and you just slink back to the front range. Leave damnation and perdition to the experts. Leave the woman to take care of herself, and leave the old man to take care of his own magic mountain. Lets just get out of here without hellfire raining down on anyone. I bet all your wives and children be glad to see you back so soon. Lets go back down to the front range. Hows that sound?"

But it didnt sound like much to Joe. He just went back to chunking and chipping.

"Right now the only place I have to go is through this wall. And Im going."

The going took a lot longer than we had anticipated. Me and Joe, and mostly Joe, spent most of the night gouging and sweating, but eventually we loosened a cinderblock, and then another. And that was all there was, just an old crumbly cinderblock wall that was built a hundred or more years ago to separate rooms and not to keep men prisoners. Getting out hadnt been much of an obstacle. Sometimes thinking about an obstacle is the worst part.

We squeezed through the wall into an empty hallway, and then we scuttled up some stairs and out a window into an alley. We heard, but did not see, any more shinyboots. I doubt the Bishop would be pleased to learn that his walls were crumbly and his shinybooted guards lazy. He would be set on some atoning for sure after he found out we didnt stick around for hanging.

After the darkness it felt good to be out in the night. But we had been lucky, and I didnt want to push our luck. I still wanted to skip out, but Joe was more ambitious.

"We gotta climb and get some elevation. We gotta climb so that we can cross over to them buildings above town, where they took our packs and mules. Maybe we can get the woman too. We can lay up in one of those old mines if we need to."

Joe didnt wait for a response. He moved off towards a dark side street, heading uphill, moving quickly in the predawn, leaving me to follow.

A couple blocks away we crouched in an alley behind the stump of an old tree, catching our breath, listening, feeling the relief of escape. Nineveh was quiet, and only twice had we seen a window lit up with the paleyellow light of a candle. We were trying to decide the best route to take, and we had no idea where the streets ran.

Joe was right about climbing above the town, especially since he was not particularly fond of large bodies of water. I could swim some, but I generally was not all that seaworthy either. Yet Joe was not much better than a large rock when dropped in water. I had seen him try to swim once, and it wasnt pretty. I would hate to be trapped against the shoreline. Among the high rocks and ridges in the forest, though, we had a fair chance. But against a couple hundred armed and righteous shinyboots we had little chance. The two of us, with only a couple of blunty brokentipped knives and nails, werent much of a crusade. I scrambled after Joe hoping to talk some sense into him.

But Joe wasnt interested in talking sense. We got to an outcropping of rocks near an old mine above the town and tried to sort out what to do. Off to the far right was the flattened low ridge with the brick buildings where the shinyboots had led away our mules and packs. We could see it better now, and I kind of recognized it. An old school of some kind with lots of windows and playing fields in back. A place where kids had learned stuff, like words and numbers and the names of rivers, before the power shut down and all the kids got sent home to wait out the Fires. There was a central core and three wings, each with three levels. Behind it was a small stadium where kids kicked balls. A mass of shinyboots seemed to be garrisoned there now.

"You want the salvation or the destruction part?" Joe asked.

"I want out of here," I said. "I figure if we stay high on the ridge we can slink our way back to the pass and get out of this happy valley."

I had tried to offer all the fairminded practical reasons for cutting our losses and returning to more familiar places and practices, but Joe just squinted off into the early dawn, watching the town. There was enough light to see a couple of sleepy boys herding sheep off to the side of us, and a few scattered individuals moving in the town below. Out in front of the school a pack of shinyboots were getting lined up to march off somewhere, and maybe to our hanging. So far, there didnt seem to be any notice of our escape. I was hoping the Bishop would choke on his atonement when he found out we had slunk out.

"Okay then, you can do the salvationing, and Ill take the destructing. You go on down behind those grassy fields and get ready to get our stuff

The Lords of Leftovers

and the woman. Keep an eye out for the crazy old man too. Maybe they dragged him over there too. I will meet you back on the far side of the pass we come in on, only stay off trail or else youll get knocked on the head again. Stay high as you can with the mules and the woman on the south side of the ridge. I will find you. Dont light no damn fires tonight."

Joe nodded, as if agreeing with himself, as if satisfied his strategy was sound. I knew what he was planning, at least in a general way, but it didnt seem like much of a plan. He was going to get the shinyboots attention while I was slipped in and slipped out. Even if he managed to stir up the entire nest, and even if I could get in and get out, I was not about to slip away unseen with a string of mules and a brokenfooted woman, especially past those concrete buildings and the big spitterguns at the head of the valley. But before I could explain the laws of probability, he threw me a bluntbladed knife, and in the next instant he was up and striding downwards towards the town center.

"Trader, youre a generous man for putting people ahead of profits."

I didnt feel too generous. Hungry more than anything. I sat for a while thinking about canned peaches and chocolate. I like the thick syruppy-sweet kind of peaches, and I put chocolate right up next to good meat and good whiskey. Funny how a little can of slurpy peaches or a chocolate bar can make things a whole lot better. I wished I had one or the other right then. Little pleasures like that can turn big problems around sometimes. People back before the Fires never stopped to think how good they had it, but then people generally have a hard time appreciating what they got. Seems like most people back then were conditioned to think more about what they wanted than what they had.

I started thinking about where I might stir up some peaches and chocolate. We had some tucked away in the packs that the wildboy hadnt found, old stuff that was maybe still good, but good enough. Maybe I could get to our packs. I got up and started picking my way across the rocks towards the school, wondering what shinyboots fed themselves. I didnt imagine Gods army feasted often on peaches and chocolate.

I found the mules first. They were roped into a grassy slope near the playing fields behind the school, and there was nobody around. If all I wanted was to steal a bunch of old mules, it would have been a perfect day. Nintendo and Eveready ambled over to me right off, looking for sugarcubes or a bucket of oats. The others came after them, all except

Duracell, who was always contrary in the mornings. It was a good sign to find the mules right off.

But Joe was right. I didnt feel right about not making a try for the packs. Leaving without at least a quick glancearound for the packs wasnt a good idea. All our scavving for the whole winter was loaded up in those packs, plus all of our guns and just about everything else we owned. Without the packs, we were no better off than the old man or any other starving ragpicker. We might as well just scratch a hole in the ground someplace and crawl in.

So I left the mules and huddledup behind a little shed above the school, trying to think up some way of getting inside. A fair number of shinyboots were marching around now, and twenty or so of them had already outfitted themselves and moved off towards the head of the valley. I had no idea how many more were inside, and I also had no idea about the best way of getting in and out. But the biggest no idea I had was wondering where our packs might be. I thought about the woman too, but I already had decided that if I got inside okay, and if I found our packs okay, then I might look around for the woman on my way out. Just so Joe wouldnt bother me about her afterwards. So I watched and waited. Id go after the packs and then maybe the woman.

Before too long, though, Joes destructing started up. Below in the towncenter gunfire suddenly broke the mornings silence, crackling pops in the wind, distinct and unmistakable. Someone or ones cut loose long bursts of automatic fire. In the distance I could hear yells and then a bell began to ring. Across the way I could see smoke beginning to rise and drift out flat across the lake. I smiled, knowing Joe enjoyed a good fire.

Then the school exploded in shinyboots, and someone began ringing another bell. A host of fifty or so shinyboots poured out of the front entrance and lined up in little groups of ten, and then after they were all lined up a couple of the purpledribbons got in front, and one of them blew a whistle, then they all began to jog towards town, following the road that switchbacked back and forth down the hill. Pretty fancy drilling. I thought the Princes boys, who were generally louts and thugs, could learn a thing or two from these shinyboots.

There wasnt much point in waiting any longer, so I slunk down towards the school. I thought I would feel myself along until I found some way of getting in without getting myself in trouble. But the problem was that, when I got close enough to see, I could be seen. All of the old classrooms had plenty of windows.

I circled around and came in at angle to the corner of the upper wing, and I was in luck. Several of the ground level windows open. Even better, no one started shooting at me, or even yelling.

I slipped into the nearest window and found myself in a barracks of sorts, a dozen beds, six by six. All of them empty. I looked around for a moment, hoping to find something lethal but there wasnt anything like that. There were trunks, though, and a couple of lockers, so I helped myself to some camo fatigues that were a tight fit. But I didnt find any shiny boots.

I creeped along an empty hallway and headed towards the doors at the end. All of the other classrooms had been converted similarly into barracks, and they were similarly empty. Beyond the double doors, though, there was a desk, and behind it sat a fat shinyboot. He was older and whiter than most I had seen, and he had a round overfed look to him. A big head set on top of a big belly. He sat behind the desk with apparently nothing to do but feed himself out of a leftover red can. With Joes knife in my hand I took a breath and pushed through the doors.

He saw the uniform first and did nothing but look startled, unable to comprehend the surprise of someone coming out of the empty barracks. Then he saw my face and pushed himself forward, dropping his can and fumbling at a cutter laying on the desk. But I was already on top of him with the knife poking against his throat before he had a chance to do more than fumble at the weapon. His can had spilled on the desk. He had been eating red beans. With my free hand, I pinched some up and ate them.

"You got any canned peaches? Im hungry for peaches, the real drippy kind in thick syrup. Or maybe some chocolate. You got any chocolate?"

I grabbed his shoulder and, keeping the knife close to his throat, moved him around back through the doors.

We looked at each other sideways, and I smiled.

"What do you want?"

I looked around and listened. So far okay.

"Peaches and chocolate, mostly. What else you got? I like apple sauce. You got any of that? Freshbaked bread is always good in the morning. And coffee, not that rootedup stuff people been drinking but real leftover coffee."

I tickled him a little with the blade, and he looked at me like I was crazy.

"I used to have some apple sauce," I said, "two whole crates filled with these little kiddycans. And I used to have a ton of other stuff too, all kinds of leftovers, canned goods and hardware, practically new blankets, and all sorts of good stuff. I even had juiced batteries and some moderately good whiskey and real leftover toilet paper. And we had stashed away a little supply of peaches and some old chocolate bars. But I am fairly sure the wildboy ate all them little sardines, though. You know what Im talking about here?"

He looked wildeyed at me and shook his head. So I poked him, just a little nudge. Then I slipped his handgun out of its holster and traded the bluntblade for his cutter.

"My things were stolen by your shinybooted soldier friends. A bunch of you shinyboots jumped us out on the old road and stole my leftovers. I want them back. If you want to keep your neckbones together and your blood pumping, you tell me where my things are."

"We are soldiers in Gods army."

"I aint asking who you take orders from. Im asking if you want to live."

We came to a quick understanding, my round friend and I. Although he swore he didnt know exactly, he told me that all supplies and materials were stored in the lower wing, while the two top wings were used for barracks, one for the officers with ribbons, elders he called them, and the other for the rest of the shinyboots. He said he didnt know how many were left scattered around the buildings but that he had heard the bells ring for six squads when the shooting started. I hoped Joe was happy with his turnout.

He seemed fairly certain and sincere that my packs were in the lower wing. He also seemed fairly anxious to get rid of me, so he laid out the safest route to the supplies. Going through the central core was not a good idea, since this was where the assembly and offices were. He showed me a side door to the outside and pointed to what he called a receiving station in the lower wing but was kind of indecisive about how many of his shinybooted friends would be there to receive me.

"One more thing," I said, pulling him back into one of old classrooms, "I lost something else." I was just about done with him, and I was in a huff to go after the packs. I had his pistol stuffed into his lower spine, and I had most of the information I needed. I looked around trying to figure what to do with him. Then I suddenly had a thought that I might stuff him into one of the cabinets. I thought they might be big enough to store a fat man full of red beans, and they latched from the outside.

"See, when your friends stole my packs, there was this woman."

He looked at me like his eyes might pop. He knew who I was talking about.

"Shes a witch."

"No, shes just a brokenfooted woman."

He looked at me strangely. "But shes the, the Bishops —"

"The Bishops what?"

I poked him a little. I thought I was all done poking him, but apparently not. The woman was more of a problem for him than my leftovers.

"Theyve taken her to the courts for inquisition."

"The what?"

"The old gym underneath of us. Its beneath the elders. Thats where they take them."

"Them who?"

He looked around like he was hoping someone else would answer for him. "You know, witches, heretics, outsiders, and all them."

"Oh yes, I know, and I bet theres a lot of them too needing to be inquisitioned."

Chapter 8

I stuffed Redbeans in one of the big cabinets towards the back of the room. Tied his hands with his own belt, stuffed his mouth with an old towel, and then I stuffed him in. And he fit, mostly. But there were problems, so I shoved, and swore.

I had to act quickly, if I was going to act at all, but I was not exactly sure what to do. I told myself that I was for going after the packs, which made good business sense. But Joe had this thing about the brokenfooted woman. I couldnt carry her and the packs together. I couldnt even carry all the packs. I hadnt heard any more of Joes fire and damnation in a while, and I wasnt sure how much time I had before the shinyboots returned, or before Redbeans spit out his towel and started screaming. I didnt think my chances were good for going after both packs and woman, even if I could figure out a way to cart them away all together. I considered unstuffing Redbeans as my pack mule, but I knew hed be more trouble than he was worth.

Just a couple of the packs would be far more valuable than a brokenfooted witchy woman. Even just a couple of food sacks and a handful of cutters would serve us better. I thought about this, and I remembered the pretty view off the rock face when I first came upon the woman. Maybe I should have left her there.

But I wasnt going to leave her. I knew it even if I couldnt fully admit it. There aint much profit in stealing witches, something even the most cacklebrained wormeater knows. And I surely knew it, but then I knew I was going after her even while I was telling myself I wasnt. I slipped out a window and headed around back to see if I could find a way to find an entrance to the lower gym. I knew that it didnt make any sense, but then nothing was making much sense since we left the front range. No sense, and certainly no profit, but thats just the way it was. But once I was headed towards the gym I told myself that I was going after the woman because Joe wanted her, and me and Joe had partnered too long to disregard each other.

The sun was fully up now, shining over the east ridgeline, but no one stopped me or shot me as I came around and found a tunnel of stairs behind two big doors. I had wanted to borrow Redbeans shinyboots, but for a big man he had small feet, so I was a little selfconscious scuffing along in my old boots and new camos. Maybe no one saw me, or maybe no one noticed that I was the only soldierofgod in the whole world without a nice pair of shiny boots. There was still smoke in the air, and I guessed everyone was still too occupied with worrying about Joe than to worry about me.

I followed the tunnel downward, and sure enough, there was a whole sports complex underneath, although I doubted anyone had bounced any balls lately. There was an open area with a big reception desk in the middle and big, wide arrows pointing the way to various courts and rooms where years ago young people sweated and strained and considered it fun. Somewhere beyond was a swimming pool.

There were two problems now. The first was that I didnt know where the woman was, and two, there were three guards at the reception desk one all purpledribbons and the other two armed with cutters. There wasnt much I could do. So I started yelling and slammed through the front doors.

"You wont believe what just happened. You wont believe it," I yelled and ran at them. I was holding Redbeans handgun at my side and carrying his cutter strapped over a shoulder, and I kept swiveling my head backwards like I was looking behind me. "Ive never seen anything like it. Youve got to come see it. Its the apocalypse."

It was the longest thirty yards I had ever run, and the strangest. They all stood at once and stared at the crazy wildman waving, screaming, and running at them. In a moment, though, one of the guards raised his assault rifle to cut me in half. Still running I pulled up the cutter and fired. The shots exploded in the enclosed area, the noise louder than any gunshots I can remember.

The guard flew backward and dropped into an awkward lump before the echo of the shot died out. Before the other two had time to look down and then back at me, I was on them.

The guard I had shot groaned. He was bleeding from his belly and dabbing at the flow with his left hand. The other two stood like rocks. With an automatic weapon in their faces and blood on the floor, they made no attempt to try their luck.

"You there," I said to the other soldier, pointing the cutter at him, "take off your shirt and press it firmly against your friends belly to stop the bloodflow. You move otherwise and you both die."

I gestured towards PurpleRibbons and tried to look as threatening as I could. "I want the brokenfooted woman, now!"

"There will be fifty armed men here in a moment." PurpleRibbons said but did not resist while I separated him from his handgun. Then I gathered up the two cutters and a couple of spare clips.

"And theyre going to find you dead." I jammed the cutter barrel into his mouth, which did nothing good for his upper lip and a couple of teeth. "I want the woman, now! You take me to her, or you die. Its that simple."

No doubt thinking their friends were about to bust in and open me up, he obliged me with some hesitation, walking me down a dark corridor. The smell was not pleasant, and I was not having fun. I was angry, and getting angrier. I had three assault rifles, two handguns, and enough ammunition to wreck my own damnation the instant someone popped in front of me.

We went down a candlelit corridor to a row of racquetball courts, and the smell did not improve. PurpleRibbons wiped his bloody mouth and pointed to one of the courts. All of them had been rigged with crude bolts on the outside, and I encouraged him to unbolt this particular door. When the door swung open, I encouraged him to go in.

She was there in the dark court, which stank worse than the hall. She had an old blanket, two buckets, and nothing else.

"Im looking for peaches and chocolate. You got any?" This was my attempt at humor, figuring if I was about to get bloodied I might as well enjoy myself. She hitched herself up using a wall. Above us there was a viewing area that opened up into another hall, and someone had left a candle burning on the ledge, but the light was not enough to see whether she smiled or not.

"I have only unclean water."

"Then lets get out of here and find something better."

We went back up the dimly lit corridor, her limping against me and Bloodymouth ahead of us, half shield and half guide

"You are both going to die," Bloodymouth informed us. "You are both damned to eternal fire."

I cracked him smartly in the back with my rifle. Nothing I could have said would have mattered to him. As I turned the woman was strapping one of other cutters around her outside shoulder. I wondered if she knew how to shoot. Being a midwife and all, she was more experienced with the other end of the life cycle.

"You too, Bloodymouth, you too. Were all going to pass to the great beyond in a moment or two if we aint careful."

From up ahead came a noise of several people running, their shinyboots clickclacking against the hard tile floors. Down the other way stood another set of big double doors with little windows, and I could see light on the other side.

"Whats down there." I cracked him again.

He gave me a bloody sneer. "I shall be rewarded with salvation. I shall be received into paradise by the angels of the Lord."

I thunked him hard on the head with the rifle butt, and he went down. He was still conscious, but was moaning and rolling around enough not to give us any trouble or any more heavenly harangues.

"You just got rewarded with a sore head. Now whats down that way?"

"The Inquisition court. Its a big room with a wooden floor. Those who are taken for heresy are taken there. The townspeople come to watch the atonements."

We left the soreheaded fool to his rewards, bumped along and pushed through the doors and began hobbling up a small set of steps. The brokenfooted woman done ok, hobbling and hopping, clutching me when she she needed to. Though I had been hauled into the Princes court a few of times over minor misunderstandings, I had never attended an inquisition or atonement before, but I sorted out the general idea. The Bishop was peeing on his little treestump of a town. And I recognized the place, an old basketball court. I remembered seeing pictures in leftover magazines and books of people playing basketball, and these days down in Aurora the Prince even has his own team. Good basketballs are scarce, though, and I have always kept an eye out for ones that can still bounce and hold air.

But here they didnt need any baskets or balls. In front of the seats were various platforms and racks that had nothing to do with sport. But the one good thing about the whole scene was that there were plenty of exits. There was yelling and more clickclacking behind us, so we headed towards the nearest door. I was not in a mind to attend my own public atonement.

But we didnt make it. Before we were halfway to the nearest door five shinyboots exploded up the steps behind us. I grabbed the woman roughly and held the gun to her head.

"Get the other one. Quick. Before he gets away," I screamed and pointed to the opposite end. Three of them looked where I pointed and took a couple of steps, while they other two kind of hesitated. That killed them, or nearly. Before I could blink the woman opened up on them. Her first burst went high and wild, jerking her arms around, but in an instant she steadied the gun and fired again, shredding one and sending the others scurrying back down the stairs for cover. I fired another burst after them. I almost paused to admire her shooting, but she hopped ahead of me towards the nearest door, and I followed to keep her upright. She looked grim and determined, despite being brokenfooted. Which I admired.

We got out, and I got her to the tree line without getting struck by lightning or shot by the Bishops shinyboots. Our luck held. Before too many of the heavenly host spilled out after us, we found the mules, and I hefted the woman on top of one. The mules didnt seem too impressed, like rescuing damaged women was an ordinary kind of occurrence. I wished the boy was still around, him being impressionable and all. I didnt have much of a chance to say much to the woman. While making our way around the rustedup spectator stands and the far edge of the field, with me carrying a fair portion of her, we hadnt had time to say much to each other, and now there was even less time for trading words. I could hear the remainder of the shinyboots we had spilled on the basketball court calling to each other as they ran looking for us.

I pointed the woman towards the south crest of the ridge and told her to make her way up and around and then on towards the head of the valley. She was of a different mind, having her own contrary set of intentions and directions.

"Ill go up to my cabin. You need to come with me."

"I need to keep watch around here for a bit. Maybe find Joe. Maybe go after the packs."

She eyed me a moment.

"Are the things in your packs so valuable?"

"Nothing that can be traded is of much value. But I aint ever going to get locked up in the dark ever again, and the Bishop done that to me. So

I owe him."

I already had added up my debits and credits. I had the mules back, and the woman, plus cutters and enough rounds to spread my own fire and damnation. But I didnt have any of the packs, any profit, any satisfaction, and certainly anything to eat. So far, my account with the Bishop was still tilted in his favor, and I wanted to balance the scales, if only for a few moments. So I took a couple mules, turned myself around, and headed back.

"Stay high and keep in cover. Dont go to near your cabin, which is likely to be filled with shinyboots. Keep moving towards that south pass and head out of this valley. Joe will find you."

But I couldnt tell what she had a mind to do. I had put her on Mitsubishi, which was, more or less, a tractable creature, and I started to head back towards Nineveh. I thought she would call to me, but she didnt. When I glanced back she was heading north, more obstinate than the mule she was riding.

I made a wide circle and came out below the school. There were a couple of side streets littered with cracked and smashed houses, and I stashed the two mules in the overgrown back yard of the one nearest the forest. The houses had all been pretty well scavenged. All the glass was gone, and the doors, and most of the good wood, wiring, and plumbing, leaving only splintery frames, broken pipes, and chunks of plaster and drywall. I crossed to the upper street and picked my way through the rubble and rubbish of a house at the end of the block, hoping to hide out for a few hours until the shinyboots had all settled down. I figured no one would suspect I was fool enough to return.

I perched near an upper window that gave me a good view of the school, or at least its lower wing, and a partial view of the road that snaked upward from the concrete buildings below. If I was going to get myself bloodiedup, I figured I would at least pick my time and place.

My chances of getting in and out were slim and miserable, but without a couple of food sacks and water bottles, and maybe a couple other guns, our chances overall were slim and miserable. And if I have a choice between eating bark and bugs, and stealing real food, Ill always prefer stealing. And I had always been a lucky thief, which most times is the same thing as being a good thief.

Once I overheard a fool of a man boast that his prize racehorse could not be stolen. Just a big dumb flatlander, who lived on a ranch down south of Aurora in the dry flats. At night he kept his horse locked up and guarded, safe from wolves and thieves. When I heard this mans boast, I could not but help to take his words as a challenge. A week or so later I rode up to his barn on a borrowed horse, and when I was accosted by his guards I told them I had been sent by the Prince to warn all of the ranchers that thieves and robbers were loose in the area. We fell to talking about horses and thieves and the Fires, and I produced a nearly full bottle of leftover whiskey, which I had earlier dosed with a handful of painkiller pills. As they swigged and swallowed, and I talked, I gave the fools a description of myself, telling them to be on a sharp lookout for this particular horsethief, as he was the worst scavving thief on the front range. Within an hour the guards were asleep, the barn unlocked, and the prize horse in my possession. Back then I used to take thieving to be a public service, teaching fools not to boast and misers not to hoard.

But that was before Joe, though, when I was crazier and younger. I generally never went too far out of my way to take something, but if it came down to stealing or starving, I admit that I gladly stole. Thieving was just another way of doing business, just another way of moving stuff around, and in some ways I reckoned it was more honorable than the bloodywork that many others were doing back then. But trading goes a lot easier. Once we started dealing we didnt have to worry every second about everyone with a cutter trying to stitch us apart us in the back. All in all, we found dealing more profitable than stealing.

I propped a couple of old boards across the window, so I wouldnt be seen, and I sat there watching the school through the broken wood, waiting for the dark. There was still the heavy scent of smoke in the air, and I wondered what Joe had lit up. Probably something big enough to keep the Bishop and his boys scurrying for a time. I watched, and for a while the general area was swollen with clumps of shinyboots, all looking alike and outfitted alike, all keeping themselves busy trotting around in all directions, including mine. After a couple of hours, though, about a hundred or so lined up in front and then headed out. They carried packs and looked like they meant to stay out for several days. I figured that they were after us and that they intended nothing good for us. With a couple of PurpleRibbons in the front, they marched off in a hurry back towards the pass we had come through earlier. I wondered if there was another way out of the happy valley.

For the rest of the day nothing much went on, just handfuls of guards buzzing around every so often. I got real hungry after a while and wished I had taken Redbeans leftovers, and I wondered what kind of life Redbeans had lived. He probably had never been stuffed in a cabinet before. He probably had never done much of anything except eat redbeans and take orders from the Bishop and those with purple ribbons. I wondered what he had dreamed as a boy, what he dreamed he would be, and if he was happy being swollen and subordinate. Most people can function as long as they know their place, their own little rut of ground.

I aint exactly figured out yet where my place was. Me and Joe moved around enough to keep our paths from ruttingup. As a boy I mostly dreamed of filling my belly, keeping out of dark places, and getting some of what most others seemed to have. I think after a while I slept a little.

Towards the afternoon a dozen shinyboots came back up the road, only they werent alone. There were six or so of them that werent all fittedup like the shinyboots and seemed kind of irregular and out of place. Given their wild appearance and arsenal, they seemed more like wackers, or something in the line of a backshooters and rampagers. One of them was big, almost Joesized, and he had long scraggly grayblack hair and a beard and altogether a spiteful mean look about him. I doubted that there was more than one wild man loose in the mountains and figured that this was Smoke, the manstealer and womanstomper. He looked grim too, as if he was intent on further bonebreaking. He skipped along in a hurry, and the others quickstepped to keep up with him. He certainly wasnt trussed up or under guard like we were when we came in, and he seemed to know where he was going. I watched as he went up the hill and disappeared into the school. Part of me wanted to meet up with him, at least under my own conditions, but the other part of me wanted no part of him. I hoped he would head out before I headed in.

The late afternoon cloudedup and rained a little, and I waited, getting hungrier and angrier. Generally when I get in a waitanddonothing situation, I get bored and irritated, since I am inclined to talk, even to the point of talking to myself, but here I was more inclined towards staying shut up and silent. I certainly wondered about how I was supposed to get back in and out of that school without being inquisitioned, but there really wasnt much I could do in the way of planning since I didnt much have a plan. Sneak in when its dark and quiet, and then try to sneak out. And since I calculated that my chances were not good and that my life was not particularly marketable, I just kind of thought about my favorite subject. Which happens to be my health, happiness, and prosperity. If I knew any other subject as well as I knew myself, I might have thought about it. But I am less familiar with most other subjects, and there always seems to be an endless stream of me, myself, and I topics.

More than anything, I wondered whether I would continue to have a life to continue wondering about. And thinking about my chances put me on to thinking about balancing all my accounts, all the pluses and minuses. But I wasnt ready for a final reckoning. I wished I had that wildboy around. For a wildboy of infinite appetite and shifty inclinations, he wasnt so bad to have around. I got to enjoy recounting my stories to him, threading together the different pieces of my life. He never interrupted, objected, or disputed.

I wished he was around now. Talking is living. One of these days I am going to be bustedup and dead. And it dont seem right. I aint one of those who see dying as a natural part of living. Maybe the brokenfooted woman does. But I dont. Just because theres a lot of something around dont make it natural or right. It dont seem natural at all to me to think that Im going to rotup and disappear. Except for maybe these shinyboots and the screamers and crazies, no one wants to be dead. These days the whole world is intent on staying alive. Ive dedicated my life to it.

I never knew any parents or family, and I can only assume I had them since that is what most generally assume. I dont remember that part. I have shards of a memory where I see a big roadway with people and dead cars and big fires off in the distance, fires big enough to light up the sky, but I dont really know if this is my memory or someone elses that Ive borrowed. I remember an acrid sour smoke in the air, and I remember people shuffling forward, most everyone silent.

I remember the old couple real well. They found me scavving in the muck of the dead city, and they took me up. I was really young, and they were old and creasy, but they kept me as best they could for as long as they could in an upstairs back apartment of a broken building. They kept everything all boltedup and boardedup, and they lived like trolls, coming out at night. The old man carried a big rifle, but he was no shooter.

My best memories of that time are the two of them teaching me words. They had a fat dictionary, and they treated it like it was holy script.

We sat for hours around a candle, all huddled up and warm, and they would give me a spoonful of sugarwater if I did well. Words were the best of what they had to give me, and also the spoonfuls of sugarwater. I would scratch on some loose paper, copying words, and the old woman would correct me, while the old man looked on silently. They fed me scraps of what they could, and sometimes we went hungry, and sometimes I repeated and scratched when there wasnt any sugarwater.

They were the only ones that ever took me up. Then, when I was still little, they died, first the old woman, who just coughed, shuddered, and died suddenly one night, and then soon after the old man, who just gave up after she was gone. I remember some others from the broken building had come around and helped me drag them out and cover them up, and afterwards they helped themselves to what few things the old couple had hoarded up. Some one even took the fat dictionary.

But no one took me. I was a throwaway, a leftbehind, and there were so many other throwaways around then. No one wanted to take me on. No one had enough to eat to share. And there were too many butchers and wackers coming around killing and taking to worry much about one more throwaway. That was when I took on the business of staying alive. I became a looter, a scav, and a thief, sneaking around the dark corners of Aurora and the dead city. A young boy, I stole what I could, not caring from who. I ganged with other throwaways when I could, and for a time there was a large enough group to feel safe. But then another peacock militia came strutting through and cornered all the throwaways they could, enlisting those big enough to carry a cutter. This time I didnt want to be taken up and hid in a ratty storm drain. The peacocks shot one little boy just to terrorize the rest.

I have done lot of things since the old couple traded me spoonfuls of sugarwater for words, some good, some bad, but mostly I did what I needed to do. To survive and stay fed and wait out the Fires. I sat in the dusty shadows of that broken house thinking I had come too far to get carvedup by a bunch of murderous saints. I felt like I had a lot more things to do. And thinking about that got me angry all over again. I wasnt ready to get bustedup and dumped. But I was feeling low, all tired, thirsty, hungry, and gloomy, and I wished Joe was around.

I didnt have to wait much longer. As the hours slipped away, I was jolted from my thoughts by noises from outside, at least I think that I heard something. I was only partially awake, while the rest of me was resting, waiting, and daydreaming about the early days when the Fires were raging. But then something suddenly drew back me into a broken house at the edge of Nineveh. Something outside the house. I peeped out but saw nothing in the gray light. I waited and listened.

Slowly, ever so softly, that something became a someone, and that someone was inside the house. I heard a board creak below, and I listened hard, wondering if I had imagined it and not believing I could be so stupid to get trapped inside some tatteredup house. Someone, and maybe several someones, was creaking up the stairs.

There was no place for me to go except out the window, and I considered it, but neither the drop nor the trash underneath looked inviting. I leaned back and pulled back the cutters bolt, hoping that the someone on the stairs hadnt heard the unmistakable metal click of the cutters slide. Or I hoped if he did hear it he would alter his plans and creep another house.

There was a brief silence, as my someone waited. Then a voice called out:

"Dont shoot me. Please dont shoot me. Oh please dont shoot me, Im just a poor soldier of god seeking salvation."

I sat for a moment, startled, but not displeased. Joe came into the room, filling it up with his bulk. He carried a military pack like the ones the shinyboots had just marched out with. He also carried a cutter of his own and enough clips to carveup a couple more houses. He took off the pack and threw me a water bottle. Carefully, as if nothing else mattered, he unwrapped a piece of gum.

"Where you been, and howd you find me," I asked between gulps.

Joe shrugged and worked the gum. "Who said I been looking for you? Me and my new partner was just scouting out the area. A couple of mules aint exactly hard to ignore."

"Whos your new partner?"

He shrugged again. "Just somebody I run into that seems a whole lot more clever than to get trapped in a broken house."

I figured he had found the woman with the mules. Or maybe he had run into the old man. "We ought to give that greasy old man a name."

"What old man?" Joe popped a bubble and went out. He was fond of gum. He would work on a piece of rockhard leftover gum for hours until he could start to chew and pop. From the top of the stairs he whistled. In a moment I heard another set of footsteps clatter up the stairs. Then the wildboy suddenly burst in the room and launched himself on me. He gripped me around the neck and squawked like a big, bony bird.

"Boy, where you been? I thought you got usedup out there on the trail."

I unfastened the boy from me and stood him back. He looked about the same, maybe a little more raggy, but he still had his boots, knife, and crazywild smile. There was a dark patch of dried blood on his shoulder. I eased off his shirt and took a look. He had been touched by a bullet, but the wound was healing. I washed it with Joes water.

"He going to live?" Joe asked.

I nodded. "Lucky he didnt get feveredup with an infection. Unless we get him killed around here he should be ok. Whered you find him?"

Another pop and shrug. "He found me. After my doings this morning, I went back up above the town and circled around in case I was being trailed, and all of a sudden he came from out of nowhere and wrapped himself around me. I think he likes us."

"Awfully big forest to meet someone by chance."

"I dont think there was much chance. Hes probably been lurking around for the past couple of days. He mustve trailed us in. Hes surely hungry, but he aint starving."

"Boy, its good to see you. I am glad that you are still stitched together."

Chapter 9

Joe and the boy mended my outlook, and they also amended my plans. We waited until it was fully dark and slunk out of the house, gathering up the two mules as we went back into the woods. On the way out Joe related his activities, and I let him know of mine.

Except for disengaging the woman, much of my day had been spent rooting around in the past, mentally picking through the debris of the dead city, but Joe had been active. The first thing he had done was to locate a couple of guards who werent too guarded, and he had relieved them of their weapons. Then he had perched himself on a roof across from the brick building that we had just exited from and sprayed it with automatic fire, aiming for the Bishops fancy windows. In the confusion that followed he slipped down and around and opened up on another side of the brick building. But Joes an ambitious sort, and even though there was a plentiful supply of shinyboots in the streets, he set fire to a splintertrap of a building nearby. I dont believe he made the Bishop happy. A good mornings work.

We moved up the ridge as quietly as we could with two mules and darkness, winding our way through the twisted pine, and after a while we stopped at the edge of a steep ravine. Below us a small stream tumbled towards the lake, and the jumble of the water and the rocks covered us. We had to decide what to do. My feelings were all jumbled together.

"I know what youre after." Joe opened a can of leftover mush from his pack and gave it to the wildboy. I couldnt tell what it was, but I was hungry enough to think about grabbing the can.

"You want to go back to the front range and scrounge up some leftovers, then trade them for a weeks worth of whiskey and a soft bed."

I waited to hear what else he was stuffed with.

"Me? I think we ought to catch up with the woman and then try to find the old man." He waited for me to stop waiting. But I waited him out. "The boy misses them, and these mules here is in need some mule-company. I think we ought to get ourselves back together and then see if we cant sneak inside the old mans mountain and steal some air conditioners or washing machines or any of that old pluginthewall stuff."

"You give up on slipping back to get our packs?"

Joe yawned and scratched. "It dont seem like too wonderful an idea to go back there again. You say that Smoke guy went in but not out?"

I nodded. "I didnt see him trail back out. But for all I know that snake could be thirty yards below us waiting to slit us open."

"I expect we will be see more of him. Right now Im more concerned with all those saints marching around. You think the woman and the mules can handle them, or you think we should give her a hand? Or maybe you really think we should head back for the packs and hope everyones at a prayer meeting? Maybe you can unstuff the man you stuffed into a box."

Answering didnt seem necessary, so I said nothing. I listened while the boy finished licking his can, hoping something smart would enter my head.

We were at a crossroads, only there werent any roads. We were at one of those places where we had to choose a direction and go, but there were all kinds of possible directions to choose from, and all of them had distressful possibilities. And they all looked about the same to me. The woman was not a question, since I figured that we ought to pick her up, seeing how Joe was hot for her. He would take her back to the fronts and plant her in one of his houses. But I was confused about the other alternatives.

Once a long while way back me and Joe had been crazy lost. We had been out in the flatlands gathering up horses when a big storm had come up. The day turned black, and the sky filled something awful with thunder and lightning. In minutes the rain froze up, and we were chunked on the head with hailstones of considerable size. What horses we had spooked and took off, and the only thing me and Joe could do was huddleup and stay out of the gulches. There wasnt much shelter around. We were driven before the wind until we finally stumbled into some big rocks on a little hill, and then we waited the storm out. But it took a lot of waiting, and before the storm give out the day did, because it never got light again. The next morning, though, was one of our strangest. What light there was was all gray and foggy, and we couldnt see much in any direction except for a few scraggly yards of tall grass, rocks, and white pockets of leftover hailstones here and there that had puddledup in low spots. But the strangest part was that we hadnt the slightest idea where we were.

I mean, nothing looked familiar, absolutely nothing. No mountains in sight, no roads, no landmarks to point us somewheres, no sun either, and with all the cold fog and drizzle we couldnt even tell what direction was what. We had never been so lost before in such a strange curious landscape. We stewed for a while, deciding what direction to take and hoping the sun would burn through the thick weather. Only it finally seemed to me that the actual direction didnt matter. Sometimes theres too many directions, and you can waste a whole lot of time wondering which one to take. You just have to make a choice and start blundering ahead and not look back, not worrying yourself about all of the other mighthavetaken directions. So we just pointed ourselves in one direction and took off. Eventually we got somewheres, an old dirt road, and that took us to another road, and then we finally found a brokedown farm. It took us about several days to get back where we had started, and we near about starved and wore down. Sometimes choosing a direction dont matter. You just go.

I felt the same way now, only instead of being surrounded by mistcovered hills and washedout gullies, we had steep ridges and forest. But the choosing was the same. We didnt need to feel around for the right way to go and then start out worrying about all the other mayberightways. All we had to do was point ourselves and go, and then once gone to keep going and not get turned around. And hope we had made a lucky choice.

We caught up with the woman sometime late morning the following day, or at least Joe found her and then came back to lead me and the wildboy to her. She hadnt gotten to the end of the valley, which was probably a good thing, as I was thinking that the shinyboots and maybe her friend Smoke would be keeping close watch on that area. But she had found herself a small open area between a formation of rocks on one side and a steep rise on the other. Except for having little water and no food, she was in pretty good shape, though the mules were probably in better shape. I was glad she hadnt headed back to her cabin.

So we had a reunion of sorts. The wildboy was grinninghappy, and the woman didnt seem displeased with our company. I checked her swollen ankle, and she didnt seem any worse than before, and maybe a touch better, but it was still a bad sprain. Joe pulled a couple more of those little green army cans out of his borrowed packs, and we all ate a little. I couldnt rightly identify what it was, but it tasted somewhat familiar and I swallowed it, and it didnt kill me. I kept wondering, though, where the Bishop and the saints had gotten all their leftover militaries. Even these little cans seemed unscuffed and new. Maybe there was a magic mountain somewheres around.

We talked some, and the woman told us a little more about Nineveh. Except for the young and the old, just about every male had to join the Bishops salvation army, and they marched around practicing considerably more warcraft than priestcraft. Just another peacock militia strutting around. But it seemed peculiar to me what all the campaigning and crusading was about, since there werent hordes of infernal fiends pouring out of the hills to attack Nineveh, just a few halfstarved skinners and lost hunters. And it seemed peculiar to me that with all their military leftovers they still had to mine lead and make bullets. The old stuff tends to be more reliable, and a lot safer, than the new stuff, or at least the Princes new stuff. According to the woman, the Bishop and his elders kept up a thick stream preaching on their covenant with God to build a new holy kingdom, one that would redeem them from the sins of the past, and that their new kingdom required sacrifice and struggle. There was a glorious future somewhere.

Seemed to me, though, that the business of constructing new kingdoms had slowed up considerably. I couldnt see much use for pious militancy and militant piety. As far as I knew salvation didnt require assault rifles, and I couldnt imagine Bishop worrying about scattered packs of skinners who wandered between the peaks chasing the elk herds, or the random crazies who turnup now and then. I couldnt see what other kind of threat the Bishop was afraid of. As far as the woman could remember, there never had been an army of sinners to confront the Bishops army of saints. A couple of times tattered bands of wackers had chanced upon the Bishops sacred ground, but they were soon taken up and atoned.

There just didnt seem to be anything that required so much soldiering. Back during the Fires just about every sort of town and community put together its own peacock militia, and they all forged their own alliances, made their own treaties, and carried on their own wars and their own slaughters. But things had settled down a lot since those days when everything got turned off and burnedup, thanks in part to men like the Princes father, who was the toughest and smartest of all the early raiders. Up here so far back in the ranges, though, it wasnt like Nineveh had any contentious neighbors. I couldnt see the use of being so warlike if there wasnt a war. I figured maybe the Bishop was planning to relocate and start a new holy war, and I imagined the Prince had no idea that the Bishop and his saints were up here plotting to spread their damnation and salvation.

Eventually we had to decide on our own tactics. The tip of the valley and the pass were pretty well guardedup with shinyboots. The ones I had seen march out had broken up into several squads, and these groups were slowly sweeping their way back towards us. We figured we could probably cut our way through them, or at least a thin line of them, and race on out, but we did not have a destination in that direction. The front range was too far without a couple of food sacks, and there wasnt much in between. Joe talked about finding the old man and his magic mountain, but he had a lot of geography to consider. I still wasnt convinced there was a magic mountain, at least the old mans golden version. As best as we could get from the old man, the mountain was back towards the way we had come. But then the old man wasnt too reliable about geography and directions. Wherever hed been for so long, he probably hadnt much use for the sun or stars, or a compass.

"I think we should go back towards Nineveh."

I looked at the woman, and she seemed sane enough.

"I know where we can hide, and maybe get some food."

We had run out of the little army cans, so that settled our direction. But then setting out surely aint the same thing as arriving, especially when following witchy brokenfooted woman.

We stayed high up in the hills, staying in the woods mostly but sometimes scrambling over open rock faces and scree fields. Below us we caught distant glimpses of the town and the bluegreen lake. I was hot and thirsty and wouldnt have minded a quick cold dunking. My head was still sore, and I hadnt eaten enough, and from high above the cold, clean water seemed inviting. Thick puffy clouds floated by across the blue sky like white islands, and as spring days go this one wasnt too bad. I was in a hopeful mood. But things always have a way of getting unhopeful.

We had just started to cross another open rocky face when the world exploded. There was a loud blast, and an explosion ripped the day apart. In an eyeblink we were jerked and jolted to the ground. I was so stunned by the force of the explosion that I just lay where I had rolled, not knowing whether I was torn up and spilling out, not even knowing what had happened and what I should do about it. I tried to focus my eyes, but the only thing I could get a look at was a weedy patch of green sticking out of a crack in the granite next to my face. My ears were roaring with the explosion, but I heard a couple of mules bellowing hysterically in pain, and a strange tinny voice crying, calling for help. After a few moments I lifted myself up half up and wrapped an arm around a boulder for support.

Things were fuzzy and numb, and nothing would stand still long enough to remain in my field of vision. The whole world rocked back and forth, swinging from side to side no matter which way I looked. Or maybe I was the one swinging. Like a drunken fool lurching about not knowing which way I was going, I swayed on rubbery legs, trying to concentrate on controlling the reeling motion, trying to hold myself stiff and straight, but the whole world zigged and zagged back and forth. The seconds slowed to years.

Wisps of grayblack smoke drifted upwards in jagged swirls, and as they lifted I sorted out what was around me. I smelled cordite. Off to the side several of the mules were down, two were still twitching and bawling, but two others lay still. Panasonic had its head bent back around, like it was looking one way and going another, only it wasnt going anywhere but to rot. The bodies of the other two were opened up and gushy, blood pooling beneath them and then spilling down the rock in small red rivulets. The other mules had scattered.

I heard them before I saw them. Their shinyboots crunched and scraped against the rock as they strutted up behind us. I looked wildly around, and then I saw the wildboy and the woman. They were both down, unmoving. The boy had been leading the woman and her mule along while stringing the other mules behind. They all had taken more of the blast than me. The two of them, the boy and the woman, lay several yards ahead of the dead mules. They lay still and at odd, awkward angles.

I stumbled over to them, reeling and woozy. The woman had been thrown back, cracking the back of her skull against the rock face, she was bloody in places and breathed in uneven gasps. The wildboy lay crooked and broken, he didnt seem to breathe at all.

The first ones to get to me spun me around and down to my knees as the others surrounded the rock and blasted flesh.

"You ever eat pizza?" I asked no one in particular. The closest one to me was a boy not much older than the wildboy. He pointed a rifle at me, and I pointed to the boy. "He never had pizza. All he had were guts and bones and maybe a couple cans of smelly sardines after we found him. We were going to take him to the old mans magic mountain where there were freezers full of things to eat like frozen pizza and microwavers to heat them up in just like in the old picture magazines, and you went and blew him up. Think about it, boy, you went and broke apart a wildboy no older than you. We all couldve gone to the old mans magic mountains and eaten peanut butter and grape jelly sandwiches or cans of spaghetti with tomato sauce and little meatballs. Then we couldve drunk real bottled whiskey until we puked, and then we couldve taken hot baths until we sobered up. We couldve flushed toliets and turned on lights. And you had to go blast us apart. You better hope that wildboy lives to eat pizza, or Im going to gut you like you done to our mules."

The boyguard winced a bit, though Im sure he thought I was blast-crazy. But I wasnt about to stop. I was intending to remark further on the advantages of having a magic mountain when another one of the PurpleRibbons marched himself up. He didnt look much different from any of them, and ordinarily I would never have marked him as a mulekiller and boyblaster. He didnt waste much time with me, just kind of glanced me over once checking for guns or wounds or whatever, then he occuppied himself with the wildboy and the woman.

He examined the wildboy first, checking for signs of life. He shook him by the shoulder, and the wildboys head flapped around. But he was alive and groaned. When he got done shaking and flapping the boy, PurpleRibbons checked the woman over. His hand came away bloody from the back of her head, and he wiped it against his pant leg like it was mudstink. I wanted to kill him for that, and if I had a gun in my hands I surely would have. But he kind of felt around and jiggled here and there for other breaks and wounds. He seemed to have had some experience in dealing with brokeup people, and I wondered how many he had broken. The scumbucket wasnt much older than the boy he blastbusted.

The wildboy stirred some, and I crawled over to him, pulling myself over the rocks, the boyguard following me, pointing at me with his oversized cutter. The wildboy had been knocked down and scrapedup, but he didnt appear too broken up. Mostly he seemed just stunned, bruised, and bleeding. One hand was cut and raw from trying to hang on to the mule tethers and his shoulder wound had pulled apart. He had started to cry, and his face was streaked with dirt and tears. He reached up with his bloody hand and wiped at his eyes, smearing his face with red. He had lost one of his prize boots and his hunting knife had been yanked away.

"You all right, boy," I asked.

He didnt respond, just kept staring at the woman and dead mules. PurpleRibbons was still bending over the woman. She coughed and moaned, coming around now.

I turned the boy towards me, forcing him to look at me. "Listen here, boy. Listen to what I am saying. Dont cry about what you cant change. Think about yourself and think about staying alive. Where theres life, theres hope, and when theres hope, theres a chance for something better. Think about how youre going to hurt for a little while and then how youre going to heal up. Think about finding your boot and then finding the old mans magic mountain. The best thing you can do is think about eating pizza in a room fill of electric lights and real toilet paper. Focus on all the good and better things ahead of you. Theres a magic mountain out there, and were going to find it."

The boy looked at me. Slowly he worked his mouth and lips, and then slowly, but still quite suddenly, the wildboy spoke: "He told me."

I was stunned, blastshocked and shook up all at once. My head was still woozy from the explosion, and my ears were still ringing, so maybe I hadnt heard right. But then I looked at the wildboy and I knew I had. It was a strange moment, though, with a scrapedup, bloodsmeared, tear-streaked wildboy suddenly speaking. I worked my mouth for a moment or two, but no sound came out. I was nearly wordless.

"Boy, youre talking."

The boy smeared his tears with a shoulder. He seemed somewhat surprised himself.

"Yes," he said.

PurpleRibbons walked over to us but then ignored us. The dark stain where he had wiped his hand was about eye level. He turned to the guards around us, including the boyguard. "When Sister Bern is ready, well head back down. If these two cause any disturbance, kill them," he said,

The Lords of Leftovers

pointing at us, then he moved back towards the woman.

I took this part personally. I wished I still had a gun, and felt around to see if I still had a knife. I didnt like him for wiping the womans blood on his pants. And I didnt like him for being a mulekiller and boyblaster.

"Dont worry, boy. You just sit here and think about healing and pizza. You probably dont know what pizza is, or peaches, or peppermint candy. But theyre good things for you to enjoy. A thousand times better than little oily fish. Think about healing and good things, and better times. Dont do any more talking, either. One way or another, well get your boot and knife back."

I began to get up, and one of the other shinyboots lording over us made a threatening motion with the butt of his rifle, like he was going to clobber me. I already had a sore head and didnt need another. But a disturbance was what we needed, some sort of a little attentiongetter. I kind of halfcrouched.

"Hey, PurpleRibbons, the Bishops gonna have you sweeping the streets of perdition when he finds out you blasted the woman. Shes a holy woman, and she knows the way to Heaven, the promised land, the realm of light bulbs and color television, the keys to the kingdom of glory and groceries, the holy city of home appliances and all other laborsaving devices."

PurpleRibbons looked at me blankly. He saw me but he didnt see me. I imagined that he was well versed in the rhetoric of salvation, only he didnt care much for my salvation. He turned to one of the guards.

"Kill him," he ordered.

His response was not the response I had hoped for. The guard hesitated, looking down at me then back at PurpleRibbons, and then he slowly raised his cutter.

"Now just wait a minute, mulekiller," I hollered, "Im serious. Were supposed to lead you to the promised land. The Bishop wants us all back alive."

The shinyboots scuffed around, still looking from me to Purple-Ribbons and back again. But PurpleRibbons didnt waste more than a moment. He unholstered his handgun and strode over to me like he was in charge of the world and I was just some dirtclod he had to kick out of the way.

"The Bishop wants Sister Bern returned safely. And he does not care whether the rest of you live or die." He cocked the pistol and lowered it to my head.

I am fully convinced the man intended to send me over. I squatted there and smiled at the wildboy, I wanted him to remember my smile, not the disdain of vile heartless murderers. For the longest moment Ive ever lived I waited, and the wildboy looked back at me and began to howl. I could see it forming in his mouth, contorting his redstreaky face. There wasnt much to howl about. PurpleRibbons had no anger or regret, not even irritation or frustration. My life had no value to him, and he showed not the slightest interest in dealing with me. I was just a fly to swat away. The man wanted to kill me and be done with me. But he never got the chance.

A burst of cutterfire suddenly broke apart the stillness, instantly followed by a thump, a grunt, and then the sound of air oozing out of a sack. PurpleRibbons had been knocked down and crumpledup. A bright red flower began to bloom in his chest. His squad of a dozen boysaints hesitated, not quite understanding the what, where, and how. But I did, and I was grateful.

Joe has a delicate sense of the dramatic timing. I just knew he had waited until that handgun was poking against my head before announcing himself. I could have explained this to the guards, the suddenness of his revelation coming at the most unexpected time, but they were still trying to figure out why I wasnt the one who got chunkedup. They didnt seem like they were in the mood to appreciate Joes sense of stagecraft.

I went over and checked PurpleRibbons. His eyes were still staring with a blank unseeing expression. He was spoiled meat, and if the wolves and the nightcreatures didnt get to him he would rot, fester, and stink. Eventually his bones would bleachup and scatter, and finally he would dustup and disappear.

I dont think much about an afterlife. I have a hard enough time dealing with this life to worry about whats yonder. I know that someday Im going to rot up, and then maybe then Ill find out what follows. So Ive never been real curious about whats beyond. I have worried too much about living to worry about dying. Maybe PurpleRibbons really had been devout and well versed in the particulars of salvation, and maybe he knew all about heaven and hell and everything in between. I hoped he had found whatever it was that he had been expecting. I wasnt so angry at him now.

I picked up the handgun, and the boyguards were stirring, bringing their cutters up to fire. I held out my hands and gestured towards them, but I didnt seem to reassure them much. One of them raised his rifle towards me, but before he could get it pointed the wildboy lunged at him from the side.

A second burst rang out, and the guard spun around and dropped, letting go of both weapon and wild boy. He rolled around, crying and grabbing at a ruined leg.

I screamed at the guards. "My partners out there, and hes a deadshot. Hell cut down all of you. Drop your guns and dont move."

One moved, and a third burst was fired, and the rock underneath the guard exploded, knocking him backwards. He screamed and grabbed at his foot.

"Dont move," I screamed again. "Hes out there." I pointed up above us, but I had no idea where Joe was.

The shinyboots slithered about looking for cover, but the rock face was wide open. There were a couple of boulders but nothing else.

"Drop your guns or he will shoot."

Several of them actually paid attention to me. Others kind of rolled and stumbled towards the trees below us. The rest, including the first boyguard, just cowered and waited for something to happen to them.

I was up among them, taking their weapons and packs, when Joe came down from the rocks above. The wildboy limped over to him, and he half hugged and half carried the boy along. He dropped the boy off at the woman and then said something to her. She nodded. Joe checked the mules, but there wasnt much left to check.

We finished up with the boyguards and sent them scurrying down the hills, carrying the two bloodylegged boys along with them. I didnt know what else to do with them. We questioned them some, but they didnt have anything to trade. They were trained to follow orders, and now there was no one left to give them orders.

"Your eyes getting bad, your hand unsteady?" I asked Joe. He and the wildboy had been going through the packs, gathering the clips and what food they could find.

"Probably both." He didnt bother to look up.

"You missed a couple of times. You hit one in the leg, another in the foot, and you severely wounded a rock."

"I was aiming for, a leg, a foot, and a rock," he said. "I believe those shots were well timed and on target."

I nodded. "Couldve come a bit earlier. That puffedup peacock mightve shot me."

"Here they are," Joe called. He held up half a dozen grenades. "I knew they had to have more of these things. Bet they got plenty more down at that old school they been residing in, and ton more at the magic mountain."

Grenades are a valuable commodity. These days most explosives are cheap and crude and dangerous to handle, whatever some mad bomber cooks up with whatever volatile mix he can manage, like leftover firecrackers and match heads in a tin can full of nails, or something smelly and flammable in a bottle. But military grenades are a rare and pricey leftover, something even the Prince would trade for. I wasnt thinking about trading, though.

"Now that you found those maybe you can help the boy find his boot and knife."

"Looks like he lost some blood too," Joe said.

"Yeah, but we got a better chance of getting back the boot and knife."

Joe straightened up and looked around, ignoring the dead mules and the dead saint. He had about as much use for the beyond as I did. Gone is gone.

"Too bad we cant find the old man and his magic mountain. We could have used a little technological advantage. So far we havent done much profitable on this trip. I hold you at fault for failing to negotiate favorable terms."

"We can still find him and his mountain."

I looked at the wildboy. He started to open his mouth, and I motioned for him to be quiet, not sure if he would undertrstand my gesture.

"Theres a lot of mountains around here. Which ones you want to climb first?"

Joe was rooting through the packs again. He found a compass and tossed it to the boy.

"Here you go. Now you can keep us from getting lost. Traders liable to walk off in the wrong direction every time he moves a foot."

"The boy can take us where we want to go. The old man told him."

Joe dropped a pack and looked at me skeptically. "What do you mean? He told the boy where his mountain was?"

I nodded, and the boy smiled. Joe turned and looked at him.

"You think he can draw us a map, maybe even write us a note, or something?" he asked. "Or you think he can use that compass and lead us?"

"I dont know. Why dont you ask him?"

Joe looked back and forth between me and the boy, and smiled. "What are you trying to tell me?"

"That the boy lost his boot and knife but he found something more useful than a leftover lizard boot and an overindulged toothpick."

He went over to boy and paused. "Is that right, boy? Did you find your voice?"

The woman hobbled over and gently set herself down next to the boy. She brushed back his hair. He looked around at us, his audience, and heaved himself up a bit, him all bangedup and puffedup in his toobig shirt. He was still holding the compass.

"Yes," he said in a whispery voice.

"Can you tell us what the old man told you?" Joe asked.

"Yes."

"Can you say anything else but yes?" Joe smiled at the boy.

"Yes, maybe, I dont know."

We did the best we could for the Bishopsman. It was less than we might have done but more than is usually done. We found a crevice between two boulders at the top of the rock face and laid him out. Spoiled meat is usually best left for the wolves and wild dogs. Me and Joe knew this, but the woman and the boy seemed squeamish about just leaving a dead Bishopsman for the carrion eaters and nightcreatures. I felt more for the dead mules than I did for him. But we lugged a load of rocks around and covered him up some. We both knew that something would get to him and chew on him. He was no different than the mule meat. We lugged rocks for the woman and the wildboy, not for the Bishopsman. When it comes down to the end, none of us are any better than a lump of dead mule. We left the mules where they were, torn, gutted, and bleeding. They were an onery and untractable lot, and some of them had covered a lot of miles hauling our junk around. I was sorry they had come to a bad end on a rocky barren stretch of ground. And I mightve started feeling a lot sorrier if the wildboy hadnt given us his key.

Somewhere down below the old man had given him a fat brassy key to keep safe. The boy tugged it out of a deep pocket and showed it to us. And when I saw it, I started believing that maybe there was a magic mountain. I had been talking about it, but mostly talking like most fools talk about places that dont exist. I didnt really believe there was a freezer full of frozen pizzas hidden away somewheres in a magic mountain. But when I saw Joe take hold of that key in his big hands, seeing it was all shiny and strange, I really started to believe. I never knew a troll to carry around a big fat brassy key.

Maybe the old man did have the keys to the kingdom of glory, or at least one of the keys. It was heavy, more oval than flat, and instead of a set of jagged teeth it had funny a series of bumps, ridges, and grooves on each side. Having encountered a few locks here and there, I imagined that whatever lock this key belonged to was nothing ordinary.

Chapter 10

The woman and the boy were asleep again, though there were still a couple of hours of daylight left. But the light and the hours didnt matter much, and with the thick mist that enclosed us most of the time the days didnt matter much either. Day and night had gotten stirred into so thick a mush that time had stopped. We were living in a rift between what had happened and what would happen.

We were in a small grassy bowl between two rocky peaks, stuck between the little that was above and all that was below, living in an old herders cabin. I felt kind of stuck between most everything. A couple of times Joe had talked to me about what we were going to do, and I told him not to worry, that until the food ran we should stay huddled up between the light and the dark, the day and the night. He took the words and rolled them around, teasing me with them, breaking them down into lumps of sound and then into even smaller pieces of sound. He began to drop the words into whatever he was saying no matter what he was saying until finally the high cabin in the clouds became the place between.

"We between. We be-tween this and that. We betweening. You just let me know when youre ready to get between this place and another place."

I didnt get much humor out of it.

Since climbing out of Nineveh the woman and the boy had spent much of their time sleeping and healing. Neither was accustomed to getting knocked down, scrapedup, and bled, so there was a lot of healing to be done. Nearly two weeks had passed since we had been blasted, and their wounds were better. Even the womans brokenfoot was coming along. A couple times a day I halfcarried her over and down to a small runoff stream below the cabin. The water from the spring thaw was like liquid ice, and its coldness took away some of the swelling and the pain.

The woman had led us to the cabin. It was no more than a crude hut with a big fireplace set high up in an open bowl that curved inward around two peaks, but it held dry during the rains. Young boys from far below brought up sheep to graze when the hot months came. Despite the early spring there was still plenty of cold, especially at night, and there were still deep stretches of ice and snow scattered in the rocks where the sun would never reach them. These high peaks held ice the year around. There wasnt a lot of wood stacked for burning, and it was a long haul to treeline to fetch more. The woman and the boy each wore layers of the Bishops camos.

Often during the day we stayed wrappedup in the thick clouds that floated low over the peaks and mixed with the mist that rolled up from the valleys below, and so we lived covered up in a gray world between past and future, waiting to heal and rest. Getting there with the woman and the boy and with what we had borrowed from the saints had not been easy. But we had needed a place to rest and recover, some place where we could stay safe and hidden and where we could control the flow of events. We could stay as long as we could eat, maybe a few more days or so.

But in truth I didnt want to stay. I joked with the boy, and I helped with the woman, and I kept guard with Joe, but I wanted to get going, settling the Bishops account and finding the old mans mountain, and maybe the old man if he was still breathing. For all we knew he had been stretched on a rope or nailed to a tree someplace where we would never find him. There were a lot of wolves in the area, and at night they scuttled around the rocks howling and barking, and I felt like howling myself. Sometimes during the day I climbed a steep rockface above cabin and sat in the slowmoving clouds. Spongedup in the damp chilly mists, I sat on a smooth flat rock, letting everything inside seep out, and thinking about the distance me and Joe had come just to get lost in the clouds with a wildboy and brokenfooted woman.

Once long ago I had been hurt enough to quit living, and I had needed a long time to heal. There have been a several times when I have lived by nearly dying, but once when I was not much older than the wildboy I lived for several weeks hanging between living and dying. I was somewhere between boy and man, and I had been lurking about a rough area near the dead city, scavenging and stealing whatever I could. The militias, guards, and CoOps were still furiously going at each other for the leftovers, and it seemed like every day there were new borders and boundaries, and new alliances. And every day was marked with black smoke and gunfire.

The Lords of Leftovers

I had been hanging around an old brokedown motel on the edge of the dead city, picking up whatever fell my way. There were a hundred rooms, and most of them still had doors and glass, and a chunkedup concrete pool filled with trash and slime and general nastiness. Traders, wackers, scammers, and scavs gathered there when they passed through, and there was always dealing going on out front. Most times it was safe. Yet sometimes someone got shot or sliced and dumped into the pool, and there was always a few sharps who took bets on whether the bleeder would crawl out of the muck. But there was always a lot of trade, and you could most times find whatever you were looking for, especially guns, ammunition, and canned food.

I hung around the whiskeyshop, reading and reciting to the drinkers. I read from storybooks, but half of the time I didnt know what I was reading, just some old fat book or picture magazine lying around, but the whiskeysoakers didnt care and didnt really listen. There was a woman who sang sadsounding songs in a language I did not understand, an old rubber man who could kiss his elbow and other parts of his body best left unmentioned, a father and son who played fiddles tolerably well, and an obscenemouthed fool who juggled. I was just one of several who performed, and I got a little food for my words, and sometimes something tradable, but when seasonable I picked up loose things that were left lying around.

A man caught a hold of me with a serviceable jacket he thought was his, and we fought. He wasnt all that old himself, but old enough to be full of swagger and boast and large enough to beat me. There were, and still are, hundreds of ragged throwaways like I was back then, tatters of lost children trying to steal enough to survive, with no one to look out for them but themselves. Most people are too busy dealing with themselves to do anything but shoo them away with a kick, thinking theyll either live or die on their own, but enough scraps get thrown around to keep them coming back, hoping for a moments kindness. But this man was drunk and mean, and he took a hold of me and was beating me to make a show of how tough he was. The jacket didnt matter to him. I had never been smashed full in the face with a mans fist before, and I was bloody and hurting. I remember my mouth getting torn and one eye closing up and the laughter from the drunks.

But I hurt him back. Maybe I was lucky, or maybe I was just big enough and quick enough, or maybe he was just drunk enough, but I finally grabbed a hold of his head and clunked him good with a heavy glass mug. Both mug and head broke apart. He went down. I remember standing there feeling good that I was the one standing. Then I turned away to soak that part of my face that was all swelledup. Only I didnt get far. He hadnt gone down far enough to stay down. A couple of minutes later when I was outside with a bucket he came at me from behind with a broken bottle, all bloody and wild and drunken, and before I could run or turn he slashed me lengthwise down the back. I fell down forward on my knees waiting for him to grab my head and cut my throat. I figured I was finished with life and waited for death. But instead of finishing it quick he began booting me, taking his time and kicking me in the head and sides. I dont remember much except the first couple kicks and waiting for the inevitable stop. I knew I was hurt bad and was fixing to shut down.

    Dyings a funny thing. Theres a kind of calm when you realize you dont need answers anymore. You dont need batteries or bread or anything else that was moments before essential in your life. And suddenly you dont have to worry about whos chasing you or where youre going to hide or when youre going to eat next. No worries about staying alive. The only thing I remember was a kind of dull surprise at suddenly perceiving the boundaries of my life and feeling kind of disappointed that there hadnt been more. I remember how grimy the pavement was and feeling disappointed to die so miserably and mean. With living theres always a struggle, and like most back then I had always thought about dying, or at least I had always thought about not dying. Each day that I had lived had added to the shape of my life, and I always had been curious about what its final shape would be. I had always thought that eventually there would be more of something. Down there bleeding away on that old cracked pavement, feeling this cruel man killing me, I felt surprised at realizing the sorrowful shape of my life and disappointed that there would never be anything else. I was a throwaway, streettrash that nobody cared about and nobody would remember. I really hadnt had much of a life after the old couple and their spoonfuls of sugarwater. I dont remember feeling much regret, just a sadness, and then the pain and the blood running out of me, and the bright red splatters on the dirty pavement. And then nothing.

    Thats what dying is like, only I didnt die. I hung around long enough till one of the traders decided hed seen enough and saved me, a big round hairy bearman with a full dark beard streaked with gray and dressed in odd layers of patched leftovers. He kicked my killer aside, and he then

The Lords of Leftovers

picked me up and carried me up to a room, where he did what he could to stop me up from bleeding out. He found an old healer woman to keep my wounds clean and keep me alive. I was weak, battered, and for what seemed like forever I stayed between wake and sleep, and only gradually after more time than I knew did I begin coming around. The old woman made me drink things that were bitter, washed my wounds with something that smelled of dead leaves and chemicals, and kept me wrapped in a blanket on an old box spring bed. She and the bearman took turns handfeeding me leftovers out of cans without labels and never said much.

The bearman was sick himself with a deep cough in his lungs, and I remember waking up to the sounds of him hacking and spitting out whatever it was that was drowning his lungs. While I was recovering, he was dying. Only he wasnt ready to give it up. He would have chills and coughing fits and then he would get up and go about his business without the slightest trace of weakness. He was a big, strong man, and his dying would take a long time.

He was a scavenger, a raider who had been in and out of the dead city more times than could be counted. Others feared him. He carried pistols, knives, and a hard attitude. He never said why he stopped my killer from finishing his business with me, and I never asked. I was afraid of what he would say, so I never asked much of anything and was grateful for what I got. He scavenged, traded, and drank during the day, and a couple of times he went off for days, but he would always leave food and clean water, and he always came back. After a month or more I was well enough to get by on my own. I had thick snakelike raw scar that crawled up and down my back and a thin moonsliver scar above my left eye, but I was still young enough to heal and generally okay otherwise. I was ready to be turned loose.

He came to me at dusk and dropped a torn canvas sack at my feet. I was still in the room where he had carried me.

"Heres about a weeks worth of food, boy. Cans of leftovers and jars of pickledup garden stuff. Couple boxes of sugar too and a sack of good flour. You can eat it or trade it. If you eat it all up, then you can go back to bein a snatchthief and takin your chances."

I picked up the sack. It was a lot more food than I could ever remember having at one time. I nodded thanks.

He stared at me for a moment. "I heard you read out of a book. It was a sad story about a man, a woman, and a necklace. Dont make no sense to kill a boy that can read."

I thanked the old couple again for my life.

"Ill be leavin tomorrow. Goin south to the hot country. Maybe dry up my lungs."

I stood while he began to gather up his things. "I aint got nothing to give you back."

He shook his shaggy head and kept on rolling, stuffing, and tying. "Dont want nothin back." He stopped for a moment and turned to me. "Sometimes livin and killin get mixed up. If you live long enough, youre gonna see others gettin killed, some boys no bigger than you too, and some even younger. Maybe one time you can keep one alive, and maybe you can teach that boy to read outa a book."

My voice chokedup. "Ill do that. I will."

Then he threw me a littleblack gun and a bag of bullets. It was an old revolver, a short, stubby thing that weighted down my hand. The grip and one side of the barrel were scratched, but it was well oiled, and I thought it was beautiful and powerful.

"The next time someones trying to kill you, you kill him."

"Ill do that too."

Joe wanted to find the old mans mountain. I wanted to find answers to a handful of questions. Finding the mountain was probably the easier task. The directions the old man had given the boy were none too specific, but we had a general notion. I kept the key in a deep pocket, and I found myself touching it, gripping it, turning it over and over, rubbing it the way some skinners and crazies do with rocks and bits of wood they think have some kind of power. Maybe the key had some kind of power too. Somewhere and someplace there was a locked door, and I wanted to find out what was behind it.

But I wanted to find out other things too. Nothing had made much sense for a considerable time. Nothing seemed to fit right in a way that I could understand, especially all the headclunking and neckstretching. I couldnt seem to let go of what we had just been through and what we observed along the way. Nineveh was a puzzle missing half the pieces. Aurora, the dead city, and the front range I understood well enough. Things there were ragged and rough, but they generally made sense. One way or another, we were all scavengers down there, living on leftovers. But Nineveh was different. I wanted to know who the Bishop was and why he needed his own little army. I wanted to know why he guarded his valley against all outsiders, and what he intended to do once he had all of his shinyboots polished. I wanted to know where he got all the leftovers, including the shinyboots and greasynew cutters. Then I wanted to know who Smoke was, where he came from, and where he took all the people he stole. And I wanted to know more about the woman and the old man too. I wanted to crawl inside some heads and poke around, sort through the chunks and rocks of their pasts and figure out their stories. But my head was cloudedup and I couldnt make much sense of anything. I wished that old man was around. Every time I found myself rubbing that fat brassy key all kinds of curious notions would get stirred up in my head.

Joe wasnt much help. He seemed much more content with our between life than I would have expected him to be, with all the notknowing and the waiting. I knew he was getting impatient to get back down to his wives and kids and extended family. When he was around he endlessly checked, stacked, and rearranged the guns, clips, and packs that we had borrowed from the soldiers back at the mulekill rocks. But he also spent a lot of time roving over the peaks and dipping below, watching out if anyone came up the trail. He had a spot down below where he could watch a mile of the herding trail, and he would spend hours there. He never said much and seemed content enough while the woman and the boy healed up. Maybe he assumed I would get things figured out. But there were too many pieces missing.

I talked to the woman as much as I could, but she never come up with enough of the pieces. Nineveh had a sizeable population that was completely selfcontained. In Nineveh there was no outside. Most of the people worked at crafts or crops, or in the mines, while the young ones tended the herds, mostly sheep with a few cows. Most everyone else got a pair of shiny boots. And no one came in who wasnt dragged in, and no one ever got out, except for Smoke and his bloody wackers. The whole world, or at least the parts Ive seen, mostly gets by with the scavenging and trading of leftovers, with enough growing, herding, making, and crafting on the side to fill in what else was needed. For a long while towns and communities were just as likely to raid as to trade, which kept the Fires burning, but after years of getting charredup and burnedout enough sane people generally figured out that trading was more profitable than raiding. Whatever you have or need can be bartered or borrowed, even skills and the new stuff. But there was no dealing in Nineveh. Nothing went in or out. The people there just did what they were supposed to do, and then hunt wolves, kill strangers, and burn witches.

"We have fast days of prayer and devotion, and at evening time all of the elders and saints come out to distribute food, clothing, and house goods. The system is simple, the greater your service to the Church, the greater your rewards. Everyone is expected to work for the Church."

"You mean work for the Bishop?"

"I mean no one questioned how things were, or what else was possible. We are told constantly that the Church is our salvation, that the rest of the world is damned and defiled. The Bishop constantly preaches that we must remain faithful to the Church, or risk eternal curse. And the Church does do good things for people. The Church gives us everything we need."

"You mean the Bishop gives you everything you need."

The woman looked at me and finally nodded. We were sitting outside on a stone bench in front of the hut. A whirling gray mist pretty much covered everything around us except for patches here and there that opened up and closed with the wind. Joe was off on his watch perch, and inside I could hear the boy rooting around looking for something, which I assumed was something he could swallow.

"Yes, I suppose it is the Bishop who gives us things."

"Nineveh sure has a curious economy."

Before the Fires, before everything came all cloggedup, brokedown, and turned off, Nineveh had been an old mining town that existed mostly by fleecing outsiders that drove up to get away from their flatland lives. It didnt have factories that made shoes or chocolate. Foods and goods were brought in and, as best I understood it, exchanged for what came out of the mines or the old paper money skinned off of the flatlanders who came up for a taste of mountain life. But now nothing came in or out of Nineveh. As far as the woman knew all of the silver that was mined was turned in fancy little coins stamped with the Bishops profile. That was their money, only it never circulated.

I couldnt make much sense of a town that hoarded silver and handed out leftovers. This was no kind of economy. Even if Bishop and all his saints started out with warehouses full of leftovers after a couple decades of giveaway they must have needed some of something. During the short months of warm they could not herd or grow enough for everyone in the town. I figured there had to be stuff hauled in from somewhere, and the most likely place, the only place I could think of, was the old mans mountain. There had to be a magic mountain somewhere close by. If there was a key, there had to be a lock, and I wanted that lock opened. I also wanted to know about Smoke and his slavers.

"I dont know anything about him except that he and those who follow him are the only ones permitted to come and go. Sometimes he is in Nineveh for weeks at a time, and then he is gone for months. I do not know where he goes. Before he came for me, I had never spoken to him. He is considered unclean."

I picked at her a little more about Smoke and other outsiders but got little.

"Aside from him, I have never seen more than a few outsiders, and all of those were taken to the Square and executed. We were always told that they were devils and looters and that we must have atonement for their pollutions. Their deaths were never easy."

"Have you ever seen a devil? I have seen pictures in books. They have horns, scales, tails, and legs like mules. And I always thought they were eternal, couldnt be dangled from a rope."

"I dont know what you mean. I have not seen such strange creatures."

"I mean devil is just a word that used to mean some kind of nasty demon. Those you saw were just men, werent they? They didnt look like hornyheaded monsters, did they?"

"I dont know what you are asking."

She was trying to communicate with me as well as she could, but talking with an outsider was difficult for her. Had Smoke not stomped on her she probably would have thought I was a devil. All my questions tended to confuse the basic framework of her Ninevehcentered world. What really stuck in my mind was that she said she never thought about the world beyond Nineveh.

"As small children we are told that whatever is beyond our mountains and valley is lost and contaminated. Only Nineveh is safe, a refuge from all that is cursed. We are not hiding from the world. We are the only world that is faithful and pure, and we are saving whatever else is out there beyond the mountains by remaining true to God. We are ..."

She looked at me for a moment, thinking. "... The Bishop and the Elders preach to us that we are Gods chosen people, doing Gods work, building Gods new kingdom on earth. All else is horribly defiled and corrupted."

I had to ask the obvious question. "Are me, Joe, and the boy defiled and corrupt?"

She smiled and shook her head. "No, I dont think you are. But at first I was not sure."

"Well, glad to hear that. I would hate to think that you thought we were mouthfoaming murderous babyeating devils."

I smiled back at her, my most civilized and polite smile. I assumed all the PurpleRibbons, and shinyboots, and probably most everyone else, believed that the rest of everywhere was all wild and violent, all evil and sinful. Nineveh was a tiny gathering of the faithful, and they probably were devout in believing that they were at the center of Gods creation. All else was savage and distant.

But I wanted to know more of what they believed, what their doctrines and teachings were. A few hours earlier there had been a hard rain, and our tiny circle of stone, rock, and earth was wet and slick, and there was still a cold dampness in the air. The runoff tumbled out of a wall of grayness, spilled over the rocks below us, and disappeared into another gray wall as quickly as it had appeared. The woman had been walking too much, and she had swelled her ankle up again, and I had reminded her that she needed to stay off it. She sat wrappedup in an old bloodstained muleblanket. I asked her what she specifically believed.

She shook off my question. "I dont know what you mean."

"I mean what are the doctrines, principles, tenets of your church. Do you believe trees or birds have souls? Do you believe paradise is filled with chocolate and chewing gum and clean beds and only the pure from Nineveh get to go there? Do you believe the Bishop is immortal? Do you believe that all of the terrible suffering in the world is part of Gods plan?"

She remained silent for a few moments. "No, I dont believe in any of those things."

I waited a few more moments. I did not want to irritate her, but I also wanted to know more of what she believed, or was now starting to believe.

"Do you really believe God has chosen all of you in Nineveh as his specially appointed prophets, saints, and apostles? Is the Bishop and his saints contracted with the Divinity to do anything specific, or they just generally responsible for good works?"

She stared off into the mist, remaining silent. I had poked her until all I was getting back were shrugs and silences, and a few Idontknows. I had

The Lords of Leftovers

been half fooling with her, but I was curious too. There was a lot I was curious about, and she was the only source I had.

"Where do all those shiny boots and automatic weapons come from?"

"I dont know. We are told simply that God provides for us."

"Where does the Bishop sleep?"

She shrugged again. "He has many residences, and many are blessed by his presence."

"What do you know about the Bishop? Where did he come from? How did he get to be the Bishop? What does he do besides hang outsiders and burn witches?

She shook her head, and we both waited while the mist continued to move across the bowl.

"The Bishop has always been the Bishop. I have seen him, and listened to him, all my life. I have seen him at meetings and gatherings, and along the streets. I always thought he was watching me, but all the children thought the same, especially the girls. We wanted to be good for the Bishop. The Bishop was a distant powerful figure, and we wanted him to love us."

She fell silent for a moment, but then continued.

"He never spoke to me except for a few times. Once when I was young and still living with the old midwife he visited us, and he gave me a little sack of hard candy, all different flavors and colors. I had never tasted such things before, and have not since. He sat stiffly on an old wooden chair that creaked when he moved and told me to be a good girl and to love the Church. He sounded like he was sad and uncomfortable. I wanted so much to be a good girl. The old woman made him a cup of tea, but he didnt drink it, and he soon left. He never returned, and I always wondered if it was because I had been bad."

"Sometimes being bad aint a bad thing."

I was trying to be jokey, but she ignored me.

"Another time, after I had started midwifing and sicktending, the Bishop had stopped me in the Square and had warned me that healing was witchcraft, that only the Church could heal and cure. But I ignored him and continued, and so I was not a good girl. Not long after that, when I was wed to Elder James, I was taken to the Bishop to receive his blessing, but he barely spoke and would not look at me. There were three other young girls, and he seemed much happier with them, but by then I was so upset at being married to Elder James, who could barely walk and whose hands shook, that I did not care if I was a bad girl.

She looked at me and half smiled. Young girls had it a lot rougher than young boys. I had been in a lot of unhappy, unpleasant places, but I had never been considered a chunk of property that could be traded away.

"Then this past year I was summoned by the Inquisitors. A complaint had been made against me, though I never knew what the complaint was or who the complainers were. An Elder and some saints took me to the school, and I appeared before a panel of Inquisitors. The Bishop was there, and he remained silent while my heresies were announced. I was guilty, since the Inquisitors never summon the innocent. But before I was led away the Bishop stood up and called me to repent. He urged to beg for mercy and surrender myself to the Church."

"You mean be a good girl."

"He was angry, and he shouted at me. He said I was damning myself, and I would burn in hell. He told me that my only salvation was the Church and only repentance would save me. I didnt know what to say, so I said nothing. The longer I remained silent, the angrier he got. I thought they would hang me, or do worse."

But there had been no ritual of atonement, no whipping, no marking, no ropes, no burning in the fires of hell, and no hotburned confessions.

"I was not offered for atonement. I was kept locked in darkness for a couple of days, near to where you found me, and then I was let go. I was left alone until I was informed that I had to be remarried. I was told that I had to remarry or burn as a witch. That was when I decided to leave the Church, and to leave Nineveh. But I always wanted to tell the Bishop I am not a witch."

"You dont look like a witch. Now, I have not had much interaction with witches, and so cannot be sure of what they look like. But I generally assume witches and heretics have a wildcrazy look about them, that they have a lot of wild hair, and are all ugly, pocky, dirty, and wartedup. They dance around fires and stew babies in big stinking pots. Now you aint none of those things. As far as I can tell."

I was trying to get her to smile, but she seemed sad. I thought I would try once more, but less jokey.

"Its like I said about devils. Witch is just a word people use to name what they are afraid of. People like to believe in monsters and demons cause it makes things a lot easier to understand and accept. What you ought to do is consider what makes the Bishop and his saints afraid of you."

Chapter 11

"We should make a short excursion."

We were laying around late huddled up by the fire, and the glow of the coals cast a red glimmer around the small room. Joe was taking all of the cutters apart and putting them back together. He just smiled and kept on clicking pieces together. He had already done the same thing a few hundred times.

"No more resting up in the clouds? You ready to find the old mans mountain?"

I shrugged. "Ready to find something."

The boy came over to the table where we sat and settled himself between us on the bench. He was chewing on something. He was doing fine since he had healedup from the muleblast, and since Joe had gone back to collect his missing boot and knife. Near us the woman slept on a pile of blankets, while across the wall shadowshapes flickered in the dim firelight. Joe set down a cutter bolt and fiddled with his pipe.

"Find what?"

"Whats with Nineveh and that crazy Bishop? Be nice to understand a few things, like where all the cutters and shinyboots come from.""

Rising from the table, he stretched and yawned, acting as indifferent as a cat.

"Be a better idea to think about that key in your pocket and whats behind the door. Probably the old mans magic mountain and a whole warehouse filled with guns and boots."

The boy stopped chewing and looked back and forth at us. He looked sleepy. Joe had been keeping him busy gathering firewood down at the tree line.

"I want to know whats behind every locked door. Dont you think the Bishop will let us take a quick peek behind a few of his locked doors if we ask real nice."

Joe nodded, but he wasnt agreeing. "That right? You think hes going to oblige, him being so friendly and all?"

"Maybe if we ask nice, maybe we can borrow a few minutes of his time, him having to save the world and all, and ask about his silver mine and where he gets all his shinyboots and camos. We got off to a bad start with him. Hes probably a lot more reasonable when you get him alone and when he aint bishoping in front of people."

Joe kept on nodding, smiling. "You want to go see him? Cause I aint going. I would rather get clusteredup with a pack of knivey wackers than bother with the Bishop and his saints. You forgetting the last time we visited? I dont think they would be real gracious with us. We aint got much of a survival chance there, and I dont see how going back to the Bishop is going to increase our chances. There aint no advantage in it. You must be getting sick from being so high up with this air so thin and all. You better go rest up, and then in the morning Ill take you down a ways to the tree line so you can come to your senses."

He stretched again, raising his arms across the dim red and the shadows. The boy got up and stretched himself too, an uneven reflection.

"The woman thinks she knows where he sleeps most of the time. I figure tomorrow night maybe we can sneak in and snatch him. Those shinyboots wont be expecting us. Maybe we can get our packs back. Maybe get some payback for those stupid mules the shinyboots guttedup. Leastways get us some more food."

"Sometimes youre crazier than a nightscreamer. You got a key to a magic mountain, and all you want to is go get yourself atoned by some grayheaded, crackbrained preachy fool of a hangman. You better sleep on it and hope your minds in better shape in the morning. I aint going back down there."

I nodded, accepting but not accepting. Joe was right. There wasnt much profit in going back down to Nineveh. I didnt really think we could snatch the Bishop or find our packs, but I still wanted to take another look. Nineveh was a puzzle missing a lot of pieces. It was just an old mining town, and it surely didnt make its own shinyboots or cutters. There had to be a trade source.

"We should still slip in and take a quick look. We dont have to walk up and bang on the Bishops front door. Just a quick lookaround and then we leave before anyone notices. Ninevehs probably the quickest route to the old mans magic mountain."

"Maybe so, but I still aint going."

We left for Ninveh early in the morning, me and Joe, leaving the woman and the boy hidden between the gray and the granite. We went down quickly, each with cutters, pistols, and packs full of ammunition clips, and before noon we passed the mulekill rocks where we had rockedup the blustery PurpleRibbons. Something had been digging around at the crevice where we had stuck him and had dragged a leg out for a chew. What was left was pretty much gnawed and scattered about. Something had even crunched on one of his shiny boots. Its all the same, being chewedup or rottedup. I dont think PurpleRibbons cared, and I dont think the wolves, rats, and buzzards cared whether it was man or mule they fed on.

We hurried on by without offering more than a glance. There wasnt much we couldve really done anyway. Piling more rocks on what was left wouldnt have done much good. Something wouldve kept gnawing on him, if not the wolves and the wild dogs. I dont think we couldve piled on enough rocks to keep him getting gnawed on. Rats and the bigblack buzzy flies eventually get the same work done as wolves and buzzards. Rottedup meat is all the same.

I was more concerned with something chewing on me and Joe, and in truth I was probably gave more thought to dead mules than I did to the chewedup PurpleRibbons. The mules were sometimes more trouble than they were worth, and there were times I wouldve traded the whole pack for one gnarly old apple. But we had dragged them up a lot of hills with us, and I had grown accustomed to their troublesome ways. The wildboy liked the mules well enough. And it was good to have the mules around if you picked up a brokenfooted woman.

Me and Joe had been doing our best not to get chewedup, always trying to stay on the plus side of the ledger and to make a modest profit out of staying alive. I certainly wasnt looking forward to getting myself shoved into some rock crevice just to be dragged out and gnawed on by the night scavengers, or for that matter to be strangled at the end of a rope by some murderous maniac of a Bishop. Our primary business was survival.

Joe knew this. He trusted me for it. Hed been up and packing before sunrise, and by the time I slapped cold water across my face he had been ready to go, just smiling, nodding, and smoking. Nineveh was unfinished business, and we had to go back at least for a quick lookaround and a fast swipe. But we werent being foolish, blundering and thrashing along, and we certainly were not going to charge down screaming and gunblasting.

Joes as big as a mountain, but he moves quickly, and he can read a trail better than most skinners. He went steadily downward towards the town. Yet every so often he would hunker down and listen, and a minute would pass while we waited. We never heard anything more than the wind and a couple of squawkjays until we dropped down to the last high ridge above the Bishops mines. Below us the lake gleamed, looking like it came out of an old picturebook. Crunched up against it Nineveh looked out of place, like the tatters of an old raggy coat someone dropped by the lakeside. We rested and waited, staying low behind a fallen pine, watching until the light began to fade. Handfuls of shinyboots went in and out, some heading northwest along the lake, others climbing towards us and then cutting sharply back along the ridge towards the head of the valley. By dusk a few small clumps of miners and herders made their way back down towards town.

"Dont look like anythings stirred up. You think they have forgotten about us."

I nodded. "I believe things have settled down since we were here last. But I bet the Bishop dont often get rampaging wildmen setting fire to his town."

"I aint rampaging. I be strategic. So what do you think? Think we should rush them head on, or surround them for a surprise attack."

"I think we ought to go for a swim."

Joe stopped smiling. "I aint ready for whatever it is you got in mind."

I pointed to a small strip of land that dipped into the lake at the lower end of town. On it was a large house set off from the others around it. It was set against the shoreline and connected to a pier and boat dock.

"According to the woman, that theres the Bishops lakefront property. Maybe he likes to fish. Or sit on his porch and watch the choppy water."

"I aint goin in the water. You know how I get. Its too cold anyway. Ill surround them from the front while you rush them from the rear."

"We can go down below the houses and come up along the shore. We wouldnt have to get dunked, maybe just a little mudwet."

"What do you mean, maybe?

We ended up getting mudwet. After waiting until the dark had set in we made our way around the lower end of Nineveh and down to the lake, moving carefully. But another pack of shinyboots crunching along the shore had sent us into the lake, where we lay hidden behind some large rocks in the shallows. After that we nearly froze as we slunk along the lakeside. I thought we could hide out close by and watch what we thought was the Bishops house for awhile, and when we came up to some kind of little concrete hut below the house, filled with old pipes and a filter, we settled in.

"I be wet and cold. You think I should go rampaging and start a couple more fires? We could get warmed up that way."

But we lay still and watched. The Bishops house was large, and sharpangled, all wood, glass, and steel beams. The lakeside part was brokedup into square wedges of balconies with big windows. I didnt think we could actually to get in, get what we wanted from the Bishop, and then get back out. I thought the best we could do was just hang around long enough to lift a few things. Now that we were down there surrounded by water on one side and shinyboots on the other, I wasnt sure what we were doing or how we were going to do it. Despite complaining about wet and cold, Joe was mostly content to set by and watch. We had no idea if the Bishop was inside. The more I thought about it, the more I thought we would just sit in the dark by the little pump house and slip out before light, borrowing what was pluckable along the way. I sat watching, listening, and thinking about what it would be like to be a Bishop. I imagined it was a tough line of work. Me and Joe have met hundreds of scammers, most of moderate talent, but a few achieving the expert level, and none of them ever took on the performance of bishoping. Trading belief was a demanding profession. Making one or two people believe you enough to hand over the reins to an acceptable horse was generally possible, but making a couple hundred believe you enough to hand over their lives was a whole different matter, and which required constant labor and considerable capacity.

After a while we received an invitation, as a party of guests arrived. We heard them before we saw them, only at first we werent sure what we heard. A low hum and a chopping of water. The sound came across the lake a couple of minutes before they made it across. We didnt even know it was a boat at first—just a steady hum and waterslap that gradually kept getting louder, only it never got real loud, and then we heard the wash of the water as the boat glided towards us. The lake reflected the pale light of the night sky, and we saw their dark shapes as they slipped up to the dock below the house. Four men in a long boat filled with boxes.

"Ok, since youre so smart, what the hells that?" Joe was crouched next to me looking both hesitant and interested. Neither one of us had seen too many boats, especially ones that hummed.

"Some kind of big rubber rafty thing with an electric motor, Im guessing. We aint heard any little gas pistons sputtering."

We watched as all four got out and two of them flashed beams of bright light across the front of the Bishops house, back and forth.

"Archangels maybe. Divine messengers with the Bishops weekly load of batteries, chocolate, and toilet paper. Maybe they got whiskey and fancy smelling candles too. I wouldnt mind some new socks and underwear."

I whispered, but Joe still made a motion for me to hush up. We were crouched in some high weeds next to a big pipe that snaked out of the pump house and then ran down to the lake, where it disappeared into the water not more than twenty paces from the dock. "Come on, Joe. Lets snake down for a closer look."

I was about to start slithering my way along the pipe when Joe collared me back. He pointed up to the house. A small group of shinyboots had come out and were scrambling down a set of stairs from the lowest balcony. One held a big hissing lantern that burned bright enough to light up the whole area. The second man to scramble down was the Bishop.

"Looky there, our friend the Bishop has come out to greet his visitors. I think we should join the party. Help unload those boxes. Maybe we can get a hissy lantern to take back to the woman and wildboy."

But Joe wasnt interested in my suggestion. "I think maybe we should just shoot them all and be done. You think all the saints would come after us if we cut down the Bishop?"

Joe wasnt serious, least not altogether serious. He wasnt set to shoot, and I knew he was just as curious as I was to see what was going on. He slunked down the pipe some, and I slunk along after him.

The rafty boat was loaded up with crates and boxes, and three of the raftmen began to unload even before the Bishop and his lanternmen arrived. They seemed to be in no great hurry. Suddenly I recognized one of the men as he came up into the Bishops circle of light.

"Like meeting up with old friends, aint it." I pointed. Even without the lantern light, we couldve recognized him from his size and stride.

"Look Joe, theres your twin brother, Smoke."

The lantern lit up the dock area in a brightwhite arc of light. We watched as the raftmen continued to unload, while one stood off to the side. He was dressed like a shinyboots, but he wasnt all ribbonedup. He was actually kind of small and plain, but there was no mistaking his giving orders to the unloaders. He barked and pointed at the boxes, and even Smoke nodded. Then, while the others were unloading and stacking, he and the Bishop started back up towards the house. They moved out of the arc, but we could still see them fairly well. And we could hear them, or at least hear that they were talking. Behind them Smoke and the others continued to unload, stack, and carry.

"Theres the door you were talking about."

Joe looked at me silently and then swung back towards the dock area.

"We figure out whats going on here, and we can figure it all out. That little man barking orders is the door to the old mans magic mountain. Lets see if we can get inside."

He didnt turn to look at me this time. Instead he broke off a weedy stalk and began to chew on the end of it.

"We got to go in after them. We got to find out whats going on."

He spit out the stalk. "Dont go screamer now. You got other people to worry about. You got responsibilities. That boy and woman up between them peaks is waiting on you. Youre gonna have to take care of them. You best be careful. There aint no way youre going get in there and get out without blood and trouble. You aint invited to the Bishops party."

I leaned back against the pipe. Two soldiers all cutteredup had come out and were standing guard at the top of the stairs. It didnt seem too good a place to be holding a discussion on family responsibility. I figured he was just teasing me.

"I aint got no one to worry about. You got at least three or four families, and maybe more by the time we get back. I aint ever sure how many you got in your clan. I used to have part responsibility for some leftovers and a bunch of dumb mules, but the packs got stolen and the mules got brokedup and scattered. Now I aint got nothing except some borrowed guns and a key to some door we might not ever find."

"Cept for the woman and the boy."

"A brokenfooted woman and a near wordless wildboy? And youre the one that turned them up? You can add them to your kin."

"I already got enough wives, and they got sisters, and the sisters got kids, and soon the kidsll start multiplying. Ive got an active multiplication table, and thats more than enough family responsibility. The woman and the boy is all yours."

"Youre crazy, Joe. Your body temperature mustve dropped. Youre suffering from the cold. Hypo, or hypno, theria or something or other. You better take some deep breaths and get more oxygen to your brain."

"Maybe so, but I aint crazy enough to go up near that house."

I sat thinking for a moment. And there was a lot of thinking to do. But I didnt really know what to think. Joe was joking with me of course. He knew I wasnt a settledown person. Joe is the only person I ever stayed with and stuck to, and it was because he moved about as much as me. Besides the old couple, who belonged in a different world that got burnedup, I hadnt had much of a chance to be around people who were connected to other people. Fact is, Joe and his tribe were all that I knew, and they were more than enough for me. Down at his place in the foothills he had an assortment of wives and children, and every so often others would show up claiming kinship or begging for food, and they generally stayed. Somehow they lived together and generally got along okay, especially when Joe was around. It was that whole area of getting along I didnt know much about. I had lived pretty much my whole life scratching when I itched and drinking when I was thirsty. I aint ever had much training in being polite and discreet.

When there wasnt any place else to go, and when I wasnt scavenging or trading, or latchedup in some whiskeyshop, I stayed with Joe and his clan, all the wives, children, and whoevers, all those claiming to be a cousin or a friend of a cousin. Joe had a block of houses at the end of a long road, and he opened up a couple of rooms in one of them for me. I generally enjoyed myself, playing with some of his kids and teasing his women and not having to worry about getting chunkedup or robbed. But then after a month or so I would get restless. I aint too good at guesting to hang around for more than a month. Most times Im more comfortable in rougher places than families. I had considerable more experience with old drunken goatheads fighting with broken bottles than I did with young children.

"We better worry about family matters later. Right now Im thinking were wasting time. That little guy that showed up dont look like he belongs to the usual sort of shinyboots. I would sure like to meet him."

"I bet that Smoke would like to meet you too."

One of the guards came down the stairs and began to circle the house. We crouched down in the weeds and waited until he disappeared around the opposite side.

"You dont think we can get in unnoticed and unannounced?" I asked

Joe just shook his head. "Not now. Maybe later when the companys gone. Maybe another night."

"Then if I cant get in the back, Im going to go around to the front."

"Youve really gone screamer now. You say youre gonna do what?"

I pulled out the old mans fat brass key and handed it to Joe. "Im going to go up and knock on the front door. Im going to offer them a deal, the woman for our packs. See what kind of response we get."

"Youre the one who has gone dumbcold? Theyre gonna to shoot before you get in the door. Then theyre gonna spread your body parts around town. Maybe put your head on top a little pole for the birds to peck at."

"Maybe."

"Theyre gonna hang you in the morning, stretch your neck from a rusty streetlamp."

"Maybe."

"Theyre gonna do a lot worse when they find out youre scamming them."

We watched as the guard finished circling the house. He climbed back up the stairs, a black figure set off against the grey wall of the house. All the unloading and carrying was done.

"And even if they let you go, theyre gonna follow you. Theyre gonna find some way to scam you."

"Thats when youll come charging in and rescue me."

The Bishop was amused. He sat back in a big leather chair and looked almost like he was pleased to see me. Smoke was less amused. He stood at the end of the long table and stared coldly at me, looking as scary and mean as he could. He also looked a little out of place, being so lumpy, big, and mean. He was even more wild and nasty up close as he was from a distance, and I preferred the distant view. I had tried to engage him in conversation, but he didnt want any part of it, and at the same time he made it clear that the only thing he did want of me was a part of me he could cut out. Evidently he had me confused with Joe, thinking I had been the one to jack the woman. But the Bishop acted like he was happy to see me. Which was a relief.

Getting in hadnt been a problem. I circled around and just went up and banged on the front door. There were voices inside, and after a moment two shinyboots opened up and pointed their cutters at me. And at about the same time the one from around back came running up behind me. They didnt exactly know what to do with me, and all three of them just stared, pointed, and poked. But while I was in the middle of announcing myself Smoke stepped out from behind the door and swatted me on the side of my head. Then he and the others dragged me down a dark hallway where suddenly the world exploded with light.

The room was bright like daylight, maybe brighter, and looked like a fancy magazine picture—a big room with a fancy polished table a mile long in the middle and lined with big bookcases filled with books. In the corner there was a big round globe, all blue and green. As I walked the carpet squished under my feet. I was more surprised by how nice everything looked than I was by the Bishops electric lights.

"What an interesting and unexpected surprise," the Bishop said as they led me up to him and stood me opposite Smoke. "I thought we might be meeting again. But I confess my surprise at your sudden arrival. I dont get many visitors at this time of night."

I just sort of looked about as stupid as I could for a moment. "I like your house. What will you take for it? Ill give you ten pounds of mulemeat for that globe."

The Bishop smiled. "What else do you want—besides sanctuary of the Church?"

I looked around. "Can I have some of them books? I can read fine. The old couple taught me back during the Fires. I would like something to eat too, since I havent eaten today. You got chocolate? And then maybe a piece of this nice blue carpet to take with me. I aint ever stepped on something so soft."

Smoke skipped around the table and swatted at me some more, smacking the side of my head right where he had cracked me before.

"Can you tell him to hit me somewhere else? This side of my head is still sore from my first welcome."

The Bishop motioned Smoke back. There was no mistaking who was in charge.

"I do not have time for foolish banter. You have come at an inconvenient time. You will tell me why you have come, or I will have you taken

The Lords of Leftovers

outside and shot."

"Thats what Im here about. Im not in favor of getting myself shot or hung or hit in the head or atoned or burned or whatever other cruelty and violence you practice here. Twice you all have tried to take the only life I got, and Im hoping we can come to some kind of arrangement so that there wont be any more critical situations. All I want to do is to go back where I come from without getting rottedup in some garbage pit."

The Bishop didnt smile. Instead he got up and heaved himself forward, leaning across his shiny table, looking a little more like Smoke than he had a moment before. "Your life is no concern me. I do not care whether you live or die. You are an outsider, an unbeliever, a pestilence from the corruptions beyond. Your presence in this valley cannot be allowed. We are building a new civilization, one that will never be brought down by the old contaminations. We live as God intended us to live, doing his holy work. You and all others from the outside pollute our order and interfere with our struggle."

"That big ugly brute who keeps hitting me on the head, is he doing holy work? Cause I thought he was just a mucksucking manstealer and backshooter." I pointed at Smoke, but he was on me before I could do much more than kick his shins. He threw me down like I was nothing but rags and bones.

"Enough." shouted the Bishop.

I raised myself. There was a big plate on the table, and I wondered if I could grab it up quick enough to smash on Smokes head. But I gave up the idea. "All I want to do is to go back to the front range. You can do whatever you want in your holy valley. I came up here to trade, not to pollute. Im just a poor trader with a sore head and no mules."

The Bishop paused and faintly smiled again. "What is it you want to trade for your life?"

"The woman."

"What woman?"

"The ones you been hunting after. One of your shinyboots told me you wanted her back alive. I got her stashed away."

The Bishop leaned forward. "You have seconds to preserve your life. Tell me what you want and what you will give to get it."

I eased back some, shrugging, thinking I might finally I have an edge. You can always tell when someone wants something. Thats when you start to trade.

"She got brokedup some, but shes still alive, though shes still limpy thanks to Smoke here who stomped on her foot. Your salvation boys didnt do a good job of saving the woman. They nearly chunked her apart like they did to my mules. We got away ok. After one of your PurpleRibbons got himself shotup, the rest scattered back down the slope without worrying too much about us unbelievers."

"How do we know shes still alive. What proof do you have?"

I shrugged again. "I didnt exactly come in with a sworn testimony. I can tell you how I healed her broken foot after your mantrader stomped on her. I can tell you how we spent the last few weeks dreaming about the old mans magic mountain."

"The what?" the Bishop exploded.

With a murderous beast behind me, I didnt feel comfortable about my chances, but I did feel like I was getting somewhere. I had the Bishop wanting information, and all I had to do was figure out how to trade it away.

"A magic mountain, at least thats what we been calling it. Its some kind of old leftover military complex with stockpiles of leftovers and people living like they did before the Fires with all kinds of foods, gadgets, and contraptions, and with turnedon electricity and hot water. The greasy old man told us about it. We thought he was a screamer, but he kept telling us about it and then he give us a key. But you know all about this. You been eating off the candy mountain. This room come out of a picture book before the Fires."

The Bishop settled himself back in his big chair, looking pleased and comfortable, but I could tell he was interested.

"Where is this key?" he asked.

"My partners got it."

"Your partner has it and the woman?"

I nodded.

"And now you have someone else with you?"

"No one except the wildboy, and you cant rightly depend on him much. He aint exactly been brought up to be too civilized or articulate."

"I see. So that makes four of you then, counting Sister Bern, and all of you know about this key and this strange story of a magic mountain?" The Bishop coughed up the last two words. He wasnt happy anymore.

"The wildboy might know a heap more, since he and the greasy old man got along so well, but like I said, you cant count much on him. We caught him in the forest, and he dont seem to know more than a handful of words. He eats a lot, though. Got along well with the mules when we had mules."

"What is it you want to trade?"

"Me and my partner and maybe the wildboy just want to go back where we came from. You can have the woman if you let us go."

"And the key?"

"You can have the key and the magic mountain and whatever else was stuffed inside the old mans head. Just let us go."

"Is that all? You just want safe passage back through the valley and down the pass?"

"I wouldnt mind getting our packs back. I dont know what happened to the mules that didnt get blown apart, but maybe you got some others we could borrow. Packs and mules would be nice."

"I see," the Bishop said, only I wasnt sure what he was seeing. He looked over to Smoke and motioned to him. "Take him outside for a few minutes."

A few minutes turned out to be more than an hour that lasted more than forever. I sat on a bench by the door, and I couldnt do much except wait and worry. I figured maybe the Bishop was saying goodbye to the little soldier in the rubber boat. And I also figured that somewhere outside Joe was tucked away doing his share of waiting and wondering. But then after a while the door opened and lit up the hallway. While I was still blinking Smoke jerked me up and pushed me into the light. He wasnt happy with me.

The Bishop sat alone at the table. Only he wasnt alone. He was surrounded by more food than I could remember seeing in one place. And real food, not leftover canned mush either, and all kinds of it, sandwiches made out of white bakery bread with thick slices of meat and cheese, big dishes filled with lumpylooking baked cheesystuff that smelled spicy and sweet, and a big bowl of beautiful red apples. In the middle of the table there was an unopened bottle of leftover whiskey. I had seen pictures of it before in old magazines, squat square bottles with labels that said it came from Tennessee. I wasnt sure where exactly Tennessee was anymore, though maybe I learned it once, but I hoped it was still a place where old men in overalls sat on porches sipping sourmash and spinning stories while packs of lazy dogs slept in the sun, just like I seen in pictures. But I did know about the value of leftover whiskey. I knew that more than a few men would kill for that bottle. If I was trading it, I could get a handful of gold.

I was a little disappointed that the Bishop had so little regard for me. Only dolts and toothless dribblers would have fallen for his soft approach, but I figured I was smart enough and hungry enough to keep my balance.

"Please, help yourself." The Bishop spread out his arms over the table like he was a big bird getting ready to flap away. I began reaching with both hands, grabbing a sandwich and a big bowl of the lumpy stuff. It smelled tangy and cheesey and wonderful enough for me to want to stick my whole head in it. I grabbed the whiskey along with the lumpy stuff.

"I didnt catch your name," the Bishop said, lowering his wings.

I chewed, swallowed, then said: "I didnt throw it."

The Bishop smiled and let me gobble some more, which I was not reluctant to do. He asked me again about my name, and I went through the usual response between bites and swallows. Somebody always wants a name from me, and I get on telling them that different people give me different names at different times and about how I aint decided yet which one I liked best. I told him names never mattered too much to me. I dont mind it anymore, not exactly knowing my birth name and all. Like most, the Bishop tried out a couple and soon settled on Trader, since I just aint Jim or Bob or JimBob. He talked like he was my friend, asking me about what I had done and where I done it. He sounded like he wouldve never in the world want to choke the life out of me with a rope.

When I slowed down, and my belly swelledup, when I was just more or less picking at the plates and bowls, the Bishop opened up with his direct attack, asking me if I liked the food and if I would like to have more of it every day for as long as I lived.

"You got any chewing gum, the old leftover kind that you can pop bubbles with?"

The Bishop looked a little surprised. "I dont know. Perhaps. Why? Is this something you crave? Cravings are a sin."

"Not me. I crave chocolate and canned peaches. My partner, Joe, has a real strong inclination towards wadding up his mouth and popping gumbubbles. He likes to chew when he aint got his pipe stoked or whiskeyglass filled."

The Bishop leaned back and looked pleased. There was sort of smiley, icy moment. Then he asked me if I enjoyed my life, if I wanted to go on

The Lords of Leftovers

enjoying my life, and if I was afraid of dying. I poked around among the plates, wondering what to say. I had three fat apples in my pocket, but I considered stuffing a few more. I wondered how far the Bishop would let me go. I could probably have filled my pockets with apples.

"I guess I aint afraid of dying, but I am right particular of how Im going to die. Being dead aint an uncommon thing. But I been practicing survival for a long time."

"Then heed my words. I can give you to the Inquisitors, who will burn as a heretic. Or I can give you a pleasant life. If you help the Church, if you commit yourself to serving the Church, I will give you a house, and you can fill it with whatever you would like from our storehouses. You can have cases of whiskey if you like. But you have to remain in Nineveh as one of us. You have to become one of us. Forever."

"What do you mean?"

"You will join the Church, and you will work for the Church, helping to build the kingdom of God, and after you have proven your faith you can become an Elder. Perhaps one day you can even undertake some of our special missionary work. Your knowledge of the mountains could be useful to us. What you called the front range."

I chewed on a piece of soft bread. "I dont know. I dont know if I would be much good at the peculiar kind of missionary work Smoke does for you. I aint never been a mucksucking mansteal, and I only shoot at people when theyre shooting at me. I dont mind borrowing things, but people-stealing is different. A man once wanted to give me his wife for some old junk I had, and she wasnt all that ugly or old either, but I wouldnt deal. People aint all that great a value as commodities, and they take a darn lot of upkeep. And as for the Elder business, I aint much on being devotional. Is that a requirement for sainthood? I am just trying to be honest with you. Joe aint exactly set out for the sacred order either. Me and him been trucking up and down the mountains for a long time. We just want to slip away and keep on dealing leftovers."

"I see," he said, and paused. "You dont think the advantages of the Church and Nineveh are great enough for you to consider a different life?"

"I dont know. I would have to think about it some. Whats the other half of the deal? I give you the woman and the key?"

The Bishop give me another one of his icy smiles. " The key. The boy. And your partner. You must give everything up to the Church. You must surrender all to the Church. You must shed all of your former life. You must stand alone before God, renouncing your sins and pollutions."

I coughed a bit, swallowed, and then coughed again. "What do you want with Joe? He aint good for much."

"Your partner must be surrendered along with all vestiges of your past. You must enter the Church naked, stripped of all your former life. I must know that you are willing to sacrifice everything for the Church. You must give up your friends and your past. There have been transgressions, and there must be atonement. I cannot save you without offering your partner and the boy to divine justice. Sin and sacrilege cannot go unpunished."

I sipped a little more of the Bishops whiskey, taking my time and thinking. I aint never had nothing that I wouldnt trade away, not one thing no matter how bright or shiny. You can always get another gun or horse, but you cant get another Joe Cruz. He was the only one I ever encountered. Partnering with Joe had lasted me longer than any other thing in my life.

"Why dont you just let me and Joe slip back down to the front range and let God and all the heavenly host worry about divine justice? We been trading a long time, and we aint never before stumbled over your town, and we aint likely to stumble over it again. Ill give you the woman and the key, and you let me, Joe, and the boy out of this valley of tears. You can keep the packs and whatever mules wander up."

The Bishop kept smiling, but he didnt sound smiley. "I do not bargain with unbelievers. If you wish to live, and live well, you will surrender up all of your companions, and you will remain in Nineveh serving the Church."

Chapter 12

Me and my new partner Smoke and a pack of the shinyboots made good time getting back up into the mountains. With a couple of hours of sunlight left we had nearly reached tree line and were only an hour or so below the cabin. We were hauled up for quick rest and mapread below an outcrop of rocks, and Smoke stayed close to me while a couple of the PurpleRibbons conferred, tracing possible routes with their fingers on an old crinkled map. They seemed to know exactly where we were headed, and I didnt doubt they knew exactly what they wanted to do once they got there.

I had gotten one of my wishes, only now of course I wished I had wished for something else. I had a nice new pair of shiny boots. Only the boots were a little tight and stiff, and my feet were sore from the climb. I had also new creasey camos and a new greasy cutter, so that I looked just like one of the saints. But someone forgot to give me bullets to load up a clip, and I couldnt persuade anyone to loan me a handful. I looked like a saint, but I wasnt a saint. For some reason, although I had done my best to act helpful and sincere, Smoke and the PurpleRibbons didnt seem to consider me entirely reliable. Especially Smoke, who kept a knifeswing behind me the whole time we trekked up into the elevations.

I couldnt blame them. I generally dont think of myself as reliable either. Never have in most ways. Not the kind of steady responsible living that comes with looking after something or someone. Most things that fell in my way needing to be looked after I sidestepped. But I didnt let on that I was anything but saintly, or that my thinking and my doing had been at odds from the start. I was headed up in one direction while I was intending a far different route to a different place. But then Smoke and the two Purples probably knew this, and they were intending a far different destination for me than a safe return to Nineveh. I imagined Smoke was looking forward to this, hoping for a chance to slice me apart with his bigugly knife.

The shinyboots had heaved and humped around me the whole time, not saying much, working at appearing indifferent to me, and I couldnt get more than a grunt, shake, or cough from them when I asked social sorts of questions. Not even a response to a polite howyadoin? Several were just boysaints, who looked away, almost shyly, but a couple of them needed to prove themselves by giving me tough shinybooted looks. I doubted any of them had a purple snakescar running up his back. A few, the older ones, generally eyed me over like I was some kind of nasty sludge needing a wipe, but most others at most gave me quick sideways glances and looked away. I assumed that theyd been ribbonedup not to fraternize with me. Or maybe they all were convinced I was a bloodsucking maneating pagan, a lost sinner without a chance of the Bishops blessing and salvation. But Smoke was especially attentive. He kept close to me, like he wanted to help me up if I stumbled.

I wasnt sure where Joe was, or what he was thinking, but I hoped he was thinking about when and where he was going to kill Smoke. I knew Joe being Joe that he was somewhere around. I figured he trailed us back up over the ridges until he knew where we were headed. Then I figured he probably cut ahead of us to get the woman and the boy out of the cabin. Probably, I figured. Only I couldnt be sure. Joes steady, especially in tight places. But when theres a devil with a bigugly knife getting ready to butcher you up, you cant be sure of anything.

Trust is funny that way. I knew I could rely on Joe, but I also knew I could rely on the fact that Smoke, sooner or later, was going to try cutting me apart, and probably sooner than later now that we had gotten close to the high ridges and the Purples had figured out where they were headed. Smoke wore his knife on his belt, never far from fingertips, and I could easily imagine the quickcold feel of it gutting me open like a fish. My old snakescar itched the whole time we were headed up. And so worrying about getting all cutup and spilledopen started me doubting what else I could rely on. I knew Joe wouldnt believe I had turned saintly, no matter what I was wearing or where I was headed, leading a pack of the shinyboots. But I wasnt sure what he could do to keep me intact and uncut. There wasnt much I could hang on to the hope that Joe could figure out a sure way to separate me from Smoke and the shinyboots before they managed to separate me from me.

I began to feel more hopeful when we entered the misty world between the high peaks. Once the PurpleRibbons had decided where we were headed and how to get there, we hiked up to the final sloping cut below the herdershut, and I welcomed the mists and light rain, hoping to lose myself in the gray drizzle. I was hoping I could slip away before Smoke slipped out his knife. He always managed to keep a pace or two behind me, no matter how I moved my sore feet.

But I wasnt expecting the woman. We came over the last hump below the bowl and there she was, standing on a small rockledge a couple hundred yards above us. She stood there, all wet and intense, holding on to a cutter, and for a moment all of us stopped to look back at her. Then one of the PurpleRibbons barked, and shinyboots began to spread out, scrambling to flank her.

She opened up, and the clatter of her rounds scattered all of us below, except for Smoke, who grabbed a hold of my hair and yanked me back. I twisted away, flapping my arms, trying to get away before he brought his bigugly knife to my throat. But he held on.

Then the world burst apart in a thunderous explosion, followed seconds later by a second blast, and instantly, before the sound of the detonations rolled across the peaks, a huge form burst out of the mist and knocked Smoke to the ground, breaking his grip on my head. I fell to the side, rolled up, and ran off with most of my hair. Behind me there were several bursts of fire and shouts, and before I could turn Joe was next to me, running hard, pushing me forward, nearly carrying me along. He was laughing and whooping it up.

We ran downwards, off the left, then broke direction and came back around, still heading down toward the thick forest. After a minute or two, Joe suddenly veered off and dragged me up behind a steep rock outcrop, and we settled in behind a couple of large boulders, watching and listening. Joe unstrapped a cutter and jerked its bolt into firing position.

"Guess Ill have to shoot you," he said, squinting back through the mist, "now that youve joined the salvation army. Aint got no more grenades left to blow you up."

I squinted along with him. "Seems like you went to a lot of trouble just to shoot me. You couldve got that out of the way back up a ways, or just waited till your big friend did it for you. Only hes more a slicer than a shooter."

"Anxious was he? Even with you all decked out like all them other saints?"

I nodded. "I dont think he wanted to waste a bullet."

"I figured," he said quietly. "He was quick with that blade."

"Did you get him?" I was hopeful.

"Get him? You mean kill that monster? No, I banged away at him and then cracked him on the head, but he was too quick for anything mortal. But I mightve have trimmed some flesh and made him leak a little, though, cause I heard him grunt some."

"Thats a start. You can keep taking chunks out of him until you take him down to shoebox size."

Joe grunted. "That mustve been his intention too." He eased away from the rock and turned his back towards me. The whole area from his shoulders to his lower back was one large dark stain. "What do you think?"

I wasnt sure, but I thought Joe might bleed to death.

It took a lot of stiches to close Joe up. When I finally got a chance later on, I closed him up with some heavy blue thread and a sewing needle the woman came up with. Joe squawked some, and cursed me repeatedly for my lack of sewing skills, but he never complained too much. And he didnt bleed to death either.

How close he was I dont know. Several hours later we met up with the woman and the boy up on a rocky crest behind her old cabin down below. Joe was quiet and slow the whole way down. I had done the best I could for him at the rocks, binding him up as tight as I could. But the gash was deep and ran across his right shoulder. Smoke had slashed him after they had collided, cutting more than stabbing. Had Joe not been moving when the blade came down, the damage would have been worse. But it was bad enough. With all the running and dodging we done, the cut wouldnt close, and my binding his shoulder didnt do more than slow the flow. So the woman took a chance and went back to her cabin for a needle and thread. Joe wasnt particular about the color of the thread, or my sewing. Nor did he seem particular about our intentions and directions. He seemed more sleepy than interested, despite his curses.

We were eased back, feeling almost content. The woman had taken us to an old mine shaft, and we had cozied up inside. We had a couple of blankets and a few things from the borrowed packs, the boy was already asleep, and the world was strangely silent. The only thing we could hear was our own breathing, the steady drips off somewheres in the darkness,

The Lords of Leftovers

and the far off sound of the wind.

"I bet you want to go down into that town again and knock on a few more doors. Or maybe go back to the Bishops for another feast. Enjoy his hospitality some more. Drink some more of his leftover whiskey."

I had already made up my mind long before Smoke started shadowing me up the slopes me. But I waited a bit before responding, listening to the drips and the wind, wishing I did have some of the Bishops feast. I didnt even get to keep one of my pocketed apples.

"Maybe. He does have a nice table, a big old long shiny thing, big enough for a host of saints and sinners alike. And he has lots of scarce foods I aint encountered before, like that cheesytomato stuff. I did enjoy his hospitality. But I was also thinking that we might try a change of scenery. Seems like every time we go near Nineveh we get in some kind of trouble. We aint had much of a chance to do much else except try to get out of the trouble. I think we ought to try a different direction."

"A different direction to what? Why dont we just direct ourselves back to the front range by retracing our way out of here? We come back emptyhanded before. Aint no big deal. We could restup and healup and then head out somewhere else. Maybe go south into the hot flats."

"You just want to head back to your wives and children."

"Wives? How many wives?"

"Its not a set figure. Joe, you remember that redheaded woman a while back? She didnt stay all that long, and then way back you showed up with that sour prickly woman, but she couldnt get along with the rest of your clan."

Joe knew I was teasing, so he went grumpy and mute, which pushed me further.

"What ever happened to that prickly woman, anyway?"

"How many wives does he have?"

I was about to attempt a second answer when Joe interrupted.

"So youre finally ready to find the old mans magic mountain? Is that the direction youre thinking about?"

"I am thinking we ought to take a boat ride, that is, in a couple of days after youre closedup."

Joe nodded. "That little guy who snapped his fingers and the others hopped? You want to see where he come from? Its got to be the magic mountain. Wait until you see what he took back with him. While you were inside enjoying the Bishops blessings, the little guy slipped out and loaded up your greasy old sardine man. They had him chained and gagged, and he didnt seem too conscious of what was happening to him. No doubt the runty man was hauling him back to the magic mountain. That old man was worth a rafty boatload of something after all."

It was good news, mostly. I was glad the old man was still alive, and I was even gladder that he had been taken across the lake. Where he went we wanted to follow.

"Aint no question, then. The boy here wants to see the old man again. And the rest of us want to see what they got squirreled away on the other of the lake."

Joe repositioned his back, wincing some as he lay down on his side. He looked at me shaking his head.

"I aint swimming, and I aint gettin in no creaky little boat. I will walk around that whole lake if I have to, but I aint gonna get in no tiny flippy canoeboat. You already got me wet once already, and I didnt enjoy that, laying cold in the mud and weeds all night while you were inside stuffing yourself and getting saintedup. Lets just burn down the town and clear out of here. I aint gettin wet."

We were standing by an old boatramp next to a little beach a couple hours before sunrise. The water was calm and glassy, and there were small blankets of mist floating over the lake.

"You ought keep your voice down. Ive heard voices travel far over water. You dont want the Bishop and a pack of shinyboots joining us, do you?"

"I would rather deal with them than this little flippy boat." Joe kicked the canoe nearest him.

After three days layingup in the old mine, the woman had led us down to a set of docks on the lake a couple miles below Nineveh. But she didnt think much of the water either.

"Sometimes people will fish from the shore, but no one ever crosses to the other side. It is forbidden, and those who venture across the water never come back. As little children we were told that the lake is haunted on the other side, that there are evil spirits who inhabit the water and who wander the far shore."

I didnt see any evil spirits, just three crumbledup buildings, and some docks that were mostly kicked over and broken, leaving jagged splinters sticking out above the water. I couldnt really know for sure, but it looked like a place where people before the Fires played on the water, zipping around on speedy little boats, or on little sailing boats. Now there wasnt much left except for a couple rowing boats sunk at the waters edge and a handful of canoes that had been hauled up and abandoned. The woman had been right about one thing. There was no one around. Except for Joe, the only sound was the steady softslap of the water against the shore. I dont put too much stock in evil spirits, or haunted shores, so I thought it was safe enough as long as the water stayed calm and Joe didnt tip himself over.

"Yall go on. Ill see you around on the other side. I aint getting in no flippy little boat. And I aint wearing one them floaty ratty vests either."

But he did both. And eventually we got somewhere.

Across the lake the slopes were steep, rising sharply from the lakeshore. There werent too many handholds up the rocks and slopes, and there wasnt much around except patches scrubpine and bushes growing out of the rocks and along the ledges. Every so often there were ugly yellowbrown tailings that had been pushed out from a mineshaft and dumped down, and at the upper end there was a long rocky avalanche shute. It wasnt a hospitable shore.

We paddled across in our borrowed canoes, all of us bundled up in old moldy life vests, me and the woman in a dark blue one with what was left of the borrowed cutters and packs, and Joe and the boy in a green one with Joe taking up most of the room, leaving the boy just space enough in the bow so that he could dip his paddle. Joe was grumpy, but after a bit the grumpiness was more to pick at me than express any real complaint. He took to canoeing well enough, while clunking his paddle against the sides, and grumbling. Canoeing was a new challenge, and Joe rarely refused a challenge. We werent on the water all that long before he and the boy were trying to race ahead. But I could tell he was still hurting. He held his body frozeup, unwilling to move anything but his big arms. I had taken his blue stitches out, and he looked like he had closedup without infection, but I could tell he was favoring his uncut shoulder. Progress was slow.

Me and the woman were ok with the canoeing business, though not great. I didnt want Joe to get too far ahead, and I figured I could get the hang of it if I did it long enough, but the more I strained the more I seemed to scrape and splash. Canoeing wasnt much called for in our line of work. I didnt suppose the woman had much use for it either, being in the midwifing business and still touchy about evil spirits. Only the boy seemed to enjoy himself, which was hard to do with Joe grumbling behind him.

The weather and the water held for most of the day, calm and sunny, but in the late afternoon the sky thickened with black clouds, and a sudden rain soaked the world. The wind blew hard across the lake, rippling the dark water into waves. We had made it across the lake and were paddling parallel to the demoninfested shoreline, so we hauledup and huddled when the storm broke. But everything got soaked in the downpour, and we didnt have an easy time of it. Especially with blistery hands, sore backs, and an unknown destination.

Thinking back on it, though, it strikes me as curious work. We were a miserable lot, paddling around a big lake, and none of us knowing much about the business of canoeing, all bundled up in moldy old life vests and hoping to stay out of the cold water. We didnt know where we were going, and aside from a handful of candles we had no way of seeing much of anything in the dark. Besides being wet and cold, we had little food and few supplies, and what we had was as soaked as we were. We werent a formidable lot at the start, and the best one of us was still mending from a knife wound. The only one of us who had any enthusiasm was the wildboy, but he didnt know enough to realize he didnt know any better.

Across the lake we found nothing that would hide a big rubber boat or a magic mountain. The shore was so steep in most places that you couldnt stand without gripping rock or a runty pine, and along many places we passed there werent too many of those. We werent too far from the head of the lake up at the end of the valley where we had come in, so we headed west down the shore, hugging close to the shoreline, looking for something, but not knowing what to look for. After the storm we took to the water again, hoping to find a better place to haulup, but we couldnt see more than darkshapes around us and stars above us. The water had calmed after the storm, and we paddled slowly. We were wet and cold, and as night came on the air chilled, which made us all the more miserable.

Joe wanted to pull up somewhere, anywhere, and after a time we found a small shelf cut into the hillside. We pulled the canoes up and hid them the best we could behind some rocks, then hauled ourselves, the packs, and cutters up to the shelf. Joe did most of hauling, with the wildboy trailing after him, while I tried to be helpful with the woman, but none of us was in particularly high spirits. Though glad not to be dunked, we were still cold and wet, and all Joe wanted to do was wrapup in a blanket and get warmedup. The wildboy and the woman got themselves wrapped and planted as best they could, and soon they fell silent. I wasnt much sleepy, so I leaned back on a flat rock and stared across the lake. I wasnt displeased with our canoeing.

Nineveh was up a ways hidden behind a bend in the far shore, and there wasnt much to see except jaggy lines and shapes against the night. It was hard to tell that there were people anywhere within a hundred miles. I saw no lights and heard nothing that came from people. The world seemed dark and empty.

I always like to imagine what things were like before the lights went out, before everything began to runout, breakdown, and rustup, and before people began to fight over what was left. The old couple used to tell me about the dead city before the Fires. It was litup so much at night that it was like day, and there were all kinds of shops, filled with whatever you wanted, that were open day and night. They said the city glowed so brightly you could see it hundreds of miles away, and they said that when you looked down at it from the mountains it looked like millions of dazzling diamonds, all litup and aglow like the night sky itself. Then the Fires got going, and the fighting heated up, and most of the city was burneddown or shotup. Pretty soon the lights started popping out all over, not all at once, but more like a steady stain of dark that kept spreading every night, some sections going all at once, some just a little at a time, flickering, sputtering, then blacking out. With the dark all the killers and the wackers ganged up to swarm on those who were left, fighting for leftovers, butchering anyone and each other. In the daylight the scavengers picked at the wreckage when the militias werent hoarding over what they claimed was theirs. But I was young enough not to know any better, and after a while the wackers and the scavengers seemed normal enough.

The best I can figure it is that centuries of stumbling forwards got all muckedup in a decade of falling backwards. Older people, all those who had been around before the Fires, mustve been awfully sad and surprised when the lights blinked off and the stores got looted. And awfully desperate when the Fires got whitehot and the starving began.

Thats why people still dream about magic mountains and happy valleys, dreamy places where the lights never went out and where people live like they did before the Fires. Places where people wont kill for a pair of shoes, or a chocolate bar. Places where hot water and cold beer can be had any time of day or night, and where electric lights are aglow at night, and where stores are filled with endless rows of all kinds of food, clothing, and hardware. Such places are nice to daydream about, or argue over with the drunken fools. I think most people hanker after a place where the lights never went out, where theres tons of food and barrels of whiskey. And these days there are more than a few who believe someone like the Prince is going to popup and turn the lights back on. Everbody is always spinning dreamy stories because stories can be hopeful even when there is little to hope for.

Which was why I wondered if the old man wasnt just some crazy jackassed fool who wanted to climb out of his greasy pit long enough to see the world before he kicked over and died. Maybe the little military man was taking him back somewhere to keep him locked up safe. Maybe the old man was a madman needing to be chained and gagged. And even if there was some sort of magic mountain down at the lakes end, it was probably just some old brokedown military installation that wasnt much better than any other crumbly stack of splinters and chunkedup concrete. Things aint often what you imagine them to be, or what you hope them to be.

And things aint never going to be like they were before the Fires. Not ever. Not for a moment. They cant be, and shouldnt be, and Im glad of it too. There mustve been a lot of dumb, wasteful people before the Fires, people who didnt realize the value of what they had. But people always want to dream of lights, and heat, and candy, and shops filled with endless rows, because dreaming is hoping.

The Bishop is right about one thing. Everybodys after some kind of salvation. Me and Joe trade old magazines with shiny pictures of life before the Fires. Nobody can read much anymore, but most like to look at the pictures and dream about a different world.

We paddled along the lakeshore all the next day, and it didnt seem like we were going to find anything other than rockslides and waterfalls. Even dry, Joe stayed grumbly, not saying much, and his mood spread to the rest of us. There were long silences filled with nothing but the sound of wind and water and paddles whacking the sides of canoes. There wasnt much left to eat, and the hours of paddling had worn us down. We kept following the shore west, haulingup and resting ourselves at midday and then later in the afternoon at a couple rocky points, and for a second night we dragged ourselves up on a little hill, only there wasnt much that was soft and flat enough to stretch out on, and we had to wedge ourselves in to keep our heads pointed uphill.

By the end of the second day I had blisters oozing, and I was sore in the shoulders. The others were much the same. The woman was the worst off, but she didnt say much, and she didnt turn back to look me in the eye when I asked her about the Bishop or Nineveh. I studied her back mostly, or at least I studied the back of an old patchy gray sweater. She had cut much of her hair, and it seemed about as patchy as her old sweater. Every so often I saw her wince when she rubbed a blister or moved a sore muscle, but she didnt complain. She paddled with strips of rags wrapped around her hands. Like we all did.

Maybe she just figured there wasnt much use in complaining. And maybe thats why Joe went mostly silent. We hadnt seen anything that looked like a big rubber boat or a little general. We hadnt seen much of anything unusal except for packs of wolves streaking across a hillside high up on the other side of the lake, and the only unusual thing about that is that you dont usually get a chance to see them in daylight.

We finally came up to a small notch of land that was only slightly less steep than the one we tried to sleep on the previous night. Joe and the boy pulled up to it, and before the boy could fling himself out Joe had already jumped and dragged the canoe up behind him, the wildboy falling backward for a canoe ride over rocks. Joe grabbed his blanket, chose a spot, and lay down. We gathered around him. It had generally been a pretty day with a lot of sun, blue sky, and big shaggy clouds that floated over us. But in the last hour the clouds had balled up and had turned grayblack. There wasnt much to do but put the guns and packs underneath the canoes and get wet again. Which didnt help Joes mood much.

"What were gonna do is paddle ourselves straight back across this lake, hike back to Nineveh, borrow whatever we need to get ourselves home, and then go back home. This trip aint turned out to be the high point of my professional career. I would rather run with the wolves on the others side of the lake than paddle anymore."

"You ready to call it quits?" I asked.

"Been ready."

I was ready too. Another couple of days and we wouldve been left eating grub worms and gnawing tree bark. There aint no advantage in starving. At least we could slink back to Nineveh and steal something to eat. The boy was halfstarved already. He sat by Joes head digging at a rotten stump with his big hunting knife. I asked him what he wanted to do, but he just shrugged and kept on stabbing the soft yellow wood.

"We have to go on another day. We have to be getting close to the end of the lake, and there must be something there. There must be people there. Maybe thats what were looking for. Maybe we can find food and a place to sleep there. We cant go back without knowing whats there. I cant go back without knowing whats there," the woman said.

I was a bit startled. It was more than she had said to me all day. She was perched on a rock and had turned her face away from us.

I admired the woman. I might have been admiring her for longer than I would have admitted to myself, but at that moment I admitted some of it. She could barely close her hands with the blisters and rags, and she wasnt exactly a wormeater.

"Something there?" I asked.

"What?" She turned back to us.

"You said there must be something there."

"I dont know for sure. Ive never been down to this part of the lake. We were told it was an evil place."

"Who said it was evil? Places arent anything but places. People are evil. Water and rocks aint evil, and we aint encountered any lake demons."

The woman hugged herself and looked out across the lake. "Everyone. Or maybe no one. Maybe just the Bishop and the Elders. Little children are told that if they are bad the ghosts from across the lake will carry them away." She paused, then looked back at us.

"Please understand. We were always told that the whole world, everywhere beyond Nineveh, was evil and filled with contagion and corruption. Everything beyond Nineveh was cruel and ungodly. That everywhere there were devils who killed, tortured, and ate people. That the whole world had gone sinful and wicked. We were told that we were the only good people left in the world. We were the only chance for goodness ever again. Everything else was spoiled and destroyed. And I never went anywhere to find out what things were like. I never went anywhere. I never even went to the end of the lake to see if it was really haunted. Nineveh was my world. Everyones world. I brought babies into this world, and the only world we had was Nineveh. I never thought about other places except to think that they were terrible places. None of us did. Then you came, and now I know that there are other places that maybe arent so sinful and wicked, that maybe not everything is evil. Now I want to find out about other places. Theres got to be something at the end of the lake."

She took a breath and looked back out over the lake again. The wind had picked up a bit, and out on the lake there were a few small waves capped with white froth. It had been a pretty speech, and I think I understood what was gnawing away at her. I thought about back when we had climbed up the rocks above the river and saw her for the first time, and I thought about that old school where I had found her squatting in a small court where years ago kids played with rubber balls. Me and Joe had already made our choice, but it was a pretty speech.

"Maybe it wont storm after all," I said turning to Joe.

He peered out from his blanket and then rewrapped himself. "Maybe."

So the woman, wanting to see what was at the end of the lake, kept us going. I washed and wrapped her hands, and then she leaned forward in the front of the canoe and paddled, never complaining. Me and Joe didnt either. I just watched her from the back, thinking she was a little crazy and thinking too that sometimes being crazy wasnt all that bad a thing. All of us are crazy one way or another, and sometimes theres good craziness. Joe and the boy kept up pushing ahead of us, but me and the woman stayed with them. Aside from the blisters the canoeing business had gotten easier.

By the afternoon we got to the end of the lake. Gradually the steep walls of rock fell back and gave way to rolling hills and broken cuts, and the shore began to curve in and out from the hills, no longer such a sharp rocky line between land and water. Then we came around a bend and saw the boat landing. Or what was left of it. There was a long, wide concrete ramp that poured down a little hill, and on top of it there were a couple small brick buildings set in an old asphalt lot. We paddled out in front of the ramp, staying a hundred yards off shore, and looked the place over. The ramp was like an old road the came down the hill and disappeared into the water.

All was still and empty, the only sound was the hollow sound of water slapping against the sides of the canoes. The ramp was crumbly and chunkedup, and patches of weeds had broken through the crumbly spots. The roofs of the two buildings had collapsed. Scattered around there were a few concrete tables and benches. It wasnt much of a door into a magic mountain.

Joe paddled up and gripped the side of our canoe. He had two cutters strapped across his front. The boy had no gun but looked just as grim.

"Looks like a nice place to launch a rubber boat," I said.

Joe nodded and squinted.

"Is it deserted?" the woman asked.

Joe shrugged. "If weve been seen, then weve been seen."

"Maybe we should put out some fishing lines, and make a couple sandwiches for a picnic." I said.

"Maybe we ought to paddle on around over yonder out of sight, then cut back through the woods. This place dont feel right to me. I would rather be shot at behind a rock or a tree than in a little flippy plastic boat," Joe said.

"Canoe. This heres a canoe."

Joe looked at me, then back at the shore. "You worry too much about words. Theyre like grenades. You get one near enough to what youre aiming at, and it will do the job. Canoe, boat, gunwale, or rudder, I dont care. I am ready for the shore. Wish I had some more of those grenades." He picked up his paddle and with a couple of strokes shot ahead of us, heading towards a point of land a ways down from the boat launch.

When we landed, Joe picked up his guns and a pack with ammunition clips and walked off into the forest. "Good bye boat. Ill see the rest of you back at that ramp. Trader, you take them up by the shoreline. Ill find you in an hour or so."

Which is exactly what he did, only it might have been more like a couple of hours. We left the canoes and moldy life vests and edged our way along the shoreline, getting wet and muddiedup, so that by the time we got to the ramp and nosed around some we settled down on a concrete bench in the sun. We had a picnic of our own with a couple leftover cans of the shinyboots field rations. Tasteless for the most part. The boy was sucking at one, licking the last possible slurp out of it, when Joe walked up. He set his pack and guns down and leaned back against the concrete table.

"How many of those we got left?" He pointed to the boy.

"Wildboys? Why, hes our last. We best conserve him."

"Youre about as funny as a canoe."

The woman smiled.

"How many of those little green cans we got left?"

The Lords of Leftovers

"About ten or so. Depends on how many the boy has sucked up lately. And a couple packets of the mushy stuff. You want to join our picnic?"

He shook his head. "You take ten little green cans and ..." Joe stopped and looked around. He began to sort through the remaining packs, pulling a spool of thin nylon string out of one, candles and a couple handkerchiefs out of another, a rubber ground cloth out of a third pack, and then finally a pretty good blanket.

"What a minute," I said. "Ive been sleeping with that one. What are you fixing to do? Why are you always giving away my blanket?"

"We all got to make sacrifices." He took a pocketknife and a box of matches out of his pocket and threw them into the pile. The woman added ten little green cans to the pile. The boy set down his own can and then looked back and forth between us and the pile. He reached into his own pants pocket and pulled out the compass Joe had given him, brushing a bit of lint and dirt off of it.

"Thats all right boy. You can keep your compass. I think we can get by without giving it up. You might have to find your way one of these days."

I looked around and couldnt see much but what was obvious, just the broken asphalt, the old concrete tables and benches, and the forest ringed around us. But I knew Joe was seeing something else

"You planning on making friends?" I asked.

Joe nodded. "Too bad we dont have fish hooks. Then we could really make a lot of friends. I seen a couple of young boys fishing with spears."

"Who are they?"

"Skinners I guess. I didnt stop to introduce myself. Just some crazy wildmen hungry enough to go poking after fish with sharpened sticks. Only saw a couple. But I suspect theres a few around. They dont seem to be enjoying too many of the comforts of civilization."

"They know were here?"

Joe nodded again. "I was watching them fish at runoff below a dam down a ways, and all of a sudden another called from the woods, and the two bolted like deer at a gunshot."

"Im not sure I understand. Who are these people?" asked the woman.

Joe shrugged. "Skinners and hunters. Wildmen. Savages. Devils and demons. They get stuck with a lot of names. Call them whatever you like."

She still didnt look like she understood, so I set in.

"I guess the Bishop dont invite too many over for dinner, but theres lots of small clumps of people roaming all over these mountains. Most have gone primitive and live as nomads, hunting and gathering, raiding whenever they can, and stealing when they can get away with it. We trade some with them, those back near the front range mostly, but generally they dont like to be sociable. They tend to think were all wicked and corrupt too. People call them skinners cause they live mostly by hunting. When things got bad and the Fires got out of control, a lot of people decided civilization wasnt exactly a successful venture, and a lot of them just gave up trying to be civilized in cities, and now those that are left dont know no other way to live. They dont live much better than the first natives who came creeping through the mountains after elk and buffalo."

The woman nodded. "The Heathen. The Elders say they are evil and blamed them for raiding our herds. The saints hunt them down, and sometimes they bring back prisoners for atonement."

I looked at the woman. "Sometimes you sound like one of them shinyboots."

She looked back at me with a sad smile. "They were burned."

Joe whistled softly. "Maybe we had better throw in more gear. We better make a lot of friends."

"Or else paddle ourselves back out of here." Though muddiedup, I was still outfitted like one of the salvation boys, and I didnt want to be mistaken for one.

Joe shook his head at me. "I already said goodbye to them little boats. Im for making friends." He dumped the trade pile into the blanket and moved off with it. He hiked up a ways to another picnic table at the end of the clearing, where he spread out the blanket and arranged everything. Then he turned back towards us.

"What do we do now?" the woman asked.

"We wait. See if anyone wants to make friends."

Joe strolled back to us. The woman and the boy watched curiously.

"What are we trading for, exactly?" she asked.

"Our lives first, and then well see what else we can get." I smiled at her.

Chapter 13

The first one to come out was a wildboy not much older than our wildboy. We hadnt heard him come up. In a suddenflash, he jumped out from behind a tree, howled something wolflike, and exploded in a jerky run towards our offering. Except for a necklace with a chunk of skyblue rock and a patch of rag, he was naked, all smeared up in green, black, and mud, and carrying a spear with a jagged metal tip. He ran up to the blanket and barked some more, and shook his spear at us.

We had waited on the fat side of two hours, long enough to start feeling sleepy and dullheaded, and long enough for the light to begin to fade. The wildboy was busy making splinters out of a fallen log with his knife, the blade nearly as big as his forearm. The woman had turned herself around and was staring out across the lake. She had been silent for a long time, and she stared without moving, almost without breathing. It was hard to tell what was rattling around in her head. I had been watching the woods, only not really watching, since I took that to be was Joes job. He was best at watching for sudden appearances of wolves and wildboys. So I watched without really watching, thinking more about myself as some preFire cityperson driving up to the mountains in a sleek rustless tankedup car, toting a slick little boat with a motor on the tail and a basket full of white bread sandwiches and fried chicken and a barrel full of ice and beer. I had seen pictures of such things, of handsome people who laughed as they pursued their pleasure and their leisure, people so comfortable they never suspected that hot times were coming. I was having a little trouble making this picture work in my head, though. Its hard not thinking something youre knowing. All I could think of was how I wish I could have told some of those handsome people what was coming.

Then the skinnerboy ran up and howled at us. He stabbed at the air with his spear, issuing a series of unintelligible challenges and insults as he howled and barked. Then he turned his back to us and bent forward, still shaking his spear with one hand and buttpatting himself mockingly with the other.

"What is he doing?" the woman asked.

Joe gave me a youtellher look.

"Thats universal sign language. There are some slight variations in the translation."

The woman looked at me but didnt give me any sort of smile.

"I can see whats hes doing. Why is he doing it?"

"No way of knowing for sure whats inside his skull. I imagine hes just showing us he aint afraid of us. It aint personal or anything. I suspect hes as afraid of us as we are of him. Hes also showing off for the rest of his band, who are no doubt off a ways watching."

"Are you afraid?"

I shrugged. "No telling what can happen. Skinners aint exactly stable and predictable. Most of the ones Ive known talk to rocks, feathers, weeds, and little pieces of wood and think theyre carring on conversations."

"What are we going to do?"

I shrugged again. "Wait until he gets tired of slapping himself and howling, and then see what he does."

"Im not waiting."

With that the woman got up and began to move towards the skinnerboy. I rose to tackle her, but before I could take more than a step the boy, our wildboy, was up and loping after her. In a moment the skinnerboy straightened up and turned around. He growled some and jabbed his spear at the woman a couple of times, but it was clear he didnt expect his challenge to be taken up by a limpy woman and a bootedup wildboy, both without even a spear.

Joe grabbed at me. "Hold on, this might work out okay."

But I couldnt let things rest. It wasnt just having the woman confront a nearly naked skinnerboy with a spear that bothered me. I judged she was a match for him, no matter how greased up and crazy he was. But if there was one, there were surely others, probably a packful of others, and any one of them might be unhinged and crazy enough to kill an unarmed brokenfooted woman and a halftamed wildboy. I handed Joe my cutter and, sticking a handgun down my back, I went towards the blanket.

When I got there the skinnerboy was growling, only not so loud as before. He stood on the other side of the table and hopping around as he growled, poking at us in the air. I couldnt tell if he was growling words or just sounds, or sounds he thought were words. It was a lively flow, though, and none of it making any sense.

"Whats your name? My name is Bern, and I live, or lived, across the lake. I have never been to this end of the lake before. The Bishop said it was forbidden. We just want to find out where we are. We mean you no harm."

The woman waited for a response, but the skinnerboy didnt respond. I couldnt tell if he understood or not. I couldnt tell what he was capable of comprehending or doing. But I didnt think that exchanging names mattered much to him, as he probably had a dozen different names. I stepped between them, trying to move the woman back, but she shuffled back around to my side. The skinnerboy kept jabbing with his spear, which was tipped with a long, jagged piece of sharpened metal, shrapnel from some sort of unidentifiable leftover. Its edges had been scraped razor thin. I let him jab away on his half the table, thinking that if he invaded our half I would smear red into his green, black, and mud.

But then the wildboy, our boy, began stabbing at one of the little cans. He gave up in a moment, sticking it in my hand, wanting me to open it.

"Aint much of a can opener, are you?"

So we had a picnic. Me and the woman and the wildboy on one side of the table, and the skinnerboy on the other, trading hard crackers and field rations with each other. We would put something down on the table in front of him, and hed eye it and then us again and then snatch it up. Even when he was chewing and swallowing he kept up a steady stream of barks and grunts, and every so often a nearly intelligible word or two tumbled out, a regular chatterbox he was. I was fairly certain I heard the words, snake, dog, and eat.

At first it was just the one skinnerboy, but then after he had set to swallowing three others straggled up and joined in. Just boys really, none too old or too young, all of them smearedup and muddied in various shades, and all in various stages of dress and undress. All of them carrying spears and knives, and one toting an old leftover axe. None carried guns, but that didnt mean a couple others werent off somewhere close enough to cut us down. Skinners will usually trade for guns and ammunition and then more guns and ammunition. Back on the front range the Prince has laws against trading guns to skinners, but then the Prince has a lot of laws, and me and Joe cant never keep them all in mind. Always seemed to me that without guns skinners couldnt really do much to protect themselves from wolves and wackers, and now sanctified unholy shinybooted saints. Everyones got guns. Why not a few scraggly wildmen?

Our scraggly boymen barked and grunted back at each other and at us, while the woman kept trying to have a conversation with them.

"Have you seen men with boats come through here? Are there other people living around here? We are looking for someone. Where do you live?"

The skinnerboys mostly ignored her, eyeing her for a second and then refocusing on something to stuff into their mouths or a pouch. But the woman was persistent, and she kept picking up our trade goods and handing them over. Even as she was handing things to them they did their best to ignore her, taking something from her hand like they were picking it up from a stump. She was giving everything away, and I was trying to slow her down some, trying to get her to understand the illogic of giving away without getting back. But I didnt get much of a chance to explain the principles of fair exchange to her.

Before I could slow her down a few more come up, another half dozen, followed by a tall one on the tail end of them. He was as nearly as tall as Joe, maybe even a lick or two taller, only a lot thinner, like if he turned sideways he might disappear. But he wasnt skeletal and wasted away like Ive seen some that were starving and diseased. His muscles were hard, lean, and all sinewy, and he had long arms that looked like twisted pieces of steel cable. He come up behind all the rest, and every one of us quieted. He had on some shorts that might have been pants on someone else, and he had them smudged up in green, black, and mud like all the rest of them, so that he was pretty well forested. But to complete his attire he had added a few leaves and twigs to his hair. He looked like he was kin to a tree.

No doubt about his authority, though. He carried a cutter and enough clips to chop down any forest.

"I am Captain Treetop of the United Armies of America. You are all my prisoners."

For a moment we just sort of stared at each other. No one chewed or swallowed or grunted. Even the original chatterbox boy looked a bit bashful.

"You call to the big otherone and tell him come out. I make him prisoner too."

I smiled and tried to look relaxed. The wildboy, our boy, reached over and handed the Armies of America a cracker spread with something meaty out of a can. He took it and chewed it in half.

"Well, Captain, the big otherone wont come over as long as youre pointing a gun at us."

He looked at us for a moment and then shrugged, setting his cutter down on the blanket.

"Youre still my prisoners," he said, and snatched up two of the remaining field rations from across the table.

Treetop and his skinnerboys took us back to their camp, and we shared what was left of our food. We happily gave him the canoes too, so that Armies of America could become the Navies of America, but he seemed a little shy like Joe about them and was more interested in raking through our packs. In return we got some gnarly roots that I hoped were edible, the bony remains of some smoked fish, and a couple of their spears. They were camped close to the lake not too far from the boat ramp, just a few small tents of hides and old canvas. There were no women, and none too old or too young, so I figured they were part of a larger group. Hunting perhaps. Probably raiding.

"Captain, we come from the east where the mountains rise from the flatlands. Where do you come from? You up here fishing and hunting?"

The Captain was busy examining Joes pocketknife that that he had dug up from somewheres. He closed it up, and the knife disappeared into his pocket.

"We come from there," he said, pointing generally towards where the sun had set, "and we come to kill the man in the wall."

"Who you after?" I asked, wanting to be sure I heard right.

"Man in the Wall. He shoots at us. I am going to kill him. Then we will see whats in the wall."

Joe walked over and sat down with us, nearly filling up the log we were perched on. The skinners had started a fire, and the light danced in the shadows of the trees.

"Man in the Wall, huh?"

Both the Captain and I nodded.

"By wall, you mean the dam over there that holds up this end of the lake?" Joe asked.

Treetop nodded again and went on rummaging. He had found a folding tin cup that he fancied and was carefully opening and closing it.

"I know the wall you mean, but what man do you mean?" Joe asked.

Treetop stuck the tin cup into his shorts, then paused for a moment to compose his speech. He seemed not to understand our not understanding. "The man in the wall who lives there. He comes out and shoots at us when we climb up on the wall near the big pipes. I want to shoot him now."

"Captain, can you show us where this man is? We are up here looking around for some few people too, and maybe hes one of them. Can you take us to where he comes out of the wall? There were some people that must have come through here a few days ago. They snatched a friend of ours, and we want him back." I was hoping he would take a kindly view to our search.

He nodded, gathering up the pack I had been carrying. "In the morning we can go. But I get to kill him."

The dam was a threehundredyard moonslice of concrete, and about fifty feet wide at the top, quite a respectable little dam for being so high up in the mountains. It rose out of the lake and dropped away on the other side, dropping as much as a couple hundred feet down into a deep gorge. Two huge gray pipes like giant hooks came out of the dams center and snaked downward. Between the two snakes the runoff spilled over and gathered into a deep narrow pool before crashing over the rocks and logs, and it was here where they speared their fish.

High above the runoff, about two thirds of the way up, was a small, rectangular balcony cut into the side of the dam. Since it had a slight overhang, we hadnt seen it from above, and it wasnt too noticeable from below either. But this was where Captain Treetop pointed us towards. It wasnt much more than a ledge, but it was like a window into another world.

Down below, back on the front range and out in the flats, some people had generators stuck away. I had seen them, mostly old rusty little engines that sputtered and coughed. Some people stashed away fuel or bartered for it, and every so often they would fire up their generators and turn on what lights they could and heat up water just like before the Fires. Out on the south flats I had even seen one hooked up to a windmill, and the man come in from his horses and cows and sat up at night listening to a leftover music box and looking at picture books. He said he could even watch movies, but I was skeptical. I wanted to see his movies, but a couple of weeks after I met him he got himself spoiled in a raid and his house burned. The wackers even burned his windmill.

I had lived being skeptical, not believing all the fools and their foolish stories about how all the lights were suddenly going to blink back on, and about how the secret government was going suddenly to come out of hiding one day and sweep all of us into a new age of leisure and technology. Like gods out of the sky, a pack of fancy presidents and presidents men, all sincere, kindly, and concerned, were going to pop up and start handing out light bulbs and water heaters and candied popcorn. I mean, I always heard this blather and babble, even decades after all civil authority pretty much went bust, but I was never willing to plunge into such dreams. Stories of secret governments and secret installations were about as plentiful a crop as happy valleys and magic mountains. Or paradise islands. Or secret underground bunkers.

But here for a moment I was not so skeptical. I looked where Treetop was pointing, and I began to think that maybe, just maybe, there was a door that led somewhere. I had already seen a little general in a rubber boat that hummed. I was ready for light switches and hot water faucets. I wanted in that door.

We were clumped behind a stand of pines near the runoff, all of us. When we set out the woman and the boy had come too, and then all the rest of the Treetops band joined the parade. We were all squatted down and whispery. I was thinking I really wanted to see this man in the wall.

"Is the man in the wall up there now?"

Treetop nodded. Then to show me he motioned Chatterbox to go out into the clearing. The skinnerboy was a bit more attired than before, having put on a raggy shirt he had dug out from somewheres. The onceblue shirt hung down to his knees, and the skinnerboy probably couldve stuffed both his arms into one of its. As soon as he parked himself next to the runoff, he set to wailing and barking, and if that wasnt enough he picked up a few rocks and began chucking at the balcony. He wasnt a real good shot, but he mustve landed at least one. Then he began to climb up one of the gray snakes towards the mouth of the runoff, stopping every so often to bark and launch another rock.

And then, suddenly, the man in the wall came out. I sat there amazed, wondering and believing. He was dressed like the shinyboots, all done up in camos like a regular little soldier, and he came out on his little ledge and began hollering and flapping his arms, trying to get Chatterbox to clear out. But the skinnerboy kept on scrambling and chucking, barking and grunting. The man disappeared for a moment only to reappear holding a gun, not the usual cutter but some kind of longscoped rifle. He waved it in the air to show Chatterbox, and then he fired off a couple of aimless rounds. When these had no effect, he aimed and fired again.

A piece of the concrete retaining wall near where Chatterbox was perched suddenly chippedup, and the skinnerboy slipped down the snake and squished himself underneath as far as he could fit. The man in the wall began yelling again, but I couldnt make out what he was saying above the crash of the water. He fired off another round, chipping some more concrete a few yards from the boy. As soon as the firing stopped, Chatterbox was up and scrambling down the runoff towards us.

In another instant, before I could grab him, Treetop tumbled out from behind our tree and began whooping it up, waving his cutter, and behind him the rest of his band spilled out. They danced, jiggled, and barked, and a few of them bent over and buttslapped. The man in the wall disappeared into his wall.

The man in the wall turned out to be two men. I had no way of knowing this until Joe lowered me to the balcony, but by then it was too late.

We had to negotiate with Treetop both for the privilege of using our own rope and for the privilege of being lowered down the concrete cliff. But we got it done by trading away an extra cutter and by promising Treetop that he could roast that man in the wall when we were done with him and keep anything he found inside the wall. Treetop had a pretty fair head when it came to trading.

So in a short time I was hanging around next to the balcony by a rope, with the rope so tight around my middle and thighs that I thought I was being cut in half. I was waiting for Treetop and Chatterbox and all the rest of their skinner band to start whooping it up down below. I had done my best to explain to them all not to launch any rocks or spears my way, and I was just hoping they would understand and comply. But for Treetop, they still werent communicating too much, except by grunts, barks, and a few words here and there. With that rope cutting me in two, I was just hoping they would cooperate before I passed out.

But they did, eventually. Down below by the runoff they suddenly appeared, wild dancers. They skipped and jumped about, and they hollered and threw rocks, most of which landed well clear of me. And I waited. And waited. No one appeared though. Even after Chatterbox and a couple of others began clambering up the pipes no one appeared.

I wouldve had Joe haul me back up, but I was suffering and suffocating too much. I wanted to at least rest on the balcony and adjust the rope, so I turned, twisted, and swung myself around until I planted myself.

But there wasnt anything there. Just a little ledge with a bit of iron railing, then a little steel door. Not a big door, not hardly some kind of grand portal into another world, just a squat, heavy little half door, which was rustedup in places, and which was of course locked shut. I couldve banged on it, and I couldve shot at it, but all I did was just untie the rope and set myself down. The view below was pretty enough.

The sun had slipped beneath a layer of clouds and shone brightly in the crack between earth and sky. It was already past midday, and in a few hours it would start getting dark. I was hungry, not having had much to eat since we traded away the rest of saintly rations. I sat there wondering about whether I wanted Joe to lower something to eat and a blanket, that is, even if I could make him understand what I wanted above the roar of falling water. Being stubborn, I thought about just hunkering down on that ledge until either the man in the wall appeared or I died from starvation and frustration. But the prospect of leaving my bones on that little ledge to windrot didnt appeal to me, and I was just about to tie myself up for ascent when something clanked and clanged on the other side of the door, and it began to open with a loud scrape.

I didnt wait for an invitation but grabbed at the door and swung it wide with all my strength. I wanted inside so badly that nothing could have stopped me then, not even a hundred screaming wackers, and when the door was open I butted and bulled my way in, pushing and shoving myself past the quite startled man in the wall. I threw myself across the little room and rolled up against the wall. I pointed the cutter back at the man in the wall, who merely dangled his rifle at an odd angle. I pointed again, and he laid it down.

He didnt look like anything fancy, not like some sort of godpresident out of someones whiskeysoaked dream. He was just an ordinary looking man, somewhat old, somewhat pale, and somewhat markedup and worndown, and after a moment he looked more tired than surprised.

I didnt know what to say. I looked around the room, but there wasnt anything in it, just a bare concrete room. Yet it seemed alive. I was surrounded with a deep hum of heavy machinery spinning. The man in the wall and I squinted at each other.

"I got in," I said finally.

The old man in the wall nodded.

"You got in, but youll never get out. This heres a federal installation. You are trespassing on property of the United States of America. We are under military marshall law, and trespassing here is a capital crime. All violators will be shot."

Chapter 14

We had a standoff, me and the old rifleman. I had Armies of America, and he had the United States of America, and I figured I had a definite edge in this deal. I had an automatic weapon poked in his belly, and after a moment I had his fancyscoped rifle on my side too. I motioned him out in the hallway. Down to the right there was a large roomfull of panels with gauges, switches, and monitors, stuff I had never seen put together and running before. Up ahead of us there was nothing but hallway and a couple more doors. I had pushed my way into another world.

I was a kid with a mountain of candy, wild with excitement, wanting to jump, dance, and grab everything at once. I wanted in those doors. I wanted to start flipping switches. I wanted to go up and down that hallway. I wanted to sniff around those gauges and start pulling and pushing at things. I wanted whatever was there. I knew I was like some fool who didnt know better than to bang his fool head against a wall, but I didnt care. I wanted whatever I could find, and I absolutely believed that I had a right to it. I had survived by grubbing in trash heaps and garbage dumps, and now I had pushed my way into someplace where lights came on at the flick of a switch.

"You eat people?"

I looked at the exrifleman and considered his question. We were standing at the doorway. He had a curious notion about people beyond his little balcony.

"Not often. I prefer chicken. And sometimes I will feed on an old goat. But maybe every once in a while a nice plump tender baby will do. Youre too old and gnarly. Youd be all leathery and full of gristle. Probably sour, too. You look a bit yellow. You got any babies around?"

The old man snorted.

"Aint no babies around here."

"That right? What about peaches and chocolate? You got any bubbly gum? How about applesauce? Lets go up here and see what you got. What do you eat around here?" I pushed him out in the hall up towards the doors.

Now most people being held captive by a hungry cannibal holding an automatic weapon wouldve turned silent and sullen, or maybe all moany and weepy. But the exrifleman man seemed downright expansive.

"You dont look much like a savage."

"A what?"

"A savage. You know, a barbarian. All outsiders are savage and wild and dirty. You know, like savage barbarians. All you do is kill and eat each other."

"Dont believe Ive seen too many barbarians in these mountains. A pack of hungry thievish skinners, maybe. Maybe you mean some other mountains. Theres lots of mountains and places I dont know about. Now wild and dirty is another thing. Theres quite a horde of wild and dirty people out yonder. But they aint nothing special or out of the ordinary." I stopped him by the first door. "Okay, whats behind door number one."

"Open it and find out."

I shook my head. "No, you open it and find out for me."

He shrugged and opened the door. For a moment we just stood there and looked in. I could see a cot and some crumpled blankets. The room smelled rank and unaired. I shoved him in and followed.

Instantly the old man dove forward and rolled, and as I turned towards him I heard something behind me. I twisted back around enough to glimpse a second man come out from the corner. He was twofisting a handgun, which he poked in my direction. Then the room exploded in a quick series of three shots.

I didnt make a decision. I didnt even think. Instead I lunged, going low, and came up swinging the buttend of the cutter towards that handgun. Something stabbed me in the side as I came up, but I connected with gun and fingers. Before he could bring it up again I smashed a second time. The man howled, and the gun clattered to the floor. Still reacting, I grabbed the gun and shoved the two men together, then headed them both back out into the hallway.

"Anymore of you damnfools around?" I screamed at them. The first old man shook his head. I poked him hard with the gun.

"Thats the truth. Theres just us here. Theres no one else."

I pushed them both down to the floor and slid down across from them. We were all in shock. You just cant stand around in a tight space while some fooljackass bangs away with a handgun and not get your brains rattled. The firing had been deafening, and all I could hear were the shots echoing in my head, all I could smell was the acrid smell of the powder. I took a few slow, deep breaths and surveyed the two men. Both looked a lot alike. Not only were they both oldish and wrinkly, but both were pale and sallowlooking. One, the first one, had more hair than the other one. The second one was wincing, cradling his smashed fingers. He was squatter than the other and had a fat rolly chin that dribbled into his neck. I checked myself over and found that I had been touched in the fleshy part of the hip, more of a gash than a wound. But I knew that soon it would begin to hurt like crazy.

"Im leaking a little here. I aint happy with you old yellow men."

"Just get it over with." The exrifleman looked at me glumly. Number two was licking his hand.

"Get it over with?"

He nodded. "Yeah. Get it over with. Kill us. Shoot us quick. But damn dont eat me. I dont much care about anything except getting ate up."

I wondered at this. First the old man thought I was a cannibal, then a savage, and now a bloodlusting wacker.

"Shoot you?"

"Yeah. You aint nothing a murdering savage. All of you are just a bunch of crazy killers."

I shook my head. "All of whom? Mostly Im a trader. And then maybe sometimes a thief. Often a scavenger. And Ive been known as some other things, and some aint always polite. But generally I aint been labeled a murdering savage. Maybe you got me confused with the last wild man you tried to backshoot."

They both looked at me. Number Two blinked and rocked and looked upset, but Number One looked more incredulous.

"You aint going to shoot us?"

For a moment I considered whether shooting the damnfool would an appropriate response to his question.

"I dont think so, maybe a little later, but then I aint altogether sure. Sometimes I feel downright murderous, but usually I prefer whiskey to blood. You got any whiskey? Maybe after I get oiled up I can torture you some, skin you alive and that sort of thing."

They didnt look like they either understood or believed. They were just two old men, palelooking and ranksmelling, not supermen, not supernatural, and certainly not magical.

"A trader," I repeated. "I trade leftovers and find lost things. Sometimes I tell a fortune or two. You got anything you want to trade? You want your fortune told? Do a little doctoring too. Ill fix up Number Twos hand for something to eat."

Number Two snarled at me. "We called the base. A squad of troopers will be here soon, and then youll be dead."

"And you call me savage? Here I offer to fix up your hand for a little chocolate bar, and you offer me back death and violence. I dont think youve had much experience in the trading business. Youre supposed to make the other guy think hes getting something good while youre getting something better from him. Dont you know how to barter?"

Neither one appreciated my irony. Number One had turned silent and sullen, but Number Two was still snarly. "Youre all diseased and ignorant."

"Yeah, well, maybe so by your standards. But Ill tell you what. Pretty soon Treetop, that is Armies of America, is going to come tearing in here and shoot one or both of you. Hes got his own standards, and hes taken an oath, and I guarantee hes interested in roasting your flesh. He aint polite like me. Fact is, he just might be a savage wild flesheating barbarian."

They didnt seem overwhelmed with the prospect of being roasted by the Armies of America. The ringing in my head had not faded much, and my hip was starting to burn.

"So, while were waiting for your roasting, tell me about the base and all these troopers who are going to shoot me dead."

I never got a chance to set Number Twos hand, but I did get a cube of ice, and I wouldve gotten a lot more if Treetop hadnt shown up.

Number Two was a man of peculiar notions. I offered again to set his hand, but he wouldnt let me near him. He was under the distinct impression that, in addition to being a murderous savage barbarian cannibal, I was contaminated with all manner of infection and contagion, and he reacted to me as if I was a walking pestilence of misery and death. He would have preferred getting shot to getting close to me, but he did throw me a little chunk of ice. He come out from another one of the rooms with his hand stuck in a bowl of ice, and in exchange for a promise to leave him alone he threw me a piece and showed me where he got it.

I wouldve done a lot more than look at their kitchen, but suddenly I

The Lords of Leftovers

heard a whoop and a holler and Treetop really did come tearing up the hallway. He was all smeared up in black and made quite an impression on One and Two, especially Number Two, who dropped his bowl of ice and locked himself in the bathroom.

    I would have preferred One to follow Two, but he favored a different strategy. Every time Treetop tried to shoot him, he danced around behind me. And his dancing set Treetop to dancing, which made me in the middleground kind of jumpy too. It took a whole lot of soothing to sort out. Treetop wanted to keep his vow, and for a time I wasnt sure if he didnt mean to shoot both of us. As we danced around, One kept screaming that neither he nor Two had shot at them to hurt them, so after hopping around long enough to get winded Treetop finally calmed down, and I convinced him that shooting two unarmed old men was probably not a good idea, that if he waited he could probably shoot up a whole squad of old yellow men.

    I traded Treetop a freezer full of frozen leftovers for his deathoath, and I traded the lives of the old men for information about where they come from and who was coming at us. Seemed like good deals at the time. I got Two out of the bathroom easily enough but not Treetop. He stood there crunching nuggets of frozen corn and flushing water for the longest time.

    One didnt much take to us at all, but he warmed up some. Two never did like us a bit. He was surly and stony and kept reminding us what the troopers were going to do to us for trespassing in a restricted area and sundry other violations. And worse, he made fun of us, especially Treetop for his flushing. People have despised and detested me before, of course, but usually after I had done something to them, like skinning them in a deal, or after I showed up with something they wanted, but here was Two just hating us for being us. Of course, I did crunch his hand, but what he felt went a whole lot deeper than a couple mangled fingers. To him we were outsiders, aliens trespassing where we had no right to be, which to him meant something a lot worse than what he flushed away in his fancy pipes.

    So I wasnt happy with my deals. Here I was trading to save his life and he didnt think I had one, not a good civilized human kind of life. I was just some sort of sickdirty animal that got all tangledup in a fence. It was a mighty challenge to maintain my dignity with him thinking I was dangerous, diseased, and disagreeable. And it made me think that maybe I ought to let Treetop shoot him and be done with him, but that didnt seem to be the thing to do, with me trying to prove how civilized I was and all, and for some reason I wanted to appear civilized. So Treetop loaded himself up with frozen fish sticks and assorted chunks of frozen vegetables, and the old men got to live. For my part I got a fancy rifle with a killerscope and a bloody crease in my thigh. I wasnt none too happy.

We waited underneath the road, all of us savages. Except for Treetop and Two. They were down the road a stretch sitting on a big rock, waiting for the troopers to show up. Two wasnt nearly so scornful now. He knew Treetop had his mind set on shooting someone, and he naturally preferred for that someone to be someone else. He was easier on Treetop than he had been on me.

The rest of us were waiting to ambush whatever showed up or slowed down. We had rolled some rocks onto the road around a sharp curve, trying to make it look like a recent slide, and we figured that the rocks, the curve, and Treetop would be enough to slow down a truck full of magic mountain men. So all of us wild cannibals waited to come spilling out from underneath the road, all trollike, full of savagery and bloodlust. We were a half mile or so up from the dam in a fairly roomy but fairly wet culvert. A steady trickle ran down alongside the road and through the culvert, and we waited with muddywet feet. All of us except for Joe. He had taken an instant liking to my killerscopedrifle and then had taken himself up the slope to test the rifles accuracy.

And so we waited for Twos troopers to come rolling in, and we waited. We waited for what seemed to be a considerable amount of time, and then when I started picking at One about the lightning response of his rescue party and noticed he was wearing a watch that worked, I traded him a piece of candle wax for it that the boy had stashed away in his pocket and give it to the boy. Then we kept time together and watched the hands go around a couple of times, and the whole time I was trying to explain to the boy the notion of time, but he didnt seem to care too much for the concept of minutes and hours. He just liked to watch the second hand zip around and hold the watch up to his ear. He was right proud.

After a while Treetops bunch spilled out from underneath the road and went up to sun themselves on some rocks, where they feasted on the rest of our food and the rest of Treetops soggy chunks, so I was pretty much left with One, the boy, and the woman when the jeep finally showed up.

The boy heard it first and was tugging at us back down out of sight, and we waited some more. But the jeep didnt come charging down the hill with guns blazing. It just sort of rolled along, making clangy metalgrinding noises every time the driver shifted gears. When it came around the turn, it stopped with a couple of exhaust stutters. There were four men, two about as old and sallow as One and Two and the other two on their way to getting there. I could almost hear what they were saying, or rather arguing about, when the driver started grinding some more gears and began to back up the road.

Suddenly two quick shots rang out and both the grinding and the jeep abruptly came to a halt. Joe had tested his accuracy.

I came out from the culvert thinking maybe one of troopers was grinding gears in another world, but I found them all crouched safely behind the dead jeep. I surprised them, only not in the usual way. I climbed up to the road, and they just looked surprised, staring back at me, especially when I raised a cutter at them. By the time I had lined them up Treetop and his skinnerboys came boiling up. They poked at them, emptying their pockets and stripping the jeep of whatever they took a fancy to. The wildboy helped with the collection, while the woman and I admired Joes work. He had put two shots neatly into the jeeps front, which hissed and sputtered, dripping a lot of greenbrown muck underneath.

"You see what you done to our jeep? Now how are we gonna get back?" The first one, the driver, asked when I went around to them.

"Wheres back?"

He looked about fifty or so, graywhite hair and a square reddish face.

"Or you gonna shoot us?" he asked, ignoring my question.

I ignored his question and watched as Joe strolled down the slope. The rifle looked like a stick in his hands. He looked pleased.

"It was in great pain, so I killed it," Joe said, nodding toward the jeep.

"He wants to know if were going to kill him." I said as Joe ambled over.

"Dunno know. Is he in great pain too?" Joe asked.

I shook my head, "I dont think so."

"Well, you can bet that Treetop wants to shoot someone."

Which was true. Treetop had finished his plundering and had added

One and Two to the others. Now he paced around us excitedly.

"Which one?" he asked

"Which one what? Whats he want?" Whitehair asked.

I shrugged. "He wants to know which of you he should shoot. Hes promised himself he would shoot the man in the wall, and now we got a handful of possible candidates. Hes also partial to roasting alive and other savage torments."

"Roast one of them idiots," he said pointing to One and Two, "All we done is come down here because they were screaming they were under attack. And all we were supposed to do was to see what was happening and then report back. Now we cant even get back."

"Wheres back?"

Whitehair wasnt the least bit snarly or sullen, although his three companions tended towards the direction One and Two had started. Not being accustomed to savage wild flesheating barbarians, they seemed equally convinced that we were about to torture them until they slowly expired and then barbecue their remains. They were surprised when I told them I preferred roasted chicken to roasted people. Whitehair was amused.

"Maybe we ought to let Treetop shoot Two. He aint been too polite. I think hes a reasonable solution."

"You think hes the best candidate. We got a half dozen to choose from. Maybe Treetop should shoot one of the others for torturing this old jeep vehicle."

"Youre not really going to let him shoot one of them, are you?" the woman interrupted. She seemed concerned.

We both shrugged.

We followed the road all night, me and Joe and all the rest. Whitehair and the magicmountainmen complained most of the time, that the road was too steep, that their feet hurt, that they couldnt see, that there was nothing to eat but soggy vegetables and soggier fish sticks, but mostly that the distance was too far to walk. Walking up a mountain road at night was not one of their favorite customs. Seemed like Whitehair wasnt accustomed to doing anything much but mourn the loss of his jeep. The distance from the lake to their base was maybe ten miles or so on a twisty gravely road, but they made it seem a whole lot longer. Towards dawn they finally gave out and lay down in a convenient patch of pine needles by the

The Lords of Leftovers

road. I figured we were still three miles or so from where we wanted to go. All of us diseasebearing heathen maneating savage barbarians were in a bust to get there, but there wasnt any use in trooping the troopers any further.

"Yous might as well shoot us, cause youre killing us this way," Whitehair panted.

I had taken a liking to Whitehair. He grumbled a lot, especially about his dead jeep, but there was nothing too tart in his mutterings, and sometimes he was funny.

"I wouldnt be saying that around Treetop, if I were you. Hes liable to forget about his promise."

Treetop had promised not to shoot anyone else in exchange for as much food, clothing, and guns as he and the rest of his band could carry. In return, Whitehair had promised to turn us loose inside one of the storage areas as soon as we got inside.

And being inside sounded like a great idea. For most of the night me and Joe had been thinking about taking possession of the storage areas and everything else inside. We figured if all the rest of the magicmountainmen were like Whitehair and his bunch, we could pretty much have our way. We had got the boy and the woman fired up too. While Whitehair was gathering in his breath, I nudged him with a couple of questions. I had always spent most of my life on the outside of places, even when I was escorting the Princes mother around for a time, and now I imagined myself on the inside.

"Cant say for sure how big it is or wheres everything at. The installations huge, thats for sure. Theres some places Ive never been. Like some of those upper levels where they stash the whitecoats and officers."

Whitehair wasnt exactly a fountain of information, but I sat there pulling awhile at him, and he would mumble some to get me to shut up. But I kept pulling, and he wasnt really opposed to being pulled at.

"Dont know how old it is or when construction started. Damn thing is more than a hundred years old I guess, but the military kept digging and building right up until everything went crazy. Now theres a whole honeycombed city underneath the three peaks. Down below at the bottom theres a massive horseshoe shaped tunnel and the front gate built to withstand multiple warheads. Thats where they started tunneling."

"Multiple warheads?"

"Yeah, you know, rockets inside of rockets, the big bombs."

I nodded, knowing but not really knowing. I knew the dead city.

"Theres a series of seven levels carved like giant steps, each one dropping off into the other, and each one carved up into hundreds of storage areas, personnel quarters, and all the different posts, units, and work stations. The installation was built to withstand any sort of attack and survive a siege of centuries. We brought in as much of everything as we possibly could. Thats what I remember most. Dragging in tons and tons of stuff in and then packing it away. Fitting up the place with everything that was needed to withstand time and war. All the generals and all the politicians had us pack everything away that they thought theyd need, or might need. And we got supercomputers and power systems that will run everything forever. They got good and ready to dig themselves into a big hole in the ground and then they got all of us good soldiers to take care of them, the high command."

"How many of they and us are left?"

Whitehair looked at me for a moment. He had spent most of his life guarding something I wanted to pry open.

"Hundreds, thousands maybe. They reproduce and multiply, whats left of the generals and politicians. But like I said, theres places Ive not seen in years, and some places Ive never seen. Like up on top, the penthouses that open up on the cliffs and have real windows, glass as thick as your arm and reinforced with steel, but theyre still windows. Me, I got a sun lamp."

I studied him for a moment in the gray light. Next to us, the boy twisted pine needles and listened to the soft hum of his watch. Joe had disappeared ahead of us. The woman sat behind us, listening.

"Monks in a monastery, thats what we are, keepers the holy word of E Pluribus Unum, Microsoft, Google, and Playstation."

"Whats Google?"

Whitehair snorted and shook his head.

"Nothing but a bunch of old useless stuff. All of us have spent most of our lives playing games on computer screens."

"Ive seen lots of computers. Plenty. The Prince has a sizeable collection that he turns on when hes got his generator humming. And Ive seen movies too."

Whitehair was kind enough to step politely around my swagger.

Chapter 15

"What are you going to do when you get there?"

I shrugged. Whitehair had asked a good question.

"Dont know. Pillage and plunder, the usual barbarian horde sort of thing I guess. Maybe some atrocity, the usual havoc and destruction. Two over there thinks we eat people, being so savage and all. We are all wild and crazy with bloodlust and wickedness. He also thinks were diseased carriers of mortal sickness."

He nodded. "Most of us have never been up close to people from the outside before. Theres all kinds of stories about outsiders, about those that were left behind."

"What about the inside? What do you do in there all the time?"

He rolled his head and hitched himself up to his elbows. "Different things, but not much of anything. A lot more got done years ago, back when we were all young and foolish. Now we just go through the days out of habit and cause we dont know any better. Ive been a sergeant, a noncommissioned officer, practically forever. Was a lieutenant once, but got busted for drinking, fighting, and insubordination. Used to be Intelligence and then Security. We used to hike around patrolling, checking cameras and all that fancy electronic stuff, walking perimeters, chasing out the strays and crazies, sometimes slipping out of the valley to check on the roads. All that stuff is still out there, and all them satellites are still up there," he waved his arm around, "but nobody bothers much with watching and listening anymore. We still keep watch on them on the other side of lake, but now it seems like they do most of the watching."

"Them? From Nineveh?"

He nodded. "Bunch of crazies and getting crazier. Especially the Bishop. Hes been trying to dig us out ever since he stole his first goat. Way back the command negotiated a trading alliance of sorts, trading crates of junk here for fresh meat and produce. Long time ago, before the Bishop come along, we would send rangers out on extended patrols, and theyd mix with the townspeople, and a few of the towns young men would come over to mix with us. The base kept the town alive, and I guess they kept us alive. Before the Bishop climbed into the pulpit Nineveh was our window to the outside."

"Was?"

"Yeah, was. The Bishop and the General dont exactly see eye to eye like anymore, each thinking what he has is more valuable than what the other has. We still try to trade supplies for whatever the town raises or grows, but we havent had fresh meat in a long time, not even an old gristly goat." He paused and sat up. "Somebody ought to bust the Bishop down to private for insuborndiantion. I bet the General would if he could. That Bishop doesnt have much respect for military or civil authority. Nothing means much to him and his Elders except the Apocalypse or some other crazy madness stuck into their foolish heads. But then I guess there arent really too many of us around anymore that care. I used to care, but now I got rheumatism instead of patriotism."

He stopped and held up his hands. The knuckles were large, knobby, and red.

"You ought to give up the security business. Retire someplace south on the dry flats. Raise corn and maybe some goats of your own. Find a nice woman and a jug of whiskey."

He laughed. "I wouldnt do well as a sheepherder or chicken farmer. I havent been anywhere in years, except to the dam and the other side of the lake, a few times in Nineveh when we were still allowed there, and then down the range some. We were always told there wasnt any place left to go. I thought about it, though, and some did a lot more than think about it. We dont really number in the hundreds or thousands. We used to have a lot of desertions, but now the ones who wanted to leave have mostly all left, and the ones who stayed will probably stick around until they get boxed up and buried. But theres a few who still get out. One day youll see someone, then theyre gone. A few weeks back we were sent out to chase an old fellow who took off, one of the white coats who sit upstairs with the computer terminals. His name was Newlin. The General wanted him back real bad, but we never found him. The General offered rewards. Even had the Bishop and his boys out looking for him. Not too many of them wizards are left. Supposedly he left some sort of virus that is going to shut everything down. I guess by now hes probably starved out there on his own. There arent many of us that can tell the difference between an ear of corn and a goat."

I thought about the old man all bruisy and trussedup going for a boat ride.

"Maybe hell turn up yet. You cant ever tell when you might kick up an old leftover can of sardines."

"Theyre not going to let you in, not the officers, and not the troopers. Our job has always been to keep people like you from getting in." Whitehair was trying to be helpful.

The entrance was something like the entrance to a mine shaft. A tunnel had been drilled into the bottom of a steep hill at the base of the first mountain, and tons of concrete had been poured to build it up with thick vertical walls and a thick overhang. It mightve been a tunnel entrance for a fourlaner, only our side of the road stopped dead before a set of two massive steel circular doors, fifty yards or more in diameter. These doors were in turn protected by a series of three circular razorwire fences and concrete barriers. Everything looked a bit worn and rusty, but still functional.

"See, this is the main entrance, but it was built to keep people like you out. No offense or anything."

I saw, but I didnt really want to see. We were hunched down a few hundred yards down the road in a ditch behind some stubby pines. Before us everything had been cut and leveled and the barriers erected. It was a killing zone.

All of us outsiders wanted inside. The dam had only been a trace, but this was truly the mother lode, the fattest, richest vein of leftovers that me and Joe had ever come across in all our years of scavving. I didnt take offense to Whitehairs referring to me as "people like you," but I surely wanted to change my status. I wanted inside.

"How do you get back in?"

"Unlock the first gate with a pass code, then radio in for someone to come out and unlock the other two. That last wire fence there is electric, and I wouldnt suggest trying to climb it. Youll get fried. Our generators are still working fine."

"What would happen if you just walked up and said your jeep broke down?"

Whitehair shrugged. "Dont know. Those who have watch duty would probably turn on the cameras and send a couple guards out to check. We could probably get back in," he gestured to his friends, "but if they saw you they wouldnt open up. Theyd just let us all rot out here. If they didnt kill us all. They got enough automatic weaponry to turn this whole slope into gravel. From here to the entrance there are more than enough automatic gun installations thatll cut down anything that moves. And then there are explosive devices that can be set off if things get really hot. Plus they got listening devices and motion detectors, and I guess all that stuff still works. I dont mean to be discouraging or anything, but you cant get in unless youre invited in. And no one is going to invite you in, not even if youre holding a gun to my head."

"Tell me this, if getting in is so impossible, how do people get out?"

Whitehair shrugged again. "Hell if I know. Like I said, theres places inside Ive never been. Like way up at the upper levels where all the real fancy electronic stuff is located. Theres three large airshafts that connect all the levels, and theres maintennance passageways for all the wiring and plumbing too. And up at the very top theres even a heliport and a radar installation. As late as a handful of years ago I saw helicopters come in and take off from up there. I imagine there are ways to get in and out up there, but I just dont know about them. With all the security devices getting up theys impossible anyway. Theres antipersonnel mines planted around these slopes and ridges. Down below here we got a couple of emergency tunnels that lead to the outside, but theyre sealed, and I never knew anyone who could unlock those seals even to get into those tunnels, and their outside doors are probably buried by now. Most who left waited till they got a chance to go outside, and then slunk off. I dont know how the computer guy made it out. This installation was created to keep outsiders on the outside."

The boy broke in between us. Slowly he reached inside his tentlike shirt and withdrew a string that he had tied around his neck. At the end of it was the old mans key.

"Here," he said solemnly.

Maybe there was a door.

The camera was like a mechanical eye, only it never blinked, just squeaked a little as it tracked us. We were crossing a rocky avalanche chute halfway up the south slope when we heard a click and a whirring sound as the camera focused on us. The camera was set in a little metal box high on a rockface fifty yards or so above us, and as soon as we came down the ravine into the clearing it opened up on us. Treetop threw a rock at it and then wanted to borrow the hunting rifle from Joe to shoot it. But this, we thought, was unnecessary.

We had been switchbacking back and forth up a steep ridge until it crested. After crossing the ravine we debated whether to attempt the avalanche chute, but Whitehair had convinced us that no one would be watching. He had been wrong.

"What should we do?" the woman turned to me. The boy was ahead of her with Joe and Whitehair, while Treetop and the Chatterboxboy ranged back and forth between us. We had left the rest of Treetops bunch down below to watch the main entrance and to keep track of One and Two and the three others, who had attempted to sneak off during the night.

"Try to look invisible."

Joe looked at me. "I aint the invisible type." He moved forward.

We followed him, and after a dozen steps the camera clicked, whirred, and squeaked as it followed us.

"We aint going to be much of a surprise. Maybe we should reconsider our strategy?"

Joe paused midstride and tried to stare down the camera. Neither blinked. Then he turned to me: "What strategy would that be?"

The strategy had been to climb to the top of the south peak, the point furthest away from the honeycomb cliffs, and then to cross a high rocky spine over to the other two peaks until we found a way inside. A simple plan, go forward until we were stopped, or until we got in.

The boy pushed us forward. He would get ahead of us, then with one hand clasped to his chest he would wait for us to catch up, then he would squirt ahead of us again, his big boots clickclacking over the rocks. He was in a hurry. Not long after the avalanche chute we came up to a small marshy table, nothing more than a flat chip stuck on the side of the mountain. There was a lot of grass and mud and a small shallow pond. I thought the boy would get stuck, his boots getting sucked down into the mud, but he hardly slowed down. He was in a big hurry and skated across the bog. And I guess the rest of us were too.

We didnt lag far behind, either in rocks or mud. Even Whitehair wanted to get it over with. He wasnt much at rock scrambling or clambering up mountainsides, but he kept at it, despite rheumatic joints, short breath, and red face. He couldve dropped off to the side and set himself down, puffing for air, and we wouldve kept on going. But he wanted to see what we were going to see. So he wheezed along with us, complaining about just about everything he could think to complain about, including his dead jeep. But we were all pretty wheezied, muddied, and redfaced. We had worked our way up some steep rocky inclines, and the higher we went the harder it got. There was probably an easier way than the angle we chose, most often there always is, but we kept scraping along mountainside, moving back and forth across the rocks and steep slopes, pausing only to check our line of ascent and catch our breath, hoping not to take ourselves into someplace that we couldnt take ourselves out of. Tree line was a ways below us, and all around us was a pretty view of thick green forest broken by the jagged graysilver rocky tops.

We hadnt encountered any automatic gun installations, or mine fields or cameras, or anything related to lockedaway people. We had the ridge to ourselves, and we kept pushing, hoping to stumble into something like a magic door.

Which is what happened when the boy screamed. We had been stopped on the side of a craggy rock, but the boy had rested only a few moments before darting around to the side and up. Then he screamed.

My first thought was that he had lost his hold and had fallen. We hiked ourselves up after him, the woman out front hopping around like shed never been brokenfooted, the rest of us not far behind.

The boy hadnt fallen. He was standing and staring, and when the rest of us came around we stood and stared too. In front of us was a small concrete square, the first thing constructed by people since the camera had clicked on us. We had struggled up a mountain that belonged to another world where time was still measured in centuries, and in this world there were no lost things or leftovers. Just wind, sky, and rock.

So it was more than a little surprising to look upon the little squat building with its thick lines and stubby shape. It had been cut and poured into the base of a sheer rock face that loomed above it, and it measured maybe a dozen yards across and another dozen in heighth. In the front there was a long rectangular window of little glass squares, and over to the side there lay the rusty skeleton of a broken radio tower.

"What is it?" the woman asked.

The boy was already moving towards it, followed by Treetop and

The Lords of Leftovers

Chatterbox. Joe edged around to the side. I stood with the woman and Whitehair, wondering myself. We were pretty high up, but with all the rock formations and false peaks there was no telling where the real peak was. I thought maybe this was some kind of weather station or observation post, but there was no telling what it was or how old it was. The only thing I could tell was that no one had been around in a long while.

We trudged up and peered into the bunker. Others had been here before us and had tried to break into the building by smashing the window, only the glass panes didnt smash. They broke into a million tiny powdery spider lines, but they didnt break. So with the dark inside and the spider lines outside we didnt see much.

"Theres a door around the side," Joe said, coming from around the far end.

"And I bet its unlocked too, and inside theres a chocolate cake."

Treetop turnd to me. "What cake?"

"Dont worry about it none. Hes just trying to be funny. I dont think theres anything worth anything inside. The doors thick as a brick and all rusted up, and there aint been no one around here for a long time."

We followed Joe around to the door, which indeed was all rustedup. But it was still a formidable barrier. We thumped on it some, and it felt cold, heavy, and immobile. Whoever had smashed at the windowglass had scraped some against the door, leaving a few scuffs. But there was nothing on the outside, no handle, knob, latch, or lock of any kind. This was not a door for outsiders.

Joe stood back and studied the door. "I dont have a friendly feeling for it."

We had an itch to get in, but no way of getting in. I wanted to scratch but had no way of scratching except kicking, and kicking had a no effect on the door. Treetop and Chatterbox kicked and thumped but got nothing more than a deep dull bangy echo. Joe gave us a disgusted look and walked off.

"I dont think kicking the door down will work. Why dont you try chuckin rocks at it?" he called back to us.

Only he wasnt joking. In a few moments he came back hunched over and straining, his arms and chest full of the biggest hunk of granite I had ever seen a man carry. I knew the old birds down in Auroras whiskeyshops would love to tell this story. He dropped it with a thud about five feet back from the door.

"Lemme see you throw this," He bent over to catch his breath.

Treetop went over to the rock and wrapped his long arms around it, but he couldnt do more than rock it an inch or two.

Joe looked at me and smiled.

"I aint even going to try, and youre crazy to try. Youre going to hurt yourself, busting something up on the inside, and I dont want to be the one to go back and tell all your wives and children that you died throwing rocks at a rusty door on top of a lost mountain. We can find another way inside."

"Hes right. It aint worth it. Theres gonna be better ways. Lets keep on goin up further," Whitehair said. "We can find the heliport and radar installation."

But Joe just give us a tired sort of smile. Then he leaned over and wrestled with his rock. He squatted down and got his arms around it enough to heave it up about six inches off the ground, then he let loose a scream and jerked it to his knees. His was straining harder than I had ever seen him strain, harder than I thought it was possible to strain, and I thought he surely would burst. I didnt wait to see it, though, but stepped in and tried to jack up the rock from my side.

"Help me get it to my chest, then get out of the way," he grunted.

Treetop pitched in too, then even Chatterbox and Whitehair leaned in, and all of us boosted the rock up to chestlevel. Together the bunch of us were stretched and strained, and I didnt see how Joe was going to take the load by himself.

"Now," he screamed, and suddenly he hoisted the rock up even higher, out of our arms.

We fell back out of his way as he lunged forward at the door, running several yards until colliding. There was a loud jarring crash of rock and metal. The door exploded inward. Somewhere inside both rock and Joe rolled to a stop. A wave of dust blew out past the broken doorframe. For a moment we stared, then we plunged in after him.

"I could have lifted it up by myself." Joe sat up and nodded towards the rock. It had chipped and bustedup some.

I knelt next to him. He was bustedup too, rubbing his chest, and there was a gash on his chin that dripped blood. I looked back at the broken door. Joe had snapped off a steel bolt as thick as my wrist.

"You all right?"

He shrugged. "Better check to make sure the rocks okay."

We didnt know where we were or how long it took to get there. We had groped and poked our way along a dark passageway that tilted down into the mountain, and whatever sense of time or distance we had when we started we had lost somewhere back up on top with the daylight. There was nothing but the black, not even a thin line of light that slipped past the crack of a door, just a heavy thick darkness that felt cool on the skin and which filled our lungs every time we took a breath. We were all heaving hard, and I thought I was going to suffocate.

After a while I eased up some, but not much, and I tried thinking about the outside, about Joe heaving that big rock. The others seemed lost in their own thoughts, and I wondered if they felt less frantic. I wondered if they had given in to the dark, accepted it like it was a natural and comfortable element. I didnt and couldnt. I felt boxed up and afraid that I would never find my way back to the light.

Which was why I was more than a little startled when the woman flipped on a light switch.

We were blinking, rubbing our eyes, squinting at each other like we had just woken up and were surprised to find out that someone else had been in bed with us. Sort of shy and embarrassed. The woman looked the most surprised of all.

"I didnt think it would work," she said, and pointed to the light switch.

But it did, and after our eyes quit blinking and squinting, and after Treetop quit flipping the switch back and forth, on and off, we adjusted enough so that we see that we were in a wide concrete passageway. Overhead there was a string of lights in little cages every forty feet or so, just enough so that the circles of light nearly touched. We had changed directions a couple of times, zigzagging our way down, so that we had no idea about where we were headed. Just deeper and downward. Ahead of us there was a bend, and behind us the string of lights ran up to another turn. It was a lot better to have flipped a switch and discovered electricity, but it had been a curious experience to grope along a concrete wall in the dark without even a stub of a candle.

Maybe we had only been bumping and groping along for only a few minutes. In the dark everything got mixed up and confused. Time and distance are things that belong to the light.

Yet we had passed through a door into a strange world. And not just the big old rusty one Joe had knocked down and or the flimsy things we had kicked in to get into the passageway.

The woman discovered electricity, and then all of us discovered that we were someplace where we had never been before, a dank musty place of concrete, dust, and silence, but it was another world, and one we didnt belong to but wanted to inhabit just the same.

From the flimsy doors we had gone down several flights of steep stairs in the dark, and then we creeped along a wall, telling ourselves that we would only go another few yards or so to see if we would come to something. Only there was nothing but the dark, nothing but our breathing, snuffling, groping, and shuffling. Even Chatterbox had fallen silent.

I thought that maybe this was like death. Maybe hell wasnt so fieryhot and boily after all, just someplace where you got lost in the dark, someplace where you just edged along all numblike and stupid, never knowing where you were or where you were going.

After I quit blinking I was happy to have escaped back into the light.

Chapter 16

Hell didnt last forever. After what seemed like endless stumbling we came upon another steep set of stairs. There was a steel door, but this one wasnt even locked.

The boy and Treetop began running along the walls hunting for more light switches to flip, hoping to find the switch that would light everything up and open all doors.

We followed, thinking we would arrive somewhere eventually, and thinking that place would take us closer to where we wanted to go. Generally its safe to assume that roads, stairs, and passageways lead somewhere, or at least point somewhere, though maybe they dont in hell. Me and Joe had been fooled before thinking we were headed somewhere while going nowhere. But we followed the long passageway, and into another, heading somewhere.

And eventually this somewhere turned out to be a broad tunnel road that was five times as large as the previous one. We could have driven a half dozen muleteams all yokedup through without scraping the sides. It was all bright and paintedup with yellow and white lines for the traffic flow, only there was no traffic flowing. It was as silent and still as the catacomb we had just come out of. There was a thin current of cold air blowing through.

"Maybe nobodys home. Maybe we should come back later."

Joe wasnt serious. We are all firedup and feverish. Whatever feeling of dread or fatigue we had felt before was gone. Every couple hundred of yards or so there was a set of large double steel doors on both sides of the road. I could feel my blood pounding. I thought I was burst apart. The wildboy, Treetop, and Chatterbox took off full tilt towards the down slope.

"It all looks familiar, but then all these tunnels look alike. Theres more than a hundred tunnels extending more than fifty miles. Ive never been assigned to the Supply Depot or had to work audit or inventory details." Whitehair stood in the middle of the road, looking one way and then the other.

He was using words we didnt hear much, but they sounded good.

"Me and Joe is always real careful with our audit and inventory details."

I tried the nearest set of doors, and they were locked. Treetop was pushing and kicking every door he saw, enlisting the rest of us but only Chatterbox and the wildboy answered the call. The doors were pretty solid, and there werent any big chunks of rock lying around. They might as well have been trying to move the mountain itself. Treetop wanted to shoot the locks, but we werent ready to announce ourselves, or shoot ourselves with our own bullets bouncing back at us.

"Keep trying all the doors. Youll find one thats open," the woman urged, but Treetop needed little urging.

There were dozens of them, and he sprinted off again down the line yanking on all of them, Box and the wildboy keeping pace with him. They got far enough ahead of the rest of us so that when they finally dipped out of sight they were no more than wild stick figures jerking their way along.

We heard them before we saw them. Shouting and a scream. Then a short burst of automatic fire from a cutter. When we caught up with them they were as out of breath as we were. They had found a set of doors that was wide open.

"Two men, and they ran away from us," Treetop said, pointing past the doors.

We followed him in and then pulled up short. Inside was a storage area as large as a large building, or larger. A hundred feet or more high and filled with an endless network of rafting and shelving, and everywhere we looked there were boxes, crates, barrels, and bins stacked to the ceiling, thousands and thousands of leftovers that never got left over. Just stored away underneath a mountain. All numbered neatly.

"What is all this stuff," Joe asked. He walked over to the nearest aisle.

"Looks like mostly engine and machine parts. Maybe appliances and plumbing. You can tell by the numbers. Everythings got a number." Whitehair picked up a large cardboard box. He opened it and spilled a dozen thin rubber belts on the floor. Back in Aurora me and Joe could trade those away in a moment for making slingshots and gate fasteners. I

The Lords of Leftovers

looked around and then considered all the other doors and tunnels. Surely we had struck the motherlode of all leftovers, but suddenly I didnt feel too good about it. There was too much stuff.

"They were over here," Treetop pointed us away towards another aisle. "And they ran down there." He pointed again. The far end of the aisle looked distant.

"Did you shoot at them?" I asked.

Treetop shook his head, but then nodded. "I wanted them to stop, but they ran."

"What were they doing?" Whitehair asked.

Treetop shrugged, and Chatterbox confirmed with his own shrug.

"They were here," he said, and pointed us down the aisle.

Box and the wildboy took us to an intersection where two of the big aisles crossed. Parked in the middle was a small oddlooking cart with stubby wheels and a flat back. The runaway men had been loading a small wooden crate on the back of it. The little vehicle was a little scratched up some, but there wasnt a spot of rust on it.

Whitehair inspected the crate. "An electrical motor. Somebodys dishwasher mustve broke down."

"Dishwasher?" Joe asked increduously.

Whitehair ignored him. "Least we dont have to walk anymore." He gestured to the vehicle. It was painted gray, and had black numbers stenciled on the side. "This heres a gopher. Itll go for anything." He dragged the crate off and let it crash to the floor. "All aboard."

Being accustomed to gophering, Whitehair was better at it, but I got to drive. And despite rolling Joe off once when I creased a wall starting out, and I wasnt especially unsafe or unsteady. I believe Joe rolled himself off for the effect, and then for further effect he didnt want to get back on, but when he saw how the thing could scoot he gave in and climbed back on.

"Im still sore from rockchucking, you better not crash me into another wall."

I knew Joe was muttering for the sake of muttering. The others didnt hardly mutter at all, except Treetop, who was mad because he wanted to drive. We had agreed to take turns, and I had climbed on to take the first turn, though we had forgot to agree on how long a turn should last.

"It is my turn to gopher. You are still my prisoner."

Treetop had clapped a long bony hand on my shoulder, giving me a slight tug.

"Wait until we go down a ways and get somewhere. Then itll be your turn. Im just starting to ge the hang of gophering."

So we went tearing along, and I got kind of comfortable. There wasnt much to do except keep my foot pressed to the gopedal and maybe once in a while step on the stoppedal to slow down. I steered by pointing the steeringhandle where I wanted to go, but we only had one direction, so the only thing I had to watch out for was creasing the sides and scaring Joe. Every time I gave the handle a little shake the cart would suddenly swing out, which was how I scraped the wall starting out. I had pretty much come to believe that the best way to steer was by not steering until we came to the crazy corkscrew.

I eased up and rolled to a stop. In front of us the tunnel dipped sharply down and around. Since I had never been on a gophercart in a giant corkscrew before, I only wanted to prepare myself for the experience. But Whitehair had other ideas. He reached over and pressed his foot on my gofoot, and then he jerked the handle, and we plunged ahead. The fool was laughing and wouldnt get his foot off my foot, so in seconds we were going faster than people were supposed to go while careening down giant corkscrews. I knew this for a fact because we whizzed past big red and yellow signs that said "CAUTION—SLOW."

The whitehaired Fool was laughing and screaming, and the wildboy was laughing, but no one else was laughing. We were spiraling downward, scraping walls, and I was grappling with the Fool while the woman and the wildboy were hunched down like ticks and Treetop and Chaterbox were screaming and Joe was screaming that he was going to shoot somebody, and I wasnt sure if he meant me or the Fool.

But luckily we had our accident before Joe shot anyone.

We smacked them nearly deadcenter, another gopher like ours, only this one didnt have a rheumatic whithaired Fool shoving his foot up against the gopedal. This one had two more sallow soldiermen in it and was stopped in the middle of the corkscrew where no rational creature shouldve been stopped. We come ripping around the curve, and both men stood up bugeyed like they had never before seen a runaway gopher filled with cannibals and savages. They both jumped and bumped out of the way, but all I could do was stand on the stoppedal and scream at the Fool next

The Lords of Leftovers

to me. He was still laughing.

We skidded and then smacked into the other gopher. For some reason I jerked the steeringhandle at the last second, turning my side into its front so that I got the jolt and then a broken headlight stuck in my sore side.

We were lucky only getting scuffedup and bruised some. Treetop had banged up a knee pretty good and was hobbling around trying to pull the bolt back on his cutter, wanting to shoot the two men who had left their gopher where I could run into it. Joe was of the same inclination, only he seemed a little more dangerous because he had kept a grip on his guns. He glowered at the bugeyed men, then the Fool, who was still snickering, and then at me. I went over to the woman and the wildboy. They were huddled up over on the side. I asked them how they were.

"That was my first cartride," the woman said, and then smiled, "Im not sure I care to have another."

Across from us the Fool giggled, and Joe went over to him.

"Whats so funny?"

"Racing gophers. Thats what we do for fun. Everyone does it, even the officers when they dont think the rest of us are around. Didnt you enjoy the ride? Youre not going to shoot the gopher, are you?"

Joe studied the Fool for a moment. "No. I didnt enjoy the ride, so maybe I should shoot it, or you."

"It was fun, but I was not comfortable," the woman said. She and the wildboy got up and patted themselves over.

The wildboy was smiling. "Big fun."

I was siding with Joe but gave up worrying about being gophered to death. Treetop and Chatterbox had both settled their cutters on the bugeyed men. Both were still smeared up and wildlooking, and they were making quite an impression.

"Who are you?" the first man asked me. He was round and heavy. The second one was less round and heavy. He was squareheaded and thicklipped. Neither looked happy. They were dressed out like soldiers, but they didnt seem too soldierly. They, the Fool, and all of the mountainmen, were definitely leaning on the wrinkled side of life.

"We are diseasebearing, maneating savages, barbarians from the lands of fire and chaos. We are ignorant and cruel and know only blood and pain. Which of you wants to be the first to be sacrificed to satisfy our unnatural appetites?" I tried to look savage and fierce.

The two looked at each other, then the second one blurted, "Dont kill us. We aint done nothin to you." Joe dragged the Fool over and set him down next to the two men. He was still smiling, still trying to get Joe to give in.

"Wasnt it fun? We always race through these tunnels. Ask these two." The Fool nodded to the men next to him. Both looked back at him.

"I know you. Youre Security, right?" the first man said. "Are you their prisoner?"

"We captured a dozen men down at the dam. He is the last to be eaten. But he is a rheumatic fool and would give us cramps. Now we will eat one of you," I said, still trying to look savage and fierce.

I looked at Joe. He was enjoying himself despite getting knocked off a gopher. I was enjoying myself too. Being a flesheating savage was about as much fun as gophering.

Once the Prince asked me why me and Joe joked around so much when everything else was so serious. He even used the word, irreverent, which made me wonder if he had been looking at my dictionary book. I had tried to explain to him, somewhat seriously, that joking around was a good thing, that with all the Fires and the wackers and the screamers it was a necessary and natural thing. Though I wouldnt tell him, I didnt mind so much that the Fool nearly killed us. And I wouldnt tell the two gophermen that we werent savage cannibals.

"Dont kill us. Please dont. We aint done you no harm. We will do anything you want. Look, we got all the keys and pass codes to Levels 4 and 5. Level 5 has all of the military gear. You can take anything you want," the second man said. He was about the same age as the first, and carried less weight, but he had more chins and wrinkles, as if his skin was loosefitting and creased. Both still had their buggyeyed look. I was sure they had never encountered anyone like Treetop and Box, and even like me and Joe. The woman and the wildboy came over to us, and all of us pressed the three mountainmen into the wall. I thought that it was as good a time as any to get somewhere.

"Treetop and Chatterbox want unlimited supplies of food, clothing, and guns. Joe wants a dishwasher, bubblegum, bullets for his new hunting rifle, and all the gold and silver you got. The woman and the wildboy just want to see whats going on and then a fair portion of whatever Joe gets. All I want is a little general who struts around giving orders. Then I want our old man back."

The Lords of Leftovers

* * *

"We will have you all shot," the little impostor said, and slapped the table for effect, "this is a classified federal installation essential to our nations future. Anyone who trespasses, anyone who threatens the security of this installation, is subject to military law and summary execution. We are at war."

I sat in a long rectangular room with a fancy polishedup table looking out a long slit of a window. My room was one of several that were lined up in double rows overlooking a small rocky escarpment and then a sudden drop. Out beyond there was a series of high ridges and peaks that were streaked with deep pockets of yeararound snow. The rooms reminded me of a honeycomb, but the only buzzing around was the little impostor, and I had grown tired of him.

"Who you at war with? You aint got either a nation or a future. Maybe I should have you shot for impersonating a little general."

The gophermen had hooked me up with the wrong general, and I wondered if maybe there was a pack of runty generals hiding out someplace. This one looked sort of like the little general who had visited with the Bishop. He dripped ribbons and medals and little shiny stars, and he strutted around the room like the world was his barnyard, but I knew he was a fake, so I didnt mind him buzzing at me about treasonable trespass and summary execution. I was waiting for the real general to show up

Me and the Fool had been brought to the little fraud in an elevator. Four soldiers and some kind of officer had escorted us. The soldiers looked like the Fool, only they acted more soldierly than I had ever seen him or the two gophermen act. I assumed that they didnt try to gopher people to death and then cackle about it. Shoot us maybe. They carried cutters, locked and loaded, and they trooped about like they had metal spines and wooden brains just like the Bishops toy soldiers.

The Fool had tried to engage them in conversation, but they didnt have much to say to him, and the officer barked at him to shutup. He didnt seem to like the Fool much, which I could appreciate. The guards stood two in back and one on either side of us, while the officer placed himself in front. I had nothing else to do but watch the little lights pop on and off and wait for whatever was coming. Except for once being carried half drunk up several flights of stairs by a woman twice my size, this was my first elevator ride. But maybe I am misremembering how big that woman was or how far she carried me.

I had agreed to go unarmed to meet the general, while Joe and the others were holedup down below. Our two gophermen had taken us to a couple of compartments and then glued themselves together while we loaded up our damaged gopher with food and cutters and whatever else looked good. They never quite caught on that we werent really going to torture them, eat them, or infect them with grievous diseases, and they guided us through a maze of passgeways in moods that were slightly sullen but largely aghast, and bordering on hysterical. I began to like being a savage barbarian cannibal, and I growled some for dramatic effect, but I couldnt get Joe to make more than a couple uncivilized sounds, and they were mostly directed at either the Fool or me. And the woman was downright polite. She wasnt much good at the barbarian business.

Down below most of those we had seen were unarmed gophermen like the first two, and they mostly scattered or stared when they saw us. They werent exactly ready for the enemy within, especially flesheating cannibals.

Treetop and Chatterbox acted their part well enough. They scrambled and grabbed, hooting their delight at everything they touched, accepting whatever was available whether they had a use for it or not. In addition to every cutter, gun, and military belt, they took hold of a rather large electric coffee pot, spilling the coffee, a picture of a fancywhite building with a big dome, a dozen loaves of white bread, and they threw it all on the back of the gopher and then sat there munching two loaves at a time while wrestling with the others. I aint usually of a thievish mind, but I got touched by the spirit, and I picked up a little fat book with a picture of a halfnaked smiling woman on the cover, a little pocketsized telephone, and a little flat lugalong computer, which I confess I had about as much use for as a dozen loaves of soggy white bread. The Fool had made use of my telephone, though, calling upstairs to set up our meeting. He had spoken for a long time, and then had answered a lot of questions with a few yesSirs and noSirs. It didnt sound like the upstairs crowd was pleased with our arrival. But it was set up that me and the Fool would go get elevatoredup to meet the general, while Joe and the others locked themselves away with the two gophermen.

I had been trying to be polite, but after while I have to swat at whatevers buzzing around my head, even if its a runty redfaced reproduction dripping ribbons and sweat. I was luckier than the Fool, who had been dragged off roughly as soon as the elevator spit us out. Until the little fraud marched in and began sputtering, things had been quiet and polite, but his forecasts of my immiment dispatch soon became tiresome. Particularly since everyone seemed in favor my imminent dispatch. Other than a few barbs, there wasnt much to trade.

"Tell your friends to lay down their weapons and surrender. Immediately." The little fraud slapped the table again for effect, and I considered reaching over and slapping him.

"You surrender to us, you feeblebrained fraud. I dont want to hear any more about getting shot, or hung, burned, or shreddedup. I aint going to listen to it anymore. You hear what Im saying. Ever since me and Joe came up to this magic mountain paradise people have been trying to bring our lives to violent conclusion. I came here peacefully to do a little trading, and I have been robbed, smacked on the head, dragged through the forest, nearly hung like meat on a market day, chased through a school for the dead, shot at, robbed again, and exploded with grenades. Ive had guns held to my head and knives to my throat, and Im sick of it. What is the matter with everyone up here? The worst sort of the wackers and screamers down in the flats are more civilized than any of you crazy saints and soldiers. You should get out more, mix with people, and learn how to act out more civilized. Youre all crazy from being ratholed for so long."

"We are defending civilzation," he screamed at me, his redface contorting, "and you are a petty thief who has committed treasonable trespass. This installation is vital to the preservation of our most sacred national offices, and it is being attacked daily by forces you couldnt begin to understand. We are at war, and our mission is to preserve and protect our national heritage.

I breathed deeply and let go of my anger. He had been tunneledup until he had become unhinged.

"Whose national heritage? I think youve been stumbling around in the dark too long, maybe bumped your head a few too many times. You aint preserving anyones national heritage. Youre just a bunch of scaredyrats hiding in a hole in the ground, afraid to show yourselves. Your nation got burnedup and abandoned years ago, and whats left is out there grubbing in the heaps and muck of what you left behind, getting along the best they can without any help from you. People out there dont have use for your nation or heritage. They live the best lives they can, and without any help from all of you hideaways. You want to help people, you go on out there and help them plant and rebuild. You aint but a pack of grimey rodents scared of the light."

The Impostor slapped the table and came strutting around towards me. I got up to squash him and the four toy soldiers standing behind him.

But before the battle began the real little general walked in. "At ease," he snapped at the others, and at me, "Sit. Please resume your seat. There will be no shooting or executions today."

I sat back down but the Impostor glared at me. "Shoot him. Shoot them all. Lets be done with them," he hissed. "Our mission hasnt changed and will not ever change."

The Little General shook his head. "No, it hasnt. But shooting them all might not an option at this point. His friends are secured in Central Three and evidently they have hostages and sufficient firepower to make shooting them difficult and costly. I think that we will negotiate with this gentleman," he turned to me, "you have come to negotiate, havent you?"

I nodded. "The Bishop stole my packs and mules."

"Oh yes, the Bishop. And he stole your packs and mules? And is that what you want?"

I shrugged. We stared for a moment, then he turned to look out the slitwindow. The sun had broken through the clouds and patches of sunlight and shadow shifted over the high ridges in front of us. Without looking at him he dismissed the Impostor and ordered coffee.

"The Bishop tempted me with food and whiskey."

"Undoubtedly a holy sacrament. I also have taken the communion at the Bishops table, many times in fact."

"I had something cheesy."

For several moments the General said nothing, nothing about food or whiskey or cheesy sacraments. Instead he slowly pulled out a pack of cigarettes and offered me one. I took two and pocketed them, and then watched while he carefully lit one with a silver lighter with an eagle crest. He sucked hard and then exhaled slowly, a stream of white smoke curled between us. The General had his own rituals.

"You really have created quite a problem for us, and Major Ridley was correct. You really do not see the significance of who we are and what we do, nor the implications and consequences of your actions. There are much

The Lords of Leftovers

larger considerations that you are not aware of, a much bigger picture than you can imagine. You have blundered into something of far greater matter than packs and mules. What we do here is much more important than you can possibly imagine."

I played his game and was silent for a few moments. Outside it had darkened up again. "Ive seen a big enough picture. Ive traveled around the ranges and the flats my whole life, and Ive seen all kinds of people struggling to get back what they had before everything got charredup and cindered, before people like you decided that you had to save the world by destroying it. Only in your madness and arrogance you couldnt possibly realize that life would go on without you. I survived Fires and the dark that youre so afraid of. Theres lot of people out there who got through it, people with nothing but pain and wreckage in their lives surviving on nothing but the grit to stumble forward, and keep going, day by day. Most cant read and dont wash, but they were the ones that got left behind when the likes of you like flew off to your magic mountains and happy valleys, and now theyre the ones left to clean up your mess. What have you seen holed up here like tunnel rats?"

The coffee arrived and he had it poured. For a few moments we sipped and he puffed. The coffee didnt taste much like the jars of leftover powder. We again traded silences and stared through his smoke.

"I have seen the lights go out. I have sat at computer screens and video monitors and watched them go blank. I have watched as the most sacred and profound hopes of our forefathers have been trampled and destroyed." He stopped, offering up another silent moment before continuing. "And I have watched as armies have annihilated one another and as nations were consumed in war."

The General shifted himself around, setting off in a new direction. "Now I watch as everything we have struggled to protect is being threatened by a common outlaw who grows more deranged and dangerous with the passing of each day. While we grow weaker, he grows stronger. Everything we have worked and sacrificed for he will soon destroy. All the work of our lives will be ruined."

"The Bishop?"

Instead of answering, the General again changed directions. "I understand that you have refused to give your name. Are you hiding your real name, or do you really not have a name?"

I gave him back another one of his silent moments. "I had a

birthname, but nobody remembered to tell me what it was. So along the way people called me different names. An old couple had me for a while, but they generally called me boy."

He nodded. "I see. In my world names are, or were, important. My name is General Jonathan Scott Winston. My father, grandfather, and great grandfather were also named Jonathan Scott Winston. I am a descendant of the original General Scott Winston. Do you know who he was?"

I didnt and didnt care. "Did your mother name you General?"

He smiled. "She might as well have. It was my destiny. I was destined to receive a military command. I was commissioned to defend my country before I was born."

"What country?"

This was another question he wasnt excited about answering. We sipped some more, and he lit another cigarette. I was thinking about how much a carton of leftover cigarettes would be worth down in Aurora. Probably enough to start a considerable skirmish fighting over it.

"The Bishops real name is Bobby Tanner, and his father was also Bobby Tanner. Concerning previous generations I have not been informed. His father was a tanner, a hide dresser, and a tallow maker. The Bishop might well have been named Bobby Tallow. Then he might not want all of our hides."

He looked at me and waited. But I said nothing.

"I often think about the past, the flames of past military glory, the fires my descendants were fighting. Bobby Tanner dreams of the future, and his flames are burning out of control."

He looked at me and again waited.

"So whats this got to do with my packs and mules?"

The Generals request was simple. He wanted me to kill the Bishop. I explained that killing him might be a problem since he was intent on killing me. But this didnt seem to matter. Nor did it matter when I asked why the General couldnt do his own killing, seeing how he had troops and a mountainfull of leftover weaponry, and I only had me and Joe and maybe a wildboy and lamefooted woman. But this didnt matter much either. He had his reasons, he said.

He took me on a tour, and while we walked I tried to sort out his reasons. I figured he needed the Bishop, or rather he needed whoever was next in line after the Bishop had passed beyond. Or maybe Bishopsblood didnt wash off.

We went through a corridor of shiny floors and bright lights until we came to what mustve been familiar ground to the old man. There was a large open area filled with rows of monster machines that blinked and hummed as if they were alive. Sitting at a dozen or so terminals were a handful of whitecoated men and women who didnt seem half as alive as the machines. Some clicked away at keyboards, the rest just stared at us a moment and then returned to stare at the screens in front of them. None of the whitecoats were young.

"What are they doing?"

I paused in front of a large window that overlooked the computers. The General and the toy soldiers paused with me.

"Mostly gathering and storing information, monitoring, searching for signals."

"What information?"

"All kinds of information. Do you know about satellites?"

He was treating me like the others, as if I was an ignorant savage. I started to tell him that I could read and that I knew all about a lot of things, some maybe he didnt even know about after being ratholed for so long. Instead I coughed up a couple of words.

"Sputnik, Apollo, Challenger, one small step for mankind, and the right stuff."

The General smiled. "Sorry. I just have no idea what you know or dont know. I dont talk to people from the outside. We are linked up a variety of satellites that track and observe the world. Every day we are saturated with information. The computers process and store the information."

"What for?"

"Good question. To make the world a better place I suppose. We used to be connected to other bases and installations all over the world planning our recovery, but now we have lost most of those connections. Now we mostly listen and watch to see whats happening around the world."

Whether he was serious or not I couldnt tell. "Whose world?"

He was delusional, convinced that there was only one world and that his satellites and his computers and his ratsoldiers and his eaglecrested lighter gave him some sort of insight into it, and privilege over it.

I didnt push back. Theres not much anyone can say to crazies. But in my thinking theres thousands of different worlds, maybe millions, all of them dissimilar, all inhabited by one, two, or a handful of people, all thinking their world is the only world or the best world, all in some kind of strangled orbit around themselves, and only seldom do a couple of them ever randomly bang into each other. It dont take all that much to create your own little world. We all do it. Even me and Joe who generally cover more ground than most.

    I didnt like hearing the General talk about the world as if it was his, and as if it was the one and only world. I walked along with the general and his guards, looking at what he pointed at, but I concluded he was crazier than the little Imposter, and maybe crazier than the Bishop.

    As much as I know about life before the Fires, or what I think I know, and not just what it looked like in those old magazines, I think a bunch of worlds collided, big and little ones, and each one of them was well stocked with little generals and politicians who thought theirs was the one and only world and who were all overstocked with too many things destructive, and all them believing their world was so sweet and righteous that it truly ought to be the only world. I had no doubt that the General had no doubt about his one world theory. The world according to General Rat. I didnt believe his was better than mine, or the wildboys, or even Treetops.

    I doubted mine, though. Always have. Its righteousness that kills. I always thought carrying around a little doubt aint a bad thing. Maybe its just how you use the words, and maybe words dont really mean all that much anymore. I thought the General mightve been better off carrying a few doubts of his own. I have found that it is best not to put a lot of confidence in people who put too much confidence in themselves. But as generals go, he wasnt a bad sort, and I liked his lighter.

Chapter 17

The General gave me a tour and a promise of paradise. Not the Bishops squirrely kind with pearly gates and golden streets, but a string of trucks filled with whatever I wanted to cart off, fully juicedup batteries, goldbars, toilet paper, heavy weaponry, and chocolate, peaches, ketchup, gasoline, cigarettes, coffee, even generators and light bulbs. He had it all figured out. I would eliminate the Bishop and his pack of apostles, then with his help I would set myself up as territorial governor and save Nineveh from a plague of saints. I could have as much electricity, hot water, candy, whiskey, bubble gum, and wild times as I wanted, and all I had to do was take over after I took out the Bishop. It was a swell deal.

From my perspective, the Generals gold was considerably more practical and attractive than the Bishops streets of gold. And I liked the idea of carting off tons of anything I wanted. After the Bishop was launched into the next world, I could gopher my way through the Generals underworld, and anything I pointed to I could have. Lord of Leftovers. King of Rats. I could mine the motherlode for as much as my trucks could carry.

But then trucks will eventually run down or run out of gas, and even if they didnt most of the old roads are all chunked up, caved in, and overgrown. It would be nigh impossible to get down to the front range with the Generals trucks. I couldnt really go any place, though I enjoyed the image of driving up to the Princes palace in my leftover trucks. But chances were that I would never get there. Too far to go, too much to carry, and too many wackers and screamers along the way. The plain fact was that the General had thousands of tons more of everything than I could possibly drag off, including gold. I had no use for a caravan of trucks. A couple bags of gold coins would be plenty enough.

The fact is, the more you got, the more trouble youre going to have hanging on to it. Me and Joe would just end up hunkered down in some hole like the General, always afraid to let anyone know where we were or what we got. We would end up more worried with hanging on than letting go.

Dealings a better way to get by. Dont attach yourself to anything that you cant carry, and keep everything else moving. Me and Joe get by living off the laws of scarcity. Too much of anything reduces its value. Trucks with big boxes of greasynew handguns aint worth all that much more than carrying around a couple if you know how to strike a good deal. With trading, the only worry me and Joe ever had was with wackers and screamers, but theyll kill you just as dead if you were a mudgrubber weeding beans or a scav picking at scraps. I would just as soon know that a pack of bloodsoaked backshooters was trailing us up a pass than be grubbing in the dirt and never know what was going to come screaming over the hill.

Trading is a more honorable profession than bishoping or generaling. When me and Joe meet up with a cluster of people, everyone knows we are there trying to get an edge on them. Thats the nature of the deal. And theyre trying to do the same. Its out in the open and well understood. Everyone wants a good deal. Always seemed fair enough to me. Each side is trying to take advantage of the other, and everyone knows it. Cheating aint cheating when two people are trying to cheat each other. Thats just business. What gives me and Joe an advantage is that we know most people are dumb enough to think theyre smarter than everyone else. We just let them go on thinking theyre smarter.

But being a bishop, a general, or a governor seemed a lot like preaching a whole jumble of words you dont believe in but want everyone else to believe in. Its cheating without letting the other person know youre cheating. You got to do most things underhanded and slippery, and even if you feel righteous you never feel righteous enough not to know youre underhanded and slippery. You want others to believe what you cant wholly believe in. Being a trader, or even being a lurker or snatchthief, was more respectable than being a bishop or a general. As much as I admired his lighter and strut, I didnt trust this general too much.

"Isnt this beautiful?"

The General wanted me to agree with him, and was so convinced in his perception that he assumed I would agree with him. We were standing on a little grassy knoll overlooking his garden. Only it wasnt real.

The Lords of Leftovers

We had elevatored down a ways, and then he had led me through a hallway until we came to two large doors, which two toy soldiers opened for us, and he walked me through a large underground garden, all litup with racks of overhead lights. It was intended to impress me, only it stirredup a general uneasiness, and made me a little sad.

"These lights you see do a better job at photosynthesis than real sunlight."

I nodded, thinking I probably knew what photosynthesis meant, and wishing I was out in real sunlight. We walked along a pretty walkway through terraces of flowers and bushes, and even two rows of stubby apple tress dotted with small green apples. And there was a little stream that ran underneath a little wooden bridge that curved across the walkway, only the water ran from one side of the chamber to the other and then got flushed back to go again. There were no birds, no insects, and the only sounds were the flushy water and the General. It all seemed more unnatural than natural to me, and I thought the Generals garden was a good example of what he was trying to sell me, something pretty that wasnt quite real. We paused on the little grassy knoll overlooking his garden. The air was warm and moist and smelled musty. Out beyond I could see walls and the top part of the doors we had come through.

"We can make the world look like this, a beautiful garden."

I kept my mouth shut. The last thing the world needed was orderly rows of flowers, or someone thinking weeding and pruning would be enough to control the chaos of natural growth. Whats naturally wild needs to stay wild. I doubted the General knew much about gardening.

I wouldnt make too good a bishop or a general. Or a prince. I can usually make someone think he wants something he doesnt need, and make another person think something is more valuable than it really is, but I dont think I could stand up in front of a couple hundred people and make them believe in a lot of flapdoodle that I didnt believe in and that wasnt true. Joe would probably be better at it than me, him being an imposing sort and all, but he would never give up his wives and children to take on the territorial governor business. I dont think he would feel comfortable with it either. All in all, I figured we were better off with a pack of mules than a parcel of trucks, and a lot better off moving around than burrowing in. You got to distrust those that pant after power and authority. People who think theyre naturalborn leaders ought not to lead. Theyre the real scammers, the burners and the scorchers.

But I couldnt tell the General this, and I couldnt tell him his garden sucked. He really believed that it was beautiful, and he really believed that I needed a convoy of trucks, and that the world needed his weeding and pruning.

Nor could I tell him that I wanted to keep my word to the old man. I wanted to find the old man and help him bust the Generals mountain wide open, scattering all of his rats and gophermen out into the blinking daylight. The General and all his fools werent exactly hurting anyone staying underground with their property and pretensions, but there wasnt much profit in it either. For them or for anyone. It wasnt a natural situation, hiding in the ground when there wasnt anything left to hide from. Life gets built up and then knocked down and then built up again. Nothing stays the same. Life grows wild and unorderly. You cant hunker down and hang on, no matter how glorious your moment was. I was betting that deep down behind all his generalspeech, the General knew this. And deep down he probably knew his garden sucked.

The Generals deal was sour anyways. He was giving away too much for too little in return. Every thickheaded fool stumbling around a market would know that his deal reeked. The General couldve found any old bloodyminded brute to kill the Bishop. For most wackers, killing is just standard business. Cruelty dont seem to be so cruel after it gets to be ordinary. For those turned savage, the hurt and suffering of others dont matter. For a pack of leftover tobacco the General couldve found a handful of brutes to go after the Bishop. He probably couldve turned Smoke for a quarter what he was offering me. Something didnt set right with the Generals offer, and I thought it likely that he intended to have me dispatched after I concluded his dispatching. I was disappointed he thought so little of me.

The General sat across from me and carefully scraped away the ash from his cigarette. Except for a slim young man in a blue jacket, we were alone in a large dining area. I had been loadedup with biscuits, honey, and a large glass of something thick, sweet, and yellowwhite. Off in a corner the bluejacket man hovered about in case the General ordered something else. I pocketed a few biscuits and crumbled up another, thinking the wildboy would stuff himself sick if he were around.

"So what do you think?"

I dipped a piece of biscuit into the honey and tasted it. The honey was

The Lords of Leftovers

sweet and kind of smokey. "I think that it must be difficult to keep bees underground."

The General squashed out it his cigarette and began his ritual to light another. "You know what Im asking."

I was thirsty but hesitated over the chalky drink. The General had called it a protein supplement, but I decided I didnt need supplementing that looked and tasted so unnatural. I asked for more coffee and Bluejacket hurried off.

"Youre asking me if I want to kill the Bishop, and I aint too sure. I aint had much experience in the assassination business, and I dont think what youre offering is exactly what Im looking for. Why me anyway?"

Ignoring my last question, he blew smoke between us and asked the obvious question.

"What is it you want?"

"Most often I dont know what Im looking for until after Ive found it. Guess I want something more than smoke and promises and garden tours. Are you actually going to communicate with me and tell me what it is you want? How long do you think you can stay tucked up here in these mountains?"

"Until we are called to stand down."

"And whos going to be calling you?"

Instead of answering the General puffed while the Bluejacket poured. The dining was large enough so that sound seemed to echo. He wasnt going to communicate.

"And after the Bishop is out of the way, what then? Another Bishop will come along. Theres plenty more of them around than there are of you. Even if me and Joe would stick around, which we wouldnt, some other fool tanner or candlestickmaker with fancy dreams would come along thinking your magic mountain ought to be his. You sit on a dunghill long enough some will come around and want to sit where youre sitting. What is it you really want, General? I dont mean a dead Bishop and a fresh supply of mutton. What is it youre really after? Why are you hiding underground? What do you expect will happen? Why dont you just bust this mountain apart and come down with us back to the front ranges. The Prince would love you. You could rebuild the dead city. You could turn the lights back on for good. You could do a lot more good there than youre doing here."

The General scraped some more ash. "There are vital issues and situations that you do not need to know in order to carry out your mission.

There is a greater mission that all of us here are committed to. We can never relinquish our responsibility to carry out our orders."

I batted away some of his smoke, and crumbled up another biscuit, thinking that there was no real deal here.

"Your mission aint compatible with my basic mission."

"Your basic mission can still be splattered on a wall by a firing squad. Major Ridley would be happy to carry out that mission," he snapped.

I considered how long it would take me to snap his neck before Bluejacket or anyone else could stop me. But exchanging deaththreats is usually useless. Negotiations are best carried on without each side trying to bully the other.

"Threatening me probably aint the best way of persuading me to help you. Are you going to start telling me what it is youre after?"

The General blew some more smoke. He was good at that. My eyes were starting to sting.

"You must understand the importance of this installation. Our government is protecting our heritage and ensuring our future."

"Whose government?"

More smoke.

"Whose heritage?"

The General crushed out his cigarette. "Yours. The government is here for its citizens. It always has been. It never left, the people left it. The government was betrayed by its own people. There was war and civil unrest, and then more war. All the utilities and the electricity were eventually lost, stores were looted, there were riots and killings, the material infrastructure was destroyed, and in a remarkably short period of time the social fabric torn apart. People panicked when they couldnt turn on lights and faucets. But Ill tell you, during that whole terrible time the government and the military did everything possible to protect its citizens, maintain order, limit the destruction, and preserve the union. It was too much, though, just too much. So the government, all of us in every branch, locked down to wait out the anarchy of civil collapse. And thats what weve been doing, waiting until the time is right to restore the union and recover the greatness of our heritage. We will rebuild and restore. We have everything we need. When the time is right the government will come out and return to its citizens their freedoms and security. And when this time comes, it will be even greater than before. The whole hemisphere will be united. The glory of our past will open into an even more glorious future."

The General was so excited he forgot to light another cigarette with his fancy eaglelighter. I gave up thinking there was any use talking with him. Crazies wont listen to reason, and he struck me as the king of crazies. He had everything he needed but people. I knew I should keep quiet, but I couldnt keep my mouth shut.

"A Second Coming, huh? I heard about that. Read a book about it once. You and your rats going to raise the dead too?"

Suddenly the General began beeping. He pulled out a little black box no bigger than his lighter and stopped the noise. In a second Bluejacket was all over us with one of those little pocket phones. The General croaked some into it and then listened some.

"Can I talk into it too? I aint had a conversation with nobody I wasnt facing before. I would like to call Joe and see what he thinks of your offer. Hes a far better assassinator than me. Ill tell you, he can shoot a fly off a nail at three thousand yards. Ive seen him do it."

The General ignored me, and the phone got bluejacketed before I could have a go at it.

"I got a phone. Down underneath somewhere. Joes probably talking on it right now. Get Bluejacket to bring yours back, and Ill talk to Joe on it."

The General looked at me blankly. If I was beeping, he wouldve reached over and switched me off. I was nothing more than buzzynoise to him.

"I would prefer that you talk to the Bishop. He has arrived at the main gate. He and the rest of his militia."

"Whats he want?"

"To get in, of course. And then to get everything. But right now he says hell settle for you. He is making several demands, including you and your friends."

From underneath the table the General pulled out a silver pistol with pearly grips. In the moment he took to target me Bluejacket reappeared with a cutter, which wasnt as fancy but just as instructive. Seconds later the four ratsoldiers from the elevator came charging in loadedup with cutters and clips. Everybody had me pointed.

I bent over and peered underneath the table. There was a little shelf next to the Generals knee.

"You got anymore of them fancy guns? Ill trade you two bottles of sealedup whiskey. I know a fool back in Aurora thatll give fifty pounds of beans and potatoes for one of them. Ill throw in a genuine hunting knife all shiny and new without even a speck of rust on it. Ive been eyeing your eagle lighter too. We can strike a deal here."

The ratsoldiers gathered me in. They had taken my bootgun and a pocketknife, so there wasnt much I could do but amble along all friendly and goofy. They were all silent and serious. The General too. One of the guards had handed him a fatblack combat belt, which he had hung around his belly, and now he had two silverandpearl pistols holsteredup and ready for business. He led us back to the elevators.

"So General, you still want me to dispatch the Bishop? I believe I will need sufficient firepower. I might need to borrow one of your fancy handguns. I aint assassinated a saint before. I think a fancy silver pistol is required. Aint saints supposed to live forever anyway, or rise from the dead or something? Maybe Ill need a grenade and one of them big old spitter hellfire guns. Or maybe you got some of them citykillers leftover somewhere, some of those big rockets thatll rain everlasting fire and desolation. Whatdya say?"

Our negotiations were interrupted, but this time the General buzzed instead of beeped. He folded out his little phone, and for a moment there was silence, nothing but the hum of the elevator while the General listened, then suddenly he exploded. He threw the phone against the base of the elevator door, where it broke into pieces. One of the guards eyed the dead plastic then quickly looked away. The General stared straight ahead.

"Whats the matter? Run out of protein supplement?"

The General said nothing, and the ratsoldiers said nothing.

"Come on, General. These men here are as curious as I am. I aint never seen a general bust up a tiny foldup phone before in an elevator. I confess I aint exactly had much experience with either elevators or phones, so maybe its just a normal way of doing business. To tell you the truth, General, I aint exactly had much experience with generals either. But it dont seem to me to be an efficient form of communication, you breaking up that little pocketphone and all.

The General wouldnt answer me, and the ratsoldiers wouldnt look at me. We just hummed along.

"Thats the trouble with your kind, General. You always think you got to know more than anybody else, always got to have secrets so you can feel important. You all think holding secrets is like holding power. You ought to let everything out, get everything out in the open. Telling always makes you feel better."

Before I could say much else he gripped one of his pearly grips and cracked me on the side of my head. I fell back against one of the rats who pushed me back into the General. I started to bleed a little.

"You damn little runt, dont you know you cant break me apart like one of your little phones. Beating a man to death is a whole lot nastier, and I bet you aint exactly had much experience with it. You better be prepared to finish what you start."

"Say one more word, and Ill have you bound and gagged. You have caused more damage than you can possible imagine. You have jeopardized the lives of millions and the fate of this nation by infiltrating this installation. If the Bishop didnt want to kill you and your friends, I would kill you all myself."

The General pressed his fancy pistol up against my head. He didnt seem nearly so friendly now as before.

"Careful. Youll get your pearly grips all bloody."

I sat chainedup in a little closet room, waiting for something to happen. My ankles were shackled together, and my hands were handcuffed behind me. I sat on a hard metal chair, and every time I tried to get up my own personal ratsoldier pushed me back down. There wasnt much else for me to do but wait for whatever was to come. I wasnt happy, and I wished Joe and Treetop would come busting through the door and unhitch me. I would have even been happy to see the Fool in a gophercart.

Me and the General had hummed along until we bumped against what the elevators panel of lights called G1, which I hoped was JoeCruz level. All hell seemed to have broken loose with clumps of ratsoldiers running around everywhere, all of them with cutters and outfitted multiple clips and considerable clutter, all of them hurrying down another huge tunnel. A couple of big blocky armored trucks topped with spitter guns rumbled past, dragging stubby little cannons behind them. Everyone and everything was pointed in the one direction. Going to be a great show somewhere.

But the General had me draggedoff and chainedup. My ratsoldier was too scared to disobey orders and tell me what was going on. He wasnt so old and sallow as most of the others, still young enough to think of a life ahead of him. We both stared at the door, listening and wondering, and every once in a while he would push me back down when I tried to get up. All of the uproar lasted for a while, making me think that the General wasnt preparing for any sort of routine reception. More like a final battle. But I couldnt even get the guard to open the door, let alone call out to someone to find out the who, what, and where of the generals reception.

So me and the rat waited, and while we waited I told mostly true stories about wild times back in Aurora. He listened but tried hard not to let on that he was listening, but I could tell his attention was divided between the whiskey and women and what was happening out in the tunnel. Him not knowing a thing about the heathen world outside, I had him pretty much interested in the pleasures of dissipation when some more rats showed up.

No one spoke except an officer who decorated himself with a couple of gold bars on his shoulders, and he didnt say much except to bark at me to stand up while one of the rats unshackled my legs. He and three rats stuffed me on the back of a gopher.

"Can I drive? Ive had considerable experience gophering down tunnels at breakneck speeds carrying packs of women, children, and fools. Can we take my personal ratguard with us? Weve been getting on right well together."

We came to a large open chamber filled with a hundred or so ratsoldiers all gunnedup and pointing in one direction. In another world it had probably been a central depot, sometime type of staging area for distributing supplies. It had been built in four tiers, and both the back and horseshoe sides had balconies, loading docks, stairways, and open elevators, each connected with the main floor. Towards the far end there was yet another highway of a tunnel that snaked upward. I took it that a remarkable gathering was about to take place.

Me, my rats, and our gopher were loaded on to one of the elevators and carried up to the top tier, where the General was barking into another little black phone. Along the whole ledge there were a handful of sharpshooters cradling shiny black rifles with big scopes and silencers. I knew Joe wouldve loved to have had one of those gravediggers.

"General, can I get one of these big scopey rifles for Joe? A pair of pearly grips for me and a big black scopey rifle for Joe, and we will slip out of here. Wont ever come back either. I promise. We got a deal?"

The General walked over and shoved me backwards, knocking me off the gopher. I came up in a rage and kicked the stuffing out of Goldbars, who happened to be standing in front of me, and charged the General.

"You little dopeyheaded fool. I will kill you if you touch me again." I bumped the General back and was about to kick the stuffing out of him when the rest of my rats wrapped themselves around me. The General looked a little surprised.

He turned away and began to speak into his phone. A moment later he held the phone up to my face.

"Speak to your friend. Tell him to come out and lay down his weapons. Tell him to tell the rest to do the same."

"Take these locks and chains off of me. A fair trade. It aint natural to speak with my hands cuffed behind me."

The General pushed the phone closer to my face.

"Come on, General, you want me to speak on that little phone, you free my hands. Its a fair trade. No hands, no mouth."

The General paused long enough to let me know that he was in charge, then he nodded to Goldbars, who unlatched me. I rubbed my sore wrists until the General pushed the phone into my hands. I considered pushing the little black phone down the Generals throat. Though a crazyman, I had taken a liking to him before, but now he didnt seem so likeable.

"Talk to him," he barked.

I lifted up the phone carefully and stared into it.

"Speak. Tell him to surrender."

"Just hold on. I aint experienced in the phone business."

Then a voice in the phone laughed at me.

" Hey Joe, is that you?"

There was nothing but fuzzy sound for a moment, then Joe whooped out at me. "Hey, where you at? We got food and beer down here. Beer in little red and white cans. Aint no one coming in or going out as long as we can eat and drink. You gotta see Treetop. I dont think he ever drunk out of a can before, or drunk anything that would get him drunk. And he sure hasnt drunk beer before. Hes spilling it all over himself. We got us a wild time."

"Stop yelling. You dont have to scream into these things. Talk normal." There was more of the fuzzy noise. "Joe, you there?"

"Im here. You there?"

I nodded then felt stupid nodding at a phone. "Yeah, Im here. Im in a giant beehive where the Generals planning a party for the Bishop. I dont think they like each other anymore."

"Did the Bishop and his boys get inside?"

I nodded again. "Looks that way. Looks like the Bishop already had a few saints on the inside who opened the front door. Course the General aint trading much, so Im just guessing. The General cracked me on the head with a pearlygripped pistol and I had to kick him and a couple other ratsoldiers. Now he wont tell me a dang thing. Maybe you should come up here and shoot the whole bunch."

The General pushed me hard on the shoulder. "Tell him to come out."

I thought again about offering the General a chance to eat the phone, but I liked talking into it. "The General has asked me to ask you to unlock the doors and come out."

"What for?"

"He didnt say."

"Whats he trading?"

"He didnt say that either."

"Dont sound like much of a deal. Maybe youd better ask him to surrender to us. Tell him well give him back his two gophermen and all the canned beer he can drink."

The General grabbed the phone out of my hands. "Listen. Ill have your partner shot, and then Ill have all of you destroyed. I can have you blown to pieces in seconds," the General yelled.

For a moment there was nothing but the fuzzy noise, then Joe spoke. "Hello General, is that you. You dont have to yell into these phones. They work pretty well if you talk regular."

The General hit me with the phone in the chest. "Theres no time for this. If you want to live, if you want your friends to live, youll start cooperating."

I paused for a moment and looked out at all of the rat soldiers below. "And what will you give if we do?"

The General turned away and eyed his rat squad.

"What do you want?"

Chapter 18

I got shoved back into the assassinating business. I was supposed to walk down the big snaky tunnel and take out the Bishop. Just walk up casually and shoot him. I was supposed to take Joe and the woman with me and act like we were delivering ourselves up to divine retribution, then pop the Bishop when I got the chance. They give me a little black pocketgun for my belt and another for my boot if the saints found the first one. I only had a couple bullets. It wasnt much of a plan, seeing how the Bishop seemed smart enough not to let a man with a gun walk up and shoot him, I figured it was noplan. I was bait.

Joe and the woman werent cooperating with the Generals plan, deciding that Treetop and the beer were a better show. Seemed like a better deal to me too, but I got pushed along by Goldbars and a rat squad until we were at the tunnel entrance. Goldbars was still mad because I had kicked him, so we didnt exchange pleasantries. He eyed my like I was a savage cannibal.

"The Bishop has given his word that, if he receives you and the others, he will leave the installation."

"So all he wants is to take us back to Nineveh to atone for our sacrileges? He has been wanting inside these tunnels for practically forever, and now that hes in hes going leave? I dont believe the Bishop and all his shinyboots humped over here just to gather us up. I dont believe you and the General believe that either."

But what I believed didnt matter to Goldbars and his rats. They were intent on taking me forward. Both the Bishop and the General were liars of sizable magnitude, and I was bait for the one just as I was bait for the other. The Bishop wasnt about to leave the holy mountain now that he was inside, which every fool that breathed mustve realized, including the General. The two halfwitted clowns were going to have a run at each other, and I was just part of the opening procession. Goldbars didnt have much to say about the truth of the matter. But the truth is that ultimately arrogance and ambition kill more than mindless brutality. If someone had been smart enough to pack up all the bishops and generals before the Fires got sparked off, we might all be sitting around in fancy houses flipping on lights and flushing toilets.

I was between two heavily armed worlds about to bang up against each other, all crazed and intent on destroying each other, with nothing standing between but a couple of little pocket guns and an idiot plan that even a screamer wouldnt bother with. I had been better off shackledup and left behind with my pushmedown ratsoldier.

I was hoping I could walk down a ways then slip out, thinking there might be some kind of hole big enough to squeeze through. I hoped I wouldnt have to kill Goldbars and one or more of his rats, but what I didnt figure on was Goldbars and his guards jumping me from behind and handcuffing my hands behind my back again. Goldbars told me the handcuffs were only to make it look real, like I really was a prisoner they were exchanging. I asked him to explain the difference, and I asked him to step a little closer so I could listen better, that I was hard of hearing, but he did neither. I kicked one of his rats who misstepped too close in front of me.

The tunnel bent around a long halfcircle that sloped downwards, and as we went further around, me shuffling and Goldbars and the rats keeping a safe leggy distance away. Suddenly there was a loud scream and a squealy sound as a gopher popped out of a set of double doors and came tearing down a little ramp straight at us. The Fool was screaming and laughing and waving a pistol in one knuckly hand and steering with the other and heading straight at us. We icedup for a moment, trying to comprehend the unexpected possibility of being struck down by a fool in a gopher, and thats all it took. Goldbars come up to grab me, but he was a universe of late. I dove, and there was a whack and a shriek and the sound of rubber skidding and squeaking along the concrete floor. When I got up Goldbars was still down all scrunched up and rolly, while the rats were scattered and seemed somewhat disbelieving that theyd been gophered by a fool. He probably didnt even need to be waving a pistol at them.

"Well, you done it now. You finally run someone over."

The Fool jumped out and rolled Goldbars over, pulling at his pockets.

The Lords of Leftovers

Goldbars screamed louder, clutching at a leg bent where it shouldnt be bent.

"Sorry Sir, got new orders. Got to take the prisoner back upstairs."

Grabbing the handcuff key, the Fool rocked his head back at me and shouted. "Come on and get on. Aint got time to waste."

The Fool raced us back up the tunnel a ways, twitching at the handcuffs with one hand and steering wildly with the other.

"Youre gonna kill us if you dont watch out. You already bustedup Goldbars. He aint gonna be walking tomorrow."

The Fool finally clicked the key into one lock and bumped off the side of the tunnel like it was a natural part of gophering. "Damn that was fun. Never run over a Major before. Never liked that one anyway. Just another one of them brass and feathers birds that never gave a thought to the rest of us. I think I could get to enjoy running over officers."

The Fool screeched to a sudden stop in front of a large air vent. "Come on. Gotta get outa here. Someonell be after us soon as you can blink. Those guards back there aint used to having full clips and their safetys off. There liable to kill someone."

All I could see was a huge fan and a jangle of pipes and cables behind it. The Fool pulled back the screen and scooted inside as if it were as natural as taking a gulp of air. Without waiting he dropped to his knees, stuck an iron rod between the fan blades to stop the turning, and began to worm his way through a small space between the bottom two blades. "Come on. You gotta crawl."

I got scraped along, following the Fool and through to the other side. The Fool sat hunched half over and gleaming with satisfaction. We were in a narrow crawl space filled with an endless knot of pipes, cables, wires, and big gray boxes where all the wires got hookedup. There was room enough to stand, but in most places the wiry tangles filled up the space.

"Welcome to my home away from home. Years back we used to spend whole days hiding out in here. The lieutenants never could find us. Dont think any of the brass and feathers upstairs remember much about these service areas."

I looked around at the confusion of angles and shapes. "You hid out in here?"

The Fool shrugged. "Maybe not so much at first, but after a while almost always when some officer was looking for volunteers for some stupid detail. Come one. We gotta go." He squirmed his way around a fat gray pipe and began to move forward.

"Go where?"

He looked back at me like I was the fool. "Get your friends and get out of here. Theyre all crazy. Theyre all gonna kill each other. Boom boom. Hot times in the tunnels tonight. My enlistment is up."

Eventually, we emerged in a brightly lit hallway of blue tiles and gray floor. We had scuffed around for what seemed like forever, twisting and ducking, going up narrow ladders and squeezing our way back down again, until finally coming to a little halfsized door.

"Where are we?"

The Fool looked around and heaved up a laugh. "Here. Were here."

"Wheres here?"

"Here. Where your friends are."

We were standing in an empty bluegray hall filled with nothing in particular. "Where are they?"

The Fool heaved up another laugh. "Dont know exactly. Somewhere around here. This heres the living quarters for the main gate. Heard your friends were holed up down here. My rooms up a ways. This is where I live when Im not on duty, or not hiding in a service shaft."

"You mean when youre not worming your way through the walls."

"Come on. Come on. Well find them and then get outta here."

But they found us. There was a clattering up a ways, and suddenly Treetop came tearing around a corner. When he seen us he whoop-whooped and was on us before we could whoop back at him. He slapped and shook us up like we was all old friends, and I guess we were, although I felt raw from getting bangedup, trussedup, and squeezedup. But then the wildboy come tearing around the corner, barking his own wildboy whoops, and then Chatterbox and last the woman. Me and the Fool got backslapped up some more, but I didnt mind.

"This heres a cafeteria," Joe announced. We were in a large cavern of a room filled with long tables and benches and bright lights overhead. It was something like the room back up on top where the General tried to poison me with his liquid chalk. "Over yonder theres a kitchen big enough to feed a hundred hollow mountains."

Treetop straddled himself up next to me, perching on the bench like he was about to take off. He slapped a beer can in front of me and scraped up the poptop. Instantly white foam exploded and spread across the table, spilling into my lap. They all bust out laughing and hollering, even the woman, but especially Treetop and Chatterbox. Joe shook off a few drops.

"Hes been shakin that one up for you ever since we come back."

I looked at Joe and eased up some, letting trickles of beer run free without the interruption of my lap. "You all been drinking white foam? Little gassy, aint it?" I settled back down on a dry spot. Treetop produced another beer but before he could pop it I caught his hand.

"Hes excited. He likes this place. He found a barrel of some thick syrupy stuff that hes been gulping as fast as the beer. Hes drunk a gallon or more of alcohol and sugar." Joe said.

"Were going to have to get out of this place. General says hes gonna blow us up. Him and the Bishop are fixing to blow each other up too." I told Joe about the Generals party, and he seemed to study on it. "I dont know how he got in, but the Bishops in and he says he wants us to atone for our sacrileges, though I aint sure what sacrileges hes thinking of. But the Fool here says he can get us out. He says even the tunnels got tunnels around here. I dont think we got a lot of time."

"Where you wanna go?"

"Aint all that particular at the moment. Out of here. Maybe back through Nineveh and pick up a few things on our way back to the front range. I dont expect too many saints will be back home in Nineveh. I say we hike on home and pick up the Prince. By the time we return to this happy valley maybe the General and the Bishop wouldve whittled each other down a size or two. Or maybe we could just stay down in the flats for a while."

"And take these people back with us? I dont think Treetop is ready to leave."

At the end of a long table the woman got up and wandered away. The wildboy followed her. Against the far wall there was a large painted mural of a pretty mountain scene, painted in such detail that you could almost step into it and be surrounded by pine and rock. Joe got up scratching and stretching.

"Be a darn shame if those two idiots destroyed this mountain and us in it. Lot of nice stuff around here. Aint a lot of profit in total destruction."

"Aint a lot we can do to stop it. You aint thinking about getting in the middle of these ratbrains and try to stop them, are you?"

"Me? No. Im thinkin thats your job. I shoot. You negotiate."

Dan Williams

Off a ways the woman and the wildboy were staring into the mountain scene. The sky was a sharp blue fluffed in the distance with little white clouds. Through the center ran a silver stream that spilled over pockets of boulders in a waterfall. From where I sat I could almost smell the pine and hear the water splash against the rocks. Like the Gernals garden, the mural was so real it was unreal. I guess when youre living in a hole in the ground you want to be reminced of whats on the outside.

Getting outside was the plan, but it wasnt much of a plan. Get the Fool to lead us somewhere safe from the crazies below. We thought the General was crazy enough to be truthful about destroying the base in order to save it. Seemed like before the Fires, destroying something in order to save it. But we thought we owed it to the old man to try to get him out too. He only had wanted to get out and see a little blue sky, and he had only wanted the same for everyone else hunkered down inside the Generals tunnels. He certainly hadnt wanted to get dragged back through every prickly bush and thunked on every big rock just to get locked up back where hed started from. I figured we could slip out and then slip back inside after the shooting and exploding to pick up the pieces. Most times its always better to let a fire burn itself out and then sort through the ashes for whats leftover.

So we all squeezed into the wall and began climbing up a series narrow ladders in that ziggzagged through a forest of cables and pipes. The Fool said he could get us to what he called the detention corridor, where he suspected the old man might be locked up. It was a couple of levels above where we were and across a ways. But what was a ways to the Fool turned out to be a hike for the rest of us. The ladders were like little spines, and they werent exactly made for comfortable climbing, since there wasnt much of a place to grip or to step. Treetop had the most problems, which might have been because his feet were too big or because of all the foamy beer he carried in all his pockets and belly. But I figured he was safe enough, since a body couldnt fall more than a few feet without getting snagged on something. It was a dense forest.

After a couple levels we pulled ourselves out of it, arms and legs aching and chests heaving. We were in another shiny hallway, but without any pretty pictures. Just a series of large rooms with tables and chairs and then farther on gray metal doors with little windows. There wasnt anybody around, including the old man. We sat in one of the large rooms, rubbing our bumps and modifying our plan. We generally agreed that going up was better than going down, but we split on the method of ascension.

"I aint goin climb any more spindly little ladders. Im for elevatoring."

We found the nearest elevator, and I tried to get Joe excited about riding all the way to the top, but it was the others that got excited. Treetop got so excited he punched all the buttons, which made us all pile out and into another.

The Fool took us up a couple levels to the detention corridor, which seemed to be a little prison inside a much bigger prison. We tumbled out into a small reception area that funneled into a hallway, and we got about a quarter of the way down the hall when three rats came out of a doorway and pointed cutters at us.

They stared and we stared back, and for what mightve been hours but was only seconds no one moved. Then I slowly edged the wildboy behind me and tried to confuse the general confusion.

"The General sent us up here to tell you boys to march on down to him. Hes fixing to give the Bishop a hot hello and he wants everyone down at the beehive. Theres going to be blood and smoke."

The three just stared like I might have been talking some other kind of language. Maybe I was, cause I certainly didnt know any of the right words.

One of the three finally spoke. He was big but not nearly Joesized. "Throw down your weapons and raise your hands. This is a restricted area. We have orders to shoot to kill. No one is allowed here."

The Fool raised one hand enough to wave at them like he was annoyed. "Who do think youre guarding? Stop pointing those weapons at us. All hells broken loose down at Stage I. Well all be lucky to live through the day."

The Fool walked towards the guards shaking his head. He gently laid his hand over the barrel of the tall guards cutter and pointed it downwards. "You ever shot one of these anywhere other than the target range? I know you never shot a person. Dont start now."

The tall guard tried to raise his cutter, but the Fool kept his grip on it. One of the other two reached over with a free hand and grabbed the Fools shoulder. I figured if the Fool could be fool enough to grab a weapon pointed at him, then I could be too. I went up and reached out to the second guard, but he jumped back . I smiled at him.

"Killing aint a business to get into if you dont have to, and here you dont have to. Were just passing through trying to get out of here. You three ought to get somewheres safe too. There aint any use in hiding out in these tunnels anymore. If it aint the Bishop this time, somebody equally bloodyminded will come after you. This mountain is coming apart. Go on outside while you have the chance. All of you have been tunneledup for far too long."

The one I tried to grab looked squinteyed back at me and then over at the tall one. The third one come around and swung a cutter in my direction. This one was sandy haired and even paler than most, and he didnt look like he wanted to kill anyone. Joe and the others had come up behind us and crowded around. The woman came out and stood next to me. I knew then there wouldnt be any shooting.

"Weve come to get an old scrap of rags, and then get out of here before the killing starts. We aint your problem. You got an old man stuffed somewhere around here?"

The three hesitated for a moment, and then without speaking the tall one nodded and the three backed off slowly down the hall, the Fool following at their heels, talking at them like we were all old friends and that the cutters pointed at each other hadnt really been pointed at all. They led us through a series of three locked doors, and at the last the tall one pecked at a little keypad in the wall. A large gray door slid back and we walked into a halfmoon shaped room filled with blank screens set into tables filled with dials and buttons. Beyond the tables there was a large window that looked out on a walkway leading to a balcony, and beyond that there was a double layer of identical cells. There were two tiers on each side with maybe twenty cells on each level, and between them there was nothing except a dirty green tiled floor at the bottom with a few bolteddown benches and tables. At each end there were huge ventilation fans that turned slowly.

"Nice accommodations. Bet all the prisoners love this place. Wheres our old man?" I turned back from the glass wall that looked out onto the honeycomb. Two of the guards had disappeared, leaving the tall one.

"You dont talk much, do you?" I asked.

He shrugged and looked around. Joe, Treetop, and Chatterbox were once again running around pressing bottons, turning knobs, and flipping switches. Some of the screens had lit up to show empty cells. Somewhere below I could hear doors clanging open and shut. The boy and the woman had moved out onto the balcony overlooking the honeycomb.

"Never spoke to an outsider before," Tallboy finally said.

"Well, words are cheap, but sometimes theyre useful. We come for the old man. Hes mostly grease, appetite, and trouble, but the wildboy is fond of him."

He nodded again and sidled over to one of the consoles. He turned on a screen and then dialed in a fuzzy graygreen picture. Slowly a shape emerged, the figure of a man rolled into a fetal ball.

"That our old man?"

Another nod.

"Wheres he at exactly?"

Tallboy pointed off to the left. "Level two, B7. Press this button and you can talk to him." He pointed to a little square of a speaker.

I went over and stood next to him. "See how useful words are."

I pressed the button and then unpressed it.

"Go on, talk to him, get that old man up." Joe and the others had come up behind me. Treetop was trying to mash my hand down on the button.

"Just hold on. Its not every day I get to speak in a little box and make myself heard in a maze of human deprivation." I pushed him away and the wildboy reached through to press the button. I edged him out gently. He turned and ran out, followed by Chatterbox.

"Ah, Professor Newlin? Can you hear me Professor Newlin? This heres General Napoleon Alexander Augustus Sherman Winston Rat the Fourth, and Ive come to enlist you in my army of liberation. We will fight the great battle of freedom, electricity, and whiskey." I unpressed the button and turned back to Joe. "Didnt think I knew his name, did you?"

Joe edged me out none too gently and had his turn. "Come on, Greasy, were all here. Wake up. Weve got to get out of here before we get caught in a crossfire."

We watched the screen. Slowly the ball began to unwind, but before he could straighten out the wildboy and the Chatterbox burst in on him. They pulled him up and patted him down.

"Careful boys, youre going to hurt him. He probably aint accustomed to having visitors slap him with such enthusiasm."

The Fool reached around me and pressed the button. "You forgot to press the button. They cant hear you unless you press the button."

Dan Williams

I considered shooting the Fool, but instead I mashed his fingers down hard on the button. "Hello Professor Newlin, time to get out of here. We got business to tend to."

For a moment the old man stood unsteadily between the two boys, then he raised his head and stared directly back at us, smiling.

Chapter 19

"Hes fixing to get everyone killed down there, aint he? The General knows his rats aint much of a match for the Bishops shinyboots, but hes set on a fight anyway. "

The old man nodded back at me. We were sitting in the dining area up on top where the General had tried to poison me. At the end of a long table Treetop and Chatterbox were dipping bread into a giant gallon can of red tomato ketchup theyd found somewheres and were washing it all done with foamy beer. Joe had taken the Fool and had gone off to look around, leaving me with the woman and the boy and old man. He wasnt greasy like before, but he was pretty unsteady on his feet and most of the time used the wildboy for a crutch. Since leaving the guards to guard their empty prison, we hadnt seen another person. The whole top of the mountain seemed to have been pretty much cleared out. Even the whitecoats sitting in front of the computer terminals had disappeared, leaving rows of screens with nothing but identical pictures of an eagle clutching a handful of arrows. Our footsteps echoed as we clattered down the long empty hallways.

"You cave dwellers aint exactly had much soldiering experience in a couple of decades. The Bishops going to cut through you like a hot knife in a tallow pot. I cant see why the General would go to all the trouble of getting ready for a fight he knows hes going to lose. Hes got a whole mountain full of killing things. Why dont he just point some kind of big gun down the tunnel and bust the Bishop apart? Why dont he just fire off a couple missiles or something? Why drag in a bunch of men with little guns they dont know how to shoot?"

The old man stared out the slit windows like he was wishing for something. Outside graywhite clouds drifted across the ridges and peaks, their shadows darkening the rocky slopes beneath them. There was really only one answer.

"The General wants to go out in one great glorious battle, dont he? Hes spent his whole life being a night watchman in a warehouse, and now he wants to do what soldiers are supposed to do. A general aint a general unless he can lead men into battle. I bet hes sorry he got stuck away in here and missed all the Fires."

The old man turned back to me and nodded.

"What are you thinking, Mister Newlin."

"Thinking I liked it better when you didnt know my name." He looked back towards the clouds. There was a pale sliver of a scar on the side of his head where he had been rifle butted. "But Im also thinking that we could turn out the lights. They cant do too much damage in the dark."

I considered the possibility. "You can do that? You can flip a light switch?"

He nodded. "In a fashion. Everythings run by these computers up here. All I have to do is shut down the program that maintains the power grid for the Stage I, or really all of the other power grids. No power, no lights. No ventilation fans and no climate control either. And no automatic doors or electric locks. Theyre going to be stuck in the dark for a few minutes until the first backup system kicks in, but even then its going to be dark and stuffy. And even when the first backup system is running we can still shut it down. We can keep everyone down below pretty much in the dark."

The Bishop fumbling in the dark was a sweet thought, but then I thought of a question. "The General, he know about this stuff. Wheres all his whitecoats?"

The old man nodded and shrugged as he stared out the slit windows, looking like he was counting clouds.

"He must really want to have his final battle, doesnt he. He must really want to get shot out of the saddle and take everyone with him, doesnt he?"

The old man kept staring out the window, not bothering to nod this time.

"Well, Mister Newlin, I would be grateful if you would turn out all of the lights. I aint fond of getting shut up in a dark place, so I can imagine how all of those down below will react. Shut the place down."

The old man led us back through the eagles and arrows.

"Pity to lose all of this," he said. "Theres a million times more stuff stored up here in data banks than down below in the depots. Millions of data archives and programs. Whole libraries were scanned and stored. All of the major computer centers from around the country transferred their files to us for storage. We just sucked up everything we could, sucking up entire storage libraries. The federal governments intention was to stockpile all possible knowledge. All this around here is the most complete and comprehensive encyclopedia that was ever created. Think about it. Most everything useful that was ever known, its all here." He waved his hand around at the computer terminals. The woman and the boy seemed impressed. Maybe I was too, but then I had lived for a long time without having much use for computers or data archives.

"You think all of this in here is worth more than a half a dozen barrels of freshharvested of corn? I aint never seen someone eat a computer, raw or cooked."

The old man looked at me. "Guess the value of something always depends upon where youre standin. When I was outside I ate some things I wouldnt eat in here." He nodded at the thought and shuffled across a long room filled with computers and into a back hallway. "The operations center is down here. I used to have the pass code to get into it, but I am sure its been changed. But theres always a way to break into it using a backdoor."

"There is?" I wasnt quite sure I knew what he meant. Most things I broke into didnt quite fit back together again afterwards.

He walked us up to a large metal door at the end of the hall. I thought Joe might have to go back and fetch his rock.

"Theres always a way to get in. This one has several back doors we built over the years."

The door seemed pretty massive, but the old man punched some numbers into a keyboard on the wall, the electric lock clicked, and the door swung open as if it had been on greased wheels. The old man saw me staring.

"Backdoors in the computer programs, I mean. Ways to sneak into a program. Long ago I created my own emergency entry code."

Compared to the large open areas outside, the room was fairly small. Against one wall there were four computer terminals and keyboards set into a long series of cabinets. Both sidewalls were lined with what looked like metal closets. There wasnt much to indicate human habitation except a couple coffee cups and notepads and a small picture taped to the wall of a sailing ship slicing slantwise in a full wind across a blue sea. Far off in the distance there was an island with a white, sandy beach.

"Doesnt much look like your lake," I remarked, but the woman ignored me, studying the picture. The old man sat himself in front of one of the terminals and began tapping at the keys. The wildboy pulled up a chair and sat next to him. The screen came to life and filled up with something like a diagram of lines, numbers, and colored boxes. The old man tapped some more.

"Okay, now were ready." The old man turned and got up. He seemed to be moving better than when we first uncurled him.

"Need the key I gave you. Need to unlock a cabinet. This is where we store the master programs that were used to create the security system."

I had almost forgotten about the fat brass key, almost. The wildboy reached into his shirt and nearly ripped his neck off pulling it out. The old man smiled as he took it and went over to one of the metal closets. He slipped the key in and twisted. There was a solid clunk, and the door popped open. Inside from floor to ceiling on three sides there were shelves filled with notebooks and folders, all unmarked except for a small series of numbers and letters on the spines. The old man stood for a moment.

"Nothings changed here. Those idiots didnt even bother to change the code after I run off." The old man turned back to us. We were all crowded around the door, staring like we had just come down from the mountains for a market day.

"This is where I spent most of my life, nearly all of it with these programs. Heres my lifes work."

He went over to one of the shelves and fingered his way through a series of notebooks until he finally stopped at one. He opened it up and withdrew a small round disc.

"Know what this is," he asked.

I knew. The streets of the dead city were littered with computer cds. As a boy I had slung them through the air, trying to hit rats. I didnt say anything, though. I was thinking more about having to spend a life in a metal closet full of notebooks with nothing but numbers. Maybe I had come out ahead scrabbling in the trash heaps.

"This is our backdoor."

The wildboy nodded enthusiastically and the woman smiled, faintly.

"Now were going to turn off the lights."

The old mans cd was a repair program that, he explained, allowed him to get into other programs. Within a minute or so after fitting the disc into a slot next to the computer screen, he pulled up another strange looking diagram.

"I can shut down the main power to everywhere but up here. Theres actually four different backup systems that will come on, and I cant shut down everything. The last is an emergency system that is entirely separate from the others and runs on battery packs independently powered with solar panels. But it wont do much more than offer a minimal amount of light and ventilation. Its to keep people alive, not allow them the chance to kill each other. It wont operate the electric doors. Itll stay pretty dark and hot down below."

"Then what?"

The old man looked at me. "Dont know. Guess eventually the General will send someone up here after us."

Eventually came a lot sooner than we imagined it would. Before I could say another word there was a burst of automatic gunfire back behind us, followed by screaming, then followed several more bursts.

I went to the door and listened, but as suddenly as it erupted the gunfire and screaming stopped. The sudden silence was a lot thicker than usual.

"Had to be Treetop and Charterbox. Im going to go back to the dining area." I turned to the woman. "You stay here with Mister Newlin and the wildboy. Keep the door locked. Dont make any sounds, and no matter what dont open the door for anyone and dont leave."

The woman started to follow me out. "Im going with you. Im not helpless."

I looked at the woman and handed her one of the little pocket guns I had been carrying. "No, you aint helpless, but they are." I pointed back to the old man and wildboy. "You keep the door locked, and let the old man turn off all of the lights and shut this place down."

I gave her both of my assassinator guns and threaded my way back towards the dining area. I had two cutters and four clips, plus another handgun squirreled away. I thought maybe the General had sent some of his men back up top, and I was hoping they would be as helpful as Tallboy had been. But then Tallboy hadnt ever fired his weapon.

I heard them before I saw them. More screams. The closer I got the more I knew it was Treetop and Chatterbox. I came out into the main hallway leading to the dining area and inched along. Every minute or so one of them would let go a scream like someone was giving him a bad time.

I came to the open entrance to the dining area and risked a quick glance around the corner. I started to feel real sick and wished Joe was close by. I was wishing he had heard the shots and the yelling and was coming up the other side with considerable rage and fire power. I was also wishing I was long ways off sipping leftover whiskey and resting on a rock ledge overlooking a silver river as it curved its way through a quiet green valley. And I was wishing I was sitting there with nothing to do but sip and shift to the patches of sunlight and watch the river and a few wisps of white cloud in the blue sky.

Smoke the womanstomper and backslasher was standing over Treetop and Chatterbox, poking at them with his bigugly knife. When he poked, they screamed. He had six of his throatcutters with him, two of them standing around taking in the bloody show while the other four made their way around the halls perimeter. In a minute or so two of them would arrive at my entrance.

They mustve surprised Treetop and Box while they were still dipping and slurping. Both Treetop and Box were spottedup with what I hoped were bright red tomato ketchup flowers. I couldnt tell why Smoke was sticking them. Nor could I do much about it without getting myself slathered up in ketchup. I aint none too accurate for shooting across wide open spaces with a cutter, and my chances of spraying enough bullets around to catch all seven of the devils before one of them sprayed me were slim. But I couldnt slink on back and let Smoke keep sticking them. It was another one of them hard places that, when you consider what it is and who you are, aint really all that hard. I stepped out into the entrance and pointed a cutter across the hall at Smoke.

"Hey you Smoke, you scumsucking, scuzzbrained miscreant, what happened to you back on that trail up the mountain? I waited around for you, but you ran away."

Smoke straightened up and smiled, pointing his knife back at me and sliced up a bit of air. "Im going to kill you."

I nodded. "You tell your partner over here to back off or Im going to kill him and you." I pointed the cutter at the wacker slipping up the wall nearest me. Smoke picked up his own weapon and moved towards me, motioning for the man to ease off. He stopped about fifty feet away.

"I killed a lot better men than you," Smoke said.

I didnt think getting killed was a much of a competition. Seemed to me that just about any fool could get himself killed. We stood for a moment while Smokes wackers began to converge on me.

"Better? What do you mean better?"

"I mean better. Better shooters. Better fighters. Better killers."

"If they were so good, what are they doing dead?"

"Cause I killed them, like Im goin to kill you and your friends."

I felt my whole world knottedup in a hard, tight ball. It was an intense feeling of anger and fear and yet also of the strange curious cold feeling of standing between being alive and being dead at the same time. I didnt want to die. I didnt want to compete in Smokes game. For a few seconds I waited.

"Come on then you rancid sack of pusrot."

Smoke laughed. His silver skunkstreak and scars rippled as he bellowed. The two wackers behind him spread out in a loose line.

"You a talker, aint you. Im goin let the air outa you. Then Im gonna drain you of blood, guts, and whatever else you got inside you. But first you talk some more. Im lookin for the old computer man, the one I chased down to the river valley, and the woman too. I want them back. They cost me plenty. Where they at? I want them both. Maybe Ill let you live a while if you tell me where they at."

I shrugged. "Dont know. What do you want them for? The womans all healed up. You want to stomp on her some more? I dont think shed agree to that."

"Dont matter what she wants. You just tell me where they at. I know you come up here with them."

"Maybe I did. Whatll you trade for them?"

Smoke spat, and his killers laughed. "Nothin. You die easy or you die hard. Makes no difference. Ill find them up somewheres, and youll be dead all the same."

Moments can last forever, but most dont. Mostly, your life is filled with whats already flashed by. I caught a quick glimpse of myself all bloodied up in a butchered heap.

"No deal then, you ratbrained mucksucking maggoteater."

Smokes smile lasted half a second, then the hall exploded in gunfire and powdersmoke. I dove to the left and flattened as best I could, firing the cutter wildly. But they were equally wild, shredding up the wall, floor, and ceiling all around me in seconds. I emptied one cutter and then let go, and rolling to the left, firing the second cutter as I pulled up. I squeezed off a burst at what I hoped was gutpainful level. One of the wackers to the right of Smoke folded up and dropped, groaning as he went. The other five were running the sides to catch me in a crossfire. Smoke dropped and threw a table on its side. I rolled up and skittered further to the left, thinking I couldnt let them catch me in one place. I came up firing another short burst just as Smoke raised his frightful head and fired back at me, his shots breaking apart the table and benches next to me. I felt the fragments chipping at me. One of the wackers had almost circled around me and was firing at my back. I pushed back, firing at him, while Smoke leveled his fire in front of me.

I was exactly where I didnt want to be and had no real plan for getting somewhere else. I threw myself blindly to left, crashing into the legs of another table. Smokes fire followed me, ripping up the floor tiles in a jagged pattern.

But then he stopped and turned. I dove again to the left and kept rolling until I came up in a crouch. I raised up and bolted towards the far wall, raising my head far enough to catch a glimpse of that crazy Treetop blasting away with a handgun, his long bony arm jerking up and down with each shot. He had probably never fired a handgun in his life and if he didnt duck down I didnt think hed ever have another chance to practice. His chest and arms were dotted with bright wet red catsup flowers.

As I sprinted away I glanced back and saw Treetop jerked backwards in a half spin and go down. Hed been hit, probably more than once. I was still pumping legs when I heard Smoke scream for the others to go after me, while he took off at an angle trying to cut me off, but he didnt have much chance. I aint exactly light of foot, but that bloodsucker lumbered after me like he was made of stone.

I was breathing hard when I came up to the opposite entrance and ducked around the corner. The hall was open and empty, and I could choose any one of several routes out of this mess. I clicked in another clip and waited, though, listening for the wackers as they clattered up behind me.

When I judged they were right up to the door, I jumped back around, firing a steady burst. There were three close together, and I crumbled one up immediately, while the other two rolled off to the sides. I followed one with a second burst and caught him in the side. Behind them Smoke came up firing at me, forcing me back around the corner. I stuck the cutter out and fired a wild burst, hoping to force Smoke out of the way, but he kept charging and firing.

I darted across the hall into an open doorway, waiting for Smoke to come around the corner so I could cut him apart. But suddenly all the firing and clattering stopped, and the eternity of killing that had lasted less than half a minute slowed down to a silent stop. I waited, wondering if I should take off down the hall and come around the opposite end of the dining hall where I had first come in. Maybe I could take another run across the dining area so that we could start the whole thing up again, or maybe I could get to Treetop and try to patch him up before he spilled out too much of himself.

I fired a short burst around the corner into the dining area and took off down the hall, running in a wild zigzag, but no one fired a weapon at my back. I came around into the large open area and slowed. I rested up a moment behind a long wood and glass display case filled with little medals, ribbons, plaques, and shiny toysoldier trophies.

I was about to step around into the dining area when the lights flicked off. They came back on and then flicked off again. I smiled thinking the old man had done it, thinking about the General and the Bishop all huddled up in suddenly dark tunnels. After a few seconds the lights came back on again but then flicked off a third time. While they were still off I went around into the dining area and crouched against the nearest wall. Far off at the end of the hall where I had just come from there were several bursts of gunfire, the muzzle fire sparking up the darkened room.

When the lights came back on, they stayed on, and I raised up enough to see Smoke come plodding along between two rows of tables next to the wall. I dropped back down hoping he hadnt seen me. He hadnt. He was looking around the lights in the ceiling. I raised up and steadied. He was twenty yards or so away and walking towards me. The old man had given me an edge.

"I thought you devils could see in the dark."

Smoke whipped around and leveled his gun at me. We both fired at about the same time.

At that second the world was abruptly reduced to a thin strip with nothing inside it but Smokes gunfire coming at me. But then just as abruptly the world exploded outward again, and I was alive, back in the empty dining hall. I looked out through the narrow slit windows opposite me, thinking it would be nice to climb on top one of those ridges and cool off in the cold mountain air, rub some of the summer ice on the back of my neck.

Smoke was dead. Although I had tried to fire low enough to bellyshoot him, my rounds had gone high, puncturing his neck and and skull. There was a lot of blood from the neck, but it didnt bother me too much. Maybe I was accustomed to blood, or maybe I just thought that Smokes lifeblood was just a drop of what he had spilled. To be honest, I dont think I thought much of anything except relief. I was happy to be alive.

"I thought he was mine." Joe came up with his hunting rifle and poked what was left of Smokes skull. He had been down below and hadnt even heard the shooting until the last few bursts. The Fool came up behind him, grinning, rubbing his two knuckly hands together.

"Sorry. I should have let him kill me. Then you could have killed him."

Joe nodded. "It would have only been fair. Im the one he backslashed."

I didnt think being dead was being fair. "You and that Fool better squat down some. Theres still a couple wackers around here somewheres."

"Theyre back there," he said, pointing his rifle back towards the end of the dining hall. "But they aint in much better shape than Smoke here. Hard to believe a man that ugly could be dead. You sure hes dead? Maybe hes trying to fool us." Joe nudged the body with his foot. "You think I ought to shoot him some more?"

I looked at Smokes skull. The bullets had broken it apart, shattering the bone and gouging out chunks of brain. It was all rotten meat. "I believe you might be right. I believe he survived and is just playing dead. You better shoot him some more before he gets up and starts some more trouble. You better go at the legs and arms to immobilize him. You get the other three?"

"Not me. I am innocent of all this bloodletting" Joe smiled broadly.

"Not the Fool?" I was incredulous.

Joe turned to him, and the Fool shrugged. "No, he cant shoot any better than you. It was the woman and Chatterbox. She come up behind them other two while they were trailing after you and took them both down. Shes a steady shot. Then Chatterbox popped up and knocked down the last one. We better go gather him up before he takes a trophy."

I was grateful and sad at the same time. "She did? Wheres she at now?"

Joe motioned off to opposite side, near where I had first come in. "Shes over there with Treetop. You best get over there, hes leaking out his lifeblood."

I waited a moment, looking out through the big windows. There were clouds coming in. "Treetop gone? I saw him get knocked down."

Joe shook his head, smiling. "No, he aint gone where this ones gone. At least not yet." He nudged Smoke again. "But he sure needs you to plug up a couple holes."

Chapter 20

Treetop had his head stuffed with the idea that he was dying, and to avenge his death he wanted me to drag Smoke over to him so he could carve on him some. But I told him to rest easy until Joe finished up abusing the dead.

I wasnt sure if Treetop was right or not. Hed been hit twice high in the chest and shoulder area and then touched in his left side and arm. He had also been cut multiple times with Smokes bigugly knife. He had lost a lot of blood, and for a skinner who lives outdoors he was beginning to look fishbelly pale. His breathing was shallow, but his breaths were steady enough, and he wasnt coughing up blood, so that I didnt think hed been nicked in a lung. But he was so weak and so bloodied up that I couldnt tell. The chest shots had punched through, so I cleaned and patched both entrance and exit wounds to stop the flow. There wasnt much else I could do except keep cleaning and binding, and hoping. I aint got a magic box full of tricks. Hed lost a lot of blood.

The Chatterbox sat next to us playing with Smokes bigugly, gouging holes in the tiles. Hed taken it as a trophy. That and a lot more. Hed also taken the time to fit himself with a nearly new pair of shiny boots and then had drug over a pile of guns, knives, rings, belts, and whatnot that hed scraped off the rest of the meat, and which he piled up next to him. More clutter than he could carry. He even found himself a watch, though I was betting he could not tell its time. But if he wanted it, I thought he should have it. Better a watch than some poor fools scalp.

I was more concerned with carrying Treetop. Most times the only difference between the dead and the seriously wounded is the amount of time it takes to die. Sometimes when someones been seriously bloodiedup most people will move off a ways to smoke or drink and feel good or guilty that it wasnt them that was bloodiedup. There aint a lot of healers around, and most times wounds will rotup quickly and finish what the bullets started. Infections mostly kill those that dont die the first day. I had always tried to clean and patch what I could, and I had been around enough wounds to know how much blood a man can spill before he gets passed beyond. Treetop was real close, and he was still leaking some. Trying to cart him off some place would keep the wounds open.

"Will he be all right?"

I turned to the woman and shrugged. "He wants me to help him carve on Smoke so that he can die avenged. I take that to be a good sign."

She said nothing further and settled on a bench nearby. I thought about what she had done, which likely had saved my life. "I asked you to stay with the old man."

"Yes, you did."

I busied myself with Treetop, checking bandages that I had already checked, and finally turned back to her. "Those two you shot wouldve killed me. You and Chatterbox saved me."

She looked off a ways. "I shot one of them in the back. I fired without meaning to. I ran in here and then I shot him. I will live with what I have done."

She looked off, tightlipped and pale, and she twisted the strips of cloth I had cut for Treetop like she was trying to wring them dry. "The boy wanted to come, but I made him stay with Mister Newlin."

We holed up in Mister Newlins backdoor room when the little pocketphone started beeping. It was loud in the small computer room. The phone beeped several times with me and Joe and everyone else looking at.

"You pick it up. You shot Smoke, so you have to answer." Joe took a step back and leaned against a wall.

"I aint touching it. I dont like talking to people I cant see. You make the Fool answer it. I got nothing to say to people I cant see face to face. It aint natural."

The phone beeped impatiently, refusing to go away. Finally the wildboy picked it up and slowly raised it to his head. He listened without speaking. All of us could hear a muffled voice coming through. The wildboy pulled the phone away and shrugged. He handed it to the Fool.

"Hello. Security Zone II speaking?" The Fool smirked. The voice continued and seemed to get even louder. The Fool held the phone away from his head and waited.

"No sir, I cant do that. I dont think anybody else will either." The Fool turned towards me. "The General wants to talk to you. Says hes gonna blow up the mountain."

"Tell him Joes going to come down there and break him up into little general pieces."

"Sir, they said they are willing to come down and negotiate the situation with you."

"Tell him Joes going to stuff all his little general pieces into a fancy white flushing commode and flush his generalship away."

"Sir, they said that they are willing to cooperate with you in every way to preserve the integrity of the bases perimeter. They say they are patriots, Sir."

"Tell that muddlebrained lunatic that its time to end all this foolishness and start living above ground like most folks."

"Sir, they regret their incursions and are leaving now to consult with you on returning the base to order."

The Fool put the phone down and shrugged. "He would like all power, programs, and facilities restored immediately. He said that he will destroy the base before it falls into the wrong hands."

Joe held up his hands. "We the wrong hands?"

"Probably so. To him we aint any better than the Bishop and his saints, us being savages and cannibals," I said studying my own hands.

"I guess we should go down there and give the little general a big flush."

"Im gonna shoot the one and then the other," Joe said and punched a clip into a cutter. He had it in his mind to shoot both the General and the Bishop. "Being a savage and all, its its my nature to kill, especially them that bothers me."

I nodded. "Especially if youre hungry."

We were huddled up in a hallway that the Fool had steered us into, which he swore would open up into the beehives fourth level. We had elevatored and switchbacked our way through a series of levels, and all we had to do was go down some stairs and spill out on a balcony. Every so often an emergency light had popped on, but the light was murky and dull. I still had my doubts about meeting up with the General, but Joe wasnt in a mind to argue.

"Fairs only fair. You shot Smoke, so I get to shoot both the General and the Bishop, seeing how I am bigger than you and therefore have more savagery inside me."

"As long as you can see in this murk, you can have them. I dont want them, not to shoot, shake, or shove. Theyre all yours. You want em, you shoot em. But then you got to skin em and clean em if you want to eat them. I aint helping with that."

Joe looked at me and grinned. Behind him the Fool grinned right along. If the wildboy and the old man had been with us, they probably would have thought it was great fun too, but we had left them tucked away back on top locked away with Treetop, the woman, and Chatterbox.

"Youre just saying that now. I know when we get down there youll try to shoot one or the other. I know you. Youre not an honorable man when it comes to shooting Bishops and Generals and such."

I didnt have to be honorable, though, and Joe didnt have to shoot anyone. By the time we creeped our way down to the open balcony the Generals big battle was all over except for a couple of boys who were too scared to shoot, run, or surrender. One of his own men, a recent convert to the Bishops path to salvation, had come up behind him and clunked his generalship on the head, and without him there was only a token resistance when the Bishop brought his shinyboots up. No big guns, no big blowup, no great battle strategy, no heroic charge. The General was overwhelmed before his big battle even got started. Now there was just a little old delusional man all ropedup and bloodyheaded.

We came out slowly and peered over the balcony, but down below the Bishop was already packing everybody up and beginning to head off towards the tunnels. There were small pockets of light around the chamber from the emergency backup system, and we could see the General was laid up on top of a gopher waiting to be delivered somewheres. I imagined the Bishop wanted to take him back for atonement. A few of his men, half dozen or so, were trussed up like him and sitting along the entrance to the first tunnel. Another clump of ratsoldiers were crouched in a circle under a guard of shinyboots. The rest of the saints were spreading out in all directions, looking through the shadows to round up the rest that had run off, or looking to cart off what they could carry.

Joe watched them for maybe a second and then suddenly straightened up to lean over the railing. He fired a long cutterburst, sending the soldiers below ducking for cover, scattering the hot brass around us. Then he switched to his fancyscope and methodically banged a couple more shots.

The Lords of Leftovers

"You think I got their attention?"

"I think you did. Now what are you going to do?"

Joe looked over the balcony and leaned back quickly. We were starting to draw return fire. "Dont know. I dont have enough bullets to kill them all. You and the Fool are gonna have to help me out. You want to rush them, or you want to sneak around behind them and surprise them?"

It was an old joke, and I smiled, but I didnt feel too cheerful. The Fool was rubbing his knuckly hands and staring at us, probably trying to figure just how crazy we were. But there aint no qualifying craziness. And maybe we had gone fulltilt screamer. If I had been any less crazy I would already have been slinking down the backside of the Generals mountain.

I waited another moment for the return fire to quit and then stepped over to the balcony and fired a quick burst towards an empty patch of concrete.

"Hey, all of you saints and sinners. We want to talk to the Bishop. Where you at Bishop? Come out of the shadows and talk with us. We got business to discuss with you. We got all the keys to the kingdom of God and all the electricity. We got fishy sticks, beer, computer cds, and archangels with backdoors and master programs."

The Bishop wasnt happy with us. He strutted around below us, scowling at us.

"How you doing Reverend? Save any souls lately? Hows the Lords work coming along? Has the Kingdom come?"

The Bishop looked at me and paused midstride.

"What is it you want?"

I shrugged. It all seemed pretty obvious to me. "Me and Joe just want to tuck our tails and get out of here. Go back to where we come from. We just want to go back where we been meaning to go since we got dragged into your happy valley."

The Bishops shinyboots were spilling back out of the tunnels, gathering around him. A couple of groups broke off and headed towards the tunnel below us. I hoped the Fool had figured out a way to lock the doors.

"Why should I let you go?"

"We got the old man and his light switch. We got the witch woman. We got the keys to the kingdom. And we got your favorite manstealer assassinator, Smoke. You want him back, dont you?"

"I want full power turned back on. If you want to live another ten minutes, youll return the power and surrender. We have you surrounded. If you do not surrender, you will die."

I could tell that me and the Bishop werent about to meet on any common ground. He probably just wanted to keep me talking until his shinyboots gunned me down.

"Actually I was hoping to live more than just a couple minutes. Dont you think you could give me another twenty or thirty years. In health, I mean. Dont want to get laidup stinking and drooling on myself. Ill tell you what. You give me another thirtyfive years of health, strength, and mental clarity, and Ill let you go. Joe and his clan too. Can we strike a deal here?

The Bishop was about a seventyfive yards below and in front of me, and I thought in the shadowy murk he mightve cracked a smile. Wasnt much of a smile, though.

"You give me all that, plus your holy blessing, and then let me and Joe slip away with that wildboy we been dragging around with us, and maybe also a new pack of mules that you been owing us, and we will let you go to live a couple more minutes."

The Bishop stopped smiling. "You are wasting my time and interfering with Gods work. You have nothing to offer me. Nothing."

Down below some place there was some door banging followed by a spray of bullets. I had hoped it was the Fool doing the spraying.

"Health, strength, mental clarity, we get to go with the wildboy, mules, enough leftovers to impress the Prince, and also maybe well take the woman and the old man with us too. We have got used to their company. And we been packing around a couple of beersucking skinners, and well also take them out with us. One of them is hurt pretty bad and aint good for much. In return you get the magic mountain. Seems like a fair trade to me."

"This is not yours to give," the Bishop suddenly screamed, throwing out his arms and gesturing at the underground world around him. "This is Gods."

"Ill tell you what. I think well take the General too. He aint much fun sometimes, and he can be right troublesome, but we got kind of fond of him too, and hes the only General we got. Maybe you ought to have one of your saints untie him and send him on this way."

The Bishop whipped himself over to the General, and with a huge roundhouse swatted him in the back of his already bloodied head. The

The Lords of Leftovers

General bounced once and tried to roll away from another blow. "This man is an idolater. You are idolaters." The Bishop turned away from the General and pointed up to me.

"Well, Reverend Sir, I hate to drop all my cards on the table without holding something back. But Im going to tell you what the deal is here. Me and Joe squeezed into the magic mountain first and have claimed salvage rights. It might be Gods, but until he comes down and tells me what he wants done with it, me and Joe are going to handle things. You and your pack of clatterbrained killer saints are trespassing on our claim, and youre going to have to get out of here. But before you leave, I want you to let the General go. And dont go beating on him anymore, or you wont live to take another unsanctified step. We been trying to bargain nice with you, but me and Joe are getting tired of your bullheaded foolishness."

Joe stood up and made himself known. The Fool had moved him down and around to a lower balcony on the right. There was some commotion and gun pointing, but Joe calmly leveled fancyscope at the Bishop. We had him in a crossfire, but Joe was enough. Even in the shadowy light he wouldnt miss.

"Joes a deadshot, which means youre a dead saint. Im here trading your life for our lives. You want to keep it, you better stop fooling around and threatening us with perdition. You aint immortal."

The Bishop paused for a moment, and in that one moment he lost the one chance he had. If he had jumped the second Joe popped up, he might have squirted behind a gopher or a clump of his own men. But he was too convinced of his invincibility, too sure that he was on top, too sure that he was righteous, and too arrogant to think he could get knocked down by a savage with a hunting rifle. Now he was nothing but blood and guts waiting to be spilled.

"Let the General go, and let us all get out of here. Thats all we want right now. You want the mountain, its yours."

The Bishop paused, gauging his chances. But after a few seconds he decided not to take a chance. He dropped his shoulders and motioned for one of his Ribbons to go to the General. The man cautiously approached the General and began untying him. The General rolled up and sat, rubbing his wrists.

"Come on, General, we got things to do. This battles over. Well go find you another."

The General slid off the gopher, but before he could take two steps the

Bishop pushed his Ribbons in Joes direction and dove back at the General. Ribbons started to pull a handgun, but before he could clear the weapon Joe dropped him, ruining him. But the Bishop had his own gun out and had collared the General around the neck, trying to use him as a shield.

"Kill them, kill them all," he screamed.

A hundred or so guns erupted, forcing Joe back and me to flatten out and stay low, which is something I am uncommonly good at. In moments the beehive was filled with a lot of yelling, smoke, bullets, and the clink of empty shells scattering. I thought that surely this was a likely taste of the Bishops perdition.

I didnt exactly see it, but in the midst of the smoke and fire the little bloodyheaded muddlebrained General twisted away. When I looked up he was rolling around on the yellowstriped concrete floor with the Bishop, grabbing at his holinesses handgun with one hand and trying to strangle him with the other. I popped a few rounds down in the general vicinity to keep the saints back and the fight more or less even, but with the rattle and shot and dark around me I didnt see much except glimpses of a twisting mass of GeneralBishop rolling around on the floor. Then I heard the shot, or at least I think I heard the shot above all other shots. I risked a peek over and saw that the General was kneeling over the Bishop. He must have ripped away the Bishops gun enough until he could point it gutlevel at the Bishops. The shot had punched a hole in the Bishops belly, and even from where I was standing I could see the dark wet patch.

Quickly the General fired a couple more rounds at the shinyboot nearest the Bishop, collapsing him in a heap. And just as quickly the General came up with the heaps cutter and began spraying bullets at any and all saints in his general location. Within moments, after dropping or scattering all of the immediate targets, the General rushed towards the loading docks, trying to scare up a fresh batch of saints.

This was the Generals final battle. Any fool could see that, including our own, who came out on a lower balcony to scream at the General to stay down. But there was no staying down to be done. The General charged towards anyone he saw, firing clips off as fast he could load and fire, wounding some, sending most for cover, almost begging someone to kill him. I fired a short burst in front of him, trying to head him away from his glorious death, but there was no stopping him. Like a screamer run amok he darted about wildly. He was so crazed that he didnt even try to aim or consider where he was charging. For nearly an eternity of ten seconds or so no one obliged the General, but then suddenly, just as he was about to spray another batch of saints, a couple slid behind him and stitched his back with two long bursts. The General was knocked forward and rolled once till he lay still. His final glorious battle hadnt lasted long.

Chapter 21

The Bishop didnt want to die. He had shinyboots out hunting around in all directions for what was left of the Generals medical staff, but so far they hadnt scared up anyone willing to take on a bloodiedup Bishop fixin to die. Seemed to me that the crowd of PurpleRibbons who had collected around the Bishop were of a mixed mind concerning which way they wanted the him to lean, and which they were leaning. There was a whole magic mountain still to fight over.

Trying to save the life of someone who has been trying to take my life aint exactly a good business, but it seemed to me that if I could strike deal with the Bishop I could get me and Joe and the others out without getting into more trouble. But I didnt think I could do much for him.

"Youve got to save me." The Bishop was a little whispery and a little slurry but not too bad considering the blood loss and pain. He clutched at my arm with a bloody hand.

I had been easing him back, trying to loosen his clothing enough so I could get at him. His personal shinyboots had sat him up against the side of a gopher, which hadnt helped him any.

"You got to save yourself. You got to stay with us, stay alert, stay on this side of the living if you want to live. Dont let go. Keep focused on me."

There wasnt much anything I could do. Maybe if there was a real doctor around he could keep the Bishop from leaking his life away. I couldnt do anything to repair the damage inside. His guts were all torn up, and he was slowly dying. He needed a miracle, and I didnt have any.

I had slunk down to the Bishop after it appeared all his PurpleRibbons and shinyboots werent going to do much more than watch him expire. The PurpleRibbons were already jockeying around for the title of "Whosin-Charge" and didnt pay me much mind. I could see right away why they werent paying the Bishop much mind. Sometimes power can shift suddenly. I busied myself trying to clean the wounds and stop the blood flow.

"Wheres my daughter?"

I thought the Bishop was starting to slip and paid him no mind. I certainly had no information about his family. Up to that point, I hadnt ever considered the Bishop a family man.

"Wheres my daughter?"

This time I looked back into the Bishops eyes. He was in pain, and he was weak from the blood loss, but he held his gaze, and he seemed lucid. I wondered who he was asking about. And then I knew. I aint no General or Bishop, but it didnt take too long for something to make sense.

"Shes safe. Shes up there on top tucked away. She saved my life earlier. Shes a strong, brave woman."

The Bishop raised up slightly and winced in pain, but he looked around a moment before lying back down.

"If I die, theyll kill her."

"They" were his own saints, those supposedly building the new kingdom of God. His loyal brothers in the struggle for salvation. As I looked up, two of the PurpleRibbons broke loose from a knot of shinyboots and came towards us.

"No they wont. Me and Joe will keep her safe."

He nodded ever so slightly. "Theyre afraid of her. She has followers in town, many of the women and some of men. Theyll think she would seize power."

I tried to busy myself with cleaning the Bishop up and keeping him calm, but there wasnt much I could do except wipe away the muck and think about the woman.

"Am I going to die?"

I had heard that question once or twice before, and I had never known how to answer, even when I knew the answer.

"I dont know. Probably. But I really dont. You aint in good shape. Youve a bad gut wound, and theres not much I can do for you. I cant go in there and try to sew things back up. But only you can really say whether youre going to live or die. If you hold on, if theres a real doctor around here somewheres that can pull out a bullet and sew guts, if theres medicine around here that can kill the infection, then maybe. But only maybe. Gut wounds are usually killers, and the dying aint easy."

The Bishop looked at me for a moment, and I thought maybe I should have answered him differently. I thought he was going to say something else to me but he didnt. He pressed his eyes shut a moment and then opened them to motion the two Ribbons over. He spoke to them in a voice firmer than he could have felt.

"I have negotiated an agreement with this man. Give him and his friends as much as they can carry away and safe passage out of the mountain. They will return power to the base before they leave. Let the woman Bern go with them."

The two PurpleRibbons stared at me. They were both pretty well layered up in ribbons and glory. Finally, one nodded.

Chapter 22

Theres not much left to tell. Stories will always have a beginning and an ending, but they get tacked on so that people will think theres order and structure when usually there aint. People generally like a good ending, but they aint often found. Theres always a few raggy threads that somebody will start tugging on, and whenever something comes to a conclusion theres always a drift into the next part. Life is one constant persistent stubborn flow, and there aint much difference in where you start and where you end.

We got out of the magic mountain. After a couple days hiding out on top we slipped out with everything we could carry, and then some. Food, clothing, tobacco, shinyboots, greasynew cutters, chocolate bars, and all other sorts of tradables that were light enough to lug up the pass and then drag down towards Aurora. Joe was loaded up with more than two of me could carry, but then he had more people to take care of back down on the front range.

I had tried to get Treetop interested in gathering up his band to follow us down when he healed up, telling him they could live a lot easier as scavengers in Aurora than they could as skinners in the mountains, but he wouldnt have none of it. Once we got him and Chatterbox reunited with his band, all he wanted to do was go back into the mountain, healed up or not, figuring he had as much right to it as the remaining saints. Said he was the General now. I patched him up the best I could, and I showed him how to keep his shoulder immobile so it could heal, but he was tugging at it just as soon as I finished wrapping it. I gave him the Generals eaglelighter when we parted at the dam, and he gave me back a little chunk of skyblue rock that he had dangling around his neck. I hoped I would see him again. For being savage cannibals, he, Chatterbox, and the others were alright.

None of the saints seemed interested in leaving the mountain, especially the two PurpleRibbons who seemed most intent on carrying forward the Bishops good work. There was already a commotion when we left, several groups pulling apart to have a go at each other. I feared for the woman and the old man, but we were able to slip them out with the Fools help. There were still a few ratsoldiers scattered about, and a couple Goldbars were trying to rally them together. It was a good time for slipping out. Mister Newlin had turned the lights back on, but only long enough to satisfy the saints and soldiers so we could disappear. The Fool got us down to the main entrance easy enough, and we walked out. Everyone else was too preoccupied sizing each other us.

I kept the Generals fancygrips, which I eventually traded to the Prince for future favors. I knew he would take an active interest in what was left of the magic mountain, and all along I figured he would charge up the mountains just as soon as we told him our story. He was as good a leader as his father, and maybe better, and more than a match for whichever saints or soldiers were left when he arrived. Having some experience in reconstructing, he would do more for the people of Nineveh and those left in the magic mountain than either the Bishop or the General had ever done.

The Fool and the Boy stuck with us. We probably couldnt have got shut of them if we tried, and we didnt try. I had filled them with stories of whiskeyshops and market days, and they were hot for Aurora. The Fools a naturalborn, rheumatic clown who laughs too much, complains too much, and who really aint good for much, but he helped carry our packs, and after a bit me and Joe couldnt see much difference between us and aintus with him being around. And after running over that one Goldbar there was no way he was going to stay hunkered down in those tunnels. He was a part of us before we realized he had joined up. And I owed him.

We straggled back down to the front range, and when we got there Joes tribe took to the Fool like a flock of birds to a seed patch. Within a week he had all the wives, sisters, children, and cousins pawing over him, and within another week Joe had installed him in one of his houses with a couple of his frolicsome female cousins. I tried to explain to them that the Fool was not to be trusted with guns and gophers, but they paid me no mind. Me and the Boy were there for the installation, and the Boy ate his way through every course of the feast, and then went back for more. I give the Fool a bottle of the Generals best whiskey, without an expectation of a return.

The Boy got more sociable, and more comfortable talking, especially when the tribe began pawing over him too. Someone was always jabbering at him, not knowing that he was only an unlettered wildboy, and quick enough he got adjusted to jabbering back at them, though sometimes he didnt make much sense. Maybe me and Joe just hadnt been talking enough to him. Some of Joes women took to calling him Daniel, but I dont know where they got that name. Hes a naturalborn thief and ought to be called Sneak, or maybe Eatalot. But Ill leave it up to him to decide what he ought to be called. Me and Joe are fixing him up to take over the business when we finally get done.

We dragged Mister Newlin down with us, and quick enough he also got himself adjusted to life without tunnels and generals. He got on well with the Prince, who was pleased to have someone around who could work on his computers. I believe the Prince was more taken with Mister Newlin than he was with the fancygrips I gave him. He had been trying to get some his computers hookedup and running for a long while, so Mister Newlin was indeed a heavenly gift. Now hes got notions about returning a power grid to Aurora, and hes got Mister Newlin settled down on the top floor of a building near the palace, where he can work his magic. He gave him a title too, CityWorks Manager. Great times are coming to Aurora.

The Prince has it in his head not to wait till after the snows to visit Nineveh with his rangers. Hes fixin to leave. I suspect he wont need a lot of manpower, or firepower. Mister Newlin had arranged things so that, a couple days after our departure, the magic mountain shut down for good. Its just a big cave now, and when the snows come its going to get awfully cold and dark inside. He also scrambled the pipes at the dam so that the water flow stopped and the generartors shut down. Now the magic mountain aint much of a place for the living. But its a good enough tomb for two pitiful fools who didnt know any better than to faceoff against each other.

Which about brings me up to date. Me and Joe are gathering another pack of mules to make the trip up with Prince. We think theres business yet to be done. We have three mules already, bartered for fair prices with magic mountain scraps. I have named them Eveready, Duracell, and Rayovac after our old mules. I have my eye on a fourth mule, which I will name Harley. Or maybe Healey depending on its personality. Naming is a serious business.

In a few days we will head back to Nineveh and the magic mountain, hoping to make a few trades, and hoping to pick up another magic mountain load. Being a savage and a cannibal I expect we will still have an edge when dealing with the rats, or those that are left. Im guessing most of those still sane will have lit out for new territory.

I never said much to the woman. Not about the Bishops dying, not about what he said, and not about going with us. After parting with Treetop and his bunch, we rubberrafted over to Nineveh and there was a bit of a stir when we got there. Everyone over there knew about the magic mountain only they never could let on that they knew. But with the Bishop being gone and the woman returning, there were enough ripples to get the people milling around the town square, ready for some big times to come. The woman got to talking to different clumps of people, and they seemed to believe her that there was a bigger world than the one the Bishop had given them. I suspect shes liked enough to get herself elected the next Pope. Within a day after getting back to Nineveh she already got herself installed as Interim Mayor.

I reckoned the woman would have come with us if she had been a mind to, so there wasnt any asking or discussing. At least with me. I really didnt know for sure what she intended until we got to the top of the pass and looked back over the Bishops valley. It was a pretty scene. The day was warm and sunny, and the lake was a dark bluegreen streak that sparkled in the light. It was another one of those prettypicture scenes that makes you think that the passage of time is all some sort of grand illusion. Overhead a couple hawks turned slow circles.

"Pretty valley." I couldnt think of anything else to say. The woman didnt say anything.

"Theres other places just as pretty. Sometimes the flats seem almost as pretty when the evening sky lights up the whole world with the glow of a golden sunset."

She still didnt say anything, so I shut up for a moment and started to hitch up my packs one more time.

"I would like to see such a sunset someday."

Of course, I knew she hadnt been planning on going with us, but then I had thought that, well maybe, I didnt know. But she couldnt really leave Nineveh with so many saints and wolves running loose. I thought maybe Joe had talked to her about our leaving, and maybe her leaving, so I knew she had it mapped out in her head. She had qualities.

"You will come back with your Prince?"

I nodded, though it had been more statement than question.

"He aint exactly my Prince, but I am sure he will take an active interest in your valley, and in the magic mountain. He definitely will want to get up here soon, and Im guessing he wont wait till after the snows. Hes a decisive man. Im glad we get along most times. "

She nodded. I got one pack up on my back and was lugging another. I turned towards the downward path of the east slope. The others had already started down. The wildboy had shot ahead but stopped to look at us.

"Whats my name?" she asked suddenly.

I twisted around, thought for a moment, and finally shrugged. I knew what others called her, what she considered her name, and it was a pretty enough name.

"Dont have no idea. I aint good with names. They come slow to me, and they dont stick. I aint decided what I should call you."

She smiled. "Nor do I know what to call you."

"Maybe when I come back up we can figure all that out."

"Maybe." She smiled once more and then turned towards her valley.

Which brings me back to the where I started, sipping rotgut whiskey in a spidertrap. Me and Joe and wildboy Daniel, along with the Prince and a sizable portion of his rangers, are fixin to head on back to Nineveh. And maybe by the time we get there Ill have figured out a couple of acceptable names. I have some old picture books stashed away, and I will give them to the woman. I will show her pictures of distant worlds, and I will tell her stories of these places. I will enjoy those stories.

Book Club Discussion Questions

1. Trader and Joe exist in a world where the traditional social order has broken down, where many of the old rules and regulations, customs and conventions, have collapsed. How have these two men adapted to the lack of an established social order?
2. Examine the ways Trader and Joe change during the course of the novel. How do they begin behaving differently as the novel progresses?
3. What kind of town is Nineveh? Why would you want or not want to live there?
4. What has brought Trader and Joe together as trading partners, and why do they stay together?
5. During their journey to the Magic Mountain, Trader and Joe encounter the wild boy, the brokenfooted woman, the old man, Treetop, and the fool. Who are these people, and how do they contribute to the journey?
6. The Bishop and the General are figures of authority in the novel. What kinds of power do they have, and what are the sources of their power?
7. Who is the Prince and how does he function in the novel?
8. As the novel ends, Trader and Joe are ready to take the Prince and a troop of his Rangers back to Nineveh and the Magic Mountain. What might they find at both places, and what might they do when they get there?
9. There are a variety of faiths and beliefs in the novel. Of the major characters, who believes in what, and how do their beliefs guide them?
10. At the end of the novel what evidence can you find to say that readers are left with a vision of the future that is either hopeful or bleak?

CPSIA information can be obtained
at www.ICGtesting.com
Printed in the USA
LVHW041520080722
723063LV00005B/675